Praise for

THE RIPPER'S HELLBROTH

"A very clever weaving of factual material with imagination. The result is a very entertaining read that should enthrall lovers of fantasy and the great Jack the Ripper mystery of 1888. A wonderful adventure."

—*Stewart P. Evans, author and co-author of multiple of works to include* Jack the Ripper: First American Serial Killer, Jack the Ripper: Scotland Yard Investigates, Jack the Ripper: Letters from Hell, *and* The Ultimate Jack the Ripper Sourcebook.

"*The Ripper's Hellbroth* was delightful to read not only for its gripping story and stark contrasting plot-lines the author brings masterly together, but for real understanding of facts and theories on Jack the Ripper and his victims. The portrayal of modern forensics and Victorian detection create the setting for an original mystery novel based on the Whitechapel murders I can highly recommend."

—*Spiro Dimolianis, author of* Jack the Ripper and Black Magic: Victorian Conspiracy Theories, Secret Societies and the Supernatural Mystique of the Whitechapel Murders.

"A vigorous mixture of facts and fiction that constantly entertains."

—*Joe Chetcuti, co-author of* Jack the Ripper: The Suspects.

"The best novel ever written on the Ripper subject—bar none!"

—*Jonathan Hainsworth, author of* Jack the Ripper: Case Solved, 1891.

The Ripper's Hellbroth

THE WATCHMAKER REVELATIONS

MICHAEL L. HAWLEY

HELLBENDER BOOKS

an imprint of Sunbury Press, Inc.
Mechanicsburg, PA USA

HELLBENDER BOOKS

an imprint of Sunbury Press, Inc.
Mechanicsburg, PA USA

For information about special discounts for bulk purchases, please contact Sunbury Press Orders Dept. at (855) 338-8359 or orders@sunburypress.com.

To request one of our authors for speaking engagements or book signings, please contact Sunbury Press Publicity Dept. at publicity@sunburypress.com.

ISBN: 978-1-62006-835-9 (Trade paperback)
ISBN: 978-1-62006-836-6 (Mobipocket)

Library of Congress Control Number: 2017943693

FIRST SUNBURY PRESS EDITION: July 2017

Product of the United States of America
0 1 1 2 3 5 8 13 21 34 55

Set in Bookman Old Style
Designed by Crystal Devine
Cover by Amber Rendon
Edited by Jennifer Cappello

Continue the Enlightenment!

Author's Note

The sections of the story taking place in the nineteenth century are based upon true events. A serious effort was made to be historically accurate, including people involved, locations of events, and documentary evidence presented, as revealed in my nonfiction book, *The Ripper's Haunts* (2016).

The transformation of *The Ripper's Hellbroth* from an intriguing idea to a beautiful work of art can be attributed first to my amazing readers: Nick Vanderhyde, Joe Chetcuti, Nick and Jenn Rastelli, Anita Hawley, and Jonathan Hainsworth; and second to my editors: Scott Benson, David Grundy, and Juls Duncan. Many thanks go out to Tom Balk for sharing with me his detective experience; to Larry Maglietto for letting me "build him a watch" (the Watchmaker); and finally to all of my fellow ripperologists for continuing such an addicting field of research.

chapter one

Buffalo police patrolman Aaron Phelps stood next to the bus stop on Elmwood Street along the popular strip of small storefront specialty shops, cafes, restaurants, bars, and homes, staring at the flashing lights illuminating the dozens of century-old, three-story homes along the street. The flashing blues and reds bouncing off the buildings gave the impression he was at a light show, but instead of hearing synchronized music, he heard the sounds of distant sirens from police vehicles making their way to the crime scene. The 911 call came less than an hour ago, yet uniformed officers and local residents already crowded the sidewalks and street, especially near the narrow alleyway three houses down.

A uniformed officer began blocking the entrance to the alleyway with police tape.

Phelps turned as a police car sped toward him, then watched as its driver parked halfway on the sidewalk. A balding elderly police officer jumped out of the vehicle and approached him.

"Whatcha got, Phelps?"

"Looks like our perp stuck again, Sarge," Phelps commented then turned and escorted the police sergeant toward the direction of the alleyway. "We have a deceased college-aged female in the alley. Mutilated." He pointed to a distraught young man speaking with a uniformed officer scribbling in his notepad. "That's her boyfriend. Her apartment's just down Elmwood."

"Who found the body?"

Phelps pointed up at the adjoining home. "An old lady who lives there." He paused. "Well, her dog found the victim. The dog was barking up a storm in the alley, so the curious lady took out her flashlight and was shocked by a dead body. Her scream caught the attention of the deceased's boyfriend," Phelps pointed back at the bus stop, "who was waiting for her at the bus stop. He was the one who called it in."

"Same wounds as the others?"

Phelps glanced over at the police sergeant. "Prepare yourself, Sarge. It's nasty. Neck cut to the spine and abdominal mutilation, just like before. I'm sure there's missing organs."

The police sergeant ducked under the police tape then entered the dark alleyway, now filled with police officers. The body was illuminated by their lights. He stared down at the dead girl for a moment.

A police officer leaning over the body popped his head up. "I'm not a detective, Sarge, but if I was a betting man, I'd say the Niagara Falls Ripper has struck again."

"That's what Phelps thinks. Don't touch anything, Jenkins." The police sergeant shook his head then turned around and eyed Phelps. "Are the crime scene specialists and detectives on their way? The faster the deceased is classified a victim the better."

"Another five minutes." Phelps approached the police sergeant, staring at the body. "Doubt CSI and the detectives will even find anything. After six months, still not a clue to who the perpetrator is."

"Well, that's why the captain's on his way to San Antonio." The police sergeant glanced over as two detectives rushed over. "Hopefully he can convince this FBI expert to help us."

"Oh yeah," Phelps replied. "The Watchmaker, right? Some lab rat turned detective sleuth. I hear he hits a home run every time. Always nails the perp." He eyed the body. "I'm not so sure this time, Sarge."

The police sergeant shook his head again. "Ya got that right. This guy's too good at killing."

* * *

Monday, September 18. San Antonio, Texas—FBI Serial Murder Symposium.

Dr. Edward Dunham, chief scientist for the Federal Bureau of Investigation's Behavioral Analysis Unit, stood anxious and uneasy behind the stage curtains of a large college campus auditorium. He gently pushed the fabric aside and peeked out. The room was filled with law enforcement officials and academics from around the country. Dunham, relatively thin and of medium height, looked every bit of his forty-eight years. Gray streaks in his wavy light brown hair, slight crow's feet wrinkled around his steely-gray eyes, and his clean-shaven face gave the impression that he was a well-read and intelligent man. His light brown herringbone tweed suit with elbow patches fit loosely on him as though he had lost a lot of weight in a short time. The suit identified him as an academic, and that's exactly what he preferred.

Heather Kennedy, one of Dunham's lab scientists, stood next to him, giving him her undivided attention—though in his nervousness he hardly noticed. Much shorter than Dunham and slightly overweight, Heather was in her late thirties with jet black hair. She wore black-rimmed glasses and preferred to dress in professional business attire. Heather was very protective of her boss. His absentmindedness was almost as infamous as his skills as a forensic scientist and detective sleuth were famous—but she did not want this to overshadow his brilliance, so she made it a point to always be at his side, coaching him through these awkward events.

"You're going to do fine, Dr. Dunham," Heather whispered as she straightened Dunham's collar and tightened his tie.

"Heather, I'm just not good at speaking in front of a crowd, especially a crowd of peers and academics. There are over a hundred fifty published subject-matter experts in the field of violent crime and serial murders out there." He glanced back at Heather. "You're excellent at this type of thing. It should be you doing the introduction."

Heather grabbed him by the shoulders, gaining his full attention. "You are the chief scientist," she said firmly. "This symposium is your brainchild—and besides, the real reason why

most of these people are participating in this week-long conference is to speak with you."

Dunham tightened his lips. "Well, I'm nothing special."

Heather smiled and rolled her eyes. "Yeah, right."

He glanced away and buttoned his jacket, then parted the
curtains again and stared at the crowd. "There are a lot more
people here than we planned on." He let go of the curtain.

Heather smiled. "And you're nothing special." She lightly
grabbed his chin. "Now look, Dr. Dunham, the reason why I
speak so well to an audience is because when I look out at
them, I don't see an intimidating mass of people, I see individuals. When you get out there, pause for a bit, glance around for
people you recognize, and when you begin your speech, pick
one of them and talk only to him."

Dunham raised his eyebrows and smiled. "That's pretty
clever, Heather. I think I'll try that."

He waited in the wings as Management Program Analyst
Janice Brody was at the podium speaking to the audience. "The
next speaker is the head of our Serial Symposium Group, Dr.
Edward Dunham, clinical forensic scientist and chief scien-
tist in the FBI's NCAVC's Behavioral Analysis Unit Two out of
Quantico, Virginia."

Audience members whispered to each other, clearly excited.

"He has been working for the FBI's lab for the last eighteen
years," she continued. "And for the last eight, he's expanded
his role by working in the field with numerous serial killer task
forces." She turned and faced Dunham. "Everyone knows his
record. I'd like to present Dr. Edward Dunham."

The audience applauded.

Dunham walked out onto the stage. Now away from the protection of the large curtain, his anxiety level increased.

The audience stood in unison and continued their applause.

He tensed up even more but continued to the podium. He
then remembered what Heather had said and decided to apply
her strategy. As he smiled at the crowd and waved, he recognized some of them, which seemed to have a calming effect. He
then noticed someone who seemed out of place in a crowd of
academics and recognized him immediately. It was his boss,
Michael Peters, assistant director for the FBI's Critical Incident
Response Group, the department that his behavioral analysis

unit reported to. Dunham knew Peters to be a man of importance, and he even dressed the part, wearing an expensive dark
suit, a pressed white shirt, and a burgundy tie. Peters was
taller than he was, handsome, clean-shaven, dark-haired, and
athletic. Dunham's relationship with the assistant director was
outstanding.

Dunham broke his gaze from Peters and glanced back at
his lab scientist. Heather nodded and smiled from offstage, ac-
knowledging that he'd just taken her advice.

Next to Peters was a man who seemed to be in a serious
conversation with him, but Dunham didn't recognize him. He
was a black man equal in height to Peters, yet slightly stockier.
He was also wearing a suit, light blue in color, and clearly made
of a less-expensive fabric than Peters'. Dunham could see that
the man's shirt collar didn't fit his thick neck, thus he had the
button undone with his tie loosened. The man's hairline was
receding, and his hair, along with his well-groomed mustache
and beard, had spots of gray. All in all, he concluded that this
man was a seasoned police officer or detective. They must've
ended their discussion, as Peters sat comfortably back into his
seat, and the other man leaned forward with his full attention
on Dunham, who had now reached the podium. Dr. Dunham
shook Brody's hand, then faced the crowd again.

Everyone took their seats as Brody left the podium.

Dunham gave the audience one more quick scan. "Good
morning. I'm thrilled that you could make it. First, I'd like to
thank the rest of the Serial Murder Symposium Group for organizing such an important follow-up to our last symposium."

Some in the audience clapped.

Dunham noticed they were a fidgety group, constantly whispering to each other. "In an effort to stay up-to-date on and
continuously improve upon issues pertaining to serial murder,
the Federal Bureau of Investigation has decided to host another
multi-disciplinary symposium. The agenda will mirror the last
conference, with serial murder topics on common myths, defini-
tions, typologies, pathology and causality, forensics, the role of
the media, prosecution issues, investigative task force organization, and major case-management issues. We will have panel
discussions, case studies, and discussion groups addressing a
range of topics related to serial murder."

Disinterested in Dunham's preliminary comments, Fred Johnson unbuttoned his light-blue suit jacket and leaned his body toward Peters. He whispered, "Have you spoken to Dr. Dunham to see if he'll join our task force?"

Peters smiled but kept his attention on Dunham. "Yes, I have. Because Dr. Dunham's invested so much energy in organizing this symposium, he has mixed feelings about leaving it." He eyed Johnson. "But believe me, he's very interested in the Niagara Falls Serial Killer Case. I've already told him that all of his colleagues are more than capable of making this another successful symposium. It should be a go."

Johnson sat back in his chair, staring at Dunham for a moment, then he eyed Peters. "I certainly hope he does. We're at our wits' end, and the killer recently struck again, as you know."

Peters leaned over. "We love the man," he whispered. "But I have to warn you. Dr. Dunham is the quintessential absent-minded professor. Brilliant, but he gets easily lost in his ever-inquisitive mind. His focus is intense, and you can see it in his eyes. It's like he's penetrating your soul." He paused. "I'm sure this focus is the reason why he can be absentminded, but it's also the reason why he's so good at his job. I'd recommend you pair him up with a type-A personality—an 'odd couple,' if you will."

Johnson grinned and nodded, then glanced at Dunham's medium, thin-framed body. "I thought someone told me he was taller?"

Peters glanced up in thought, then said, "I've heard that before. It might be the Paul Bunyan effect. He's becoming such a household name within the law enforcement community because of his success that people naturally translate this into physical stature."

"I bet you're right, Assistant Director," Johnson replied.

Dunham finished his introductory comments, then asked the audience, "Now, are there any questions before I hand the podium back to Janice?"

Dozens of hands shot up.

He pointed toward one of them. "Yes?"

The man stood up. "Hello, Dr. Dunham, my name is Dr. Henry Patton from the School of Criminal Justice and Criminalistics at Cal State. My question deals with your discovery of the Kansas City serial killer's identity." He pointed at Dunham.

"What did you do differently to break the case that the original members of the task force failed to do for a full twenty years?"

Peters leaned his head toward Johnson. "I knew this would happen. Everyone wants to know why Dr. Dunham is so successful at rooting out serial killers—a perfect record so far. My guess is every one of these next questions will be about his discovery of the identity of the Kansas City serial killer or one of his earlier cases." He looked at Dunham. "And why not? This is the perfect venue for these questions."

Dunham nodded to Dr. Patton. "Well, this particular offender murdered sixteen women in and around Kansas City between the fall of 1995 and the summer of 2009. Frustrating for the task force was the fact that the DNA analyses of the crimes scenes that occurred in the 1990s showed significant contamination. Investigators were not yet familiar enough with the DNA collection process. For example, cigarette butts were discovered at three of the earlier crime scenes, and they produced a DNA match among them." He shook his head. "It was soon discovered that the DNA belonged to a local detective photographer who was in the habit of throwing his butts on the ground as he took photos."

Johnson shook his head. "This happened in Buffalo too."

Dunham paused, drank from a water bottle, then continued. "When I joined the task force, it was quite evident that they were doing an excellent job with the case, but the problem was this serial offender always seemed to be one step ahead. I concurred with their typological assessment that the serial offender's motive was a combination of lust and thrill, also that the offender was a stationary killer, and lastly that he or she exhibited both organized and disorganized behavior."

Peters scanned the room and grinned. He noticed that the normally chatty attendees had their complete and undivided attention on Dunham.

Dunham continued. "My judgment, however, was that the offender exhibited predominantly organized behavior." He placed his hand on his chest. "My contribution that ultimately broke the case was to search for any homicides that occurred around Kansas City in 1994 and earlier. The idea was that if we identified any of these homicides with our offender, maybe he left his DNA at that crime scene." He raised his finger. "Recall that the O. J. Simpson trial took place from January to October of 1995. This is significant because it was the first time most Americans—including serial killers—knew about law enforcement using DNA analysis at a crime scene. In 1994, a perpetrator would've been oblivious to this method of identification, thus giving us hope that we might recover this elusive killer's DNA." He nodded. "It worked."

Audience members began whispering to each other again.

Dunham took another sip of water. "I discovered a homicide that had occurred in late 1994 that matched the offender's MO with a few minor variations that were not noticed before. It went unnoticed because this particular victim was discovered eighty miles to the east of the offender's anchor point, and more significantly, there was already a conviction in that particular case.

"The convicted killer," Dunham continued, "had murdered someone else just three blocks away from this particular crime scene, on the same day. Local law enforcement connected the two homicides, since both appeared similar." He shook his head. "After reviewing the two, I demonstrated not only that the person convicted of the crime did not commit this murder—although he was certainly guilty of the other—but also that the MO and offender signature matched the Kansas City serial offender's."

Dr. Dunham paused for more whispering.

"I noticed that the motives were entirely different. The first murder was a crime of anger, while the second was the result of sadistic lust. Semen was discovered on the jeans of the victim in that case, even though there was no sexual penetration."

Dr. Patton's eyes widened in confusion, and he raised his hand again. "I thought there was no semen found in the Kansas City murder crime scenes."

"That's correct," Dunham answered. "Although everything else was the same—such as evidence of frontal strangulation, and location of multiple stab wounds on the face and genitals. The serial offender later admitted he had ejaculated while killing the later victims but did it in such a way as to not leave any traces of semen. He had quickly become wise to DNA trace evidence, but thanks to excellent evidence collection, the analysts produced a viable DNA sample from the semen. We then entered the information into the DNA database. It matched a known sex offender in the area, who'd been taken off the suspect list earlier because he had a solid alibi—or so it seemed."

Numerous audience members nodded, whispering to each other.

Dunham scanned the room. "There was enough evidence to get a search warrant for his house and vehicle, which eventually gave us enough evidence to convict. After conviction, he confessed to the murders, and he even helped us locate two more bodies."

Captain Johnson glanced over at Peters, grinned, and nodded.

Dunham raised his hand to halt further questioning. "I don't want to go into too much more detail because we're actually going to use this as a case study after tomorrow morning's presentation."

Another audience member raised his hand and stood up after Dunham acknowledged him. "Hello, Dr. Dunham, my name is Dr. Francis Gerard from the Henry C. Lee College of Criminal Justice and Forensic Sciences. I would like to piggyback off of my colleague's question." He held up a hand. "I promise it's separate from the case study we'll be working on. In the act of identifying the victims of the Kansas City serial killer, I'm sure others screened the previous year's homicides within at least a hundred-mile radius. What motivated you to go as far as to evaluate murder cases where there was already a conviction?"

Dunham thought for a moment. "When I examined what was thought to be the first murder victim, I was convinced the offender must have practiced his craft prior to this, for numerous reasons. For example, his offender signature was fully developed, and as you know, many sado-sexual serial offenders adjust their methods until they settle upon a favorite signature. Case in point: if you look at the Andrei Chikatilo case, the Soviet serial killer, he experimented until he found what best satisfied his sadistic desires." Dunham shrugged his shoulders. "On a personal level, once I believe I'm on a trail of discovery, I have a habit of focusing upon it relentlessly until something is revealed."

"I'll say," Peters joked to Johnson, having experienced Dunham's relentlessness before. "He's like a pit bull."

Sensing that the audience was satisfied with his answer, Dunham took the opportunity to call Janice Brody back. He glanced over his shoulder at Janice, who was waiting to take the podium. "Here again is Janice, and she will be going over administrative issues with you."

Brody smiled at Dunham as he left center stage. She abruptly grabbed his arm, and she whispered, "Dr. Dunham, you forgot your folder."

He gave an embarrassed smile, grabbed his paperwork from Brody, then ambled offstage.

Peters got up out of his seat and signaled Johnson to follow him. "It's time to meet Dr. Dunham, Captain Johnson."

Johnson followed Peters out of the auditorium.

"Edward," Peters yelled as he and Johnson approached Dunham. "I'd like to introduce you to Captain Fred Johnson of the Buffalo City Police Department and head of the Niagara Falls Serial Killer Task Force." He glanced over at Johnson. "Captain Johnson, this is Dr. Edward Dunham, chief scientist at our behavioral analysis unit."

Johnson shook Dunham's hand. "Dr. Dunham, you've come highly recommended by—" he paused for a moment—"actually, by everyone." He glanced over at Peters. "Assistant Director Peters said he's spoken to you about our requesting you on the case. As you know, we're getting nowhere."

Dunham stared at Johnson, clearly recalling the Niagara Falls case file in his mind, then said, "I heard there's been another victim."

Johnson nodded. "Angie Sparks. A student from Buffalo State College." He intentionally gave the victim's name in order to personalize the case for Dunham, hopefully influencing a positive decision from him to join the team.

"The report said a blood-soaked parchment with smeared writing was found a couple blocks away from the body, correct?" Dunham inquired.

"True," Johnson replied. "And DNA analysis has just confirmed the blood came from Angie Sparks. The problem is, although we can make out a partial list of herbal medicines on the parchment, so far this information hasn't given us any leads." Johnson then noticed what Assistant Director Peters was talking about regarding Dunham's penetrating eyes, but he found it quite refreshing. He could understand why Dunham was well-liked. It was as if the man was thoroughly interested in what you had to say.

"I do know of the Buffalo Forensic Lab, and it's one of the best, but do you mind if our team in Virginia has a go at the parchment?" Dunham asked. "I would like to analyze it for myself."

"Of course!" Johnson paused. "Does this mean you'll be joining us?"

Dunham nodded. "Yes it does. My wife is a professor of anthropology in Virginia, and she's on sabbatical in Europe for the next two months, so I'm open for an extended trip." He grinned. "It's time to help your team catch a killer."

Johnson smiled, glanced over at Peters, then grabbed Dunham's hand and shook it aggressively. "Excellent. I'll have the parchment sent to you immediately."

chapter two

1888: Friday, September 7. London, England.

Inspector First Class Walter Andrews gazed out the window of his horse-drawn police cab at a darker-than-usual evening in London's affluent West End. As he made his way to the poor East End district of Whitechapel, the flickering dull-yellow light glowing from the gas streetlamps reflected haphazardly off the rough cobblestone streets giving the outside a hazy, eerie atmosphere. Andrews popped his head out the window, looking back at Metropolitan Police Headquarters, commonly known as Scotland Yard. He then noticed the beginnings of an evening fog in the form of a light mist encroaching on the glow of the streetlamps.

An omnibus pulled over to the side in front of a theater; its horses still moved about but began to settle down.

It was the theater district, and Andrews noticed that a long line of people filled the sidewalks waiting just outside the ever-popular Lyceum Theatre. He looked up and read the huge theater sign: Mansfield's *A Strange Case of Dr. Jekyll and Mr. Hyde.* He then realized the sky had a faint red radiance, owing to distant building fires still burning through the night. "How appropriate," he mumbled quietly to himself, connecting the hellish-looking evening not only to this particular ghoulish theatrical play, but also because he was headed to a district experiencing hell on earth due to a brutal killer terrorizing its residents.

The police cab driver snapped the reins and quickened their pace.

Andrews pulled his head back into the cab and settled into his seat. The constant clip-clop of the horses' shoes striking the street had a calming, mesmerizing effect on him, heightened by the rhythmic rocking motion of the carriage. His stout, five-foot ten-inch height, and wide shoulders made him an imposing figure, yet he knew he was beginning to show signs of age with his receding salt-and-pepper hair. He purposely kept his graying beard relatively short in order to give a more youthful appearance. He'd requested some leave in order to heal from physical ailments, but his plea fell on deaf ears at Scotland Yard because they were under a great deal of pressure to apprehend this ruthless and elusive killer. Instead, they gave him and his detective team temporary assignment on the Whitechapel murders investigation.

The powerful, wide-shouldered man sitting directly across from Andrews attempted to shine his hand-held lamp onto the paper in his thick lap, but he frowned, shook his head, and then repositioned it.

Andrews watched with an inquisitive look.

The man gritted his teeth. "Confounded light!" His thick neck gave the appearance he had none, and his shoulders and hands were massive, which contributed to his inability to maneuver his lamp. He made one more adjustment, paused, then grinned as the lamp gave a steady light to his paper.

Andrews smirked. The man was part of his detective team, Detective Sergeant Frank Froest. Froest was shorter than he was but likely the most powerful man on the force—a perfect person to have around when things got rough. Luckily, he had a great disposition and loved telling jokes. Froest kept his light-colored hair short and had a clean-shaven face. He loved wearing expensive suits and walking around with a silver-handled cane.

Froest popped his head up. In response to Andrews smiling at him, he presented a section of the paper. "Be my guest, boss."

Andrews shook his head. "No thank you, Frank. I'm not fond of reading in such dim light. Hurts my eyes."

Froest turned to his left and presented the paper to the third man sharing the cab. "Walter? Care to catch up on the news?"

"Already read it, Frank," Walter replied.

"Ha!" Froest blurted out, grinning. "I should've known, Detective Sergeant Walter Dinnie! I have never met a man more well-read than you." He looked down at his paper. "I bet there's not a fact that you don't know."

Andrews nodded and smiled. "That we can agree upon." Dinnie was a great member of his team. He was taller than Froest, slightly overweight, had much narrower shoulders, and was balding with deep reddish sideburns. Dinnie had a gift for organization, especially with paperwork, and he enjoyed working in the office rather than getting his hands dirty on the streets; a perfect counter-weight to Froest. Dinnie understood the law as well as any barrister, which was quite handy on numerous occasions. When Froest would generate extra paperwork by pushing the limits of police authority, Dinnie took care of it and magically kept him out of legal trouble. No one could argue this detective team got results.

Dinnie placed his hand on Froest's shoulder. "In the words of Francis Bacon, my friend, knowledge is power."

Andrews stared out of the cab at the cold and misty scenery and thought about the poor East End district of Whitechapel. Their chief inspector briefed them and explained that three atypical and violent murders occurred in Whitechapel. They were all within a five-month period and all women of the lower "unfortunate" prostitute class, which bore the hallmarks of a single killer. What convinced the press, and some at Scotland Yard, of one killer was the fact that all the murders occurred within a third of a mile of each other. Lastly, and more importantly, their bodies were attacked with the same inhuman and ghoul-like brutality. When the third and most vicious murder occurred, Scotland Yard reluctantly accepted the likelihood that the murders were from the same hand. Hence, they formally began a murder investigation.

Dinnie glanced over at Andrews. "I hear Inspectors Abberline and Moore have also been assigned to Whitechapel. Is that right?"

Andrews nodded. "Correct. Inspector Abberline is the perfect fit since he was inspector-in-charge of Whitechapel just before he was assigned to Scotland Yard last year. He'll take charge of the investigation so the local inspector can focus upon the usual Whitechapel crime."

"And Inspector Moore is a fine chap," Froest interrupted. "Although he thinks he's got a pint of royal blood in him."

Andrews smirked. "That's Henry Moore for you. Marrying into money would give anyone a lofty air."

Froest studied his cane. "I like the brown cane he lugs around. Word has it, his is made of iron—just painted brown to look like wood."

"It is indeed, Frank, which is why he has no fear of entering the darkest alleys." Dinnie affirmed, then he looked over at Andrews. "I'll wager a day's salary, though, if he hit Frank here over the head with it, it would bend like a spoon."

"Ha!" Andrews blurted out. "I agree."

Froest rubbed his head, then handled his cane and grinned smugly. "Jealous of my fineness, are we, Walter?"

Dinnie laughed. "I am indeed, partner, especially due to the fact that you have a full head of hair." He touched his bald head. "And I seemed to have lost mine."

Froest nudged Dinnie. "Oh, that reminds me. Walter, what do a tree and a dog have in common?"

Andrews grinned, knowing he was going to hear another infamous Froest joke.

Dinnie rolled his eyes. "I don't know, Frank. What?"

"They both lose their bark when they're dead!" Froest slapped Dinnie's knee with excessive force then let out a loud, guttural laugh. "Bah, hah, hah!"

Dinnie eyed Andrews and shook his head.

Froest started reading his paper again then nudged Dinnie. "Listen to this, a refined lady from the West End has recently been slumming in the Whitechapel District." He glanced up again at Andrews then continued reading. "Notice what she says. 'The district is made up of two main thoroughfares that cross, Whitechapel Road and Commercial Street. Off of these streets are congested narrow alleyways and side streets packed with overcrowded, filthy, ramshackle slums and lodging houses. They are ill-paved, narrow, and poorly-lit streets with very few gas lamps. They are so vile, moral sewage flows till they become hideous cesspools of vice and crime. Fine ladies and white-handed gentlemen will do no good down here; indeed nothing will remedy the evils while lighting is deficient, sanitary conveniences absent, and these filthy dark alleys exist.'"

Dinnie eyed Andrews. "Is this what we have to look forward to, Inspector?"

"Best be prepared, Walter," Andrews answered. "It's true that the East End has a well-earned reputation for vice and villainy." He tilted his head. "And I daresay unequaled anywhere in the British Isles. The district is filled with swindlers, pickpockets, muggers, and large numbers of prostitutes, many of which would steal from a little old lady and never give two thoughts about it." He paused and smiled. "In all—a charming place."

"It still sounds like a nice respite from the dreary confines of headquarters," Froest joked.

"The people aren't all bad," Andrews continued. "There are plenty of honest residents. The foreign Jews never give us any trouble, as so with the prosperous furriers and silk weavers. All these are law-abiding citizens."

An unusually loud noise emanated from outside, catching Dinnie's attention. A crowd of people were conversing at a busy tavern, which was situated at a street corner. There seemed to be just as many customers outside the tavern as inside, all apparently oblivious to the cold, wet evening. "I see we've made it to the East End."

Froest looked outside. "I get the impression that all of the women in Whitechapel are prostitutes."

"Far from it," Andrews replied. "It's relatively easy to pick the unfortunates out in a crowd, though. They generally wear bright colors, light blue mostly, and an adornment of well-worn ostrich feathers. After awhile, you'll become familiar with them. They're very territorial, so you'll most likely see them give their pitch at one location," he pointed out of the cab, "such as outside a favored market or gin palace."

"Inspector, did the chief inspector give you any more details about the case after we left the meeting?" Dinnie asked.

Andrews took a deep breath and leaned forward. "Well, we discussed how the murderer seems to be increasing the level of violence on his victims. He said that the first victim was found near Whitechapel Church on April third, stabbed with a stick-like object in the vaginal region. The second victim was found about a month ago, just a block away from the first, at the bottom of some steps leading into a lodging house—thirty-nine stab wounds in the abdominal region. And the third victim was found a week ago, just off of Whitechapel Road, on a side street, with her neck nearly severed by a knife attack, followed by a deep knife wound in her abdomen. He believes the next victim,"

Andrews raised his finger, "and he's confident there'll be an-other," he paused again, "will experience a most horrendous death."

"Didn't you tell me Inspector Abberline thought these kill-ings are probably vengeance murders from a gang of ruffians trying to blackmail unfortunates?" Froest asked.

Andrews thought for a moment and nodded. "A high rip gang, you mean, and that certainly is a possibility. The pattern of these killings and their targets could suggest some high rip gang is trying to strike fear into unfortunates in an attempt to get a message out that they mean business." He then shook his head. "But he now believes the ruthlessness of the last two murders, especially the Nichols murder, suggests something even worse—and I agree."

"Oh?" Dinnie queried.

Andrews nodded. "The killer's agenda seems to be the actual act of killing, not in intimidating unfortunates into submission. I think we're dealing with an altogether different kind of killer—a monomaniac with an extreme hatred of prostitutes, and even having a taste for blood." He glanced out the window. "Most likely some local butcher down on his luck all of his life has been victimized one too many times by the unfortunate class and has finally gone insane."

Froest pointed in the direction of the West End. "Don't you think it's odd that these murders coincide with the opening of Mansfield's *Jekyll and Hyde* at the Lyceum Theatre? It's as though the show has incited this fiend into overkill." He raised his eyebrows and tilted his head. "I'm not the first to recognize this."

"Maybe," Andrews paused. "I can see a Jekyll and Hyde scenario, but from a different perspective. The killer might be an upstanding citizen holding a prestigious position during the day in the West End, as a Dr. Jekyll so to speak, but at night, Mr. Hyde takes over his personality, and he goes on a rampage against a class of people no one cares about—and in his mind, will do nothing about."

Froest stared up in thought, then nodded. "I'm inclined to believe you, boss. This kind of behavior can only come from a life of misery. No well-bred man would do something like this." He paused for a moment and smiled. "But don't quote me on that."

"Speaking of quoting, or quoting police officials by the press," Andrews added, "headquarters wants us to remind everyone not to speak to the press for fear of us possibly revealing our intentions to the killer. The press knows more than they should. All of the public hysteria over the newspaper articles on the latest suspect, Leather Apron, is a perfect example of this."

Dinnie nodded.

"It's more like fear of political embarrassment," Froest interjected. "Someday headquarters will realize we could use the press to our advantage. Someone, somewhere, has seen this guy."

"That'll not happen in our lifetime, Frank," Dinnie replied. "Those in charge have little respect for the abilities of us lower-class detectives. My guess is, when we finally see a street-trained police officer at the commissioner level, we'll start to see effective police policies put into place."

The three merely gazed out the window, all recognizing their mutual silence as a sign of agreement.

The scenery outside clearly changed from an area of residential dwellings to a crowded area of business and recreation—albeit less affluent than in the West End. There was a constant hustle and bustle of activity from the pedestrians, horse-drawn carriages, and the multitudes of street vendors, gin palaces, and butcher stalls.

Froest tilted his head and eyed Andrews, clearly a little confused. "I thought this place was poverty-stricken."

Dinnie leaned closer to the window for a better view.

Shops lined both sides of the street. The smell of fried fish pervaded the air, bombarding the senses along with the scent of smoking naphtha lamps belonging to the many vendors. Altogether, the area had an atmosphere of a large and busy fair.

Andrews nodded. "Extremely so, but Whitechapel Road and Commercial Street hide it—it's the back streets. Where there's poverty, there's crime, which begins on these busy main thoroughfares then flows into the dark side streets," he said, pointing down a dark alley.

Andrews leaned over, grabbed Froest's cane, then knocked on the roof of the cab. The cab slowed to a stop. "How about we stop here on Commercial Street and walk the rest of the way? Leman Street Police Station is just a few blocks down. This should give you a good feel for the district."

The three detectives exited the cab and started south down the dark and damp busy street.

A police constable walking his beat northward, having spotted the detectives, approached them, beaming. "Inspector Andrews!" the constable yelled.

Andrews noticed the constable and smiled.

The constable nodded to Dinnie and Froest. "Evening, Detective Sergeants! It's great to see you again."

They all shook hands.

Andrews gave the constable a big friendly handshake. "Good evening, PC Barrett. It's great to see you again."

"Everyone in the division is looking forward to your help," Barrett commented.

"How has it been since last week's murder?" Froest asked.

Barrett shook his head. "Bloody hell, Sarge. Everyone has lost their wits. Why, just today, we almost had a riot on our hands when we apprehended a drunkard. Someone called out, 'He's the killer!' and an innocent sailor in our custody would have been bludgeoned to death if it weren't for us rushing him off to the police station."

Andrews looked south down the street. "We're headed to Leman Street Police Station to speak with Inspectors Reid, Abberline, and Moore."

"That's where I just came from, Inspector. They're all there waiting for you." Barrett turned at the sound of a commotion beginning between a vendor and two pedestrians. He started toward it then turned back. "I'd best be off, gentlemen. Again, it's great you're here."

"We won't keep you, Thomas." Andrews glanced at Dinnie and Froest as their fellow officer hurried away. "Barrett was the first constable on the scene of the second murder—the unfortunate Martha Tabram."

As the detectives continued their journey south, Andrews pointed to down a street to their left. "Just a block east down Wentworth Street here is George Yard, the location of the Tabram murder last month, and a block farther down was where the unfortunate Emma Smith was accosted last spring."

A few minutes later they came to the huge corner of Commercial Street and Whitechapel Road. Andrews pointed east down Whitechapel Road. "A few blocks east, just north of London Hospital, was the location of the last murder. The Nichols woman. Her head was cut nearly clean off, and she had a deep wound in her stomach."

Froest stared down the street. "Whitechapel Road is much wider than I expected, and every square inch is being used."

Froest looked around as they walked south, when a horse-drawn carriage popped out from the mist and darkness and came to an abrupt stop right in front of them.

Andrews and Dinnie stopped and walked around the carriage, but the inattentive Froest continued straight, walking right into the cab.

Thump.

The noise caused Andrews and Dinnie to glance back.

"Are you OK, Frank?" Andrews asked.

Froest backed away from the carriage, apparently slightly dazed. "Now, that was a close call!"

The passenger of the carriage opened the door and climbed out. He turned his head and peeked from under his American-style, wide-brim hat, almost as if to apologize to Inspector Froest, but the stranger remained silent. Instead, he shook his head, then rushed north toward Commercial Street. He wore a well-worn dark cape, and he had in his left hand a cane, which was not unusual, as anyone who could afford to travel in a cab most likely owned a cane.

Inspector Froest rolled his eyes and shouted loud enough for the man to hear, "Is courtesy absent here as well?" He hurried his pace to catch up to Dinnie and Andrews.

The man from the carriage strolled briskly away and blended into the crowd. "Idiots, these English detectives. Not only are they obnoxious, they're also blatantly obvious. Their fashion of dress and food stains scream plainclothes police detective," he muttered to himself.

He slowed and continued his way north through the crowded street stopping at vendors and eyeing the patrons. At one point, he saw a drunken, middle-aged lady just in front of him getting scolded by a vendor.

"Off with you, Poll. You're scarin' the customers away!"

"Aw, what do you know! Bugger off then." Poll turned around in a stagger and accidentally bumped into the man. She grabbed his arm and said, "Oh, what a fine gentleman, what do ya say we—"

The man jerked his arm away and bellowed, "Unhand me, you disgusting cow!" He glared at her and then moved quickly away.

Poll merely shrugged her shoulders, apparently unaffected by his nasty response, and kept on staggering down the street in the opposite direction.

The man glanced behind himself as he approached the corner of Wentworth Street, ensuring he wasn't being watched. He stopped then quickly turned east into the dark, misty street onto George Yard. He approached some familiar steps and bent down. "Oh, hallowed ground!" He kissed his index and middle fingers and touched them to a bloodstained cobblestone. He exhaled and shuddered in excitement and then left as quickly as he came. The man returned to Commercial Street and turned north until he reached the crowded market, where he again blended in with the pedestrians. As the evening wore on, he faded deeper into the shadows.

Across the street from the market was the Ten Bells Pub, where many unfortunates solicited their trade.

He had complete attention on these unfortunates, but he kept his distance. As one would walk away from the area, he would sometimes follow. Experience had taught him to never be on empty sidewalks, even in the mist. All too often, this brought unwanted attention from ruffians and even police. If ruffians did show an interest in him, he revealed his formidable cane, hidden within his cloak.

He stared up at the reddened sky. "Ah, there's no better place in the world to do Hell's business," he whispered. "Evil is everywhere. Even I must dress so as to not bring attention to myself with the gangs of thugs and loafers practicing their craft. They sleep and drink in the alleys and courts during the day and come out at night to knock down and rob anyone. The police, these bobbies, are few in numbers, but a chance encounter while I am doing my father's business would be unwanted. Fortune will favor me, for this is my deification into the service of Lucifer." He glanced around, ensuring no one heard his voice.

Two loud drunken sailors stumbled across his path.

He backed into the darkness and watched them leave. "Ah, this is the perfect dark and dreary evening to begin my metamorphosis. Which blessed unfortunate is going to be the sacrificial lamb and allow me to eat from the Tree of Life and obtain eternal existence? No longer will I be god-like—I will attain eternal life and finally become a god. She will be honored by the Most High for participating in His son's henosis." He glanced around. "It is as if Hell has arisen again and is waiting for me to take my rightful place."

A man staggered out of the Ten Bells Pub and leaned on the streetlamp.

He watched the man but continued to think about his divine transformation. "I shall offer her body and blood—Satan's Eucharist; a sacrifice from hell."

At that very moment, walking north on Commercial Street near the pub, was a short, stout unfortunate.

She was approached by a medium-height man. He then struck up a conversation with her, and it was obvious they were discussing a sexual transaction.

"Oh yes, she is perfect," the man in the shadows muttered.

The unfortunate and her client left together and walked north.

The man in the shadows followed.

The couple turned right onto Hanbury Street.

There were so few street lights on the East End side streets that it was easy for the dark figure to follow and stay hidden within the shadows, especially in the haziness of the mist. He followed as the two turned left into a fenced-in yard and began speaking in low tones. The dark figure entered the yard from a different location and strategically positioned himself in order to make a quick escape if need be.

"Will you?" the accompanying man asked the unfortunate.

"Yes," she replied.

As the two began their carnal business, the dark figure felt revulsion. How could anyone gain satisfaction with something as disgusting and low as a prostitute?

The man began to get rough with the harlot.

"No!" the unfortunate blurted out forcefully, then pushed him away.

The tussle caused both of them to fall against the fence.

The man got up, cussed at her, threw a few coins on the ground, then left.

"It is time," the dark figure whispered to himself as the man vanished around the corner. He took another quick glance to ensure there were no witnesses then pounced. He grabbed the woman by the throat with such force that she was lifted up off the ground and onto her back, leaving no time to call for help.

Thud!

He could feel her tense up and even try to scream through his choke hold. It gave him an exhilarating sense of power.

In seconds she was unconscious.

The dark figure stared at her motionless body in the low light. His heart pumped hard as he experienced the thrill of the capture. He noticed the shiny reflection of rings on her hand, so he pulled them off her fingers and placed them near her feet in preparation for the ritual.

"*Corpus donum*—I give you her body," he chanted.

He opened up his cloak, took out a knife with a long, thin blade, held onto her chin from above her head, and cut her throat, consciously keeping away from the blood flow.

"*Sanguis donum*—I give you her blood."

The dark figure repositioned himself over the victim, and within minutes he had disemboweled her, taking out her uterus and surrounding tissues. He then stuffed them into a black bag.

"*Fructus arbor vitae sumo*—I take the fruit of the Tree of Life."

The dark figure picked up the rings, covered himself again with his cloak, and rushed out of the yard as quietly as he came.

* * *

Just after six a.m., Inspector Joseph Chandler was at the corner of Hanbury Street and Commercial Street when a number of men hurried by him.

"Another woman has been murdered!" one of the men yelled to him.

Chandler immediately ran toward the commotion and arrived at a scene where a crowd was gathering next to a fenced-in yard. He gazed down and saw the mutilated body of a woman. He bit his tightened fist in disgust, paused for a moment, then decided to take charge of the area. "Back up, everyone, please," he instructed firmly. "You there, young man, go fetch me a cover."

The boy nodded his head, ran to a neighboring building, and returned with a large sack.

Chandler placed the sack over the body and turned as the constables began to arrive. They immediately assisted in crowd control, which gave Chandler an opportunity to search the yard, now a swarm of police constables from the Commercial Street Police Station, a sub-station to Leman Street Police Station. Chandler directed a number of them to begin gathering statements from people in the crowd and in neighboring buildings.

The divisional surgeon, Dr. George Bagster Phillips, finally showed up. Phillips had been working as a divisional surgeon for years and knew his job inside and out. Not only was he a medical specialist, but he was also the crime scene investigation expert.

The detective inspectors worked closely with the divisional surgeons throughout the crime scene investigation and the followup inquiries. Chandler knew Phillips had an excellent reputation within the courts.

"Good morning, Doctor," Chandler greeted. "Our killer has struck again."

"A horrible tragedy," Phillips said. He took off the cover and the tarpaulin that had been placed over the body, then averted his eyes. "What mutilation. Even worse than the last one. No one deserves this kind of treatment, not even wretched unfortunates."

"This will cause panic in the streets," Chandler added.

Phillips leaned over and began his examination. "The body is cold, but rigor mortis is only just beginning. Inspector, I estimate the time of death as approximately two hours ago." He popped his head up and eyed Chandler. "What time is it?"

"I just walked down Brick Lane, Doctor," the police constable standing next to Chandler replied. "The time on the Black Eagle Brewery clock showed six thirty a.m."

"Which makes the time of death approximately four thirty a.m.," Phillips calculated. "Her neck is nearly severed, yet her tongue is protruding. This could only mean she was unconscious before her throat was cut."

Chandler turned his head away in disgust. "He certainly ripped at her body parts."

"It appears some of her organs are missing," the surgeon commented. "What's this?" He pointed at a number of items on the ground.

"I saw those too," Chandler said.

"We need to make sure no one touches any of this," Phillips remarked.

The ambulance rushed in.

Phillips directed the body to be taken to Whitechapel Work-house Infirmary Mortuary in preparation for a thorough examination of the body.

Inspector Chandler approached the three police sergeants in conversation. "Sergeant Badham," he said. "Please escort the body to the mortuary—and take a couple of constables with you."

"Make sure no one touches the body!" Phillips exclaimed.

Chandler eyed another pair of sergeants. "Sergeant Thick, contact Inspector Abberline about the murder. I'm sure he'll want to be informed immediately. Sergeant Leach, Dr. Phillips and I are going to begin searching the area for evidence. You're in charge of crowd control."

chapter three

Dunham squinted his eyes then blocked the sun with his hand. "There's not too much shade in the front of the lab building." He glanced over at Assistant Director Peters. "Now, who again are we waiting for, sir?"

Peters smiled. "The man who controls our checkbook, Edward—Congressman Henry O'Shea. He's the ranking member of the House Committee on Appropriations and holds a position on the Subcommittee on Commerce, Justice, Science, and Related Agencies."

Dunham gazed around, searching for signs of anyone heading toward them, then asked, "Why would a man of his importance want to personally visit our FBI lab anyway?"

Peters flashed him a grin, then looked out in the distance. "Each year, the director presents the FBI annual budget proposal to this subcommittee. Of the FBI's three-part mission—protecting the US against foreign intelligence threats, upholding and enforcing federal criminal law, and providing leadership and criminal justice services to all other law enforcement agencies in the US and abroad—the congressman has a great deal of interest in the third part—specifically the FBI's role in assisting local law enforcement serial killer task forces. He's asked to have a walk-through at the FBI lab in order for him to, as he puts it, 'make more informed financial decisions.' He fights for our cause, so we want to give him all the ammo he needs. The director and deputy director thought your task force's current assistance with the well-known Niagara Falls Serial Killer Case would be the perfect opportunity for his visit."

Dunham took a deep breath. "Talk about pressure."

"I'm confident you'll do fine, Edward," Peters said. "Congressman O'Shea wanted to be as inconspicuous as possible, so he'll be coming here by himself. He asked if we could refrain from introducing him with his title to your group. He doesn't want them to get too anxious, so introducing him as 'Mr. O'Shea' will be just fine."

A middle-aged man of medium-thin stature and possessing a receding hairline stepped onto the sidewalk and headed directly toward Peters and Dunham.

"And here he comes," Peters said.

"Michael, it's great to see you, again," O'Shea greeted ash he reached out to shake Peters' hand.

"It's an honor to see you again, Mr. Congressman."

O'Shea shook Peter's hand aggressively then turned toward Dunham. "And this must be none other than Dr. Dunham. It's an honor." O'Shea shook his hand.

Dunham, a little embarrassed, replied, "How do you do, sir? The honor's all mine."

O'Shea dropped his chin and raised his eyebrows. "You'd be surprised at how many congressmen and senators know about your successes, Dr. Dunham. You have become our golden egg." He turned his gaze upon the building behind Dunham and Peters. "Michael, tell me about this place. Give me a little background."

"Well, Congressman," Peters replied. "The FBI Laboratory Building has been in operation here in Quantico, Virginia, since 1932, housing a state-of-the-art forensic facility—" he eyed Dunham—"just like the Evidence Control Unit Dr. Dunham works out of, as we will see. We have approximately five hundred scientific experts and special agents working here. Federal funding has ensured cutting-edge science and technology for the sole purpose of solving cases and preventing criminal and terrorist acts."

O'Shea nodded. "I see."

Peters directed O'Shea toward the building entrance. "It provides assistance not only to the FBI and other federal government departments but also to state and local law enforcement—forensic testing, technical support, expert witness testimony, and training. The lab has even aided foreign countries requesting US assistance. In certain circumstances, as in the case with Dr. Dunham, experts have been temporarily assigned to augment local serial killer task forces."

O'Shea paused at the entrance of the building and turned toward Dunham. "This is precisely why I'm here. From what the assistant director has told me, the Niagara Falls Task Force has sent you a critical piece of evidence for your team to analyze."

"That's correct, sir," Dunham confirmed. "It's a handwritten sheet of parchment found near one of the crime scenes, with the victim's blood on it. It clearly came from the offender."

"How long has your team been working on the parchment?" O'Shea asked.

"We received it this morning, and we've already discovered a few things."

O'Shea started toward the front door. "Excellent, I'm excited to see your group analyze it further."

"Follow us, sir," Peters interrupted. He led them through the building and into one of the evidence control unit labs where a team of six was busy operating forensic equipment and instruments. Peters extended his arm and smiled at O'Shea. "I present Dr. Dunham's team of specialists, sir. Come on in."

Two analysts in the lab, a young, smooth-faced man and a bespectacled woman, simultaneously glanced up as the three men entered the lab.

The male analyst greeted them first. "Director Peters, Dr. Dunham, we have the results of our tests on the parchment." He shoved his hand into his pocket. "Oh, Dr. Dunham, here's your cell phone. You forgot it when you left this morning."

Dunham gave a twisted smile and grabbed it. "Thanks, Jack."

"Jack, Heather," Peters began. "This is Mr. O'Shea. Mr. O'Shea, this is Jack Stride, and behind him is Heather Kennedy."

Jack reached over and shook O'Shea's hand. "How do you do, Mr. O'Shea."

"Nice to meet you, Jack," O'Shea said, then shook Heather's hand. "Nice to meet you, Heather."

Heather's eyes revealed a flicker of recognition, but she responded calmly. "Nice to meet you too, Mr. O'Shea."

Peters motioned to the two specialists. "Jack and Heather are both chemists and document analysts, and both have been employed with the evidence control unit—Jack for fifteen years and Heather for ten years," he said, nodding at each scientist respectively. "Jack is Dr. Dunham's lead scientist."

O'Shea nodded.

"What have you found, Jack?" Dunham asked.

Jack glanced at Heather. "Dr. Dunham, Heather came through for us again."

Heather beamed. "Come over here. I'll show you." She turned and walked toward a table where the parchment had been placed in a glass container.

As she donned a pair of soft, white cotton gloves, she captured the attention of not only O'Shea, Peters, and Dunham, but also everyone else in the lab. She looked down and pointed to a section of the parchment. "Notice that the bloodstains—which are organic compounds—cover much of the writing and range in appearance from translucent to completely opaque. Notice also that much of the ink in the writing has been smeared." She paused and glanced up at Peters and O'Shea. "We applied light manipulation technology in order to reveal much more than what we can see with the naked eye."

Peters' head tilted. "If I read the accompanying documents correctly, the Buffalo lab report stated they already did this. They performed ultraviolet fluorescence analysis on the parchment, and it revealed a list of herbal medicine."

Heather nodded. "Yes, sir, but we're taking advantage of additional technologies not yet available to Buffalo, thus allowing us to view the parchment through a thousand-fold more wavelengths of electromagnetic energy. Although the Buffalo lab viewed the parchment in the ultraviolet, IR, and visible range, we accomplished it with much higher resolution."

O'Shea eyed Peters, obviously a little confused.

"In effect," Heather continued, "we can identify any specific wavelength of electromagnetic radiation that works best at penetrating the stains, making the stains invisible in the image in order for us to read the underlying writing. In this case, the UV fluorescence test offered the best wavelengths. Still, we didn't find anything new, although we have confirmed Buffalo's results—that the list is a list of herbs."

O'Shea nodded. "I see."

Heather smiled and pointed to another section of the parchment. "We took it a step further. We performed high resolution infrared analysis on the smears—or, actually, on the indentations created by the author's pen. Infrared reflection on the indented sections allows us to see what was written regardless if the ink is present or not."

Peters smiled.

Heather pointed to the monitor. "Note the results. Above the list is a three-word title." She led them over to a large flat-screen computer console. "We digitized the images and used computer imaging software to further enhance them." Heather grinned at Dunham. "Dr. Dunham, you haven't seen this yet."

"Excellent! I was waiting for this." Dunham took the seat then stared intensely at the image on the monitor.

Peters nudged closer, peeking over Dunham's shoulder at the image. "Wow, this certainly does reveal much more." Peters squinted. "But it's still difficult to read."

"We believe it's a three-word phrase with the center word 'of,'" Heather replied. "The first word is the most difficult to make out." She touched the screen with her index finger. "In the first word, the first letter is E or F, then L or I, followed by three illegible letters, and finally an R. The second word is 'of.' The third word starts with M, then A or O, followed by M, two illegible letters, and finally an N or H. We're attempting to make out a cogent phrase." She glanced over at O'Shea and Peters. "The team and I agree that the third word is 'mammon.'"

"What does mammon mean?" Peters asked.

"Well," Dunham interrupted, staring at the image. "In the Christian community, mammon is used to refer to a God-substitute, such as worshiping money over God. Alternatively, and less well-known, in the Middle Ages, Mammon was referred to as the name of the son of Satan." He glanced up at Peters. "Now, keeping in mind who wrote it—a ruthless killer—I'm inclined to believe it refers to the son of Satan."

Jack interrupted, "Dr. Dunham, the majority of us are sure that the first word is 'Flavor,' making the phrase, 'Flavor of Mammon.' This seems to conform to a sado-sexual typology, somewhat like Jeffrey Dahmer eating his sexual partners. In line with your idea that this offender is a Jack the Ripper copycat killer, one of the original Ripper letters, the 'From hell' letter, stated that he fried part of the kidney and ate it."

Peters nodded. "That certainly does make a lot of sense."

O'Shea eyed Dunham. "Hmm . . . the Niagara Falls serial killer a Jack the Ripper copycat killer."

"Similar offender signatures," Jack jumped in, matter-of-factly.

"One second," Dunham interrupted, staring at the image further. "I believe I have something."

Peters caught Heather and Jack glance at each other, both frowning; then they shrugged their shoulders, shaking their heads, and he knew why. They recognized immediately the moment their boss discovered something they missed, which in this case, likely disproved their hypothesis. He grinned; Dunham's team frequently submitted to his judgment, and for good reason.

"Your evaluation of the first word has merit," Dunham explained. "Especially since it creates a coherent three-word phrase indicative of a sexually-based motive, and as you said, in line with a Ripper copycat killer. There is just one problem. The first letter is definitely E and the fifth letter is an I." He noticed Heather and Jack, along with two other analysts, take a closer look at the image.

"You're right, Dr. Dunham," Heather said, shaking her head again. "We can't go against the data." She looked over at Jack. "Well, back to the drawing board."

"Hold on," Dunham interrupted again. He paused, gazing up at the ceiling, recalling something from memory. "Could it be?" He glanced back at the image, Assistant Director Peters, the team members, and Congressman O'Shea rapt with attention, awaiting his epiphany. Dunham stared at the image. "Yes, I believe so." He paused. "Although this would change the entire typology." He tapped his lips for a moment then quickly leaned back. "Oh yes, the article!"

Jack shook his head. "OK, enough of the talking to yourself, Dr. Dunham. What are you thinking—or saying?"

Dunham turned and realized the room had gone silent. "I'm sorry. It seems to me that the first word is 'Elixir,' which means the phrase is 'Elixir of Mammon.'"

Heather peered at it again. "Yes, it does seem to say elixir." She paused. "Excuse me for being persistent, but this doesn't seem to conform to a Jack the Ripper motive."

Dunham pointed his index finger at her. "Remember, it's only an assumption that the offender's typology is sexually related, since he seems to be a Jack the Ripper copycat killer."

"Exactly, hence the confusion," Heather replied. Jack nodded in agreement.

"Allow me to clarify," Dunham said. "Jack the Ripper of 1888 was never discovered, so his true motive might have been something other than the generally accepted typology of sexually based. A number of modern experts evaluated the extant documentary evidence on his victims and concluded the motive and behavior was anger-retaliatory. The mutilations were not necessarily on sexual organs, but organs specific to females. In other words, Jack the Ripper had an extreme hatred of women, as opposed to a morbid sexual lust for them."

Jack nodded. "OK."

Dunham held his finger up. "Another motive may have been personal gain. Recently, I read an article on Jack the Ripper, which suggested the Whitechapel killer's motive was to collect ingredients from parts taken from the organs of 'almost living' women and mix them with herbs in order to create an elixir of life."

O'Shea shook his head. "Almost living—meaning just killed."

Dunham nodded. "The author discovered an old newspaper article published during the time of the 1888 murders that reported the English police investigating this very theory. Again, the Ripper's typology would be personal gain as opposed to sexually based." He shifted his body in order to include everyone in the conversation. "This conclusion would also explain the list of herbal ingredients."

Jack nodded and added, "That does give a possible meaning for the list, and the Flavor of Mammon explanation does not."

"If true," Dunham continued, "this just might lead us to how the offender selects his victims, and that could open lines of investigation."

"I believe we have a lead!" Heather exclaimed and clapped her hands together.

"Excellent job, Dr. Dunham," Peters said, then glanced around at everyone. "And congratulations to your team as well."

"Absolutely amazing. I'm so honored to have been part of this. Rest assured, everyone, you have an ally in Congress."

Jack slapped himself on the forehead. "So you're Congressman O'Shea?"

O'Shea laughed. "None other."

"Outstanding work, guys," Dunham concluded. "Jack, will you print these images out for me?"

"Already done," Heather interjected as she handed Dunham a manila folder.

Dunham smiled at her. "I should've known." He then glanced at Peters. "It's time to reread an article, then I'm off to Buffalo."

Dunham led Peters and O'Shea toward the door.

As Heather, Jack, and the rest of the team gave each other high fives an approving buzz emanated from them. Heather grabbed a phone off the counter. "Oh, Dr. Dunham, you forgot your cell phone again!"

chapter four

1888: Monday, September 9. New York City, New York—Police Headquarters.

New York City's chief of detectives, Police Detective Bureau Chief Inspector Thomas F. Byrnes, enjoyed the view from his top-floor window. His success on the job had made him a national figure, and his New York City Police detective force had become a template for other big cities to emulate. He was a large man, slightly overweight now, but he could still take advantage of his size when he needed to intimidate an obstinate politician or even an unruly prisoner. The mayor often told him he was charismatic, driven, and brilliant, and he enjoyed that, but he knew his record could speak for itself. He had risen through the ranks to the top of the police officer hierarchy in only eleven years, which was a testament to his capabilities and motivation.

There was a loud knock at the door, causing him turn around in time to see his favorite detective, Inspector Thomas Crowley, burst in. Normally, no one would dare barge into his office, but he had taken a liking to the young detective; probably because they were so much alike, and Crowley reminded him of himself years ago: daring, rough, yet bright.

Crowley rushed up to Byrnes, daily newspaper in hand. "Sir, you gotta see this!" he exclaimed, then placed the newspaper on the desk as Byrnes sat down.

"See what, Inspector?"

"The killer has struck again in London, and Scotland Yard is dumbfounded," Crowley explained in excitement.

He and Crowley were mutual anglophiles and loved to read about English affairs, but Byrnes also liked to compare his own city police force with Scotland Yard. "Let's see here," Byrnes said and found the article.

WHITECHAPEL STARTLED BY A FOURTH MURDER
New York Times, September 9, 1888—from our own correspondent.

London, Sept. 8. – Not even during the riots and fog of February, 1886, have I seen London so thoroughly excited as it is to-night. The Whitechapel fiend murdered his fourth victim this morning and still continues undetected, unseen, and unknown. There is a panic in Whitechapel which will instantly extend to other districts should he change his locality, as the four murders are in everybody's mouth. The papers are full of them, and nothing else is talked of. The latest murder is exactly like its predecessor. The victim was a woman street walker of the lowest class. She had no money, having been refused lodgings shortly before because she lacked 8d. Her throat was cut so completely that everything but the spine was severed, and the body was ripped up, all the viscera being scattered about. The murder in all its details was inhuman to the last degree, and, like the others, could have been the work only of a bloodthirsty beast in human shape. It was committed in the most daring manner possible.

All day long Whitechapel has been wild with excitement. The four murders have been committed within a gunshot of each other, but the detectives have no clue. The London police and detective force is probably the stupidest in the world. The man called "Leather Apron," of whom I cabled you, is still at large. He is well known, but they have not been able to arrest him, and he will doubtless do another murder in a day or so. One clue discovered this morning by a reporter may develop into something. An hour and a half after the murder a man with bloody hands, torn shirt, and a wild look entered a public house half a mile from the scene of the murder. The police have a good description of him and are trying to trace it. The assassin, however, is as cunning as he is daring. Both in this and in the last murder he took but a few minutes to murder his victim in a spot which had been examined but a quarter of an hour before. Both the character of the deed and the cool cunning alike exhibit the qualities of a monomaniac.

Such a series of murders has not been known in London for a hundred years. There is a bare possibility that it may turn out to be something like a case of Jekyll and Hyde, as Joseph Taylor, a perfectly reliable man, who saw the suspected person this morning in a shabby dress, swears that he has seen the same man coming out of a lodging house in Wilton-street very differently dressed. However that may be, the murders are certainly the most ghastly and mysterious known to English police history.

Byrnes finished and glanced up at Crowley. "I'm simply amazed at how the transatlantic news-cable wire system can bring news to us as the event is happening. You know, Inspector, in my day, foreign news was weeks old before it made our newspapers."

"But, sir, there seems to be an actual Dr. Jekyll and Mr. Hyde loose on the streets of London."

"Very interesting, Inspector, very interesting." Byrnes thought for a moment. "Far be it for me to criticize English law enforcement, but this wouldn't happen in our city."

"You do realize, sir, if they don't catch this bloke, the press is going to start comparing Scotland Yard to New York City's police force."

"Let them," Byrnes said with confidence. "It's time for everyone to see who has the best police force in the world."

* * *

Friday, September 17. London, England—West End, Lyceum Theatre.

Eminent British civil engineer Sir Charles Hutton Gregory sat in the center of the theater, second row back, staring at two actors on stage conversing with each other. He glanced to the right and watched the lead actor, Richard Mansfield, hiding from the two actors behind a stage prop made to look like a wall and doorway.

Mansfield was bent over, breathing deeply, wearing torn clothing, and pacing back and forth.

One of the actors to the left reached behind a stack of packing straw and picked up an ax.

Both actors approached the door.

The actor without the ax pounded on the door. "Jekyll! This is Utterson. I demand to see you!"

Mansfield stopped pacing and crouched behind a table.

The actor playing Utterson pounded one more time. "I give you fair warning. Our suspicions are aroused, and I must and shall see you if not by fair means, then by foul—if not of your consent, then by brute force!"

Mansfield rose. "Utterson, for God's sake, have mercy!"

The actor playing Utterson faced the man with the ax and grasped his arm. "Ah, that's not Jekyll's voice." He glanced back at he door. "It's Hyde's! Down with the door, Poole!"

Mansfield fell the ground, contorted, then began to twitch violently, making it appear he was out of control.

The actor with the ax struck the doorframe prop.

A couple women in the audience screamed.

Sir Charles spotted one of the women and grinned.

Mansfield stopped twitching momentarily, twitched two more times, then stopped and relaxed completely, taking on the appearance of being dead.

The ax-wielding actor struck the door again, then the two opened the door, rushed in, and approached Mansfield.

The actor playing Utterson crouched down to Mansfield's side, inspected him, then looked up at the actor holding the ax. "We have come too late." He shook his head then eyed the prone body. "Whether to save or punish. Hyde is gone to his account, and it only remains for us to find the body of your master."

Sir Charles nodded, pleased with the actors' performances. The play lasted a further twenty minutes, and after a standing ovation, the audience began to disperse.

"Come, follow me to the Beefsteak Room, Sir Charles," a handsome man with a clean-shaven face and long black hair invited. "It's time for an excellent meal and great company."

Sir Charles smiled at the celebrated British actor and manager of the Lyceum Theatre, Henry Irving. "I will indeed, Henry."

They entered the famous Beefsteak Room—meeting place of an exclusive West End gentleman's club—and Irving presented Sir Charles with a seat.

As he sat, he scanned the room and marveled at the elegant décor. "I am truly honored, Henry."

Irving sat next to Sir Charles. "The honor is all mine."

Sir Charles noticed Irving was comparable in height and stature to himself, but that's where the similarities ended. Charles was nearing seventy years of age and preferred to present himself with a gentlemanly air, almost always dressed in a conservative, well-tailored coat, plaid trousers, and a top hat. He grinned, recalling a fellow engineer saying he was a throwback from the 1860s, but this was him. He shifted his gaze toward his companion.

Henry Irving, on the other hand, was the quintessential charismatic handsome British actor, dressed in fine, loose-fitting clothing. Irving was fifty years of age with a barely noticeable receding hairline hidden underneath wavy hair, and oh did he have a talent for communication! Not only did Irving have the respect of the entertainment community, he was loved by the public—especially the upper crust of British and American society.

Sir Charles turned his attention to the walls of this opulent room. His actor friend was clearly the reason the Lyceum Theatre was one of the most successful theaters in London. "Henry, I wanted to thank you again for inviting me to the show and to this post-performance dinner," Sir Charles said to his host. "You are a credit to our Freemason Order."

Irving drank from his cup then raised it. "Thank you, Sir Charles. I am honored to be a brother in the Jerusalem Order with you. Did you enjoy the show?"

"Indeed I did." Sir Charles gazed around at all of the guests seated at the massive Beefsteak Room dinner table. The dozens of individual conversations created a low rumble, interspersed with occasional laughs. "Mansfield did an excellent job as Dr. Jekyll and Mr. Hyde." Sir Charles glanced back at Irving. "I do not see him. Will he be here tonight?"

Irving turned his gaze toward the door. "He's supposed to be, but managing a show in the acting business is so dynamic."

A few moments later, the door opened, and a gentleman dressed in flowing theatrical attire walked in. Everyone stood up and clapped loudly. Enjoying the applause, the gentleman gave a deep bow. "Thank you, thank you, everyone," he said. "Please, go back to your dinner, conversation, and spirits." The gentleman headed directly toward Henry Irving at the head of the table.

The actor placed his hand on Irving's back. "Henry, I apologize for being so late, and sadly I must go back and attend to a small crisis."

"No problem at all, Richard," Irving remarked as he shook his head. "I certainly understand problems arising in theater. Before you go, I'd like to introduce you to a distinguished engineer and Mason brother of mine—Sir Charles Hutton Gregory. Sir Charles, this is, of course, our star of the evening, Richard Mansfield."

Mansfield bowed his head and said, "It is an honor, Sir Charles."

Sir Charles returned the bow. "The honor is all mine, Mr. Mansfield. Your portrayal of Dr. Jekyll and Mr. Hyde was brilliant. Tonight's performance was an astounding success, and I applaud you and your cast."

"Thank you, and I would be pleased if you would call me Richard," Mansfield said, but then he tightened his lips. "I have pressing business to attend to, but I hope we can discuss this further in the near future."

"Of course," Sir Charles replied and gave a second head bow.

Mansfield quickly left the room, waving to everyone, and even placing his hands on the shoulders of a few he obviously knew.

Sir Charles glanced over at Irving and whispered, "Mr. Mansfield's performance during the woman's murder was much too real for my constitution, though. He's quite a convincing actor. I can see why some have made a connection between Mansfield and the Whitechapel fiend." He shook his head. "Rubbish in my opinion, though."

"I must agree. He has such a kind soul, Mansfield."

Sir Charles gazed again around the room. "And thank you again for inviting me here tonight, Henry. I am having an excellent time."

"Not at all," Irving replied. "Although we need to impress upon your fellow engineers in the Lodge the idea of enjoying the show for themselves. With all of the newspaper organizations popping up, advertising costs have skyrocketed."

Sir Charles laughed and added, "I shall certainly do my part, Henry. Oh, by the way—is there any chance I might be introduced to the beautiful actress, Fanny Stirling? I've taken a fancy to her. She did such a good job in *Romeo and Juliet* a few years back."

Irving grinned and said, "Yes of course, Sir Charles. The Lyceum Theatre will soon be blessed by her beauty again, and I will speak with her."

Sir Charles stiffened his lips and leaned over the table. "Henry, is it true that *Macbeth* will be playing at the Lyceum Theatre this December?"

"It is true," Irving replied.

"Are you sure that is a good idea?" Sir Charles asked in concern and whispered even softer. "Those supporting the crown see that play as quite subversive."

"Even my critics realize I am the last one to promote anarchy against the queen." Irving said, obviously irritated. "The Lyceum Theatre could not survive if the monarchy was violently overthrown. Wealthy patrons and beneficiaries play a critical part in the success of a theater." Irving paused, taking a sip from his glass. "Besides, it is an extraordinary Shakespearean play, and the beautiful Ellen Terry will be playing the part of the Scottish Lady."

"I agree with you, Henry," Sir Charles added. "But as you know, many see the literary and artistic community as radical, and everyone knows you promote educational and intellectual dialogue in the Beefsteak Room—not unlike your radical mentor, Samuel Phelps, did at Sadler's Wells Theatre years ago." Sir Charles quickly peeked over his shoulder. "Also, that Sunday at Trafalgar Square was all too recent. The monarchy is very sensitive."

"People forget that I turned down Phelps' request to join him," Irving replied quietly but firmly. "I certainly appreciate your directness and concern, Sir Charles—I really do—but the arrangements for the Bard's Play are complete, and the show must go on. Opening day will be December twenty-ninth."

Sir Charles sat back, and his voice returned to a normal tone. "As you know, I personally am excited to see Ellen Terry's performance." He decided it was best to change the subject. "Oh, were you aware that our brother Freemason, George, has started a citizen's vigilance committee in hopes of catching the Whitechapel fiend?"

Irving eyed Sir Charles; his eyebrows rose. "You mean George Lusk, who oversaw the remodeling and decorating here at the theater?"

Sir Charles nodded and gazed around the room. "He did an excellent job on the theater, especially here in the Beefsteak Room."

"Indeed," Irving replied.

Sir Charles leaned closer to Irving. "He and his fellow tradesmen are frustrated with the police and believe they're doing a horrible job finding this killer. Lusk is afraid that the killer will hurt business." He pointed his finger to the right. "They have their meetings at the Doric Freemason Lodge in Anderton's Hotel on Fleet Street. Some of his Mason brothers are very nervous about his plans, but they have been on board with the idea so far."

"He may be right about the investigation," Irving commented. "Lusk is a very persistent man, and I'm sure he'll do an excellent job. Just awful, those killings, especially the most recent one—mutilating her body like that."

Sir Charles nodded. "Another actor, Charles Reeves, has joined Lusk's vigilance committee. Have you heard of him?"

"Yes, we've been acquaintances for years. In fact, he introduced me to Lusk when I was looking to improve the theater. He's an interesting character."

Sir Charles noticed two men in a serious conversation at the other end of the table. The man to the right was small, thin, and fragile-looking. The man to the left was large and stocky but quite refined in appearance. He recognized this man. "Bram Stoker is your manager, is that correct?"

Irving glanced over at Stoker and nodded. "Yes, I wouldn't know what to do without him. He has quite the talent for writing."

"Who is that smaller gentleman speaking with him?"

Irving finished a swig of his beverage and wiped his face. "That, Sir Charles, is Thomas Henry Hall Caine—a brilliant poet and writer from Liverpool. Bram's best friend." He grinned. "Aside from me, of course. I shall introduce him to you later." He leaned over to Sir Charles, spilling some of his drink. "He prefers to be called Hall Caine."

Sir Charles stared at the two in interest. "They are certainly engrossed in a lively conversation. It's like no one else exists, even in this very loud and entertaining environment." He thought for a moment. "I wonder what they're talking about."

Irving took another sip, now clearly in his drink. "Oh, I don't need to wonder. I know exactly what it's about. Bram just spoke to me about it in great detail. An old acquaintance of Hall Caine's has recently approached Bram about a mutual passion, and Hall Caine has been warning him to stay away from the man—some wealthy American expert in herbal medicines—the Great American Doctor, he calls himself. Anyway, this man was introduced to Bram by Oscar Wilde, the critic, another like-minded individual."

Sir Charles' interest piqued. "What is this mutual passion?"

Irving leaned over, now bracing himself on his elbow. "Bram, and a number of other employees of mine, have been involved with a strange, Catholic-friendly Rosicrucian Order. Apparently, the man is also Catholic. They—along with Wilde—have a mutual interest in discovering the Elixir of Life."

"I'm not surprised," Sir Charles remarked. "I've read about medical doctors attempting to do that very thing in France—from ground-up animal testicles, I believe."

Irving nodded. "Bram and Wilde believe the elixir is a mixture of special herbs, which leads back to Hall Caine's old acquaintance. This man goes one step further and believes the special herbs need to be mixed with ingredients from the animal kingdom." Irving paused. "He claims he read this in the *Magnum Opus* itself!"

Sir Charles stared straight at Irving in shock. "The *Magnum Opus*? Don't tell me he is in possession of the *Book of All Knowledge*! Isn't that just a myth?"

Irving grinned. "Well according to this man, an American army general living in Washington DC told him it exists, and it was brought to London in 1745 by the Count of St. Germain, a Rosicrucian. Of course, the man claims to have discovered it." He took another drink. "With the help of a partner."

Sir Charles stared at the two in conversation. "What a discovery that would be. I'm familiar with the *Magnum Opus*. They also call it the *Sacred Book M*—knowledge universal."

Irving squared up to Sir Charles. "Be careful, Sir Charles. Hall Caine warned us of this man's incessant lying. Few take him seriously back in America."

"I thought Rosicrucianism and Catholicism were incompatible," Sir Charles said. "I know the church doesn't look too highly upon Rosicrucianism."

Irving nodded. "The Rosicrucians that Bram associates himself with are very forbearing about Catholicism, and even open-minded about having women as members, for that matter. They call themselves the Order of the Golden Dawn. The problem is Bram would be excommunicated if the church found out, so he doesn't officially call himself a member."

"Are they attempting to create the elixir?"

"No—at least not Bram and my other employees. Bram told me that Hall Caine's old acquaintance is, though, and is asking him to help finance it."

"Maybe he's merely trying to take him for his money," Sir Charles suggested.

"He'd best be forewarned, but this is where it gets strange. The herbal expert has apparently taken it in a ritualistic, macabre direction—a most hellish approach, which Hall Caine has told Bram in no uncertain terms could cause society more harm than good. The man believes the concoction requires herbs of his own discovery mixed with ground-up ingredients taken from the internal organs of an—" he leaned even closer—"almost-living woman."

Sir Charles jerked his head back and grimaced. "How revolting!"

"Hall Caine told Bram about the Rosicrucian Illuminated Brotherhood's ancient warning that reading the *Magnum Opus* for selfish reasons will cause one to be seduced by the devil himself." Irving nodded. "The herbal expert's interpretation certainly seems most satanic."

"So, does Hall Caine believe his old acquaintance might be the Whitechapel killer? Quite the coincidence we have a mono-maniac on the loose collecting organs."

Irving sat back and shook his head. "No, he's convinced the man's not capable of such heinous crimes, although he is concerned that his obsession might bring him unwanted police attention. Personally, I agree with Hall Caine, but Bram has always been interested in immortally fiendish ideas about im-mortality, especially vampires."

"Well, it is certainly curious."

Irving shook his head again and waved his hand. "No, a man of such good breeding would never be involved in atroci-ties of this nature. Besides, Hall Caine told us that he's quite the coward. I'm convinced the killer is most likely a Jew or one of those foreigners living on the East End." He took another drink. "But still, it's an intriguing motive for a person to kill. It's very Shakespearean, like the witches' brew in the Scottish Play. Medical maniac attempts to create a hellbroth in order to gain immortality. Oh, I do miss the Macbeth role," he hiccuped.

"Very interesting," Sir Charles commented. "If you're sure, then I do agree with you that this man could not be the brutal Whitechapel fiend. Nonetheless, if some medical maniac is in-deed creating an elixir of life—hellbroth, as you put it—it certain-ly wouldn't hurt informing my friend at Scotland Yard about it."

"If you could, please do not mention where you heard the story. I would prefer not to have the Yard poking around the theater. Besides, Bram and Hall Caine would never forgive me."

"Of course, Henry. Of course."

chapter five

PRESENT DAY: Wednesday, September 20. Buffalo, New York—Lombardo Funeral Home.

Celine Faulks could think of a thousand places she'd rather be than in this funeral home, but she knew it was important to her friend's family that she pay her last respects. She was still numb from the shock of Angie's brutal death. It happened just a few days ago, and it had barely set in that she'd never get to speak to her friend again. As she got to the front of the line to speak with Angie's parents, she noticed the redness in their eyes. She hesitated, then approached Angie's father.

He gently grabbed her hands. "Thank you for being here, Celine. My wife and I certainly appreciate it, and I'm sure Angie somehow knows that you gave her your last respects."

Mrs. Sparks rubbed her shoulder but stayed silent.

Celine's eyes teared up. "I'm so sorry, Mr. and Mrs. Sparks. Everyone loved Angie." Celine could feel Mr. Sparks' trembling hands tighten their grip. These last few days must have been insanely miserable for Angie's parents, finding out she was murdered by a serial killer then having to prepare for her funeral.

Mr. Sparks put on a kind smile. "My daughter actually spoke of you. She said you were the reason she'd passed a couple of her courses. She said you were the best college study-mate ever."

Celine returned the smile. "We met at Buffalo State last year. We had two classes together."

"Angie may have told you I work for the State Department, and as a result, I've been in Europe for the past year."

Celine nodded. "Yes, she told me."

Mr. Sparks closed his eyes and shook his head. "It kills me to not have been with her, her last year of her life. I had no idea that there was this Niagara Falls Ripper prowling around Western New York." He gazed around the funeral parlor. "I see so many law enforcement officers here paying their respects. Some have told me they're working as hard as they can, but nothing has come up yet." Mr. Sparks released Celine's hands.

"The sooner they catch him the better, Mr. Sparks," Celine reassured.

They kissed each other's cheeks, and Celine walked over to an empty corner of the room and waited for her younger brother, Robbie. She appreciated Robbie accompanying her, even though he didn't know Angie personally. Robbie was two years younger than she was and a senior at Tonawanda City High School. The two of them were born and raised in the small city, which was just north of Buffalo.

"Is your name Celine?" a voice whispered.

Celine glanced up at a very handsome man in his early to mid-twenties.

"Yes," she replied nervously, now overly cautious around strange men.

"I overheard you speaking to my boss, Mr. Sparks." He offered his hand. "My name is Jeff Barnes. I also work for the State Department. I'm on Mr. Sparks' staff and just flew in two nights ago. I go everywhere he goes." He grinned. "I'm kind of like his expensive baggage carrier."

Celine's tight lips relaxed into a slight smile, and she shook his hand. "It's nice to meet you. I'm Celine Faulks."

He scanned the room as he stood next to her. "Do you mind if I ask you about this serial killer?" Barnes eyed Celine. "The Niagara Falls Ripper? It's amazing how out-of-the-loop you get being stashed in Europe for so long."

Celine nodded. "Sure. Actually, I'm probably a good person to get the details from because my brother, Robbie, is considered kind of a local expert. He's always bugging me about it, so I can't help but learn something."

"When did it all start?"

Celine paused for a moment and stared at the ceiling. "Well, around six months ago, during Easter weekend I think. The police call him the "Niagara Falls Serial Killer" because he killed the first woman on the American side of Niagara Falls near the Niagara Casino. All of the murders have been in the Western New York area, and he always mutilates them, which is why the news calls him the Niagara Falls Ripper. I guess he rips their guts out just like the famous Jack the Ripper did." She paused for a moment as her stomach lurched at the thought of her friend having been torn apart like the news outlets described in gory detail.

Barnes cringed. "How disgusting."

Celine nodded, gulped, and whispered, "The weirdest thing is, he takes body parts. They say he takes them as some kind of trophy. Robbie thinks he does the Jeffrey Dahmer thing and eats them."

"I bet your brother's right," Barnes remarked and shook his head. "It's probably terrifying everyone around here."

"Everyone I know is freaked out for sure, especially women since we're his targets. The killer's roaming around freely, and we don't even know what he looks like." Celine stared around the funeral home. "He might even be in this room as we speak."

Barnes scanned the room again. "How many women has he murdered?"

Celine thought for a moment and said, "Five, I think . . . yeah, five. The second murder was a middle-aged woman just like the first, but she was killed in Delaware Park while out jogging just before sunset." Celine paused. "The third woman was I think thirty. She was found at Lewistown Art Park just north of Niagara Falls on the opening night of the Buffalo Philharmonic Orchestra Summerfest—a big thing in Lewistown. I should know, I was there."

Barnes frowned and shook his head.

"The fourth was just like Angie—in college, but from Niagara Community College—and she'd been murdered just after the Lewistown lady. She was found dead south of Buffalo, this time in the concert area at the Erie County Fair. That's one of the biggest fairs in the country, which goes on for ten days in the middle of August. She was killed on the night of their biggest concert of the year, some country singer whose latest song was number one on the charts."

"Sounds like he hasn't invaded anyone's home," Barnes said.

"Not yet, anyway."

"And the police are no closer to catching this guy?"

Celine shook her head. "Nope, at least that's what they're saying publicly."

Barnes raised his open hand, showing his fingers. "So, Angie was the fifth victim?"

Celine nodded and frowned. "Over a month had gone by since the last murder," she whispered. "And it seemed people began to forget about them." She shook her head. "But he struck again. Angie lived on the Elmwood Strip in Buffalo. It's a quaint, artsy area next to Buffalo State College with small stores and restaurants. I'm not sure if you've been there, but her apartment was right next to a renovated residential home-turned-restaurant."

Barnes nodded. "Yes, we were there yesterday. The staff is taking care of everything for Mr. and Mrs. Sparks. That's the least we could do."

Celine paused. "They figure Angie left her apartment for the bus stop, which was down three blocks, in order to go to a Buffalo Bills Monday Night Football game. She and her boyfriend won tickets just two days before."

Barnes looked around. "Is her boyfriend here?"

Celine pointed to a young man sitting next to Angie's mother. "That's him. Angie never made it to the game that night. As you probably know, her body was found . . . mutilated in a secluded alleyway three houses before the bus stop. No one saw or heard anything, and it was as if the killer was waiting for her." Celine paused again.

"This guy's bound to slip up sometime. Maybe they'll get his DNA or something."

Celine pointed toward a couple uniformed men whispering to each other. "I overheard some of the police talking about the case—well, actually, Robbie did. He said they were talking a lot about the FBI and their criminal profiling and how it's produced no viable suspects. They were talking about this guy nicknamed the Watchmaker—some serial killer expert who was just assigned to the case. Robbie said the police seemed excited about him, so things might be looking up."

"Sis, you ready to go?"

Celine turned her head toward her brother and his friend, who had just popped their heads around the corner. She raised her finger. "One second, Robbie, I'll be right there."

Robbie nodded to Barnes, then he and the other young man slipped back into the hallway.

Barnes grinned. "It looks like your brother's ready to go."

"Yeah," Celine said. "All his life he's wanted to be a police detective or FBI agent, and although he was disgusted when the serial killer killed someone I knew, he's been in his element this last year trying to figure out who this killer is. It's annoying, really, but some of his ideas are pretty good. His friend is Ralph, and they're two peas in a pod. Those two and another friend, Kyle, who didn't come to the funeral, are like the three musketeers. They go everywhere together."

Robbie stuck his head back into the room. "Come on, come on, Celine. Let's go!" he said hurriedly, causing Celine to blast him an angry look.

Barnes shook Celine's hand. "Thanks again, Celine. Now, don't be careless—keep your serial killer radar going at all times." He smiled. "The next time I'm in town, do you mind if I look you up?"

Celine beamed. "That sounds great. Nice to meet you, Jeff." They parted, and she met up with Robbie and Ralph in the hall.

"Did he ask you out?" Robbie asked as both he and Ralph grinned teasingly.

"Shut up," Celine blurted out. "Come on."

They followed her out of the building and piled into the car. Once everyone was situated, Celine pulled onto the road.

"Sis, I think I know why there is no pattern to his selection of victims, besides them being female."

Celine quickly eyed Robbie then turned her gaze back to the road. "Why?"

"No pattern is his pattern," Robbie exclaimed. "I mean he's purposely choosing random women in order to keep the police off his trail."

"I bet you're right," Ralph replied, leaning forward and joining into the conversation. "I'm kinda surprised that there was no sexual intercourse."

"These guys are so whacked," Robbie explained. "The knife is his penis. In his mind, he did have sex."

"What!? That's horse crap," Celine stated bluntly.

"I'm not kidding. Just check the latest research on serial killers. It has everything to do with what they call sado-sexual, or sadistic sexual, behavior. It boils down to primal instincts, and what's more primal than sex and violence?"

"Rob's right, Celine," Ralph agreed and raised his eyebrows, grinning slightly and reclining into the backseat. "For guys, it's all about sex."

"Well, he didn't have actual sex, so I think it has more to do with power and him getting a thrill out of watching the 'weaker sex' being tortured," Celine said, making one-handed air quotes. "They say that rape is more about power than sex, mixed with a little thrill."

Robbie nodded. "Could be. Power is very primal, but if it's true that he is trying to imitate Jack the Ripper . . . some psychologists say he was a sado-sexual serial killer too."

"Did they ever find out who Jack the Ripper was?" Celine asked. "What was Jack's last name?"

"No, it's still an unsolved mystery, and the guy probably wasn't even named Jack," Robbie answered.

"Then they don't really know, do they? They don't really know his motive was sadistic sexual behavior. He might've just hated women who looked like his abusive prostitute mommy."

Out of the corner of her eye, Celine saw Robbie stare out the window. He nodded. "I can't argue with that, sis. I can't argue with that."

There was a long silence. "Isn't it interesting that it's a sexual thing with serial murderers using their knife as a penis when they don't have sex, but serial rapists who actually do have sex are not doing it for sex, but for power?" Celine said as she glanced again at Robbie, who was now typing on his iPhone.

"Hang on . . . I'm texting Kyle about tonight. Hey, do you mind dropping us off at his house? We plan on staking out the Kiss concert at the First Niagara Center tonight. Ralph thinks the Niagara Falls murderer will do his next killing at a popular event where it's not unusual to dress like freaks. Besides, it'll be an awesome time."

"That's right," Ralph added. "If you look at all of the killings, they were at public places with some kind of popular event going on. What's more popular than a Kiss concert?" Ralph beamed. "And think of all the babes." He leaned forward. "Speaking of babes, did you see that hot girl in the second row? She was checking me out big time."

Celine shook her head. "Ralph, it was a funeral. You shouldn't have been thinking that kind of stuff. Besides, you think every girl checks you out. I'm sure it was a case of her creeping out because you were ogling her at a memorial service."

"You were getting pretty friendly with that guy!" Ralph blurted out. "Besides, she wanted me, and funerals are the perfect place to hook up if you play the consolation card right. Your brother's my wingman. He's on the same page." Ralph turned to his friend. "Rob, what'd Kyle say? Is it a go tonight?"

"Yep," Robbie responded then looked over at Celine. "You wanna skip work tonight and come with us?"

"Of course not. I make good money at the theater. Regardless, I prefer a play over a rock concert anytime." She glanced over at Robbie. "But have fun tonight."

"Celine, what do you do at Shea's, anyway?" Ralph asked.

"Well, on evenings and weekends, I work at the concession stands Shea's has in the halls just outside the theater. Most people who work there are retired volunteers, but one of their wealthy patrons, Fredrick Deckman, is a friend of Dad's, and he got me the job. He thought it might give me connections because I'm a theater major at Buff State." She shrugged her shoulders. "Actually, I just like working there because it's so beautiful, and also because I can watch the plays and performances for free."

"Maybe you can get me a job," Ralph suggested. "What do you think?"

"Actually, they did just hire a couple of other people, but the manager only wants college students. Sorry, maybe next year."

"That's OK," Ralph said. "I was just thinking that there might be some hot rich ladies there. I bet it's cougar central."

Celine just rolled her eyes and shook her head.

chapter six

Detective Sergeant Dinnie paced the briefing room with
one eye on the closed door to the office of the local detective
in charge, Inspector Reid. Chief Inspector Swanson from headquarters was in a meeting with all four first-class detective inspectors: Andrews, Abberline, Moore, and Reid.

Abrupt, loud laughter from the corner of the room caught
Dinnie's attention. It was a group of young detectives and constables surrounding none other Sergeant Froest. He grinned at
Froest, who had his clay tobacco pipe dangling from the side
of his mouth, smoke billowing. His audience was mesmerized
with story after story—typical of Froest. *The perfect medicine for
a division of exhausted police officers working excessive overtime
with no end in sight*, Dinnie thought to himself.

"Sergeant Dinnie!" Froest yelled. "Remember I told you about
Uncle Thomas and his run-in with Buffalo Bill at the Carlton
Club last year?"

Dinnie waved his hand and grinned.

Froest continued with his story.

The distinctive smells of years of burning candles and pipe
smoke embedded in the wood of the old building assaulted Dinnie's nose. He noticed the low wooden ceilings and walls—which
were in dire need of painting—the rickety old floorboards, and
the well-worn chairs and desks, which were randomly stationed about the room. It reminded him of those tough days at

a divisional police station early in his career, and in a strange way, he missed it.

An older, rough-looking detective sergeant entered the room, stopped, and glanced at Froest. He grinned. "Sergeant, are you telling lies again?"

Froest beamed back. "Sergeant Godly, you of all people should know that I am duty-bound to educate my junior colleagues about the ways of class and decorum." He paused. "There's room here for the codgers, as well."

Godly grinned, raised both hands, and flopped them forward. "Ah, codswallop!" He spotted Dinnie, waved, then marched through the room to the duty desk.

Dinnie waved back, then thought for a moment. How coincidental that on the very same day Andrews, Abberline, and Moore joined the investigation, the killer struck again. Over a week had passed since this Chapman murder occurred, and as expected, it was the biggest news of the day. These atrocious killings had become world news—embarrassing news that the British government and Scotland Yard detested.

Chief Inspector Swanson, along with the first-class inspectors, entered the briefing room, which signaled everyone to take their seats.

Froest approached Dinnie and pointed at Swanson. "It's great the chief inspector is making a show."

Dinnie nodded. "Indeed." Just like with Sergeant Froest, a visit from well-loved Chief Inspector Swanson also boosted morale. Dinnie, Froest, and Andrews had recently worked closely with Swanson at headquarters, and they knew him to be levelheaded and blessed with a keen intellect. He had a kind face and was always in a good mood. His calm demeanor tended to relax subordinates, making it easy to like him and work for him.

Swanson approached Dinnie and Froest and shook their hands. "Gentlemen, it's nice to see you again. How are you doing?"

"Fine, sir," Froest said.

Dinnie nodded. "All is well, sir."

Swanson nodded then made his way up to the podium next to the first-class inspectors. Swanson glanced out at the seated police officers. "Good morning, gentlemen. Our new boss, Assistant Commissioner Anderson, is still in Ireland, but he and I are in constant communication. He is fully aware that each and every one of you is overburdened with thirty-plus cases, only to be loaded with the responsibility of finding the Whitechapel murderer, and both of us are in agreement that this is a recipe for failure." He pointed at the inspectors. "As you know, we've assigned Inspectors Abberline, Andrews, and Moore—and their detective teams—to focus solely upon this case, in order for your division to keep up on your workload. While this'll allow you to spend time on your other cases, please continue to keep your eyes and ears open for possible leads." He paused. "Per the commissioner's directive, we've increased the number of police constables in hopes of improving the chance of catching the killer in the act. They've not been trained in effective investigative techniques as you have, but at least this'll give you more resources." He smiled encouragingly. "Good luck, and keep your chin up."

"Thank you, sir," a detective yelled out.

Swanson left the podium, shook the inspectors' hands, then quickly left the building.

Inspector Reid took the podium.

Dinnie knew Reid well. When Abberline was in this division as detective-in-charge for nearly a decade, Reid was his number-two man. Abberline told him Reid was the reason for his success. Even though Reid's weak chin—partially hidden by a thick blonde goatee—gave the impression of an ineffective leader, his subordinates knew the opposite.

Reid cleared his throat. "Good morning. This meeting will deal strictly with the Whitechapel murder case, so I'd like to pass it on to Inspector Abberline."

Abberline nodded, took the podium, and faced the detectives. "Good morning. Many theories have been proposed as to the identity of the murderer, and we would be remiss if we didn't entertain each and every one. Recently, an eminent engineer received some information that suggests we have a real-life Dr. Jekyll and Mr. Hyde on our hands."

Numerous conversations immediately sprang up.

Abberline raised both hands. "Hold on, hold on. We need to be cautious. It's true there's evidence connecting the play with the murders, but it's probably nothing." He paused. "Allow me to finish."

The room quieted down.

"According to the esteemed engineer, the killer is an upstanding doctor practicing during the day, but when the sun sets, his insanity sets in, and he becomes single-minded in his search for the elixir of life. Apparently, he's mixing special herbs with ingredients found only in the organs of a freshly murdered woman."

The detectives broke into more sidebar conversations.

Reid faced the detectives. "Quiet!"

"Listen," Abberline said once the room fell silent. "This is the kind of story the press would love to get their hands on, and if it makes the papers and we ignore it, especially when it came from one of our more prominent citizens, Scotland Yard will feel the wrath from the politicians."

"Inspector, my team will look into it," Andrews replied.

"Thank you, Inspector," Abberline acknowledged. "I'd recommend you make a few visits to local herb stores and ask if any of them have had an unusual customer asking strange questions."

Andrews nodded.

Abberline raised his finger. "Oh, also, recall Coroner Baxter's claim about some American medical student offering large sums of money for anatomical specimens. According to the medical community, the museum curator did indeed have such a request made to him, but it came from a Philadelphia physician, who has not been to our shores for a full year." He paused. "There's more to the story, but that'll be for later."

Inspector Reid raised his hand. "Speaking of museums, Constable Neil, the PC who discovered the Nichols body in Buck's Row three weeks ago, spoke to me about an interesting public complaint."

Abberline's eyes widened. "Oh?"

"His beat out of Bethnal Green Police Station covers the London Hospital area on Whitechapel Road, and as he walked by, the owner of a cheesemonger's shop approached him. The owner complained to him about a freak wax museum and live entertainment show next to his shop."

Abberline nodded. "The wax museum—I'm familiar with the place. We shut it down in '82 for violating the Obscene Act of '57, and in '84 it reopened for a few weeks, displaying a deformed person they called the Elephant Man."

A couple detectives nodded.

"The London Hospital Medical College immediately demanded we shut it down," Abberline continued. "They claimed it was affecting their medical students' morality." He shook his head.

"How ironic that the Elephant Man then moved into the London Hospital, invited by the very same physicians doing the complaining."

"The prince and princess of Wales just visited him last month," Moore interrupted.

Inspector Reid grinned. "Not surprising that you'd know this critical piece of information."

Moore smiled back.

"I remember seeing the Elephant Man!" a detective exclaimed. "What a grotesque sight. He had massive growths all over his body—sad, really."

Reid raised his hand to regain their attention. "Actually, that's not the same museum. That particular one was Ol' Man Cotton's anatomical wax museum, and it's still shut down. Just a few buildings west, a stone's throw away from the London Hospital, on the corner of Whitechapel Road and Thomas Street, is a chamber of horrors wax museum—like Madame Tussaud's Chamber of Horrors on the West End, but a penny show version. The proprietor also operates a live entertainment show in the adjoining building. It has a ghost show and a few other shows designed to bring in the public. Apparently, the crowds outside in the street are a complete nuisance to all the neighbors."

"Isn't Bethnal Green Police Station handling it?" Dinnie asked.

Inspector Reid nodded. "Yes, but the live show nuisance is not why I mentioned it. There's a connection to the Whitechapel murders, and it gets pretty strange. Neil entered the chamber of horrors museum and the main attraction. In the basement-level showroom are full wax models of the Whitechapel victims Tabram, Nichols, and Chapman—the heads nearly severed, deep wounds, internal organs, blood, the lot! Apparently, only a week after each victim lost her life, a wax model of her corpse went up in the cellar."

Froest sat up. "So, even before the bodies have been buried, this showman has immortalized the Whitechapel fiend's handiwork!" He shook his head. "How repulsive."

"What has also concerned Neil," continued Reid, "was how close the displays seemed to be to the actual murder scenes, as if the killer was involved with setting the displays up."

Abberline started pacing, stopped, and faced the detectives. "Such morbid displays at a time like this will certainly cause us more harm than good." He paused for a moment. "On the other hand, if the killer's visiting this museum—either by design or for inspiration—maybe it's the lead we've been looking for."

Andrews smiled. "Inspector, if you don't mind, my team will take this on also."

Abberline nodded. "Great. Find out how the museum owner received his information on the murders."

"Of course," Andrews answered.

Froest glanced over at Dinnie. "I was at Madame Tussaud's wax museum last January. The chamber of horrors gallery is off to the side of the main attraction. Quite the popular sideshow."

"Hmm," Dinnie replied. "If this Whitechapel museum is filled with the same gory and violent displays, our killer might be getting ideas from this museum."

"The whole gallery was wax displays of graphic executions of murderers. It even had bloody dismembered heads next to a guillotine."

Dinnie shook his head. "The more graphic the better, apparently."

"Let's you and I take this one, Walter." Froest said to Dinnie.

Dinnie smiled at Froest. "You could certainly dismantle a few exhibits in a hurry," he added jokingly.

Abberline raised his hand. "Last order of business. After my personal escort of suspect William Piggott to this station, and subsequent interrogation, he curiously went crazy. He's now at the asylum at Bow. I have to admit I was becoming convinced of Piggott's guilt, but I just don't see how someone so insane could've committed these very calculated murders."

"If another murder occurs while he's in the asylum, then we can surely take him off the list," Moore replied.

Abberline leaned over the crowd of detectives. "Are there any further questions?" After a lull, Abberline turned to Reid and nodded.

Reid faced the detectives. "Thank you, gentlemen. That is all."

Dinnie and the other inspectors rose from their seats, ready to take on their new assignments.

chapter seven

Captain Johnson rushed down the hallway from the elevator, then poked his head into Detective John Riggs' doorway.
"Riggs, meet me in my office." He quickly vanished.

"I'll be right there, Captain," Riggs replied to the empty door
as he searched his desk and grabbed his notepad. He stood up
and buttoned his tailor-made suit on his way out—something he
did every time. Riggs was relatively tall, clean-shaven, and athletically built. He knew he looked more like a high-end lawyer
than a detective in his pressed shirts and costly suits. Captain
Johnson occasionally teased him about his good looks and im-
maculate appearance, but he knew his boss favored him.

Johnson was sitting at his desk and reaching for a folder
when Riggs entered the office. "What's up, boss?"

"One of the FBI's chief scientists, a clinical forensic expert
named Dr. Edward Dunham, who's from the NCAVC's Behavioral Analysis Unit out of Quantico, Virginia, is joining our task
force." He waved the report and opened the file.

Riggs raised his eyebrows and nodded. "Dunham—isn't he a
pretty big deal?"

"That's right. But, rumor has it he's rather absentminded,
and you're the most organized, detail-oriented person on the
force, so you're assigned to him while he's here. I'd like you to
take care of him, and be at his beck and call at all times." He

dropped his chin and eyed Riggs. "He's the best, so learn from him."

Riggs beamed, thinking about the opportunity he'd have working with such a reputable person. "Outstanding! He can crash at my place."

"No need. His accommodations are all taken care of, but he prefers not to have a rental, so you're his ride."

"I'm there," Riggs replied happily.

"He just finished investigating the parchment lead in our Niagara Falls Serial Killer Case."

Riggs frowned. "That was a dead end."

"Not so," Johnson said. "Apparently, he found something."

"Excellent."

Johnson pointed his finger at the door. "He just arrived and should be up here in a few minutes."

Riggs smiled at Johnson. "We're finally bringing in the heavyweights. I remember he broke the Kansas City Serial Killer Case a few years back." He paused. "I hear they call him 'the Watchmaker.' Wonder what that's about."

Johnson shrugged his shoulders. "I have no idea, but what I do know is he's relentless and has a phenomenal reputation as a sleuth."

The front desk secretary's voice emanated from Johnson's phone speaker. "Sir, Dr. Dunham's here."

Johnson eyed Riggs. "Excellent, Mary. Bring him here."

"Follow me, Dr. Dunham," they could hear her say before the intercom clicked off.

Johnson and Riggs craned their necks toward the hallway. Mary led the way, Dunham nearly bumping into her when she slid to a stop at Johnson's office door. He nodded to her, evidently embarrassed, then entered the room.

"Thank you, Mary," Johnson said and stood up to greet Dunham as the secretary backed out of the office and closed the door behind her. "Dr. Dunham, it's great to see you again, and welcome to the team."

"Thank you," Dunham replied as they shook hands. "It's great to finally be here. The hotel accommodations are outstanding." He glanced over at Riggs.

"Riggs, I'd like to introduce you to Special Agent Dr. Edward Dunham," Johnson said. "Dr. Dunham, this is Detective John Riggs."

"Pleased to meet you, Detective Riggs."

Riggs grabbed his hand enthusiastically and gave a firm and friendly handshake. "It's a pleasure to meet you, Dr. Dunham. Please call me Riggs. Everyone does."

"We have a general task force meeting next week," Johnson interrupted. "So I'll introduce you to everyone then. We have representatives from the New York State Police, the sheriff's departments in all of the Western New York counties, and also from a number of local suburban police departments. Outside my office is the task force headquarters, but with this many police involved, we generally have our scheduled meetings in the auditorium."

"I'm looking forward to joining the team, Captain," Dunham said.

Johnson smiled. "Everyone is excited to meet you. I have yet to find someone who doesn't know of you."

Dunham grinned humbly. "Thanks, Captain. I hope I can add to all of this law enforcement experience."

"I was just telling Riggs here about your recent revelations on the Niagara Falls Serial Killer Case."

"Could you fill me in on some of the details?" Riggs asked.

Dunham nodded. "Absolutely, as you know, all of the victims were strangled from the front, nearly decapitated with a single knife-cut to the throat, and completely eviscerated—and missing at least one internal organ."

"Which is why the press has been calling the murderer the 'Niagara Falls Ripper,'" Riggs interjected.

"Precisely—a copycat killer of the original City of London Jack the Ripper of 1888, yet, this has gotten us no closer to finding the killer . . . which is quite reminiscent of the original unsolved Ripper case. Up until now, there's been very little evidence pointing to the copycat killer, but this one and only slip-up could possibly give us a lead."

"The parchment, you mean?" Riggs asked.

"Yes, as you know, a block away from the last victim, investigators discovered a small, blood-soaked, and torn piece of paper, or parchment, and DNA testing identified the blood as belonging to the victim." Dunham sat down in the open seat behind him, which prompted Johnson and Riggs to do the same. "The parchment clearly came from the killer." He nodded to Johnson. "When Captain Johnson asked me to help with the case, I asked him to send me the parchment, since it was the strongest piece of evidence available. Our lab has the latest in light manipulation technology, so we analyzed the evidence under multiple wavelengths of light. This allowed us to make out the title of the list as 'Elixir of Life.'"

Riggs grinned and glanced at Johnson. "Excellent."

Dunham nodded. "The phrase jarred my memory, and I recalled reading an article a few years back on a possible Jack the Ripper motive involving an elixir of life."

"Hmmm, a Jack the Ripper copycat killer leaving Jack the Ripper-type evidence. I think we can throw coincidence out the door," Riggs suggested.

"Ultimately, this suggests a completely different typology for our killer," Dunham explained. "Meaning instead of a sado-sexual psychopath, we have a psychopath motivated by personal gain mixed with a little anger-retaliatory behavior. This will significantly change our task force's direction."

"What does the article say?" Riggs asked.

Dunham shuffled through his briefcase. "I have it right here." He pulled out a folder and scanned it. "It's a newspaper article from the *Bridgeport Morning News* in Connecticut, dated October 8, 1888. It discusses an American from New York City, who kept an herb shop in the Whitechapel District, and was visited by an English detective about a customer asking for an unusual compound of herbs. Apparently, they had information that the murderer was a medical maniac, trying to find an elixir of life by mixing a concoction of herbs with essential ingredients in the parts taken from the female victims—creating what the reporter called a 'hellbroth.' The author then connects Ripper suspect Francis Tumblety with this American from New York City."

"Isn't this Francis Tumblety the Jack the Ripper suspect who's buried in Rochester just an hour and a half away?" Riggs asked.

Dunham's eyes opened wide. "That's right. Very impressive, Detective Riggs."

Riggs grinned and noticed Johnson staring at him. "Hey, I saw a Jack the Ripper episode on the History Channel once," he said proudly.

Johnson glanced back at Dunham, pointing to the doctor's report. "Good catch, Dr. Dunham. Mammon the son of Satan, hellbroth, elixir, and Jack the Ripper—this is just too coincidental. Now we somehow have to apply this to our Niagara Falls Serial Killer Case."

"I agree," Dunham replied. Again he retrieved an article from his briefcase. "Another article, more recently published, also connects Tumblety to the Ripper murders of 1888. The name of this particular article is 'Tumblety & the Elixir of Life,' and the author is a man by the name of Ryan Stanton. He lives in your area. Coincidentally, he's currently heading up an exhumation of that very Jack the Ripper suspect, Francis Tumblety."

"Cool," Riggs replied.

"I've scheduled a meeting with him on Monday," Dunham continued. "If our killer is indeed trying to follow in the footsteps of Jack the Ripper, specific to this elixir of life theory, who better to help us catch this guy than the ripperologist who discovered the elixir of life–Jack the Ripper connection in the first place?"

"Ripperologist?" Riggs asked.

Dunham nodded. "Yes, a ripperologist is a person who has a deep interest in the mysteries surrounding the Whitechapel killings of 1888 attributed to Jack the Ripper. Many have researched and written extensively on the subject, and there are a number of online forums and magazines devoted to it. All facets of the mystery—such as the suspects, the victims, the murder scenes, the law enforcement officers involved, the politics of the day—are researched. Ripperologists are in constant communication with each other through these online venues, discussing the details."

"I'm definitely curious to see what this Stanton can do for us," Johnson commented.

With a knock on Johnson's door, a police detective barged in. "Captain, a man walking his dog this morning came across a deceased female, just outside of the First Niagara Center in one of the parking lots, and it appears to be a homicide!" he exclaimed excitedly.

All three shot out of their seats.

"Her throat was cut just like the other Niagara Falls Ripper victims," the detective continued. "The Erie County Sheriff Department secured the crime scene and surrounding parking lots."

"How far into the crime scene investigation are they?" Johnson asked as the men rushed out the door and toward the elevator.

"Barriers have been put up with entry and exit points," the detective replied. "They just handed it over to our department, but they're helping us search for physical evidence. So far, they've not found anything, but they're still searching."

"Any other witnesses?" Riggs asked.

"Not yet. Oh, and the medical examiner has just arrived."

"How fortunate, Dr. Dunham," Johnson said. "Assuming this is our offender's latest victim, she was discovered on the day you arrived."

Riggs shook his head. "Only a week later." He spotted some luggage near the front desk. "Doctor, do you need anything out of your luggage?"

"No, all set."

"Are you driving, Riggs?" Johnson asked.

"Sure, Captain. My car's out front."

After the elevator ride down, the three exited the building and entered Riggs' car. He pulled into the street.

Dunham stared out the back window. "How far away is the arena?"

"Just a few minutes," Riggs said. "It's also downtown, but it's located at what we call the Waterfront, since it's on the coast of Lake Erie."

"What is the First Niagara Center?" Dunham asked.

"The First Niagara Center," Johnson began to explain, "was formerly known as the HSBC Arena. It's a sports and entertainment facility, home to Buffalo's professional hockey team, the Buffalo Sabres."

"The center is also the home of the national lacrosse team, Buffalo Bandits," Riggs interrupted. He glanced in the mirror quickly at Dunham. "Buffalo's a huge sports town."

"Come to think of it," Johnson added, "the center arena is controlled by the owner of the Buffalo Sabres, but the land and surrounding parking lots are public property owned by Erie County. This should help us out in investigating the crime scene."

"Does it host anything besides sports events?" Dunham asked.

"Entertainment events, such as professional wrestling championships, major concerts, circuses, and family shows." Johnson paused. "As I think about it, last night's event was a big rock concert."

Riggs turned onto another street.

Johnson pointed out the window. "That's the First Niagara Center, there."

"It appears the crime scene investigation is well underway," Riggs observed. The entire parking lot complex for the First Niagara Center was blocked off and completely filled with police and crime scene investigators.

They parked, exited, and headed toward the murder scene.

Dunham noticed that many of the police officers stopped what they were doing and stared at him, some whispering to each other. He glanced over at Johnson.

Johnson smiled. "Dr. Dunham, when I said everyone up here knows of your reputation, I meant it."

They approached the murder scene, which was at the side of a large parking lot in a patch of high weeds near a small building the size of a shed.

Dunham looked up at the underside of a large highway overpass.

"That's the skyway," Riggs said.

They made their way carefully around a detective photographer shooting photos, then neared the medical examiner, who was hovering over the body.

The examiner glanced up at Dunham. "Well hello, Dr. Dunham. What a pleasant surprise. I heard you were joining the task force."

Dunham recognized the forensic pathologist. "Hello, Dr. Fielding. Nice surprise. How's Mary?"

Fielding looked back at the body, scanning it. "The wife's doing fine, although the university has been putting pressure on her to publish," Fielding chatted calmly. "She'll probably retire instead." He popped his head up. "She told me your wife has been enjoying her sabbatical in Europe."

"Yes, and luckily it gives me the opportunity to help out here on this case. What've you discovered so far?"

Everyone gave Fielding and the body their full attention.

"Well, as you can see," Fielding began, "the murder victim is a woman in her early to mid-twenties, lying on her back, fully clothed, including a jacket." He pointed to the neck. "The deep slash to her throat was caused by a very sharp and relatively long cutting instrument, which nearly severed her head. This is clearly the cause of death." He pointed around the body. "The bloodstains and spatter pattern indicate she was murdered in situ."

Riggs whispered to Dunham, "In situ?"

Dunham pointed at the body. "It means she was attacked at that very spot."

"There's evidence of strangulation as well," Fielding explained and again pointed to the neck. "Notice the bruising above the cut, and notice her tongue sticking out." He glanced over at Dunham. "The condition of the body suggests a time of death at around midnight last night."

"That's during or just after the concert," Riggs calculated. He turned toward a lone car in the parking lot and pointed at it. "I'll wager a guess that that car is hers." He turned his head toward the arena behind them then back to the car. "It appears she was attacked while walking to it from the arena."

"Assuming the victim was going to her car after the concert was done," Johnson interrupted. "That most likely means the killer attacked her while others were also heading for their cars." He shook his head. "How'd he do that?" He glanced at the weeds. "Did he lead her to this spot, or was he hidden here waiting for her?" Johnson squinted and traced through the air with his finger the path the from the arena building to the murder site, and onward to the victim's car. "I say the latter."

"I'm not entirely sure she's a victim of the Niagara Falls serial killer," Dr. Fielding commented. "A major identifying characteristic of the serial offender's signature, abdominal mutilation, is not present. This young lady was not disemboweled." He looked up at Dunham. "Besides, it would be out of character for this particular offender to kill so soon after the last murder. Any thoughts?"

"Oh, she's his latest victim, all right," Dunham replied.

Everyone turned and stared at him.

Dunham quickly glanced at Johnson and Riggs, then at the body. "Dr. Fielding, check the abdominal region on her right side. You should fine a deep stab wound with a narrow entry point."

Fielding momentarily looked confused, then turned to the body and searched through her jacket and clothes. More and more police officers closed in to get a better view. Fielding's eyes widened, then he shot a look at Dunham. "Why, I'll be! You're correct, Dr. Dunham." He then studied the wound. "I observe one gash about four centimeters in width, and it appears to be quite deep. The lack of blood indicates post mortem. Her heart had stopped from the neck wound before he stabbed her here."

"This also tells us the width of the murder weapon—approximately four centimeters," Dunham commented.

Riggs glanced over at Johnson and back to Dunham. "How did you know the examiner would find a stab wound there?"

"Well, the autopsy reports on all of the previous victims stated that the offender eviscerated post mortem, most likely to avoid blood-spatter on himself. In each case, I saw evidence that the offender started the evisceration process in the abdominal region on the victim's right side, cutting through the clothes in two of the cases." He pointed around the crime scene. "So far, I've noticed nearly a half-dozen similarities between this crime scene and the others—the location of the murder next to a popular venue, the gender of the victim, position of the victim, and the presence of a deep neck wound with the tongue sticking out to start."

Everyone just stared at Dunham, listening intently.

Dunham pointed at the body. "In view of this, I'm convinced this particular offender was interrupted prior to completing his agenda. From where I'm standing, I noticed a small cut in this victim's clothing. Of course, Dr. Fielding would have eventually discovered it. It's clear to me this is another victim of the Niagara Falls serial killer."

Johnson smiled. "Well, a quick prediction of the location of a hidden wound proving to be correct has certainly convinced me." He pulled out his cell phone. "It's time to contact the rest of the task force."

"Also, Captain," Dunham interrupted. "If it's true that the offender felt the need to rush out prior to completing the abdominal mutilation, we might have ourselves a witness to the murderer. Whoever interrupted him may have seen him running away. If the person, or persons, did not know there was a woman in these tall weeds, they probably don't even realize they were a witness to our offender leaving the scene of the crime."

"We can start with a list of everyone in attendance at last night's concert." Riggs said. "I'll check with the First Niagara Center box office. They should have a list of most people in attendance. Of course, the arena holds about 20,000 people. The good news is the box office should have the ticket holders' phone numbers as well."

Johnson glanced around. "Maybe we'll get lucky and the event was caught on a security camera."

"Great," Dunham complimented. "I also recommend we make a public announcement as soon as possible. Once those attending the concert realize a murder occurred right under their noses, they will begin to retrace their steps as they left the arena. If we wait too long, their memories may fade."

Johnson clapped his hands and rubbed them together. "We have a plan, gentlemen. Let's do it!"

chapter eight

Sergeant Dinnie walked out the front door of Leman Street Police Station, stopped at the top step, and scanned the area. He dropped his chin so that his deerstalker hat stopped the cold, light drizzle from hitting his face.

Sergeant Froest joined him on the steps and looked up toward the rainy gray sky.

Dinnie pulled out a hanky and wiped his face. "Frank, I believe the day calls for a police cab. The wax museum is a distance away, anyway."

Froest pointed at a police cab positioned in front of the station. "Already called for one, partner."

They headed down the steps toward the police cab, and a few minutes later they were traveling east on Whitechapel Road.

Dinnie looked out his window and saw a pedestrian yelling at a carriage driver who'd just driven over a mud puddle and had splashed water on him. "The cold rain certainly hasn't stopped business." He glanced out the other window. "It's quite crowded on the streets."

"With the Whitechapel fiend killing his third victim, you'd think there'd be no one," Froest remarked. "But, then again, it is daylight. He's only mutilated unfortunates, and the killings have all happened at night on the side streets."

"Nighttime activity hasn't changed much either," Dinnie added. "I've even noticed an increase in the numbers of the affluent class visiting here."

Froest shook his head, frowning. "Here we go again. You do know that these rich clubmen and their fine ladies will soon be contacting headquarters for us to escort them."

"They certainly enjoy their slumming," Dinnie agreed. "I guess I'd better keep my uniforms pressed and practice my courteous small talk." He grinned at Froest. "Rumor has it they feel quite safe with you, Frank, so shine your shoes, my friend, and refine your jokes."

Froest snickered then stared out the window. "We're getting close to the museum, Walter." He pointed out of the cab. "There's the London Hospital over there, and it's right across the street."

Dinnie looked around. "This area is curiously close to the Nichols murder. It was just a block or so down that street. Am I correct?"

Froest nodded. "That's right. Less than a block away. Not more than a two minute walk, I'd wager."

Dinnie ordered the cab to stop in front of the cheesemonger's shop next to the museum. As they exited the cab, both noticed the museum was closed.

"How strange," Froest said. "I was told the museum was open every day of the week."

They headed up to the museum entrance. Large painted signs on the windows advertised wax displays of the executions of the 'Most Famous Murderers of Our Time.' The most prominent sign advertised wax displays of the 'Latest Three Whitechapel Murders,' and had two graphic pictures. Another sign said 'Admission Fee—One Penny Only.'

Dinnie looked up at the second floor. "Empty . . . it looks like no one lives up there."

Froest raised his eyes. "Would you want to live above a freak museum?"

Dinnie glanced at the shop next to the museum. "How about we visit the cheesemonger's shop, shall we?"

The two approached the shop.

As they entered, Dinnie noticed an elderly, frail gentleman behind the counter. Standing next to him was a large, powerful-looking younger man. "Good morning, my name is Detective Sergeant Dinnie, and this is Detective Sergeant Froest. We're here to see the owner."

The older man stared at them for a moment. "That would be me. George Hunt. Are ya here about that godforsaken freak museum and live show next to me?"

"Indeed we are," Dinnie replied.

"Ya came at the wrong time. They're closed." He shook his head. "Strange. They're usually open every day from sunrise to midnight, and even on the weekends, so I don't know why they're closed today. The owner, Tom Barry, ain't around like he used to be though."

The younger man approached Hunt and whispered in his ear.

Hunt nodded to him then eyed the detectives. "This is my right hand man, young Henry Tate. He's been seein' Mr. Barry less and less too."

Tate nodded to Dinnie and Froest. "Mornin', gov'nors," he said respectfully.

"Henry keeps my shop open into the evenin' when the boxin' matches and ghost shows are open," Hunt explained. "He also keeps the ruffians out when the crowd gets a little ornery out-side the museum."

Dinnie nodded to Tate. "Nice to meet you, Mr. Tate. You said Mr. Barry is not around as much as he used to be? Why do you think that?"

Tate glanced at Hunt and paused. "Well, sir, he's still around, but he doesn't let anyone know, especially the bobbies. I think he's scared of the police. Lately, more and more people are gettin' perturbed by them pictures of the murder victims in front of the museum. There's been lots of hollerin' and screamin'."

"I'm not surprised," Dinnie commented.

"They say he's takin' advantage of all the excitement caused by the murders, and that's just not right," Hunt blurted out. "One day just after the third killin' an angry crowd took the pictures out and ripped them apart. It started a big brawl, and an inspector and two constables had to clear out the crowd. The police were actually there before the crowd took them pictures out, so I know they were glad to see them gone. You bein' police, I figured you knew about that."

Dinnie shook his head. "We don't work out of this local police station. When was the last time you saw him?"

Tate stared at Hunt and pointed his finger to the left. "I just saw him yesterday at lunchtime eatin' at his favorite pub. I bet he's there right now."

Dinnie turned to face the front of the store. "Oh, where's that?"

"Just outside the door to your left at the Star & Garter Pub," Hunt explained. "I eat there sometimes."

"Young Mr. Tate," Dinnie said. "If he's there, would you be able to point him out to us?"

"Of course," Tate replied.

Dinnie glanced back at Hunt. "Barry's chamber of horrors museum has been around for a few years, hasn't it?"

Hunt nodded. "Almost seven years to the day."

"Besides the increase in the level of nuisance," Dinnie added, "has there been anything unusual happening, especially around the time Barry began displaying the murder victims?"

Hunt nodded. "Yes, actually—the other man."

"Other man?" Froest asked. "You mean the son-in-law?"

"No, the tall man with the large black mustache. It looks like he waxes it. He was helpin' Barry out with settin' up the grotesque wax displays of the murdered women in the museums."

"What can you tell us about this tall man?" Dinnie asked.

"He was taller than most," Hunt said. "Seemed like he thought he was better than everyone, and always acted like he was in a hurry and late for somethin'. He usually wore one of those Yankee hats. His clothes were nothin' special, but he always had an expensive-lookin' black cane."

"Anything else?" Dinnie asked.

"Just that he was always tellin' the workmen what to do, and yellin' at them. He must have been the foreman or somethin'."

"Was he yelling at Mr. Barry too?" Froest asked.

"Not that I saw," Hunt explained. "But it was the timing that was curious. I could swear that the last two times a woman got murdered, this man was hangin' around the museum a day *before* the murders."

Tate nodded. "Yep, and I've seen him in the crowds in the evenings afterward too."

"Now that is very curious." Dinnie replied. "Thank you, Mr. Hunt and young Tate. You've been very helpful. Mr. Tate, may we bother you to escort us over to the Star & Garter and point him out to us if he's there?"

Tate nodded. "Surely, gov'nors. I'll walk you over now."

"I hope you close it down—and soon!" Hunt yelled angrily after them.

As they left the cheesemonger's shop, Dinnie spotted the pictures in the museum window. He approached them and said, "Frank, the wax models in the pictures of the Tabram, Nichols, and Chapman murders do indeed look surprisingly similar to the actual victims—including the positions that the bodies were found in."

Froest stared at the pictures and nodded. "I believe we should have Ol' Man Barry give us a personal tour."

"Good call."

"Follow me, gov'nors," Tate directed. They followed him next door to the Star & Garter Pub and crossed the threshold, then stopped. Tate nodded toward a thin old man with a beard and slightly disheveled gray hair who was sitting at a booth eating a bowl of soup.

Dinnie eyed the old man. "Thank you, Tate," he said then handed him a coin.

Dinnie and Froest approached the man, who was seemingly oblivious to their arrival. "Hello, Mr. Barry, my name is Detective Sergeant Dinnie, and this is Detective Sergeant Froest."

Without looking up, Old Man Barry pulled out a parchment and gave it to Dinnie. "Ain't done nothin' wrong. I got permission papers for my museum and live shows right here."

Dinnie read the document. "We're not here to close you down this time, Mr. Barry. Actually, we just want to see your waxworks museum. It may help us out in an investigation separate from your business."

Barry's head popped up. "Them murders?"

Two men in the next booth overheard Barry and glanced over.

Froest glared at the men, which caused them to quickly turn back and act as if they were completely disinterested in Barry's comment.

"We'd prefer to discuss this in slightly more private surroundings. May we continue at your museum, perhaps?" Dinnie asked quietly.

Barry gave a quick nod. "Fair enough. Just finished my lunch anyway." He drained his drink, dropped some coins on the table, and the three of them left.

Barry started unlocking the museum door but stopped and faced Dinnie nervously. "You don't think I had somethin' to do with them murders, do ya? I can barely walk."

Dinnie chuckled reassuringly. "Not at all, Mr. Barry. There've been hundreds of theories floating about." He looked over at Froest. "And Sergeant Froest and I have heard them all. It's just that we've been ordered to investigate even the most ridiculous ones." He eyed Barry. "We're here because one wild theory is that the killer may be frequenting your museum, building up his blood thirst, you might say."

"We're trying to get into the mind of this bloke," Froest interrupted.

Barry opened the door and entered first. "It sounds a little far-fetched to me, but let me show you around."

They entered the museum and continued into the first showroom. It was a very long room with a low ceiling. Barry lit all of the gas lamps, but the room was still relatively dark. "Be m'guest."

Dinnie made out waxen and plaster sculptures placed on high shelves lining the wall. The nearer ones, which he thought were quite hideous, displayed various abnormalities.

The room was organized into long rows of wax and plaster figures and scenes, primarily of executed murderers of the most notorious homicides in recent times, some propped up, some askew, and some against the walls, with all of them dressed in clothing of the period and culture.

Froest cringed. "One certainly could find inspiration from a place like this."

Dinnie pointed to a waxen bloody figure of English doctor William Palmer, the Prince of Poisoners, which displayed him hanging from a noose. To the back and left there was a wax display showing three men in a graveyard, snatching a body out of a grave. An old sign in front stated, 'Resurrectionists.' Next to it was a display of two men in the act of smothering a woman, and another old sign that stated, 'William Burke and William Hare.'

Dinnie stared at the next display and stopped. He leaned over to Froest. "Frank, it's Pranzini."

Below him was a wax model of the dismembered head of murderer Henri Pranzini, the French Rue Montaigne assassin; next to it was a guillotine in the released position. His headless bloody body was lying on the other side, positioned on its stomach, with his arms tied behind his back.

"He was just executed last year," Froest whispered.

Dinnie nodded. "Pranzini murdered three women in Paris by cutting their throats, just like our killer. He nearly severed the young girl's head." Dinnie paused and eyed Froest. "If this chamber of horrors did inspire our man, here's the display that gave him the idea on how to kill."

Froest read the information plaque just in front of the Pranzini display. "This gives every detail on how he killed his victims."

Barry turned back toward the detectives. "This way, gentlemen. You want to see the main attraction, don't you?"

They caught up with Barry at the end of the room.

The old man led them down a rickety corkscrew staircase.

Froest grabbed Dinnie's shoulder, clearly concerned about being heavier than most and walking onto a weak flight of stairs.

They followed anyway and descended into the dark cellar showroom.

Dinnie watched Barry light a gas lamp at the entrance, then they followed him into the dingy basement room. Once Barry lit the second lamp, Dinnie could make out three waxen figures laid out on the floor, all depictions of females on their backs, with a sign in front stating, 'Victims of the Whitechapel Murders.' The figures were covered with red ocher stain, mimicking blood.

"This is something you don't see every day, Sergeant," Froest said sarcastically, pointing to the left figure. "The sign reads, 'The Tabram Murder in George Yard Buildings on August 7.'"

Dinnie studied the Tabram figure, which had on a dark bonnet, a tattered long dark jacket, a green skirt, brown petticoat, wool stockings, and spring-sided boots. Over the breasts, abdomen, and groin area were red stains representing dozens of stab wounds.

The sign over the center figure read 'The Nichols Murder in Buck's Row on August 31.' The display showed a woman wearing a ragged reddish-brown ulster, a brown outer garment frock and skirt, wool stockings, and two undergarment petticoats.

Dinnie pointed to the Nichols display. He could see the knife wounds were different on this figure. It displayed a nearly severed head with a deep knife wound to the neck exposing her spine, with blood flowing from the wound into a recreation of a gutter. There was also red stain on the left portion of her abdomen, representing a knife wound.

"The attention to detail," Froest commented.

Dinnie crouched down for a closer look at the far right figure. "This is troublesome, Frank," Dinnie whispered.

It was the most gruesome of the three: a woman in a black skirt, petticoats, and wool stockings, lying on her back just like the other two, and having what appeared to be a knife wound nearly severing her head, blood flowing from it, just like the middle figure. In front of the scene was a sign that stated, 'The Chapman Murder at 29 Hanbury St on September 8.'

Froest studied the three female figures, then whispered to Dinnie, "Not only are the wounds nearly identical to the real murders, their bodies are positioned correctly." He popped his head up and pointed into the dark corner. "Walter, have a look over there."

Behind the three figures in the corner stood a threatening waxen figure, a large hat covering his face, and wearing a long dark cape that nearly covered his entire body. In his hand was a long, bloody knife.

Dinnie eyed Froest and shook his head. "Whoever set these models up had to have seen all three murder sites." He thought for a moment. "But was it during the murders or after?"

"Having the three bodies next to each other certainly shows how the murderer is stepping up his level of violence," Froest added. "Indeed, we should have the detective division study this."

Dinnie paused. "After two failed tries has he finally achieved this murderous agenda—collecting organs?" He glanced up at Barry. "Mr. Barry, what made you decide to create this display of the murder victims?"

Barry shrugged his shoulders. "Just tryin' to earn a livin'."

"These new displays are quite elaborate," Dinnie said. "I bet they were expensive to build. Where did you get the money to build these and pay your workers?"

Barry stared at Dinnie for a moment. "Raided my savings. Already got my money back and then some."

"Was the tall gentleman with the black mustache your financier?" Dinnie asked.

Barry's eyes popped wide. He then frowned and turned away. "Don't know what you're talkin' about."

"Now, Mr. Barry," Dinnie began. "If you've read your so-called permit from the Earl of Euston appropriately, the conditions on it state that the museum 'must meet moral standards in accordance with the Obscene Publications Act.'" He glanced over at Froest. "And I'm sure I can convince my superiors that your museum does not." He shook his head. "I'd wager I could get the museum closed by tomorrow."

Froest grinned, evidently pleased at his colleague's interpretation of the law.

"Hmm!" Barry replied. "My solicitors, Abbott, Earle, and Ogle, on Worship Street, 'ev assured me my chamber of horrors museum duddent apply to the Obscene Publications Act."

"Oh, I'm not talking about your displays on the ground floor. I'm talking about this particular one," Dinnie continued. "Are you sure my superiors would appreciate a waxen display of an ongoing murder investigation?" He tilted his head and shrugged his shoulders. "I can certainly push the issue and see how the cards fall."

Barry glared at Dinnie but remained silent for a moment. "All right, all right, ya don't have to get pushy." He dropped his stare. "Best we keep yer superiors out of it." He paused. "We made a deal. He would pay fer it and get permission, and all I had t'do was hire the best wax workers from the Bell and Mackerel on Mile End Road."

"Who did you hire to get the details correct on the murder scenes?" Dinnie asked.

"Didn't have to," Barry replied. "He said he'd take care of that."

"What is this gentleman's name?" Froest asked.

Barry paused again. "He called himself Mr. Jordan—Louis Jordan, from New York City—but I knew he were lyin', 'cause I heard his driver say, 'Pick ye up at the usual time, Dr. Twomby?'"

Dinnie wrote in his notepad. "Dr. Twomby," he repeated. "Do you expect him back any time soon?"

Barry raised his eyebrows and tilted his head. "He said he'd be back next month. Had to leave town er somethin'."

Dinnie smiled and nodded. "Thank you, Mr. Barry. You've been more than helpful."

The detectives left the museum and got into a cab, which then started off to the station.

"It's certainly strange how this American knows so many details about the murder scenes," Froest commented.

Dinnie nodded. "It's as if he wants to immortalize his evil craft."

Froest looked out the window. "That makes absolute sense, Walter." He eyed Dinnie. "We may want to let this museum stay open until we contact this Mr. Jordan—or Dr. Twomby."

Dinnie stared out of the cab window for a moment. "Excellent idea. I'll check out the files at headquarters and see if I can find anything on this Dr. Twomby."

chapter nine

Celine scanned the inside of the refrigerator, all over the door spaces, shelves, compartments, and even in the freezer. "Ellen, Amy, have either of you seen the hot sauce?" she asked, frustrated.

Ellen popped her head up from the living room couch. "Sorry, Celine," she responded apologetically. "I used the last little bit of it yesterday. Check the 'To Buy' list on the fridge door. I wrote it down."

Celine closed the refrigerator door and read the list. "Oh, my bad. How about we go shopping tonight?"

Ellen smiled. "Sounds great."

Amy peeked over the couch pillows. "I'll drive."

Celine, still melancholy from Angie's death and funeral, thought about how lucky she was to have two excellent roommates. Ellen Wadsworth and Amy Carnegie were opposites, but she loved how they got along so well with each other. Ellen was a social butterfly who'd been doted on by her mother her entire life, and as a result, she tended to carry around an attitude of entitlement. She was beautiful and blond and had a handsome jock boyfriend who doted on her just as much as her mother did. Even with these seemingly annoying traits, Ellen had the best sense of humor.

"By the way, Celine," Amy said. "I rocked the bio test. Top score in the class."

"I would've been surprised otherwise," Celine replied.

Amy, on the other hand, was a geek. Her father was an engineer, who saw the world logically and sequentially and resolved everything in practical terms. Amy inherited this, but she was also very impatient.

"You're the best," Amy complimented her friend.

Celine thought herself to be a perfect middle in between these two, and she was told by everyone that she was very laidback. Nothing seemed to bother her, and she liked it that way. She was neither the best at anything nor the worst, but she knew both Ellen and Amy believed that she had the most common sense of the three.

Celine's cell phone chimed. She picked it up and read the text. "Robbie just texted me. He and his friends just parked their car and are coming up."

"Your brother's a cutie, Celine," Ellen said, winking.

Celine smiled. "He's a pain in the butt, but I love him."

"His friends are idiots," Amy added bluntly.

Ellen rolled her eyes. "Amy, don't beat around the bush. Tell me what you really think."

"Well, they are," Amy replied. "Just watch. Ralph's going to hit on you the first minute they walk in."

"He's harmless," Celine spoke up. "But why does Kyle irritate you? He's kind of like you, actually—a brainiac."

Amy shrugged her shoulders.

The doorbell rang ceremoniously as Robbie, Ralph, and Kyle rushed in.

"Celine, what did I tell you?" Robbie scolded. "Lock that door! There's a serial killer on the loose, and who knows, it might inspire other crazies to start killing too."

Robbie eyed her roommates sitting on the couch. "And that goes for you guys too!"

Amy shrugged her shoulders. "Forgot," she replied mundanely.

Ellen smiled and waved. "Hi, Robbie."

"I forgot, guys, we will," Celine said. "What's up?"

"Did you hear? The Niagara Falls Ripper has struck again—in the parking lot at the First Niagara Center, just as Ralph predicted!" He pointed to Ralph and Kyle. "We didn't see anything, but we were at the right place!"

Ralph beamed. "Yes, I'm awesome." He glanced over at El-len. "Ellen, how about we hang out tonight and discuss my greatness."

Amy glanced over at Ellen as if to say, *I told you so.*

Ellen smiled. "Not tonight, Ralphie. I have a test Monday."

"Ralph, her boyfriend could kick the crap out of all three of us," Kyle said. "Who knows, he's probably in the bedroom right now listening to every word you're saying."

Ralph's eyes opened wide, and he glanced toward Ellen's bedroom door. "On second thought, hanging with Rob and Kyle tonight searching for a serial killer seems much safer."

"Jeff's not here," Ellen replied, rolling her eyes but smiling.

Celine glanced at Robbie. "Yeah, we heard about it. It's all over the news. The girl was from Amherst and went to the concert with a girlfriend. Apparently, they got separated in the parking lot after the concert. After fifteen minutes of waiting for her, the friend felt she'd been stranded. They say she didn't have her phone, so she got a ride home with someone else who was there."

"Little did she realize," Kyle interrupted, "her friend was dead, just a few feet away in the tall weeds! Wouldn't you think the friend would've called the police after awhile?"

"Not if she thought the girl stranded her," Amy replied. "She was probably pissed."

Ellen put her hands on her temples and grabbed her hair. "What the heck," she said, frustrated. "This loser killed Angie not more than a week ago. We don't know if his next attack will be tomorrow or in a month!"

"Clearly the police are over their heads with this," Robbie explained. "I bet we'll find the killer before they do, with my knowledge of serial killers, Kyle's brains, and Ralph's—" he glanced over at Ralph—"luck."

Ralph raised his hands. "Hey, fortune favors the awesome, my friend." He raised his chin and closed his eyes smugly. "We quickly forget who figured out how this guy thinks."

"So, what's your next plan of attack?" Celine asked.

"The same plan," Kyle replied. "He's going to murder at some popular event. Since he's changed his location every time, I think it's safe to assume he won't attack someone at the First Niagara Center again."

"Any ideas where?" Ellen asked.

Robbie thought for a moment. "Well, besides coming over here to brag about how close we were to catching the killer, we wanted to see what you guys thought."

"I think you can eliminate downtown Buffalo too," Amy commented. "I bet it'll be a place like Darien Lake, forty-five minutes east of here, either at the fun park or at one of the fall concerts they hold."

Robbie raised his eyebrows. "Awesome idea, Amy."

Kyle nodded. "I agree. It certainly seems like there's no pattern to when the murders occur, so he's probably choosing events and activities that spark his fancy—whatever that may be."

"Darien Lake it is, then," Ralph concluded.

"Glad that's settled." Celine said. "Robbie, my roommates and I have to go give blood before it closes."

"Then we're outta here, sis."

"Hey, let's look up what their fall concert schedule is," Ralph interrupted. "Then go to my house and print out the list."

The three turned to leave the apartment.

Robbie waved. "Thanks, ladies. See ya."

As the boys closed the door behind them, Ellen predicted, "I bet they just might catch the guy."

"I hope they don't get too close," Celine replied.

"Those chickens?" Amy commented. "I'm sure they'd just call the police." She glanced up at the clock. "Anyway, let's go give blood."

* * *

Student Union Building, Buffalo State College Campus.

Celine stepped to the side as they passed another student coming from the building, the telltale sign of donating blood visible on her arm: a stretchy, colorful bandage wrapped just above her elbow.

"The blood drive is on the second floor in the conference room," she explained to her two roommates as they entered the first floor, which held the cafeteria a level above the basement bookstore. Celine glanced up at the donor line, which extended to the top of the second-floor stairs.

As they mounted the stairs and joined the end of the line, Ellen eyed Celine. "I never go anywhere alone thanks to the Niagara Falls Ripper being on the loose. Angie's death and the arena killing are just too close for comfort, so I force Jeff to take me everywhere." She snickered. "He hated waiting while I was getting my pedicure, but he understands."

"I get why you never want to be alone," Celine replied. "I just don't understand you getting a pedicure at this time of the year. We're wearing shoes all the time. Isn't that a waste of money?"

Ellen shook her head. "My mom pays for it, and besides," she grinned, "it's her fault that I'm hooked on it. She started taking me when I was a kid."

Amy stared around Celine into the makeshift blood donor room the Red Cross had set up in the conference room. "When I visit home, my dad doesn't let me leave our house at night unless I get picked up. He predicted the killer would go after a college student at least once, and he was right." She pulled out her iPhone. "He found this GPS app and put it on my phone, so he knows where my sister and I are at all times."

Ellen's eyes opened wide and she smiled. "That's a great idea." She then lost the smile and said, "But I'm not going to tell Jeff about that! I don't think I want him to know where I am all the time."

"I heard it's now a way for the government to keep tabs on everyone," Celine commented. "Remember what they said in *1984*—'Big Brother's watching.'" She glanced over to the donor room entrance. "Wow, this line went quick. We're next."

Moments later, an elderly American Red Cross employee directed her to a seat.

She sat in it, but she felt a little apprehensive.

The employee placed her hand on Celine's. "Is this your first time here, honey?" she asked in a motherly tone.

Celine shook her head. "No, I just don't like needles. My name is Celine Faulks. I should be in your database."

The woman typed and then stared at her laptop screen. "Here it is." Her eyes opened wide. "Oh, you have an excellent blood type. You're a universal donor. This is quite rare." She smiled at Celine. "I wish we had more like you."

Celine raised her eyebrows. "Cool."

After they finished giving blood, the three went to the first floor cafeteria for refreshments.

"Did you hear about the girl from Amherst who was attacked while going to her car in the parking lot of the Walden Galleria Mall?" Amy asked.

"No," Ellen replied. "When did this happen, and why is it not in the news?"

"It was at the *mall*," Amy explained as she removed a printed article from her book bag. "Last week I printed this off of a watchdog website. Dad said the public never knows what happens at malls because they're private property, and it would be bad for business if people knew how dangerous their parking lots were."

"That makes business sense," Celine replied.

"He said about twenty years ago, one of the inner-city gangs used to have an initiation in the mall parking lot. They would wait under a car, and when the owner tried to unlock the car, they would take a knife and slit their Achilles tendon. My dad heard that straight from a Buffalo police cop." Amy pointed at the article. "Listen to this. It says, 'An East Amherst High School student was at the Walden Galleria Mall Saturday evening, just leaving the movie theater. As she walked into the parking ramp just outside of the theater entrance, a man in a mask attempted to force her into his car. The man tripped, which allowed her to get free. She began to scream while running back toward the mall. A couple saw her, but at this time the perpetrator ran to his car and sped off. Even though he was wearing a mask, she identified him as a heavyset white male about five feet seven inches tall. The man was driving a blue Buick LeSabre. The victim had gone to the movie with a friend, but the friend was picked up by her boyfriend just before the victim walked into the parking ramp.'" Amy popped her head up. "How close was that!"

"I don't think this guy was the Niagara Falls Ripper," Celine suggested.

Ellen glanced at Celine. "Why is that?"

"Robbie is so into trying to understand the mind of the Niagara Falls Ripper, he's always talking to me about it," Celine explained. "I remember Robbie saying the killer always kills them and guts them right where he attacked them. Instead of attacking them and taking them to a private location, he just waits until an opportunity to do the whole thing presents itself.

This guy in the mall parking ramp was trying to force the girl into his car."

Amy nodded. "Well, how stupid was she for not forcing her girlfriend to stay with her, or at least have them escort her to her car."

"In a weird way, having so many stupid people out there makes it kind of safe for people like us who take serious precautions," Ellen added.

"It still doesn't help," Celine replied. "I can name a bunch of things we've all done in the last few weeks—like leaving our door unlocked."

"I guess you're right," Ellen replied and thought for a moment. "How about I have Jeff pick us up and take us back?"

chapter ten

1888: Saturday, September 29. 11:30 p.m. London, England—East End, Berner Street.

Bill Harris was one of two members of the Whitechapel Vigilance Committee on watch. He and Joe Aarons sat on the steps of Little Allie Street Baptist Chapel on the north side of Allie Street near a burning gas streetlamp. The night around them was dark and damp with a cool fall mist hugging the ground. Harris was a small, thin man, whereas his partner was tall and heavier. They both wore long overcoats and felt cockney hats. Harris strained to read a newspaper under the dim yellow light emanating from the lamp, while Aarons, eyes closed, rested his head on the building's exterior wall. Harris heard Aarons start to snore. He glanced up from his newspaper and elbowed him in the side. "Wake up, Joe," he said angrily. "If we're going to find this fiend, we have to be awake. We need to be vigilant, remember? That's why we started this vigilance committee in the first place."

Aarons slowly sat up and rubbed his eyes. "Sorry, today was a long day on the job, and tomorrow's going to be just as busy."

Harris shook his head. "You won't have a business if this killer scares everyone away, right?" He paused and glanced around. "How about we call it a night in another hour? Just after midnight. When Lusk asks us how long we were out, we'll say until three a.m. What do ya say?"

Aarons nodded. "Excellent idea, Bill. I owe you one." He leaned his head back on the wall.

Harris returned to his newspaper. He raised his eyebrows as he was reading, then he elbowed Aarons again. "Hey, Joe, check out Coroner Baxter's theory on the killer's motive. He says here, 'The difficulty in believing that the purport of the murderer was the possession of the mission abdominal organ was natural. It was abhorrent to their feelings to conclude that a life should be taken for so slight an object; but when rightly considered the reasons for most murders were altogether out of proportion to their guilt. It had been suggested that the criminal was a lunatic with morbid feelings. That might or might not be the case, but the object of the murderer appeared palpably shown by the facts, and it was not necessary to assume lunacy, for it was clear there was a market for the missing organ.'"

"Oh yeah," Aarons interrupted. "I remember. He thinks the Whitechapel fiend was some American medical student wanting to buy organs from a couple of museums, right?"

Harris shook his head. "Not exactly. He thinks the killer might be some abandoned wretch harvesting organs for profit 'cause there's a market. He's saying it has nothing to do with being insane—just someone capable of inhuman wickedness trying to make some money."

"Codswallop," Aarons declared. "This guy's a lunatic."

Out of nowhere, a tall man in a long black cape and a slouch hat sauntered up to Harris and Aarons. "Excuse me, gentlemen, would you mind telling me the location of an excellent beer house?"

Harris stared at him for a moment, then said, "The Bricklayers Pub on Settles Street. Just go north up this street and take a right on Commercial Road a few blocks, then take Settles Street north. You can't miss it."

The man touched his hat. "Thank you, kind sir." He strolled away.

As the man walked away, Harris and Aarons stared at him until he disappeared around the corner.

Aarons tapped Harris on the shoulder. "How about a spot of bitter at the Castle Pub? It's on the way home. I'm buyin'."

"Brilliant idea, Joe," Harris replied enthusiastically.

The two men got up and hurried away.

The tall dark figure peeked back around the corner at the men ditching their post and thought, *These vigilantes are idiots, especially Harris and Aarons. Not only can you spot them easily out of a crowd, their senses are so dulled, they didn't even recognize me. Proof of the effects of a lifetime of potpies, beef, and stale beer.* The man turned right onto Commercial Road, then north onto Settles Street.

Activity was bustling outside of the pub, and many unfortunates were working in the area.

He slipped into the darkness between two large trees.

Oh, the perfect location, he thought. *Jews everywhere.*

He eyed an unfortunate as she left the pub, laughing with a man. The man was of short stature and wearing a deerstalker hat. Both seemed to be enjoying each other's company.

They left the Bricklayers Pub south toward Commercial Road.

He cautiously followed. The couple turned onto Berner Street, which was much darker than Commercial Road. He was forced to tail them closer than he would've liked. He mused to himself about how his simple method of following the unfortunate and her paying customer had stumped both the police and the press.

Everyone believes the customer is the killer, but no one has yet realized it is I, following both of them, invisible to witnesses.

The unfortunate laughed at a comment her customer made. She grabbed him by the arm.

How disgusting these cattle are!

He had to admit the only reason he came up with this elusive method of stalking was because he refused to even be near the despicable gender.

The couple stopped and began cuddling each other on the opposite side of the street from a very active international worker's club, crowded with meetings and music.

The dark figure slipped into an unlit alleyway just as they stopped. He noticed a lady outside the club on the other side of the street, a distance away, listening to music. "Mr. Lusk, it was mere luck that you thwarted the completion of my sacrifice last weekend," he whispered. "Little do you realize I now attend your evening vigilante meetings. I know your plans, thus, I will always be one step ahead of you." The dark figure fondled a large piece of chalk in his pocket. "Since you're so sure a Jew is the killer—your favored 'Leather Apron'—I will lead you to further believe in this stupidity."

The dark figure slipped deeper into the shadows as a police constable ambled by the couple.

They stopped talking. Once he turned the corner, they resumed their conversation. "That bloody bobby will be back soon," she warned. "Come on, follow me."

The dark figure watched the couple cross the street and enter a pitch-black yard next to the workers' club—a yard he knew to belong to one of Lusk's Mason brothers. He scanned the area then followed them into the yard but purposely entered from the back. He sneaked closer to the couple.

Once the man was finished he wasted no time leaving.

She's alone; it's time!

As the woman was gathering herself, the dark figure attacked and grabbed her by the throat, picked her up off the ground, and forced her onto her back. Her fight for air was exhilarating.

Within seconds she was unconscious.

"*Corpus donum*—I give you her body." He pulled out a long thin blade and used it on her with excessive force. "*Sanguis donum*—I give you her blood."

A man driving a pony harnessed to a costermonger's barrow cart entered the darkened yard, nearly hitting the dead woman. But the pony abruptly stopped, aware of the man hovering over the body.

The man leapt back and hid a few yards away near his exit. He eyed the workers' club, angered that the emanating music had drowned out the sound of the approaching cart, catching him off guard. "Blasted music!" he exclaimed.

The pony became very agitated.

The driver must have noticed the dark heap lying on the ground in front of his pony. He got off of the cart, approached, and stared for a moment. "Oh my!" he yelled and rushed into the workers' club.

Damn! Hell has arrived, and I have not completed the ritual!

The dark figure rushed out of the yard. "It needs to be tonight!"

He hurried farther and farther away from the scene, searching incessantly for another opportunity. He knew once the police and the public became aware of his sacrifice on Berner Street, it would be near impossible to get a second chance to complete his ritual.

* * *

Sergeant Byfield had clearly enough of the unfortunate sing-
ing in the jail cell at his police station on Bishops Gate. He'd
dragged Catherine Eddowes in earlier in the evening in order for
her to sleep off her drunkenness. He looked up at her. "Quiet,
Ms. Eddowes!" He then eyed another officer. "Constable Hutt,
check on her condition."

"Yes, sir." Hutt crossed over to her cell.

Eddowes glanced up at him, "Officer, when can I leave?"

"When you can take care of yourself." Hutt studied Eddowes'
mannerisms.

"I can do that," she replied confidently.

Hutt paused, nodded, then opened her cell door.

She strutted out, grabbed her meager belongings from the
duty desk, and walked out of the front door held by Hutt. She
turned back around. "What time is it?"

Hutt shook his head. "Too late for you to get anything to
drink."

"I shall get a damn fine hiding when I get home," she
admitted.

"And serve you right. You had no right to get drunk." He
pointed down the street. "This way, missus."

"All right," she replied. "Goodnight, old cock." Instead of
turning right as Hutt had directed, she turned left, down the
street toward Mitre Square.

Hutt merely shook his head and went back into the station.

Within minutes of her crossing the street, a thirty-year-old
man of medium height, wearing a salt-and-pepper-colored jacket, a gray cloth cap with a peak, and a red handkerchief knot-
ted around his neck approached her. After a minute or so of
conversation, she said, "All right," and led him to Mitre Square.

At that moment, the dark figure entered the square and
spotted them. *Yes, perfect!* He slipped unnoticed into the shadows and only had to wait a few minutes before their business
was complete.

The man took out some coins, paid her, and left.

The unfortunate was collecting her things, oblivious to her
surroundings, so the sinister man quickly advanced and attacked. Within seconds she was on her back and unconscious.
The dark figure looked around for any unwanted constables

walking their beat. Seeing nothing, he began his ritual and wasted no time performing his sacrifice. As he aggressively eviscerated her in total darkness, collecting his Fruit of the Tree, he realized he had cut his free hand. Ignoring the cut, he continued his harvest, found her left kidney, and cut it out.

"*Fructus arbor vitae sumo*—I take the fruit of the Tree of Life." As he cut off a piece of the apron from his victim and blotted his cut hand, he noticed the silhouette of unfortunate's face from the distant light. It was as if she were staring and laughing at him for cutting himself! In anger, he slashed her face. Once satisfied, he thought to himself, *Well, Mr. Lusk, dinner is on me—a cuisine from hell.*

A noise came from just around the corner.

The man quickly threw his prize into a bag and rushed away. On his way to his temporary lodging on Batty Street, he realized he was still bleeding, and more of his own blood had gotten onto his shirtsleeves. He wrapped his hand in the makeshift bandage he'd cut from the clothes of the unfortunate, then stopped at a small cove on Goulston Street. He took out his piece of chalk, thought for a moment, then wrote: "The Juwes are not the men who Will not be Blamed for nothing." He grinned, then threw the makeshift bandage on the ground in front of the writing and whispered, "Just for you, Mr. Lusk," and rushed off.

October 2. New York City, New York—Police Headquarters.

As Chief Inspector Byrnes entered the police station, Inspector Crowley leapt from his seat.

"Chief Inspector," Crowley blurted out. "One moment please, sir."

He noticed Crowley had a folded newspaper. "Something interesting happened? What do you have, Inspector?"

"More news on the Whitechapel investigation, sir."

"I'm well aware of the London murderer mutilating two women a couple of nights ago. It's been the top news in the papers for two days. Apparently, he calls himself 'Jack the Ripper,' or so he said in a letter sent three days before the murders."

"Yes, sir, and the letter warned the police he was going to clip one of his victim's ears, and he did!" Crowley raised his finger. "But there's more."

Byrnes' eyes opened wide. "Oh?"

"It seems that Jack the Ripper might be an American, or so the paper says." Crowley handed Byrnes the paper.

"Interesting," Byrnes admitted and began reading.

The Sun, October 2, 1888, LONDON'S GREAT SCARE.
LONDON, Oct. 1. – There is no real news about the Whitechapel women-killing mystery, but London's fear and excitement keep bubbling over in all kinds of rumors and speculations. Queerly enough, the West End of London, and particularly maids and valets in the big hotels, who may be excused for forming queer ideas as to our United States habits, have generated the idea that some American is responsible for the crime. This original theory appears to be based principally upon the fact that some poor wretch dragged from his lodging house on suspicion in the middle of last night and released at once was described by his fellow lodgers as an uneasy gentleman with an American hat. What may be the Whitechapel lodgers' precise conception of our national headgear it would be difficult to say—probably a modified form of the sombrero made popular by Buffalo Bill.

"Well this is a different twist on the Whitechapel murder case," Byrnes commented.

"Do you suppose it's true, sir? I mean, it might be the reason why he's eluded Scotland Yard for so long."

"Could be." Byrnes thought for a moment. "If it's true that Scotland Yard is investigating the possibility of Jack the Ripper coming from our shores, we might be receiving a cable dispatch from them soon."

chapter eleven

PRESENT DAY: Monday, September 25. Rochester, New York—Holy Sepulchre Cemetery.

Riggs fidgeted in the driver's seat. "The GPS is telling us that we won't arrive at the Holy Sepulchre Cemetery for another half hour. Did you want to stop at a rest area, Dr. Dunham?"

"I'm fine," Dunham replied, staring at his iPhone map. "I didn't know that Rochester was two full hours away."

Riggs scanned the mirrors. "It's not a bad ride, really. It's a straight shot east on Interstate 90."

Dunham glanced over at Riggs. "Any update on the attendance list for the concert?"

"It's a very slow process for sure. I've got six of our task force members calling these people."

Dunham grinned. "I hope you bought lunch for them."

Riggs nodded. "Sure did. Hopefully Captain Johnson's press conference does the trick before they have to call all twenty thousand people."

Dunham peeked at his watch. "The press conference started fifteen minutes ago." He glanced out the window. "The list should also come in handy when we get a suspect—that is if he didn't fake his identity."

Twenty minutes later, they drove into a city residential area. Dunham pointed. "There's the Holy Sepulchre Cemetery."

They passed a large travel trailer parked just outside of the east gate.

"Nice camper," Riggs commented. "I've been looking for something like that." He parked in the parking lot, and they got out of the car.

Dunham stopped and stared at a group of workers with digging equipment. "That must to be it. It seems they're excavating in the older section of the cemetery."

"Those are some old-looking graves," Riggs replied.

Two of the men near the excavation site caught Dunham's attention.

One man with a patch over his eye motioned toward the newcomers.

"Dr. Dunham?" called the first man as he strolled toward them.

"Yes, and you must be Mr. Stanton. It's so nice to finally meet you."

Ryan Stanton shook Dunham's hand.

Dunham presented Riggs. "This is Buffalo Police Detective John Riggs, also on the task force."

Both exchanged greetings and a handshake.

Stanton glanced at the man with the eye patch. "My colleague here is a fellow ripperologist from Australia—Rupert Rhinelander. He's in the US for a movie production and has stopped by to see how things are progressing. It's his first time in the States."

"Pleased to meet you," Rhinelander greeted and shook their hands.

"So, are you having a good experience here?" Dunham asked.

"Brilliant, mate," Rhinelander replied but then grinned slightly. "Although, I don't understand this obsession Americans have with beer—specifically the microbrews. I personally enjoy my South Australian wines and spirits. Preferably a dry chardonnay."

Riggs shook his head, grinning. "Oh, that's sacrilege, Rupert! You're bad-mouthing what mankind has recognized as the nectar of the gods for five thousand years."

"Ha!" Dunham blurted out. "Mr. Rhinelander, your complaints are falling on deaf ears."

Rhinelander laughed. "No worries, no worries. Far be it for me to upset the heavens!"

Riggs glanced at the men working around the exhumation. "It seems to be quite a production here."

"Yes," Stanton replied. "We're exhuming not one but three bodies for DNA analysis."

"Now, remind me again what this is about?" Riggs asked.

"Well, last year two of the most celebrated and experienced ripperologists from England came up with a groundbreaking idea," Stanton explained. "To exhume a ripper victim and take a wide array of DNA samples from her body in hopes that the Whitechapel killer, i.e., Jack the Ripper, accidentally cut himself and left his DNA signature. To everyone's excitement, it worked!"

"A remarkable feat. Truly groundbreaking," Rhinelander said.

Stanton continued. "It all started with an idea that the Ripper might have accidentally cut himself while mutilating on one of victims. They found the answer in his fifth victim, Catherine Eddowes. On the evening of Eddowes' murder, the killer had actually murdered another prostitute, Elizabeth Stride, just forty-five minutes earlier. That evening is referred to as the Double Event, since he killed two women in one night. Just before one a.m. on the thirtieth of September 1888, the Ripper killed Stride, but it appeared as though he was interrupted by someone with a cart and pony. About a mile away, at approximately one forty-five a.m., a police constable found the warm body of Elizabeth Stride with her throat cut deeply and her body parts exposed. She was completely eviscerated."

"I'm glad I didn't eat lunch," Riggs replied jestingly.

Stanton grinned. "This means the killer escaped from the first murder through the alleyways, selected his victim, got the victim in a location for a safe and private murder, killed her in the usual fashion, disemboweled her, then selectively removed her left kidney in complete darkness, all in a matter of minutes!" Stanton exclaimed. "The two ripperologists correctly figured that if the Ripper had ever cut himself while in the act, it would have been with Eddowes."

"That's very impressive," Dunham commented.

Stanton raised his eyebrows. "That wasn't even the hard part. The most difficult part was getting the British officials' approval for exhuming Eddowes' body for DNA testing. The ripperology community is quite convinced that Scotland Yard has never been forthright about the Whitechapel investigation and knows much more than they are claiming. To everyone's surprise, the government agreed to the exhumation, but on the condition that it was done without any public fanfare."

"It conforms to my point all along," Rhinelander added. "The conspiratorial crowd convinced that the British government has been purposely hiding the identity of the Ripper for over one hundred years are out of touch with reality. There certainly are records still classified to this day, but it's more for protecting the reputation of living descendants."

Riggs wrinkled his eyebrows. "I don't understand."

"In British culture today," Rhineland explained, "as it was in the nineteenth century, social standing of family is everything, even for descendants. Many British citizens were investigated during the Ripper investigation, and I'm sure private dirt became a matter of record."

Riggs nodded, then said to Stanton, "So, you're exhuming a Ripper suspect's body for DNA testing to see if it matches the DNA of the actual killer?"

"Exactly, and this particular suspect, Francis Tumblety, was in the Whitechapel District during all of the murders. He was arrested at the peak of the murders in early November 1888 on suspicion, yet they didn't have the evidence to pursue a case, just like with every other suspect. Something, though, convinced Scotland Yard he might be the killer, because they charged him with two misdemeanor offenses in order to put him in jail for a while—get him off the streets as they dug further."

"Interesting," Dunham interrupted.

Stanton nodded. "The problem was, Tumblety posted bail at the end of November and fled to the US. Once here, Scotland Yard couldn't touch him since a misdemeanor offense was not extraditable." He glanced over at Rhineland. "Coincidentally, the murders stopped."

"And the guy buried here is that guy." Riggs nodded. "Intriguing."

"Interestingly," Stanton continued, "Tumblety died in St. Louis in 1903, and amongst his personal possessions were two cheap brass rings, alongside a couple of massive diamond rings and lots of cash. It was odd that a wealthy man would be in possession of two cheap rings. It makes some sense when you realize Jack the Ripper took two cheap brass rings from one of his victims."

"Now that is interesting," Riggs commented.

"So, there might have been a good reason why Scotland Yard considered him a suspect," Stanton added.

Riggs raised his hands. "I'm convinced."

"Now, he was not the only suspect," Stanton continued, "and many ripperologists put their money on a few other suspects, which is why those bodies are also being exhumed as we speak. Rupert, here, has just finished supervising the exhumation of a suspect named Montague John Druitt, a man who was found dead in the Thames River soon after the last murder. This would also explain why the murders stopped, making him an equally viable suspect. The chief constable in Scotland Yard subsequent to the murders was convinced Jack the Ripper was Druitt, and he more than anyone else had access to all of the original evidence."

"Well said, mate," Rhinelander complimented. "Ryan and I have a gentleman's bet as to which suspect will match."

Stanton smiled and pointed at the dig site. "It took me a little longer to get permission for exhuming the Tumblety grave site, but as you can see, I finally received it."

Riggs tilted his head and frowned. "Back to Tumblety. Even though Scotland Yard couldn't extradite him from the United States, if they were so convinced that he was the killer, why did they not hound him for the rest of his life?"

Rhinelander pointed his finger. "Murders continued in the East End for years after what we now believe was the last Ripper murder—the Kelly murder on November 9, 1888. Some bore the hallmarks of Jack the Ripper, and one in particular, the 1889 Alice Mackenzie murder, convinced Scotland Yard that Jack the Ripper was still in business. Since Tumblety was thousands of miles away in New York City, this immediately took him off the suspect list."

"That makes sense," Dunham commented.

"The idea that Mary Kelly's murder," Rhinelander continued, "was the last Ripper victim did not take shape until years later when a man named Melville Macnaghten—who later became an assistant commissioner at Scotland Yard—promoted the theory that Druitt was the killer. Druitt committed suicide just after the Kelly murder. Tumblety vanished completely from the Scotland Yard radar screen until a man named Chief Inspector Littlechild recollected the November 1888 chaos in a private letter to a famous newspaperman years later."

"Littlechild," Stanton added, "was the head of the secret CIA-like special branch in Scotland Yard at the time of the murders and was certainly in the know. He stated Tumblety was a very likely suspect."

Rhinelander took a quick glance at his watch. "Crikey!" He yelled. "I'm late for the airport. It was nice meeting the two of you, and keep me updated, Ryan. Cheers."

After everyone shook Rhinelander's hand, he left the cemetery.

"Didn't you say you are exhuming three bodies here?" Dunham asked.

Stanton nodded. "Yes, it's the Tumblety plot, and his father and brother are also buried here. Since they all died in old age, we don't know for sure which one is Francis Tumblety—so we're testing all three."

"Who is paying for all this work?" Dunham asked.

"An independently wealthy and well-respected ripperologist out of Burlingame, California."

"I've heard that Jack the Ripper must have had surgical expertise," Riggs commented.

"Surgical knowledge, maybe, but not surgical expertise," Stanton clarified. "Most experts agree that the killer's skill with the knife from a surgical perspective was crude, but he certainly knew how to navigate in the abdominal region in total darkness."

Dunham searched his pockets.

Without missing a beat, Riggs pulled out a small spiral notepad with a pen and handed it to him.

Dunham nodded, grabbed the notepad, and began writing.

"Do you mind if we make our way to my camper?" Stanton asked. "It's a perfect time for a break, and I have some nice cold drinks."

"Sounds great," Dunham replied.

chapter twelve

**1888: Friday, October 5. 2:00 p.m. London, England—
East End, herb store off Whitechapel Road.**

Inspector Andrews wiped his forehead with his hanky then repositioned his deerstalker hat as he strolled slowly down busy Whitechapel Road. He elbowed Inspector Moore softly in the side. "Henry, our unfortunates have smartened up." He pointed to two women loitering at the entrance of a gin palace. "They're all working in pairs ever since the last two victims were murdered a week ago."

"That has caught my attention as well," Moore replied. "Of course, staying off the streets is out of the question." He rolled his eyes.

"Of course," Andrews replied. "And thank you for joining me, by the way. I know your team is just as busy as mine."

Moore smiled. "No worries, Walter." He snickered. "My guess is you have to get a break from Froest!"

Andrews laughed. "Yes, his antics are legendary. The chief inspector has promised me a promotion if I can keep Froest out of trouble."

Moore laughed. "Impossible." He abruptly faced Andrews. "Speaking of Froest, I hear he and Dinnie had quite the experience at the chamber of horrors wax museum they visited last week."

"They did. Dinnie told me about their suspicions that if this Twomby is our maniac, he might be attempting to immortalize his actions through permanent wax displays of his atrocities."

Moore shifted his gaze to a storefront and stopped. "Is this the place, Walter?"

"I believe so." Andrews stopped in front of the window display. "Is this an herb store or an anatomical museum?"

On display were numerous items, and most prominent was a glass apparatus filled with red fluid.

Moore stared at the sign. "The sign below reads, 'The human circulatory system made healthy through herbal elixirs.'" He paused for a moment. "How ironic that a contraption displaying human blood is in the same district as the Whitechapel murders."

"And the coincidence that the Whitechapel investigation has led us to this very herb store," Andrews added, "about an elixir of life."

"Interesting indeed," Moore replied.

Andrews opened the door, and they entered the store.

A tall dark man with a prominent black mustache reclined in his chair behind the counter. He got up and approached the detectives. "May I help you, gentlemen?"

"Hello, my name is Inspector Andrews, and this is Inspector Moore. We would like to ask you a few questions, if we may." Andrews noted the store owner's demeanor change from calm to appearing quite nervous and agitated.

The store owner began organizing herbs and containers of pills on his shelves. "What is this about?"

"Nothing concerning you or your store," Andrews said reassuringly. "We're merely questioning local businesses about suspicious behaviors or suspicious people they may have seen."

The store owner continued to organize a shelf. "Oh, nothing out of the ordinary has happened here."

Moore approached a hat rack.

"So, you are an American," Andrews said, recognizing the man's accent. "Where are you from?"

The store owner paused, then replied, "New York City."

"How long have you been here in England?"

"I've offered my medical services in the British Isles periodically since '69, but my current stay began this late spring."

Moore turned and eyed the store owner. "I like your hat. It's an American slouch hat, is it not?"

The store owner nodded.

"Have you noticed any unusual customers in the last month?" Andrews asked.

"Ah, no . . . no, not here," he replied, avoiding any eye contact with the inspector.

Andrews glanced at Moore and then back at the man. "Have you ever heard of anyone mixing a concoction of ingredients from both the plant and animal kingdom in order to create an—" he paused—"elixir of life?"

The store owner suddenly stumbled into the shelf, knocking over dozens of small herbal containers. He regained his composure.

"Do you need assistance?" Andrews asked.

"No, I'm fine," the store owner gasped as he began cleaning up his mess. "No, I have not heard of this concoction." He shifted his gaze to Andrews. "Who told you this? Is this about the recent murders?"

Andrews smiled calmly. "It's of no concern. We're merely following up all theories, even, as in this instance, the most preposterous. I apologize for any inconvenience. Good day, sir." He started for the door.

Moore merely tipped his hat to the store owner and grinned, then followed Andrews.

Andrews stopped and turned back around. "Oh I'm sorry—I did not get your name."

The store owner paused for a moment shifting his eyes back and forth. "It's Twomblety—Dr. Twomblety."

Moore turned quickly toward the store owner. "Did you say 'Twomby'?"

"No, Dr. Twomblety."

"Might I inquire about your involvement in wax museums?" Moore asked.

Twomblety glared at Moore. "Absolutely nothing!" He began reorganizing a shelf of pills. "Good day, gentlemen."

Inspector Andrews gave a quick nod. "Thank you, Dr. Twomblety." He turned and led Moore out of the store.

"I wonder if Twomblety and Twomby are the same person," Moore mused.

"Well, Sergeant Dinnie did check for records on a Twomby at headquarters, but there was nothing. Maybe 'Twomblety' will show up."

"I don't know," Moore replied. "The names are unique, though, and they sound so much like each other. I'll check the next time I'm at headquarters myself."

"Do you recall what Inspector Abberline said about a sitting member of parliament dressing in disguise and personally investigating a military connection to the Tabram murder in early August?" Andrews asked.

Moore thought for a moment. "Yes, I believe it was Sir Francis Charles Hughes-Hallett. A charismatic fellow."

Andrews stared down at his feet as they neared Leman Street. "He told the chief inspector that he suspected the killer was a medical doctor very similar to this Dr. Twomblety." He faced Moore. "I noticed your interest in his Yankee hat."

"Indeed. If I'm not mistaken, I believe there was a case involving a Yankee hat. A Matthew Packer on Berner Street sold grapes to a suspicious person fitting this description."

"Then there was the Albert Chambers lodging case, the day after the double murders," Andrews added. "This man was a tall, dark American, constantly bragging to those in the house how the killer is too cute for us London detectives. He even admitted to visiting the site of the last murder."

"Did this man have a large black mustache?" Moore asked.

Andrews nodded. "Indeed he did." They resumed their pace. "Let's speak with Inspector Abberline. It's time we disseminated this information to the police constables. They need to be on the lookout for any suspicious characters in an American slouch hat."

chapter thirteen

Dunham followed Riggs up the narrow steps into Stanton's travel trailer. They slid into the bench seat in the tiny kitchen. The table was so small he bumped into Riggs and nearly crushed him into the window.

"Sorry, Detective Riggs," Stanton apologized, motioning around at the small space.

"No problem, Mr. Stanton." Riggs smirked.

Dunham accepted a drink Stanton handed to him. "Thank you."

Stanton tossed Riggs a can of cola, then sat down.

"Mr. Stanton," Dunham began. "Our concern has less to do with your exhuming a Ripper suspect and more to do with Jack the Ripper attempting to create the elixir of life. You see, we have evidence that the Niagara Falls serial killer is attempting to do that very thing, and in the very same way as your paper describes."

Stanton's mouth dropped opened. "Are you serious?" He closed his mouth and frowned. "Do you think the killer got the idea from my article?"

"Maybe," Dunham answered. "But your article does speak of nineteenth-century Freemason and Rosicrucian Orders searching for the elixir of life, and there are many offshoots of these Orders still in existence today, even in Western New York. His source may have come from them."

Stanton sat back, wide eyed. "Well, I guess so, but how co-incidental that my article gets published, and then a few years later this happens."

"True," Dunham agreed. "And we plan on investigating all leads. What more do you know about these Orders?"

Stanton placed his finger on his lips. "England at the time of the Ripper murders was a hotbed for searching for the elixir of life, which found its way into a well-do-do London West End theater called the Lyceum Theatre. Many employees of the Lyceum Theatre were involved with a Rosicrucian Order offshoot, which had as one of their primary goals the discovery of the elixir of life."

"What is a Rosicrucian?" Riggs asked.

"Rosicrucianism," Stanton answered, "is a theological belief based upon on the doctrines of Paracelsus, a Swiss physician and astrologer born in 1493. 'Rosicrucian' literally means 'rose' and 'cross,' signifying Christ's cross with a rose in its center, most likely originating with the Christian reformer Martin Luther and his connection with the rose. Paracelsus, and later the Rosicrucians, believed human beings held within them the knowledge and power of all things, including divinity, yet, this knowledge and power are untapped, or hidden. It is a type of Christian Gnosticism—Gnosticism meaning 'hidden knowledge.'"

"That doesn't sound like the Christianity I know of," Riggs commented.

"You're right," Stanton agreed. "The Christianity we are familiar with is what we call Pauline Christianity, championed so aggressively by the Apostle Paul, where justification, or how one makes it through the pearly gates to heaven, is by God's grace through faith and/or good works. Students of Rosicrucianism believe that just as Jesus the man became God, every human being has the potential to become God through studying a certain book of accumulated knowledge, ultimately becoming enlightened, or what they call illuminated."

"So, the goal of Pauline Christianity is to believe and the goal of Rosicrucianism is to know," Dunham reasoned.

Stanton smiled. "In general terms, Dr. Dunham, you nailed it. Of course the devil's in the details."

Riggs snickered. "How appropriate."

"The supposed founder of a Medieval Order," Stanton asserted, "called the Illuminated Brotherhood of Rosicrucians, located in Germany around 1407, was claimed to have translated into Latin an Arabian book containing the accumulated knowledge of the ancient masters. It was called the *Magnum Opus*, also called the *Sacred Book M*. It was said to contain the acquired knowledge from every ancient culture. Still others called this knowledge universal book the *Great Arcanum*."

"I've never heard of this before," Riggs admitted.

"Actually, you have," Stanton informed. "Or at least in an indirect way in your very own Bible. It's symbolized in the Book of Genesis as a combination of the fruit from the Tree of Knowledge of Good and Evil and the fruit from the Tree of Life in the Garden of Eden. The Rosicrucians claimed the *Magnum Opus* contained the secrets of everything, including the creation of the elixir of life, medicinal herbs for curing every disease, the transmutation of metals, and the manufacture of precious gems. They also claimed the founder manufactured the elixir of life, but of course this knowledge was again lost through centuries of time."

Riggs nodded. "I can see the connections to our investigation."

"It gets closer," Stanton claimed. "An element of Freemasonry and its rituals find its origins in Rosicrucianism, and Freemasonry was kind of the social playground for the wealthy West End Londoners. In 1865, a Freemason named Fredrick Hockley got a group of Masons together and founded the Societas Rosicruciana in Anglica, or the Rosicrucian Society of England. A requirement to become a member of this society was to already be a Freemason. In 1888—the same year as the Whitechapel killings—the Rosicrucian Order I referred to earlier was formed, called the Order of the Golden Dawn. Its members were employed by the Lyceum Theatre, and amazingly, the play *Dr. Jekyll and Mr. Hyde* was playing during the murders."

"This is getting interesting," Riggs remarked. "But if Rosicrucianism is rooted in Christianity, how could it have anything to do with the horrible Whitechapel mutilations?"

"Here's where it gets even more intriguing," Stanton continued. "The Illuminated Brotherhood gave a warning. The warning stated that if one reads from the Book of All Knowledge for selfish reasons, such as curing one's own disease or creating the elixir of life, one will not receive true knowledge and full understanding and will most certainly be seduced by Satan and become a terrible menace to mankind."

Dunham and Riggs exchanged glances.

"Wow!" Riggs exclaimed. "This fits our case like a glove."

"If my memory serves me right," Dunham began, "an 1888 letter that some experts attribute to Jack the Ripper is now referred to as the 'From hell' letter since the author signed it 'From hell.' Rosicrucians believe a person can become divine, so a Rosicrucian Jack the Ripper may have honestly believed he was 'From hell.'"

"Excellent point, Dr. Dunham!" Stanton praised. "You'd make a great ripperologist. Now, not all ripperologists believe the 'From hell' letter came from the killer—but many do."

"If this Rosicrucian–Ripper–elixir connection is true in our case, any thoughts on how this could help our investigation?" Dunham asked.

Stanton perked up. "Yes, actually. It seems there was an element of ritualism in the original murders, and if the modern killer truly is seeking an elixir of life, there may be signs of this. Color means something in Freemasonry and Rosicrucianism. The color blue means death, and the color red—as in the color of life's blood—means life. Violet is a mixture of blue and red, so to Rosicrucians it means a connection to life from death—in other words, a resurrection to immortal life. This may help. Also, diamonds were special to Rosicrucians because they purportedly possess powers, they're the hardest substance on earth, and seem to last forever—another connection to immortality."

The camper door opened, and an agitated-looking man gasped, "Mr. Stanton, four police cars just pulled into the cemetery!" His excited voice echoed through the cramped interior.

Stanton frowned, scrambled to his feet, and hurried from the camper. "What? All of our paperwork is in order. We have permission from the diocese. I just spoke with the bishop."

Dunham and Riggs followed Stanton out of the camper.

Dunham noticed six uniformed police officers and a woman dressed in regular clothes approaching them. Two of the police officers were New York State troopers, while the others appeared to be Rochester City police. In the lead was a trooper, tall with an athletic build.

"I'm sorry, have we done something wrong?" Stanton asked.

The trooper stopped and eyed all three of them. "Not that I'm aware of," he jested. "My name is Lieutenant James Hallway. We're actually looking for Dr. Dunham."

Dunham raised his hand. "I'm Dr. Dunham."

Hallway approached Dunham and shook his hand. "Hello, Dr. Dunham. I apologize for interrupting the three of you, but we have an urgent situation with the life of Mayor Armstrong's son on the line, and we could certainly use your help. May we take a short moment of your time?"

"Absolutely, but how did you know I was here?" Dunham asked.

Riggs grinned. "The Watchmaker coming to Western New York is big news."

"Everyone knew you were in Buffalo helping out with the Niagara Falls Serial Killer Case." Hallway pointed to the lady. "And it was Dr. Henderson, here, who had the idea to conference with you. We called Captain Johnson in Buffalo, and he told us you were at this cemetery, so we decided a meeting with you face-to-face was in order. Dr. Anne Henderson is our local criminal profiler and has helped us solve dozens of cases."

Henderson approached Dunham and shook his hand. "Hello, Dr. Dunham. It's a pleasure to finally meet you."

"You as well, Dr. Anderson. I'm familiar with some of your casework."

Henderson beamed then immediately regained her professional composure. "Thank you."

"So, how may I be of service?" Dunham asked.

Henderson handed Dunham a folder. "Well, Dr. Dunham, three days ago, the mayor's twelve-year-old son, Robert Armstrong, was seen leaving school at 3:10 p.m. on his way home, taking his usual route, but this time he never made it home. He was kidnapped, and our best guess is that he was taken in the most secluded section of that route. Unfortunately, no one saw anyone suspicious in the area."

Dunham sat down at a nearby picnic table and flipped open the file.

"A ransom note was found in the mayor's mailbox, and still no one saw a thing," Henderson explained.

Dunham picked up a piece of paper and stared at it. "Is this the ransom note?"

"Yes, and the kidnapper is demanding a drop-off in six hours. The instructions are confusing, and we're not entirely sure which location he means. We've narrowed it down to three places."

"The ransom note is computer typed," Dunham mumbled, "and very succinct. This is certainly not a lot to go by." He glanced up at Henderson. "Anything else?"

Henderson nodded. "Yes, there was a similar kidnapping case three months ago, which we believe is the same kidnapper." She handed another folder to Dunham. "An eleven-year-old boy was kidnapped while on his way home from school, just like the Armstrong boy. This boy, Seth, was the son of another influential person, the millionaire and owner of Printup Industries, James Printup."

Dunham pulled out the Printup ransom note and reviewed it. "I agree with you. Too many coincidences to be a separate offender. The ransom notes are very similar."

"This time, a witness saw a white, full-sized van parked in the location where he was kidnapped just an hour before," Henderson explained. "It may or may not have been the kidnapper's."

"Sadly," Hallway interrupted, "the boy was murdered on the day the ransom was supposed to be delivered because of an unavoidable delay during the delivery. The kidnapper's instructions were unusually vague, as in this case."

Dunham continued to review the Printup ransom note. "These certainly are vague instructions."

"What a frustrating time," Hallway complained. "His body was discovered a week later a hundred yards off of Highway 490, and it was burned beyond recognition with a bullet hole in the back of the victim's head, as if the kidnapper wanted to impress upon us that he meant business. Because of this, we predicted he would strike again, and here we go. Not only is the mayor well-known, he comes from a wealthy family."

"Do you have the autopsy report with you?" Dunham asked.

"Flip to the back of the file," Henderson replied. "Of interest are the stomach contents," she explained. "Since food only stays in the stomach for four to six hours, and since the victim had been kidnapped for three days, the food must have been given to the victim by the offender. The victim's stomach contained a unique and exotic spice found only in certain Vietnamese foods. There are only two restaurants in the City of Rochester that offer Vietnamese food, the Dac Hoa on Monroe Ave., and the Thai Loa on University Ave., and both receive the majority of their business through takeout. The perpetrator just might live close to one of these restaurants, and maybe he bought the food, then fed the boy leftovers. We searched both areas for owners of white vans, but all leads turned cold."

"Excellent job, Dr. Henderson," Dunham praised. "Are there any international grocery stores in the area?"

Hallway frowned. "There are two, TOPS International and Wegmans, and they certainly do have a large Oriental food section." He shook his head. "This sets us back."

Dunham thought for a moment. "It's true that the offender might've made his own Vietnamese food from ingredients he purchased at an international grocery store, but for the moment, let's assume that Dr. Henderson's suspicions are correct." Dunham paused. "We need to check your local child sex offender list and identify any sex offenders living within a few miles of either of these two restaurants."

"That can be done." Hallway turned and gave instructions to the Rochester police officers, then turned back to Dunham. "Dr. Dunham, we should have an answer for you within minutes."

"Great."

"So, you think this is a child molestation case, Dr. Dunham?" Henderson asked, confused. "We saw no evidence of molestation, and I actually didn't give it much thought since it seems to have been a classic case of kidnapping with a clear financial motive."

"Yes, I do believe child molestation was involved," Dunham asserted. "Note the chemical analysis results of the victim's rectal contents. Identified was a significant concentration of sodium laurel sulfate. That's liquid soap. Recently, child sex offenders have been using condoms in order to avoid depositing samples of their DNA in their victims. They use non-lubricated condoms, and their choice of lubricant is liquid soap."

"Why liquid soap?" Henderson asked.

"Not only is it cheap and readily accessible, it's extremely water soluble, washing away any evidence. As you can see in this case, that's not always true. A lubricated condom leaves behind a unique kind of lubrication, which confirms the use of a condom, and in a number of court cases, this was enough to get a rape conviction. The burning of the body might be a message to police, or it might be the offender attempting to hide any trace of molestation. These types of sex offenders usually have a history of child molestation, so maybe we have record of him due to a previous conviction."

Henderson grinned. "Well, I'll be."

"Dr. Dunham, why go to such lengths to molest a child?" Riggs asked. "I mean, kidnapping high-profile citizens guarantees full enforcement by police officials, thus a greater chance of getting caught."

"That's because this is not just a child molestation case or even a kidnapping case," Dunham asserted.

Riggs glanced over at an equally confused Henderson.

"Let me explain," Dunham began. "The evidence bears all the hallmarks of a sado-sexual pathological serial killer." Dunham pointed to the Printup ransom note and the Armstrong ransom note. "Notice the similarities between the two ransom notes. The offender is purposely making his delivery instructions vague, ensuring that the money never makes it to the delivery point in time. His plan was—and is—to convince police he's only out for the money, while he revels in the thrill of the chase and his lust for murder and molestation."

"I'm still not getting it," Riggs admitted.

Dunham raised his finger. "Think of the offender as pathological, as in having a mind that responds abnormally to external stimuli. They operate on a different set of mental rules, which is why it was necessary in the past to identify serial killer motives. Presently, we've identified numerous motives behind the actions of serial killers, such as sexually-based, financial or personal gain, ideology, anger and hatred, and even thrill-seeking. Many times serial killers are driven by a combination of motives. In this particular case, it may be a combination of sado-sexual and possibly financial gain, but it also seems he's thrill-seeking."

Hallway turned just as his phone went off. Staring at the lit screen of his iPhone, he said, "Dr. Dunham, we've identified eleven convicted child abuse sex offenders living near the two restaurants." He handed his phone to Dunham.

"Great." Dunham scrolled down the list. "Let me prioritize them for you. Do you have a piece of paper?"

Hallway pulled a notepad from his pocket. "Ready."

Dunham paused at one name. "Well, it's going to be a short list, actually. Dennis Cooper. His profile is a perfect match. We have his address and a home phone number."

"Got it," Hallway replied then moved briskly away.

Dunham searched his pockets, pulled out the notepad he'd been looking for earlier, and wrote down the address. He jerked his head up. "If you'll excuse me for one moment, everyone, I have to make a call." He pulled out his iPhone. "I'll be right back." Dunham headed toward the back of the camper as he sent a text message. He touched an app on his phone titled "Secured," then dialed a phone number and put the phone to his ear.

"One Alpha Charlie," a voice answered at the other end of the line.

"Winfall, One-Eight-Eight-Eight-Eight," Dunham replied.

"Our crypto-translators are in sync, and this connection is now secured," the voice said. "Good afternoon, Dr. Dunham. Please ensure no one is earshot. How may I help you?"

Dunham peeked around. "Good afternoon, Big Brother. We have a probable murder in six hours—a kidnapping of a twelve-year-old boy, the son of the mayor of Rochester. I've just texted you a name and the address of our likely offender. We need to locate his whereabouts immediately. He is most likely the same suspect in a separate, similar murder case in Rochester three months ago."

"Well, Dr. Dunham, we're in luck," Big Brother replied. "Dennis Cooper owns a cell phone, and," he paused, "it is turned on. I've triangulated his location and have just texted you the address, which is 5.2 miles south of your present position on Court Street in downtown Rochester." Big Brother paused again. "Satellite imagery shows a large building at this address with a white van parked behind it. Incidentally, this matches the description of the van registered in Cooper's name." A few moments passed. "He is at a warehouse last owned by Barnard's Shipping, which went out of business in 1994. It seems the building is abandoned."

Dunham began to pace. "That's gotta be it."

"Here's a little confirmation," Big Brother continued. "A geographic history of this particular phone IDs three hotspots within the last six weeks—his home address, his work address, and the abandoned shipping warehouse."

Dunham grinned. "Excellent!"

"One more thing, Dr. Dunham. The murdered boy three months ago wouldn't happen to have been Seth Printup would it?"

Dunham nodded as he paced. "Yes, the local authorities just informed me of his name. Why?"

"I searched for murders of juveniles in the area for the past three months, and the Printup murder site popped up as a match for the suspect's cell phone's geographical history. The location, date, and time place him at the Printup murder site in conjunction with the murder's occurrence."

Dunham grinned. "You never cease to amaze me, Big Brother. You must be operating six computers at once."

"I do have skills, my friend."

"Now, I need a cover story for knowing Cooper's exact location. Is there any place of interest within a block of this warehouse?" Dunham asked.

"Actually, the warehouse is next to where he works—the Strong Natural Museum of Play. It's less than a block from the museum and adjacent to one of the museum's parking lots."

Dunham nodded. "Perfect. I wonder how he became employed at the museum with a prior child abuse conviction?"

"Well, I found the answer to that too. He actually works for a small company subcontracted by the museum. I'm currently reading his online job application, and he stated he had no previous arrests. He lied."

Dunham shook his head and grinned. "Thanks again, Big Brother. You've earned your pay today."

"I love my job. Take care and good luck, Dr. Dunham."

Dunham hung up and approached Lieutenant Hallway. He noticed the other police officers heading for their vehicles. Hallway had a huge grin on his face and approached Dunham. "Cooper has a white Chevy van registered in his name. It certainly looks promising. We have several units on their way to Cooper's house. I want to thank you, Dr. Dunham, for all your help."

Dunham shook his head. "We're not done, Lieutenant."

Hallway stopped in his tracks.

"This man would not hold his victims in his own home. Too close for comfort. Still, it'll be in a location he's familiar with, like near his place of work. Have we determined where Cooper works?"

"At the Strong Museum," Hallway replied. "It's a kids museum."

Dunham pulled out his iPhone and opened up a satellite map app. "It's a hunch, but we have very little time. My bet is he's in an abandoned building or something near the museum."

Hallway's eyes opened wide. "There are a lot of warehouses in that location."

Dunham stared at the iPhone. "This can't be a coincidence, Lieutenant. There's a warehouse-like building near the museum, next to a museum parking lot on Court Street. At least it's a place to start your search. If he's there, I'm sure he parked his van out of sight from the road."

Hallway turned away in a hurry. "We'll take it from here! Thank you again, Dr. Dunham. I'll keep you updated."

Henderson grinned and shook Dunham's hand. "Thank you very much, Dr. Dunham. Your reputation is well deserved."

"It was nice to meet you, Dr. Henderson. I hope to see you again."

Henderson left, following the police.

Riggs, Dunham, and Stanton watched the police cars leave.

"I hope you nailed it, Dr. Dunham," Riggs said optimistically.

"Me too." Dunham faced Stanton and shook his hand. "Thank you, Mr. Stanton. We need to return to Buffalo. Do you mind if I contact you again if circumstances require it?"

"Not at all. I hope I helped out."

Dunham walked with Riggs to the car. "We need to recheck the crime scenes and evidence collected from each of the victims, such as the clothing, to see if any were wearing anything violet."

"Sounds good. I'll check the list of their personal possessions to see if anyone was wearing diamonds, as well."

They jumped into the car. "Also, let's contact the victims' family members and see if any of them received violets—as in flowers—just prior to the homicides."

Thirty minutes later, Dunham received a text from Captain Johnson. "A witness stepped forward in the First Niagara Center murder. He saw Johnson on the news," he said to Riggs.

"Great! What did he say?"

Dunham tapped the screen to open an attachment and read, "He remembered being around the little shed on his way to his parked car, apparently to urinate. When he rounded the shed, a man leaped out of the tall weeds and ran, which surprised him. He didn't think to investigate the tall weeds, but he said it was too dark to see anything, anyway."

"Did he get a description of the man?" Riggs asked.

"A partial description. He said the guy was taller than he was, maybe six foot two, with broad shoulders and an athletic build. He had dark hair and was wearing a dark trench coat. As the guy ran away, he thought he saw a straight stick in his hand."

"Well, at least it's a start," Riggs added. "I'm sure this description can eliminate some future suspects."

Dunham nodded. "Also, we now know where the suspect ran from the scene, so investigators have returned to the murder site looking for footprints. I'll text the captain and tell him we'd like to speak with the witness when we get back."

"Sounds like a plan."

Nearing downtown Buffalo, Dunham's phone rang. "Dr. Dunham speaking. Hello, Lieutenant Hallway."

Dunham glanced over at Riggs as he listened.

"Excellent, and you're welcome. Do you mind if I call you later for an update? Great. Bye."

"Did they find the boy?" Riggs asked.

"They certainly did. There was a white van in the back of that warehouse, and the SWAT team moved in and apprehended Cooper without incident. The good news is they found the Armstrong boy alive and well, although understandably distraught."

Riggs grinned and reached over to shake Dunham's hand. "Congratulations, Dr. Dunham. I'm buying the beer tonight."

"Now that sounds great," he said, then hair on the back of his neck stood on end as he realized he'd just saved a child from a horrible fate. He beamed as he stared out the car window.

chapter fourteen

Diane Barnett peeked through her blinds in the front window and watched her close friend and neighbor, Katie Jenkins,
stroll up to her house with another thirtysomething woman she
did not know. It was a dark, cool, and wet September evening,
but it was no longer raining, causing a light, misty fog in the air.

"You'll love her," she could hear Katie said to the other
woman.

Diane frowned. *Darn, I was just about to take my Wednesday evening run,* she thought to herself. She liked her home
on Florence Avenue. Not only was it a beautiful, century-old,
three-story house, but it was situated close to the Buffalo Zoo.
The neighborhood was perfect for runners. She enjoyed jogging
around the zoo in the evenings, near its exotic animal sights,
noises, and even the distinct smells.

Katie and the other woman approached Diane's front door.
"Diane and her husband, Artie, are Buffalo police officers, so
it's pretty safe around here," Diane overheard through the door.

"Oh, nice," the other woman commented.

Katie rang the doorbell. "They're also black belts in judo or
something like that, so they can kick everyone's asses. Luckily,
they're the nicest people in the world."

Diane's frown turned to a grin, and she rolled her eyes. She
popped the door open and smiled at the two.

"Diane!"

Diane beamed. "Hi, Kate." She then dropped her smile. "Why haven't you responded to my texts?"

Katie entered Diane's house with a familiar, casual air and walked past her. "I see you're going for a run."

Diane smiled and nodded at the other woman as she entered behind Katie.

The woman returned the smile and nod.

"I lost my phone again," Katie continued, "so I decided to stop by and tell you just in case you were texting me."

Diane shook her head. "I swear, Kate, you're always losing your phone."

Katie shrugged. "Diane, I'd like to introduce you to Sandy Rastelli. She and her family just moved in three houses down."

Diane shook Sandy's hand. "Sandy, it's very nice to meet you."

"It's nice to meet you too, Diane," Sandy replied. "Katie told me you and your husband are police officers."

Diane, still holding the police uniform she'd changed out of to put on her running clothes, raised it up to show her. "Yes, as you can see. Artie's not here. Lately, he's been working a different shift, but you'll meet him soon. He's back working my shift next week. Come, take a seat."

The three sat down in the living room.

Sandy gestured toward a collection of judo trophies on the piano. "I also hear you do judo. I took judo years ago. I made it to green belt, I think."

Diane crossed to the trophies and grabbed one. "Yep, Artie and I have been doing it for years." She raised the trophy. "We love the competition, as you can see. If you want to get back into it, just let me know."

Sandy nodded. "I just might do that. Where's your dojo?"

"It's about a fifteen minute drive from here. The Kin Tora Martial Arts and Fitness Center."

"Maybe I'll check them out," Sandy commented.

"So, Kate," Diane said, changing the subject. "How did the interview go? Did they love you?"

Katie turned to Sandy. "I just finished my master's degree in education this summer and have applied for some teaching jobs. This position I interviewed for opened up because the previous teacher accepted a position as an assistant principal in another school district."

"I see."

Katie turned back to Diane. "I think it went well. They'll be calling candidates for the next round of interviews on Friday. The principal said eight were interviewed, while a hundred applied!"

"Wow," Diane replied. "Even if you don't get called again, at least you know your résumé is good enough to make the first cut from such a large pool of candidates."

"It also shows how few jobs are available nowadays." Katie presented a large purse and grinned. "Just think, if my husband wasn't working, I wouldn't be able to afford my collection of purses."

Diane rolled her eyes and laughed.

"You won't laugh when you find out how much I paid for my last one," Katie confessed. "My Gucci handbag cost me four hundred fifty dollars!"

Diane's mouth dropped. "Does John know?"

Katie grinned. "Of course not, but he loves me and lets me spend his money any way I want to."

"Not if he knew how much you spent on that stupid purse," Diane warned.

Katie snickered.

Diane shook her head. "You're amazing, Katie."

Katie put down her purse and took a more serious tone. "So, there was another murder by the serial killer. A college student at Buff State I hear?"

"Oh, I heard about the Niagara Falls serial killer," Sandy added.

Diane nodded. "Pretty wild, isn't it?"

Katie glanced at Sandy. "Diane and her husband are on the serial killer task force." She shifted toward Diane. "Are you any closer to finding the killer?"

Diane shook her head. "Not at all, although the good news is our captain has recruited a top expert from the FBI, and he's joining the task force. His nickname's the Watchmaker." She shrugged her shoulders. "My personal opinion is that he won't be able to help us either. We'll see."

"Well, the guy has a nickname, doesn't he?" Katie reasoned. "If he's special enough to have that, he must be good, right?"

"I suppose," Diane replied. "So, Katie, are you going to go for a run with me tonight?"

Katie cringed and got up. "No, of course not. A candle that burns twice as bright lasts half as long. I don't want to burn out too fast in my life. Besides, it would ruin my voluptuousness."

Diane rolled her eyes. "Kate, you're skinnier than I am."

Katie led the way to the door.

Sandy followed and turned to Diane. "Well, it was nice meeting you, Diane. I hope we can get together soon."

"Nice to meet you, too, Sandy." Diane glanced at Katie. "Katie and I have a girls' night out every month or so—would you like to come out with us?"

Sandy nodded. "Sure, that would be fun."

"That's a great idea," Katie added. "Well, have fun on your run, Diane. See ya."

The front door closed softly behind them.

Diane glanced up at the clock, noticing it was getting late, possibly too late for a run. She shook her head. "Get off your butt, Diane," she spoke to herself as she got up.

After stretching for a short period, Diane left through the front door, stopped on her front porch, and peered out at the dark, misty night. As she set out, she noticed she was feeling an unusual amount of sadness, recalling being at the funeral of the Niagara Falls serial killer's college student victim, Angie Sparks. She couldn't get the emotionally draining experience out of her head, and she couldn't imagine how the victim must have felt as she was being attacked so ruthlessly by the killer.

A car drove by, and the driver waved to Diane.

Diane smiled and waved back, then she began her run. She darted around a man strolling down the sidewalk and realized she was taking a run by herself in the evening, which was probably not the brightest idea with a brutal serial killer on the loose. This gave her a sense of uneasiness. Then she remembered her husband asking her not to run alone and became acutely aware that some locations along her running path were quite dark and foggy. *Perfect for abductions*, she thought to herself. This made her even more anxious. Usually, she could zone out as she ran, allowing her to relax in the moment, but not tonight.

"Hi, Diane!" yelled an old lady from her porch.

Diane quickly glanced up at her. "Oh, hi, Mrs. Larkins."

"Be safe!" Mrs. Larkins yelled back.

The path took her away from the residential homes and along the Buffalo Zoo. The animal sounds and smells seemed to help calm her nerves. She noticed the monkeys were especially noisy this evening. She loved running by this section at night. It gave her a sense of freedom as she ran, as if she were on the plains of Africa or in the jungles of the Amazon. This particular section of her run also seemed to be the safest, since it was out in the open and the path ran next to a busy, well-lit commercial section.

"Watch to your right!" a bicyclist yelled as he passed her.

Diane moved slightly to the left but maintained her pace. She finally felt herself getting into the zone, but it was short-lived, as the path took her back into the darker residential area. Diane noticed a number of poorly lit areas ahead, and the first was about two hundred feet in front of her, where two houses were separated by a pitch-black alleyway. As she ran by the alleyway, she moved away from it, out closer to the road, and picked up a little speed. Once past it, she continued her run. The next dark area caught her by surprise. Once she realized she was running in total darkness, she became excited and rushed back into the light, which caused her to step directly into a puddle. Now her feet were wet, and she was angry. *Oh, knock it off, Diane*, she told herself. *Don't let this guy rent space in your head. Just focus on the run and ignore everything else. Get in the zone.*

She approached another poorly lit area. This time, her plan was to ignore the dark alley completely and jog right by it. As she neared the spot, a police car came out of nowhere and turned the corner onto the street at a relatively high rate of speed for the area, skidding to a stop in front of her. A male police officer got out of the car—her husband.

"Diane, what are you doing!" he roared. "You promised me you weren't going to run in the evening anymore." He looked around the area and shook his head. "I figured you wouldn't listen to me."

"Artie!" Diane yelled forcefully but affectionately, then punched him on the arm. "You scared the crap out of me!" She caught her breath and composed herself as he stared at her. "I know, I know, I forgot. I promise this'll be the last time."

"Well, I'm going to scare the hell out of you each night until you stop."

"Wait a minute, aren't you supposed to be in your firearms class tonight?"

"It was canceled, so I'm back on the streets." Artie glanced down the road. "Go ahead, Di. Finish your run," he relented. "I'll follow you the rest of the way. I'm going to go to the house with you and grab a bite to eat."

Diane beamed. "Thank you, sweetie." She kissed Artie then started running. "I'll see you in the house."

Artie got into his car and followed her around the corner.

Inside that very same dark alleyway, hidden from view, was a large, powerful man cloaked in dark clothes and holding a long knife. His target would never know that she was only seconds away from being his next victim. If her husband had waited just thirty seconds, she would have been out of his line of sight and in the midst of unbelievable horror, a participant in his ruthless agenda.

Moments later, the dark figure left the alleyway, then walked down the sidewalk, blending in with the misty fog and darkness.

chapter fifteen

PRESENT DAY: Friday, September 29. Buffalo, New York—Shea's Performing Arts Center.

Celine knew tonight's Friday evening show at Shea's was sold out, and she expected a busy evening with a high potential for raking in good tips. She loved working at Shea's, partly because of how elegant it was. The place was extravagant and beautiful. Some, she thought, might even call it ostentatious. She glanced over at her brother in the driver's seat of her car. "Thanks for dropping me off."

Robbie pulled the car in front of the theater. "Yup. There you go, sis, and thanks again for letting us take your car."

"No problem, little brother," she replied as she got out. "Be safe, and don't be stupid." She waved over her shoulder as she made her way to the front door of the theater. She paused for a moment when she spotted a friend coming to work as well.

"Hi, Cindy," Celine said pleasantly.

Cindy popped her head up. "Oh, hi, Celine. It's gonna be a busy night."

Celine grinned. "Time to make some money. We should get good tips tonight."

"I like how you think."

The two entered the theater through the main lobby. Celine stopped. "No matter how long I work here, every time I walk in, the architectural design of this lobby stops me in my tracks."

"Beautiful, isn't it?" Cindy said as she continued into the theater. "See ya."

Celine gazed around. The lobby floor was lined with huge golden tiles; the ceiling and walls were covered in artistic reliefs of arches and complementary designs, all painted with a gold base and highlighted with matching accent colors. Three of the lobby walls were beautiful portraits of what appeared to Celine to be seventeenth- or eighteenth-century nobility. Curtains with gold and maroon fabric designed in intricate detail were strategically placed along the walls, fitting perfectly into the arched reliefs. Hanging throughout the building were dozens of large crystal multi-light chandeliers.

A man strolled by and said, "Hi, Celine."

Celine dropped her gaze and glanced at him. "Hi, Mr. Scarpena," she said to her boss.

"Are you ready for a busy night?"

Her grin widened. "I'm ready." She crossed to her work station at the concession area but took a few more seconds to soak up the beautiful architecture. She scanned the main lobby and the entrances to hallways and side rooms, where massive pillars of white marble reached to the ceiling. Since her first day on the job, she liked to touch the pillars and feel their cool, smooth surface. Throughout the building were elegant chairs, seats, and small tables, creating an atmosphere of wealth and comfort. She often told her friends that working at Shea's made her feel rich.

Her concession stand was just outside the theater doors on the second floor, which allowed patrons to quickly get refreshments during the short intermission. She had the far left concession, and to her right were three others.

She and the other three employees rushed around getting ready for the crowd. One worker approached her. "I'm all set, Celine. Do you need any help?"

"I'm pretty much set too, Donna." Celine smiled. Donna was probably in her fifties and was such a nice person. "Thanks though." She eyed Donna's hair. "Oh, I love your hair. Did you just get it done?"

Donna beamed and touched her hair. "Thanks. Yes, I had it done last night. My husband thinks it makes me look ten years younger."

"I agree. I love the style."

A few patrons began climbing the stairs.

"Oh, here we go."

Celine began her night just as she always had, serving up drinks prior to the night's show.

The first half of the show flew by, with the concession crew pairing up to complete their duties. In usual fashion, the theater doors opened at intermission, and an orderly line formed for refreshments.

Celine handed a patron a drink, turned her head, and noticed a tall, wealthy-looking man in a dark suit staring at her from the next line. She was used to men staring at her, but this man's eyes were an unusual gray color, intense, and his stare and facial expression unnerved her. Two other things caught her attention; he had a beautiful cane with a massive clear crystal on its handle, and a huge diamond ring flashed from his right hand. She jerked her gaze from him but watched him peripherally.

The man moved away after he received his own order and positioned himself along a wall, still in Celine's sight.

"Hi, Celine," an older man in the front of her line said kindly.

Celine focused on her own customers and smiled. "Oh, hi, Mr. Deckman. Are you enjoying the show?"

"Excellent," Deckman replied. "Are you enjoying your job?"

"Oh yes, and thank you again for setting me up with it. It's perfect for me."

Deckman smiled. "I'll take a Coke, and you're welcome. Your boss tells me you're a keeper."

She grinned. "He's a good boss." She leaned toward Deckman, quickly glancing over at the man with the cane. "Mr. Deckman," she whispered. "Do you happen to know that tall man over there in the black suit with the cane?"

Deckman peeked quickly to his left. "Well, I do know he's been coming to the theater for years, sporadically, and he keeps to himself. A limo drops him off then picks him up at the end of the show. Why do you ask?"

Celine shrugged as she filled Deckman's drink. "Oh, no big reason. He's just a little strange. He was staring a little too hard at me, and my creeper senses kicked in."

"Having a serial killer on the loose might be the cause of that," Deckman theorized. "But keep those senses up, Celine. It's just that, this time, I don't believe you have anything to worry about. He's probably stinking rich and just thinks you're cute." Deckman grabbed his drink, gave her the money, then moved out of the line. "If anything changes though, don't hesitate to find me."

Celine smiled. "Thank you, Mr. Deckman, and enjoy the rest of the show."

"See you, Celine, and tell your dad I'll be meeting him at the casino at the usual time."

Celine nodded as she assisted the next customer. Before she knew it, the intermission was over, and they had to cash-in with Mr. Scarpena, then clean their stations. She was wiping down the final instrument when she noticed her brother's text stating he was waiting for her outside. She signed out and hurried from the building.

"Ready to go?" Robbie asked when his sister climbed in.

She looked around the empty car. "Where's Ralph and Kyle? I thought you were with them tonight."

"I was, but I already dropped them off. We took a break from our Ripper stakeout and decided just to get a bite to eat. Thank you again for letting me use your car."

"No problem." Celine eyed Robbie. "I have to tell you about this creepy old guy at the theater."

"Oh yeah, what happened?"

Celine shook her head. "Nothing, except he constantly stared at me with these intense X-ray eyes. He looked like one of those disgusting eccentric old millionaire types. Creeper to the max."

"What did he look like?"

"He was tall, dark, and wearing a suit and a long black overcoat, and he had this gorgeous black cane with a large diamond-looking crystal on the handle."

Robbie glanced at Celine. "You know, some experts believe Jack the Ripper was a rich guy, which was one of the reasons why some of them believe Scotland Yard probably knew the killer. He may even have worn a black cloak."

Celine shrugged her shoulders. "Mr. Deckman doesn't think anything of this guy."

"He was strange enough for you to tell Deckman and me about him!"

She shrugged her shoulders. "I guess so."

Robbie shook his head. "Ah, what does Mr. Deckman know anyway? He's just as rich. I say we check Creepy Dude out!"

Celine stared out the window. "The problem is no one knows who he is or where he lives."

Robbie frowned. "That sucks."

Celine held up her index finger. "Wait, Mr. Deckman said he comes to the theater periodically, and there's a new play starting up next weekend."

Robbie grinned. "I gotcha. If he shows up, text me immediately, and Ralph, Kyle, and I will wait outside and follow him." Robbie grinned. "Just think, if he's the killer—we'll be famous!" He glanced at his sister. "Now, don't back out of this, Celine."

Celine shook her head. "I won't, I won't, as long as you don't go too crazy."

"I promise!"

Next Morning: Buffalo, New York—Lafayette Hotel.

Dunham eyed his watch and noted that Riggs would be picking him up from his hotel in one hour, at seven forty-five a.m. *Just enough time to Skype my wife*, he thought as he sat on his hotel room bed, fully dressed and ready to start his day. He pulled out his tablet, turned it on, and activated Skype.

Beeping emanated from the speakers, then a female voice spoke, accompanied by her picture popping up on the screen. "Hi, honey, how are you doing?"

"Couldn't be better, dear," Dunham replied affectionately. "It's great to see you and hear your voice. How's my Maggie doing?"

"I'm doing great, and I see you've made the paper again."

Dunham looked confused. "I did not know that."

"Well, at least the CNN website, and that's national news!"

Dunham grinned. "In a way, since you're reading it from Ireland, maybe we should now call it international news."

"Well, I guess you're right, hun. Is your ego getting bigger?" she teased.

Dunham chuckled. "I guess so, dear."

"It says here that you joined the Niagara Falls Serial Killer Task Force out of Buffalo, New York—which I knew." Maggie paused. "But then, while visiting neighboring Rochester, New York, you assisted local law enforcement in apprehending the kidnapper of the mayor's son. A state police lieutenant James Hallway was interviewed and said nothing but great things about you." She smiled. "You rock, Edward!"

"Thank you, dear," he said bashfully. "I had assistance though."

"How's the serial killer investigation going?"

"It just started, so no big news yet." He raised his eyebrows. "We are, however, going to work a promising new lead."

"Excellent."

Dunham nodded. "How're your Celtic studies going?"

"Well, do you remember I told you about Y-DNA Haplogroup studies suggesting that the first contact the British Isles had with mainland Celts was most likely cultural interaction as opposed to a hostile takeover?"

"Yes, I do remember," Dunham replied, genuinely interested. He knew his wife was just as passionate about her Celtic research as he was about serial offender research.

"I'll tell you more about it later, but our research seems to corroborate this, especially here in Ireland. We have a ways to go though."

"I thought you were working on Irish myth and folklore."

"It's all interrelated," she explained. "But you're right. I only have two months here, so I want to cover as much ground as possible."

"Of course," he agreed, then smiled. "Well, Maggie, I just wanted to give you a quick hello. A task force member will be picking me up from the hotel in a few minutes to take me to the City of Buffalo Police Station. It's where our task force is headquartered. I'll be meeting the entire team for the first time. Saturday morning is the best time for all participating police districts."

"Just email me a good time for us to Skype again. Remember, I'm five hours ahead." She kissed her fingers and touched the screen. "I love you, honey, and be careful."

Dunham returned the finger kiss to the screen. "I will, and I love you too, dear." He tapped his finger to close the app, grabbed his hotel key, and headed out the door.

Dunham entered the lobby at exactly seven forty-five and noticed that Riggs was already in front of the hotel. He grinned and shook his head.

As he got into the car, Riggs handed him a coffee.

"Good morning, Riggs. Have you ever been even a minute late?" Dunham asked in jest.

Riggs grinned. "Never. Not in my nature."

Dunham opened the plastic cap on his coffee. "Thanks for the coffee."

"This is no ordinary coffee, Dr. Dunham. This is Timmy-Ho's coffee. Tim Hortons is one of our local favorites—on par with Dunkin Donuts coffee. My plan is to get you addicted to it before you go back to Virginia."

Dunham sipped his coffee. "Well, I certainly don't want to ruin your plans, especially since I'm a coffee drinker."

They arrived at the police station before Dunham had finished his coffee and were met by local police officers from around the area. Riggs introduced Dunham to almost everyone, but they started to settle down when Captain Johnson headed toward the front of the room.

Johnson faced the group and raised his hand. "OK, I need everyone's attention!"

Everyone dropped into their seats, and the room fell silent.

"Thank you for coming from your respective jurisdictions on a Saturday morning. I called this impromptu summary briefing in order to introduce you to our newest member and to bring you up to speed on a change in our task force model. In other words, we have a break in the case, and it's time to capitalize on it."

The crowd of law enforcement officers began whispering to each other, clearly interested in Johnson's revelation. Many stared at Dunham.

"I think most of you have heard of Dr. Edward Dunham, the chief forensic scientist out of the Behavioral Analysis Unit-2 Division of the FBI's National Center for the Analysis of Violent Crime, in Quantico, Virginia."

The group began to cheer and clap, then someone yelled, "The Watchmaker!"

Dunham smiled humbly.

Johnson grinned. "He joined our task force just a few days ago, and we're already seeing results." He raised his finger. "We'll be taking a new direction in the case, thanks to some of his recent discoveries, so please listen up." He glanced at Dunham. "Dr. Dunham."

The group cheered again.

Dunham stood up, joined Johnson, and faced the group. "Thank you." He paused. "Sadly, we don't have a potential suspect pool, or a list of potential suspects to narrow down, so we're going to use the sharp-shooter approach and aim directly for the bull's-eye."

Task force members glanced at each other.

Dunham continued. "First, we've narrowed our investigative focus, thanks to a clearer understanding of motive. I believe we've discovered a pattern to the homicides, which could very well lead us to the next location in the offender's plan."

"Yes!" yelled a task force member excitedly, which caused everyone, including Captain Johnson, to chuckle.

Dunham grinned. "The reason why we didn't discover this pattern earlier is because of our belief that a Jack the Ripper copycat killer is a psychopathic sado-sexual deviant, having a sexual desire to mutilate women. Our assumption was that the original Jack the Ripper was a psychopathic sado-sexual serial killer, thus we assumed our offender had the same typology. Currently, a number of Ripper experts believe the nineteenth-century killer was actually a psychopathic narcissist, having nothing to do with sexual deviancy. Additional evidence in our Niagara Falls Serial Killer Case also conforms to this."

Task force members nodded and whispered to each other.

"Now," Dunham continued. "Making the assumption that our modern-day killer fits into this typology, we began looking at the murders of these women differently. We concluded that his motive is not to satisfy a sexual desire, but one of hatred and personal gain."

Riggs elbowed Johnson in the side and leaned over with a boastful grin. "I was part of that conclusion," he bragged teasingly. "Yeah, I'm bad."

Johnson elbowed him back. "Shut up, idiot." He shook his head, hiding a slight grin.

Dunham continued. "With information provided by a local Jack the Ripper expert, we went under the assumption that he selects his victims for their organs, and he selects a location for a Freemason–slash–Rosicrucian–slash–satanic ritual for eternal life. As a result, we have a significant lead."

The group applauded.

"Working under these assumptions," Dunham explained, "we discovered that all of the victims had a blood type of O-negative. O-negative is relatively rare, with only four to eight percent of the population having it, and it's also considered the universal donor. As you're all probably aware, you can receive a transfusion of O-negative blood regardless of blood-type. If you have O-negative blood, on the other hand, you can only receive a transfusion from O-negative blood. I believe our killer has O-negative blood, and his agenda is to gain female body parts soaked in O-negative blood." Dunham glanced at Riggs. "Detective Riggs."

Riggs stood up and faced the group. "I went to the Western New York Blood Donation Organization and retrieved their donor database, and we discovered that all of the victims were on this list. Not only are all victims O-negative, they also gave blood to the same organization within the last year. Because of this pattern, we're confident that we have found his method of victim selection." He raised the document. "He somehow has a copy of this very list."

"How many women with O-negative blood are on the list?" a task force member asked.

Riggs nodded. "There are a hundred seventeen women throughout Western New York."

Johnson stood up. "So, here's the plan, ladies and gentlemen. None of this new information has changed the killer's suspected anchor point—the City of Buffalo. We believe we have always had a good understanding of his geographic comfort zone. Because of this, our task force organization will not change, and every jurisdiction represented here is involved in this next stage. We've organized the list of women's names into the representative jurisdictions in order for you to take this home and do a thorough local investigation on each woman in your area." Johnson stared hard at the group and pointed his finger forward. "Our plan is to determine this bastard's next move by identifying the next victim and to figure out his planned murder site location."

Dunham joined in again. "Another pattern we discovered with the last three victims was that they received some type of gift that lured them into the area where they were killed, such as tickets to a scheduled show at the Lewiston Art Park, as in the case of the third victim. In view of this, when you interview each woman, ask them if they've recently received a gift for something that seems to lure them. Lastly, ask them if they received anything violet in color or a violet, as in the flower."

"Dr. Dunham?" a team member asked.

Dunham acknowledged the team member.

"Why are you not considering the first two victims?"

"Well, it took awhile to discover the pattern," he replied. "Then I realized that the first two victims needed no luring. Both victims were murdered while engaging in predictable activities. The first victim was murdered during her usual gambling night at the casino. The second victim was killed while on her usual late-afternoon jog."

There was a lull in the discourse.

"Any more questions?" Johnson asked. "No? If any one of your jurisdictions needs another Memorandum of Understanding with my letterhead for resource-allocation justifications, just contact my secretary." He scanned the room. "Happy hunting, ladies and gentlemen."

chapter sixteen

1888: Tuesday, November 6. Late Night. London, England—East End, Whitechapel District.

Police Constable Tom Williams and his partner, Ralph Scott, walked their beat on north Commercial Street near Howard & Dean Street, heading toward the Ten Bells Pub. Both were fully aware that the pub and the market across the street were choice locations for soliciting prostitutes—a section of the community who had become the center of interest for the police and one Jack the Ripper. Even though the night was cold and damp from the misty fog, Williams noticed it was business as usual for the harlots. Headquarters had directed the constables to pair up while they were on patrol in order to increase police presence and to keep an extra eye on the unfortunates. Although stockier that Scott, his partner was slightly taller. Scott's night stick swung from his belt like a pendulum.

Whack!

Williams backed away. "You know, I'm getting a little annoyed at being smacked by your night stick, Ralph! That's the third time this evening," he belted out at Scott.

"Oh, sorry, Tom. Maybe I should walk on the other side of you." Scott moved and quickly changed the subject. "The evening is certainly bustling with activity."

Williams aimed his lamp down the darker and narrower Howard & Dean Street. "The night will certainly be long, I'd wager." He paused. "You know why the killer murders his victims after one a.m., don't you?"

Scott glanced over at him. "Why's that?"

"We're ordered to kick everyone out of the public houses at one a.m., so all of these people are on the streets congregating outside of the gin palaces and marketplaces. If we let these people stay in the public houses, then the streets wouldn't be so crowded that late."

"Good point," Scott agreed. A well-known unfortunate passed them, heading toward the pub. "Our ladies of the night seem a little braver lately. Less and less of them are in pairs. The last murders were over a month ago. October has been a quiet month. Maybe the killer has had his fill or moved on."

"Not a chance," Williams disagreed. "He's out there, and he'll strike again soon. Since we've been doing these double patrols, opportunities are harder to come by, so he's just biding his time. Tonight is just as good a night as any. He could be ripping a poor unfortunate's womb out a stone's throw away in these dark streets."

Both stopped and stared into a dark side street momentarily, glanced at each other, then recommenced their beat.

"I see your point," Scott replied.

"So, Inspector Abberline says a man wearing an American slouch hat was seen at the locations of the previous murders prior to the crimes being committed," Williams explained. "And we're to be on the lookout for anyone fitting his description."

"I wonder where he got his information." Scott paused. "From what I gather, Inspectors Moore and Abberline found a pattern in the thousands of eyewitness statements."

"These Americans certainly like their wide-brim hats," Williams asserted. "Everybody wants to be Buffalo Bill."

Scott stopped and faced Williams, who also stopped. "So do you."

Williams shook his head and began walking again. "I do not!"

"You do too. That's all you've been talking about ever since he visited here last year." Scott raised his hand. "As a matter of fact, your wife showed me your Buffalo Bill hat when Jane and I ate dinner with you last week."

"Ah, codswallop," Williams muttered.

Their beat took them by the Ten Bells Pub.

The street was becoming much more crowded. Nearby, two well-dressed young men laughed with a couple of unfortunates, all clearly drunk. "Look at those rich slummers in their drink."

Scott shook his head. "If they really want to experience the sights and sounds of the dangerous East End, maybe they should see what the inside of a jailhouse is like, sleeping the night off next to a loafer with a mean streak."

Williams eyed the men. "Ah, leave 'em be and let 'em spend all their money in this district. We certainly need it. Who knows, maybe with all the publicity from rich slummers writing articles in the papers, the government'll do something about it."

"I still don't like it," Scott growled.

"Besides," Williams continued, "orders are to concern ourselves strictly with lone men soliciting unfortunates." He scanned the area. "The killer being a loner makes sense to me."

As they passed the Ten Bells with the Commercial Street Market just to their left, both constables recognized a familiar unfortunate nicknamed Poll on the right side of the street, under the lamppost, having a conversation with a single male not too much taller than she was.

They were enjoying each other's company.

Williams stopped, pulled out his night stick and pointed it, then quickly glanced at Scott. "Ralph, a lone male speaking with Poll."

Scott looked over to where Tom was pointing and nodded. "Certainly is."

The constables stood in the midst of the crowded street, watching the couple. Williams then spotted a man in the shadows near a poorly-lit alley no more than twenty feet away from Poll and her acquaintance.

Williams gently pushed Scott to the side in a darkened area and whispered, "Check out the man watching Poll and her companion. He's wearing a slouch hat. He's actually wearing an American slouch hat!"

"Is he interested in Poll or what!" Scott exclaimed. "He fits the description Inspector Chandler gave us all right."

The two constables stayed hidden and watched.

After a few minutes, Williams whispered, "I think he's waiting for Poll to take this punter to a more secluded location." He eyed Scott. "Suppose our killer is not a customer, but someone watching, like this guy." He stared at the lone male again. "Partner, this just might be him!"

"If that's the case," Scott reasoned, "then how about we wait here and follow the three once Poll and the punter finally decide to go off and finish their business. Maybe we'll catch this guy in the act."

Williams nodded to Scott. "Excellent idea, Ralph."

After five minutes, Poll and her customer still had not moved, and Williams noticed the man in the slouch hat acting agitated, pacing back and forth. In an instant, he glanced behind him and caught Williams' eye, and his attention was now entirely on the constables. Williams saw the man back slowly into the alley. "Damn! He spotted us, and he's making a run for it." Williams darted toward the man with Scott close on his heels. "We can't lose him!"

Scott blew on his police whistle, then separated from Williams to the right. "I'm going around back!"

Williams knew all too well that the darkness and the misty fog were going to be this man's allies, and the longer the chase went on the greater the chance they would lose him. Williams entered the alley and shined his light into the darkness. He spotted the man exiting the back of the alley into a small courtyard.

"He's running north!" Williams yelled, then blew his whistle again. He blasted out of the first alley in front of Scott and followed the man through a private courtyard.

"He went through the alley in front of you!" Scott yelled.

As Williams exited the courtyard into the small alley, the only light he could see was from his oil lamp, which forced him to slow down. He had temporarily lost the man, but he had a feeling the man backtracked to the congested main thoroughfare. "I think he's gone back on Commercial Street!"

"I'll meet you there!" Scott called back.

Both constables made it back onto Commercial Street from different alleys.

Williams had never regained sight of the man while in the alley.

As they edged toward each other, they scanned the crowd of pedestrians. The dull yellow light emanating from the streetlamps into the mist added little assistance. The two finally met up with each other.

"I lost sight of him in the alley," Williams admitted.

Scott looked around. "Let's go south." As they began, Scott pointed at what appeared to be the very same man standing just north of the Ten Bells Pub, near the entrance of another wider alley. "There he is!" Scott whispered excitedly.

Williams spotted him, and they rushed toward him.

The man immediately backed up and vanished into the alley.

Williams blew his whistle, and the constables ran after him. This time both Williams and Scott ran into the alley together.

Although still dark and hazy, ambient light from a nearby streetlamp assisted their search.

There were multiple obstructions and large trash piles strewn about.

"Keep your eye out on the trash piles," Williams ordered as he shined his lamp on a pile of wood. He separated from Scott to search other trash piles. The alley was relatively quiet, and he noticed a musty smell was in the air combined with the stink of trash.

Moments later, two other constables entered the alley from the other end with their lamps shining in front of them.

"Did you see anyone come out?" Williams asked.

"No!" one of them replied.

Williams saw a rather large debris pile twenty feet ahead of him, stopped, and focused his attention on it. "All right, reveal yourself!" He waited. "Let's make this easy. The harder it is for us, the harder it will be for you!"

The waving lamp lights from the other constables got closer. "We're in pursuit of a suspicious man wearing a slouch hat, and we think he's hiding in here somewhere!"

Williams approached the pile quickly, fully convinced that this was the man's hiding place.

At that moment, the man exploded from a different hiding place just to Williams' right and pushed him, nearly knocking the constable off his feet.

Williams managed to grab hold of the man, and they crashed to the ground.

Scott pounced on the man's back and wrapped him up in his arms.

Moments later, the other two constables joined in, breaking Williams free from the bottom of the pile.

Williams got up slowly, grimacing from the hard fall. He noticed the man's American slouch hat sitting on the ground next to his own custodian helmet, and he picked them up. "Watch out, gentlemen. He may have a knife hidden on his person."

* * *

Inspectors Andrews, Moore, and Abberline entered the Commercial Street Police Station. Andrews noticed Inspector Chandler and Constables Tom Williams and Ralph Scott standing over a tall, dark-haired man shackled to a chair.

The man had a large black mustache and appeared duly upset, his eyes darting back and forth. He quickly glanced up at the inspectors, then stared straight at the wall.

Chandler greeted them.

Andrews' eyes met Moore's, then he faced Abberline. "That's him," he whispered, ensuring the suspect could not hear him. "He's the herb doctor Inspector Moore and I spoke to last month about the elixir theory. Dr. Twomblety, I believe."

Moore stared at the suspect. "Certainly is Twomblety." He eyed Andrews. "I'm certain he's also the financier of the wax displays of the Ripper murders at the chamber of horrors. This can't be a coincidence."

Inspector Chandler shook his head and grinned. "I don't believe it's a coincidence." He walked up to the man. "Meet Mr. Francis Tumblety," Chandler said loudly. "Or at least that's who the letters in his coat pocket say he is."

"It's Doctor Francis Tumblety, if you don't mind!" Tumblety blurted out. "And I demand to be released from these shackles at once!"

Abberline grinned. "Feisty, aren't we, Doctor? We'll be keeping the restraints on for the time being, so make yourself comfortable."

Andrews approached Tumblety. "Why, we meet again Dr. Tumblety—or Twomblety."

Tumblety glanced up at Andrews with a confused expression.

"I visited your office last month and spoke to you, remember?"

Tumblety ignored him, then looked over at Chandler and Abberline. "Where are my diamonds?"

Chandler handed Abberline a large envelope. "This is what we found on him. He had two extremely large diamonds, a large amount of money, and a number of letters written by influential people. There's one from W. H. Eccleston of Finsbury Park. He claims to be a reputable American physician temporarily residing in the West End."

Abberline scanned the letters then called everyone into the adjoining room, leaving Tumblety alone.

"So, tell me what happened."

Both constables enlightened everyone to the full details of what transpired.

Abberline glanced at Williams. "Are you absolutely certain that the man you were first chasing is this man, even though you lost sight of him?"

Williams glanced over at Scott. "We're positive, Inspector. It was the same hat, the same overcoat, the same height, and he even ran from us the same way. There's no doubt about it."

Scott nodded. "When we spotted him in front of the Ten Bells, he was panting and sweating just like we were."

"And his attention was on ol' Poll?" Andrews asked.

"Completely," Williams answered. "It was like he had no other concern in the world but her." He eyed Scott. "Wouldn't you agree, Constable Scott?"

Scott faced Andrews. "Tom—er, Constable Williams is right, Inspector, and when he saw the two of us, he acted like he was guilty of something and ran as fast as he could."

"But you found no weapon on him. Is that right?" Andrews asked.

Williams nodded, then shook his head. "That's right, sir, and we did a quick search around the area but came up with nothing."

Chandler looked over at Abberline. "I've scheduled a party to search the entire area at daybreak, Inspector."

"Excellent," Abberline replied. "Did you interrogate this Tumblety, Twomblety, or Twombly, before we got here?"

Chandler nodded. "I asked him about his interest in the unfortunate, but he denies even watching her. He claims the first time he saw the constables was when they saw him in front of the Ten Bells just before they chased him down the alley and apprehended him."

Abberline glanced back at the man. "Well, let's ask the good doctor some questions. Shall we?"

The detectives returned to the man, then encircled him.

Abberline sat in front of Tumblety. "Good morning, Doctor. May I ask why you were out at such a late hour on Commercial Street?"

Tumblety turned away from Abberline, took a quick glance behind him, and regained his composure. "Slumming, of course. Don't tell me you haven't seen other well-bred gentlemen experiencing the queer sights and sounds of the area."

"How many times have you visited the streets of Whitechapel?" Abberline asked.

He glanced over at Andrews and Moore. "As you well know, I operate an herb store here, so ever since I opened it this summer."

"So, that means you've been slumming on the streets during each of the murders," Andrews reasoned.

The man's face went red as he tightened his lips. "I was merely minding my own business," he growled. "Then, while out in front of the Ten Bells Club, these constables attacked me!" He turned away. "A case of police abuse, I assure you!"

"It's awfully peculiar of you to run away from uniformed police constables," Abberline replied. "I can understand running away from detectives dressed in regular clothes, but officers in uniform?"

The man's scowl intensified, and he clenched his teeth. "You English detectives. Your heads are as thick as the London fogs! I can't believe you're wasting your time on respectable people. No wonder you haven't caught the killer." He sat up in the chair and closed his eyes. "I refuse to answer any more questions, and I demand to contact my solicitor at once! A lawsuit will certainly be in order."

"You will be seeing your counsel in due time," Abberline replied. "Constable Williams, would you please escort the fine doctor to his jail cell?" The suspect stood and curtly said as he walked away, "Good day, sir."

Once the man was out of the room, Abberline turned to Andrews. "Inspector Andrews, I need you and your team to handle this. This sounds promising, but I have three other suspects I must deal with this morning, followed by ten others."

Andrews glanced at Chandler. "Inspector, I need you to hold Tumblety until I can go to headquarters and find out what kind of record we have on him."

"Consider it done, but as you know, the clock is ticking, Inspector," Chandler replied. "I'll have to release him within twenty-four hours or send him up to the magistrate."

Andrews smiled. "No worries. I believe that's all the time we'll need."

chapter seventeen

**PRESENT DAY: Friday, October 6. Buffalo, New York—
Shea's Performing Arts Center: "The Tail."**

Celine began her Friday-night work just as she always had,
but tonight she knew full well that her tips would be big. This
was the opening of a famous and popular play, and Shea's was
sold out. She grinned, placed an unusually large tip jar on the
counter, and added a few dollar bills.

"Good luck, Celine!" her fellow concession worker yelled. "It
looks like a big night."

"You too, Donna," Celine replied.

As intermission began, the doors to the theater opened, and
the crowd filed out rather quickly. Celine's line formed fast.

As she was serving her first patron, Celine glanced up and
caught the eyes of the same tall, creepy man in the black suit.
Surprised, she spilled the glass of Coke she was holding in her
hand.

"Sorry, sir," Celine apologized. "I'll top it off again."

"No problem," the patron replied.

She quickly regained her composure and began working as
if she had no idea the creepy guy was staring at her.

Tip jar full and intermission at an end, Celine pulled out her
cell phone and texted her brother about the creepy guy.

A return text from Robbie came almost immediately, reading, "omg, we're on our way!"

She figured with the second half of the play running for another hour, Robbie and his amateur detective team had enough
time to get to the theater.

About an hour later, another text came in. "We're in position and we see a big black limo waiting outside."

Celine texted back, "That's his. I'll let you know when I see him. He'll be wearing a long black overcoat and using a cane."

A few minutes later, the play ended, and as the audience began to leave, she saw the creepy guy as he was donning his black overcoat.

He eyed her as he crossed the atrium.

Celine quickly texted Robbie, "Here he comes. He's all yours!"

In the car, Kyle hunkered down in the driver's seat. Robbie, in the passenger seat, ducked below the dashboard until only his eyes were visible. Ralph was alone in the back, bowed between the front seats.

"There he is!" Ralph whispered a little loudly.

The creepy guy crossed the sidewalk and got into the back seat of the limo.

As the limo departed, Kyle followed.

"Wow, if he doesn't look like a Jack the Ripper I don't know who does!" Ralph exclaimed. "He's turning right!"

"I see it, I see it," Kyle replied calmly. He allowed the car ahead of him to go and then turned right, following the limo.

"Not too close," Robbie ordered. "By the way, Ralph, the image of Jack the Ripper in a black overcoat and a top hat is a misconception. No one really knows what he looked like." He paused. "I bet this guy lives in an old scary mansion."

Ralph nodded. "I hope it's a playboy mansion with dozens of hot babes greeting his limo!" He paused. "Maybe he'll give me a job."

Kyle shook his head. "I can't believe it. Even in the middle of a real-life tail of a possible serial killer, you're thinking of chicks."

"Are you really surprised? Ralph has moments of brilliance, but only moments." To Ralph, Robbie said, "Get your head outta your ass."

"Don't be dissing me, gentlemen. I have gas, and I will use it," he joked.

"Besides," Robbie continued, "if this guy truly is the killer, he won't have any women around him. I bet he still lives with his fat old mother who bitches at him relentlessly, which causes him to kill any girl that reminds him of her."

"I think both of you are off your rocker," Kyle reasoned. "This guy looks like any other rich guy. I just can't see someone this rich spending the time getting his hands dirty—or bloody in this case. What a waste. He could buy anything." He shook his head. "Why ruin the life of plenty?"

"It's all about uncontrollable urges, Kyle," Robbie retorted.

"Well, that explains why Ralph believes you," Kyle joked. "Zero urge control when it comes to the ladies."

Ralph looked at Kyle. "And that's a bad thing?"

"I'm just sayin'," Kyle replied. "If you look at all of the known serial killers, I don't remember any rich ones."

"That's just because they're too rich to be caught," Robbie argued, then grinned as he stared one car up at the limo. "We'll be the first to catch one."

A streetlight between their car and the limo turned yellow. "Oh, shit!" Kyle yelled. "We're gonna get stuck at a red light!"

The light turned red.

"Run it," Ralph ordered.

"I can't, Ralph, there's a car in front of me," Kyle replied.

"Keep your eyes on the limo, and don't lose sight of it."

Robbie pointed. "It's turning right! We're going to lose it!"

The light turned green.

"Come on, come on! Get going!" Kyle yelled at the car in front of them.

They finally got to the next intersection and turned right.

"Does anyone see it?" Kyle asked.

"No, not yet," Robbie replied. "Just go straight." He glanced in the back street. "Ralph, you look down the side streets to the right and I'll look to the left. Maybe we'll see it."

They drove by two side streets, yet neither had seen the limo.

"This sucks . . . we lost him," Robbie proclaimed.

Kyle accelerated. "There it is! It's up ahead, parked on the side of the road."

"I see it," Robbie replied. "It's in front of the convenience store." He glanced to the right. "Park here."

Kyle parked the car a few hundred feet before the store.

"That was close," Ralph sighed. "Maybe we should tail them a little closer."

Kyle nodded. "I think you're right. It's so busy with traffic around here. They shouldn't realize we're following them."

"He's coming out!" Robbie yelled.

As the limo pulled back out into the street, they began to follow.

Robbie looked to the right. "We're getting close to the river."

A few minutes later, the limo pulled into the Erie Basin Marina on the Niagara River, drove through the gated entrance, and down to the end of the drive. The restaurant and bar at the entrance of the marina was very busy this evening.

"With all these cars and people around the bar," Kyle noted, "this guy'll never know we're tailing him."

The limo pulled next to a large yacht in a very secluded section of the marina.

"Wow! Check out the size of that yacht!" Ralph commented.

Robbie pointed forward. "Stop here so he doesn't see us."

Kyle parked the car and turned the lights off.

"The door's opening," Robbie said, and they watched the creepy guy get out of the limo and hurry onto the yacht as the limo left the marina.

"Come on. Let's go see it up close," Robbie suggested.

The three got out of the car and quickly headed onto the section of the dock where the huge yacht was moored. They could still hear music emanating from the restaurant bar in the distance.

"Wow! This thing must be sixty—eighty feet long," Ralph whispered. "He must be a billionaire."

"The windows on this thing are too high to peek in," Robbie noted and glanced at the adjoining yacht. "It looks like no one is on this other boat. Let's get on it and see if we can see in his windows."

The three climbed aboard the other boat.

"There he is," Robbie whispered. "What's he doing?"

"Nothing," Kyle added. "Just as I expected—he's watching TV."

"Quite a cheap-looking TV, though," Robbie noted. "Make that two TVs. They're only twelve-inch monitors." He paused. "What's that he's watching? Isn't that a door to a building?"

"It could be one of those security monitors," Kyle reasoned.

Ralph interrupted. "Check out the room he's in. It's all flowery and light purple. I'm gonna guess he's gay and won't be greeted by gorgeous women after all."

At that moment a brilliant light illuminated the three of them, and a man bellowed, "Hey, what're you three doing?"

* * *

One hour later, Celine got a phone call from Robbie.

"Hi, Robbie. So, what did you find out?"

"Well," Robbie began, "the guy lives on a huge, eighty-foot yacht in the downtown marina."

"What happened?"

Robbie paused. "As we were peeking in the guy's windows, or portholes, as we were told, we got caught by the marina security guard."

"Crap!" Celine exclaimed. "Did you get into trouble?"

"Well," Robbie continued, "he forced us down and frisked us, then had the creepy guy come out of his yacht and asked him if he wanted to press charges."

Celine shook her head. "Wow!"

"The guy laughed and told the security guard to let us go."

"That was a close call, Robbie."

"I don't think he's the guy, Celine," Robbie reasoned. "He actually seemed quite friendly and wasn't threatened at all by us peeking in his portholes. He even invited us on board to show us around."

"Did you go aboard?"

"Are you kidding!" Robbie yelled. "We were freaked out by almost going to jail, so we took off."

Celine shook her head slowly. "Hey, we had to try. Thanks for all your help, Robbie. I'm glad you didn't get into trouble."

"No problem, sis, but I think we'll stick to casing Halloween events for the killer—and maybe not for a few days."

chapter eighteen

1888: Wednesday, November 7. Late Morning. London, England—West End, Scotland Yard.

As Andrews and Moore entered Scotland Yard headquarters, Andrews noticed Chief Inspector Swanson in the main lobby, apparently waiting for them.

"Good morning, sir, did you receive Inspector Chandler's wire?" he asked.

"Indeed I did," Swanson replied. "And Assistant Commissioner Anderson would like us to report directly to his office once you arrive."

Moore stopped, visibly stunned, and eyed Swanson. "The assistant commissioner?" he asked nervously. "Did we do something wrong? Did we go too far?"

Swanson grinned. "Quite the contrary, Inspector. There's more than meets the eye with this suspect. Follow me."

"Certainly, sir," Andrews replied. "I've had my detective team contacted, so, if I could, I'd like to inform the front desk that once they show, send them up to the assistant commissioner's floor and wait in the hallway until our meeting is over."

Swanson nodded.

Andrews rushed over to the man stationed at the front desk, spoke with him, and then rejoined the group.

They arrived on Assistant Commissioner Anderson's floor, approached his door, then paused outside his office.

Swanson knocked, cracked open the door, and popped his head in. "Sir, they're here."

"Gentlemen, come in, come in," the assistant commissioner replied.

As they entered, Andrews glanced around the room. It was large and ostentatious, adorned with high-end décor. It gave him the impression that the occupant was a very important person—and he was. The assistant commissioner had once given Andrews some friendly advice: The atmosphere in an office can be used to one's advantage. "It allows one to subtly intimidate others and converse from a position of strength," he'd said.

The assistant commissioner sat behind his oversized desk, reading. He was a thin elderly man of medium height with white hair and a white beard.

Every time Andrews saw the assistant commissioner the man was in full dress uniform, and today was no different.

The assistant commissioner lifted his head up. "Please, take a seat, everyone."

They hurried into three of five relatively small, cushioned leather seats with wooden armrests arranged amphitheater-style in front of Anderson's desk. Although the chairs were expensive-looking, they were a bit tight and uncomfortable.

Knowing the assistant commissioner's strategic mind games, Andrews knew this was intentional.

"It's nice to see you again, Inspector," the assistant commissioner said.

Andrews nodded. "Thank you, sir."

The assistant commissioner stared back down at the document. "I've been rereading Inspector Chandler's cable and Chief Inspector Swanson's comments." He paused. "Francis Tumblety certainly seems to have been up to no good." He glanced at Moore. "And you believe this man is the same man funding that god-awful wax display of the victims?"

Moore nodded. "I do indeed, sir. He seems to be immortalizing these ghastly events. He probably visits the place, enjoying the crowds' reactions to his craft."

The assistant commissioner shook his head in disgust. "I asked you to come here for two reasons, actually. First, this man seems to be the best suspect we've come across for some time, and I wanted to inform you personally of my feelings." He sat back. "We do indeed have a dossier on Tumblety, and a large one at that. He's had run-ins with the law in England since the 1870s, and earlier than that across the Atlantic—or so says Bill

Pinkerton. His record shows he's had a bitter hatred of women for quite some time, and it may not be a coincidence that his file confirms the two constables' suspicions." He eyed Andrews. "Did Tumblety have a knife on him last night?"

"No, sir," Andrews replied. "We believe he discarded it while running from the constables. We're searching the area as we speak."

The assistant commissioner nodded then looked over at Swanson. "Because he was not seen attempting to kill a prostitute, we have no concrete evidence to charge him with the Whitechapel killings, is that correct?"

Chief Inspector Swanson sat up in his chair. "Correct, sir, and to compound the problem, we'll have to release him once he goes in front of the local magistrate at the committal hearing."

"Understood," the assistant commissioner replied. "So, are you in agreement that we should execute plan B immediately?"

Swanson nodded. "I am, sir."

Andrews glanced around, confused. "Plan B, sir?"

The assistant commissioner smiled. "The second reason I asked you here is, even though he has a large dossier, you would not have known it." He sat forward. "Because of Tumblety's Irish Nationalist connections, his record was on file with Special Branch."

Andrews and Moore glanced at each other.

"Both of you know Chief Inspector Littlechild," the assistant commissioner continued. "Head of Special Branch. He'll be here any moment now."

"Well, that explains why our records search proved fruitless," Moore interrupted.

"True," the assistant commissioner agreed.

There was a knock on the door.

A relatively tall man with curly dark hair and a bushy mustache stepped into the room, carrying a large folder.

"Good morning, Chief Inspector Littlechild," the assistant commissioner greeted.

Littlechild nodded. "Good morning, sir." He glanced at Swanson and the inspectors and nodded as he handed the folder to the assistant commissioner. "Good morning, gentlemen."

They returned the greeting.

"The chief inspector and I have been familiar with this Dr. Francis Tumblety for years," the assistant commissioner said as he opened the folder. "As you can see, we have a large dossier in Special Branch on this rich Irish-American doctor. Among other things, he's a wealthy Irish Party sympathizer. As you know, the extreme wing of the Irish Party has attempted to influence government policy through violent means." He pointed to the file. "On a number of occasions they approached Tumblety for financial assistance here and in New York. Ever since the early seventies, Tumblety's been coming to England, and we've been keeping our eye on him. Early on, we noticed he is a very singular character with a taste for young men."

Andrews' eyes widened. "Interesting."

"The first time Tumblety's name came up in connection with the Whitechapel murder case was during the military investigation of the Tabram murder in early August. Back then, we didn't know it would be a series of killings, and if you recall, there was a possibility a soldier might have killed her, so Field Marshal Napier asked his old friend and sitting member of Parliament, Colonel Hughes-Hallett, to do an official investigation. He quickly eliminated a military connection to the satisfaction of everyone, and in the process, he came up with the name of Dr. Francis Tumblety as a suspect."

Andrews frowned. "Sir, I'm aware of the colonel's investigation, but why did we not know that he actually suggested this Tumblety?"

"Because Tumblety is a person of interest for Special Branch," the assistant commissioner explained, then shrugged his shoulders. "Off limits to CID, really." He raised his finger. "We looked into it and nothing came of it, since it was merely hearsay and conjecture."

"What do you mean, sir?" Moore asked.

"The colonel heard it from one of his fellow West End club men during an evening of drink."

"How curious, this same man is now in police custody on suspicion," Swanson added.

The assistant commissioner grinned. "Precisely; much of the background information we have on Tumblety came from the Pinkerton Detective Agency. We knew the Pinkertons had investigated Tumblety on countless occasions in the United States and in Canada, even as early as the American Civil War, so we asked for their assistance. Bill Pinkerton himself brought their Tumblety file to me in early August just after the Tabram murder."

"What did you find, sir?" Andrews asked.

"Mr. Pinkerton painted a picture of an eccentric character with contrary sexual instincts for older boys and young men, and also having a bitter hatred of women. He's even been known to have an anatomical museum, with specimens from the female anatomy. It's all in the dossier. Both of you are welcome to read through it, but it must stay in Chief Inspector Littlechild's office."

"Certainly, sir," Andrews replied. "So, his hatred of women is a possible motive?"

"Yes," the assistant commissioner replied. He opened his mouth to continue, but a commotion from the hallway directly outside the door caught his attention.

Two male voices were in conversation.

A loud and deep guttural laugh occurred, which caused the assistant commissioner to stare at the door. He glanced toward Swanson, who was shaking his head in irritation, and noticed Andrews rolling his eyes. The assistant commissioner glanced at the folder and said, "We have dozens of accounts of excessive hatred of women."

From outside the room came another loud laugh.

The assistant commissioner eyed the door again.

Both Swanson and Andrews stared down and shook their heads.

"Friends of yours?"

Andrews raised his hand in embarrassment. "That would be my detective team, sir. Detective Sergeants Walter Dinnie and Frank Froest."

Moore snickered, evidently enjoying every minute of Andrews' embarrassment.

Another loud laugh floated through the door.

Andrews raised his eyebrows. "Froest is the loud one."

The assistant commissioner glanced up at the ceiling in thought. "Froest . . . Froest; that name sounds familiar."

"Yes, sir," Swanson replied. "He's assisted Special Branch on a number of occasions. He's an excellent detective, and great to have around if things get too dicey. But he sometimes forgets his boundaries."

Andrews smiled.

"He's exceptionally powerful and loud, and," Swanson paused, "he thinks everyone loves his jokes."

"Is he the detective everyone calls 'the man with the iron hands'?" the assistant commissioner asked.

"Yes, sir," Andrews replied. "Froest can tear a pack of cards in half, and even snap a sixpence like a biscuit."

"Sergeant Dinnie, sir," Swanson interrupted, "has a background in accounting and is brilliant at frauds and forgeries. He's also quite adept at controlling Froest."

"I asked both to wait outside until we were finished with our meeting," Andrews stated.

"They need to hear this, too," the assistant commissioner insisted. "Please send them in."

Andrews and Swanson glanced at each other with trepidation.

The assistant commissioner nodded reassuringly. "It's all right. Send them in."

Andrews got up and retrieved Dinnie and Froest. After a moment of scolding, the three headed into the office.

Sergeant Dinnie addressed the assistant commissioner. "How do you do, sir. Detective Sergeant Walter Dinnie at your service."

The assistant commissioner nodded. "Take your seat, Detective Dinnie."

"Detective Sergeant Frank Froest, sir," Froest said.

The assistant commissioner nodded.

Dinnie sat next to Moore, but Froest was so stocky that his seat was just too small. Still, he tried.

The assistant commissioner waited as Froest slowly attempted to position himself in the seat without success.

Froest glanced at the assistant commissioner, gave him a nervous grin, then tried again to force his body into the seat. He ended up with the wooden arm rests pressing on the sides of his hips. He glanced at everyone, grinning proudly.

The assistant commissioner nodded to him then opened his mouth to continue, but Froest's chair cracked.

Froest's eyes opened wide, and he froze. Once the cracking stopped, he gave an insecure grin.

"As I was saying," the assistant commissioner continued as he eyed Froest. "The man we now have in custody, Francis Tumblety, is on our short suspect list for a number of reasons.

First, he fits eyewitness descriptions, wearing his American slouch hat, and second, he was witnessed by the police as having an unusual interest in an unfortunate. Third, he has a history of extreme hatred of women; fourth, he possesses anatomical knowledge; and fifth, he has an anatomical collection of the parts stolen from the victims' abdomens." He shook his head. "This man needs to be investigated thoroughly."

"What alarms me most about Tumblety," Littlechild interrupted, "is Mr. Pinkerton's professional opinion of him. He knows Francis Tumblety better than anyone else, and he believes him to be insane—and a demonic woman-hater at that." He raised his hands. "*Psychopathia sexualis* subjects are clearly insane and have been known to be violent."

Froest leaned over to Dinnie and whispered but was heard by everyone: "Psycho what? What kind of sex subject did he say? Sounds like a French word."

"Quiet," Dinnie whispered firmly.

Littlechild glanced at Froest. "Psychopathia sexualis is Latin, and it means someone with contrary sexual feelings."

Froest nodded but still looked confused.

Littlechild took a deep breath. "Tumblety prefers male sex partners."

Froest frowned. "Oh great. So we have a dandelion, do we?"

"Worse, Detective," the assistant commissioner responded. "He preys upon teenage boys."

Andrews raised his hand. "We still have the issue of having no evidence to hold him, and the local magistrate will order us to release him tomorrow."

The assistant commissioner grinned and pointed to the folder. "We have clear evidence that Tumblety has engaged in gross indecency and indecent assault upon young men—offenses that hold a maximum sentence of two years for each incident."

Moore smiled. "I see."

"I suggest we build a case for this," the assistant commissioner continued. "Incarcerate him for at least a year, and in the meantime do a thorough background investigation on him with the assistance of the Pinkerton Detective Agency. Also, while this social disease of a man rots in prison, we just might be able to beat a confession out of him as well."

"And if the murders stop," Moore added, "then that's further evidence we got our man. Sir, is there enough evidence in

Tumblety's file to prosecute him for gross indecency and indecent assault?"

"Yes and no," the assistant commissioner replied. He glanced over at Chief Inspector Littlechild.

"Special Branch has followed Tumblety on multiple occasions to Hyde Park," Littlechild said. "It was clear to us his intentions were to attend the pro-Irish rallies. We discovered that, after the rallies, he would stay and solicit the young military men stationed at Hyde Park."

"And they didn't shoot the bastard?" Dinnie asked.

Littlechild shook his head. "Actually, we discovered that some of these young military men got involved with an extensive prostitution ring, and they would earn extra money by selling themselves to wealthy men. Here's where the case gets real sensitive." He leaned forward. "What you're about to hear is classified, therefore, it must never leave this room."

Everyone simultaneously turned and stared at Froest.

He opened his hands and said, "What? I can keep a secret."

"On the evening after Elizabeth Stride and Catherine Eddowes were murdered, we actually arrested Dr. Tumblety for suspicious behavior at the Albert Chambers boarding house across the Thames."

"Interesting," Andrews commented. "Special Branch is indeed involved with the Whitechapel murders."

Littlechild shook his head. "Only indirectly. What caught our attention was not necessarily his involvement in the murder case, but the correspondence in his pocket." He paused. "You see, important persons in government are carelessly involving themselves in male prostitution rings, and Dr. Tumblety had a private letter addressed from a young man connected to," he coughed, "others."

Andrews and Moore looked at each other.

"We tracked the prostitution ring to a number of places on the West End," Littlechild explained, "and this young rent boy named Albert Fisher works in many of these places."

The assistant commissioner pulled out a document and handed it to Andrews. "Here's a statement from young Albert Fisher admitting to having had sexual relations with Tumblety in July of this year. We wanted to get leverage on Tumblety just in case we needed it, and now it looks like we can use it." He sat back. "What this means is we have evidence against him, but

Tumblety can afford the best of solicitors for legal help, and jury members just might be convinced that the word of a young rent boy is not enough to convict. We need a stronger case in order to ensure a guilty verdict."

"Damn solicitors mess it up every time," Froest blurted out.

The assistant commissioner stared at Froest. "I am a member of the bar, and so was my father."

Froest sat up in his chair in embarrassment, causing Moore and Dinnie to snicker. His motion caused the cracked armrest to break completely off. Froest looked up at the assistant commissioner. "Sorry, sir."

The assistant commissioner's eyebrows rose as he watched Froest place the armrest on the ground next to him.

"Oh, I meant no disrespect, sir," Froest apologized. "I'm talking about solicitors for the defense." He swallowed. "And sorry about the armrest." He then stared straight at the wall and sat motionless.

Swanson glanced at Andrews and Moore and just shook his head.

"Well, that settles it, sir," Andrews replied. "My detective team will dig up more evidence and make a watertight case."

The assistant commissioner stood up, which prompted everyone else to do the same. "Excellent. Gentlemen, because Tumblety is implicated in an altogether different investigation in Special Branch, we need to keep a lid on this." He glanced at Froest. "And, Detective, don't worry about the chair. I'll have it repaired."

"Thank you, sir," Froest replied.

The assistant commissioner sat down and dismissed them, saying, "That is all."

chapter nineteen

PRESENT DAY: Thursday, October 12. Buffalo, New York—Buffalo Police Headquarters, Task Force Office: "Preparing the Snare."

Dunham's iPhone rang, waking him from sleep. He took a deep breath, rubbed his eyes, reached over, and answered it. "Good morning. Dr. Dunham."

"Dr. Dunham, this is Captain Johnson. I'm at the task force situation room. We've got something. Can you be ready in an hour?"

He glanced at the hotel clock, showing five a.m. "I'll be ready. Thanks, Captain." Dunham hung up and slowly got into the shower.

At exactly six a.m., Riggs pulled up in front of Dunham's hotel, and Dunham got into the car. Riggs handed him a coffee.

Dunham smiled. "Thank you. Good morning, Detective Riggs. Exactly six a.m., I see."

"What can I say? Good early morning, Dr. Dunham." He paused for a moment, grinning. "Is there something else you have to do today besides going to the office?"

Dunham thought for a second. "Oh yes, I have to pick up my clothes at the dry cleaners. How'd you know?"

Riggs handed Dunham his spiral notepad. "I found this on your desk, opened to the last page. It has 'cleaners' written on it, circled, and today's date."

Dunham grinned. "Thanks. That's very observant of you."

"No problem," Riggs replied. "We'll stop by the dry cleaners at lunch."

Ten minutes later, they entered the office to see Captain Johnson and a number of Buffalo police officers and task force members huddled around a table.

Johnson glanced up. "Dr. Dunham, we hit the jackpot! A woman on the donor list from the city of Buffalo has received a gift, along with a bouquet of flowers—violets even!"

"Excellent!" Riggs yelled.

"The break we were looking for," Dunham added. "What's the gift?"

Johnson read the paper. "Two free tickets for this Saturday's Arcade Nostalgic Murder Mystery Dinner Train Ride, plus a free limousine ride to and from the event. A $160 value." He looked up at Dunham. "It's a two-plus-hour train ride and dinner on a World War II-era train through the countryside south of Buffalo, where actors from the Springville Center for the Arts put on an interactive murder mystery between stops. The letter with the gift claims to be from members of local businesses in the community, giving thanks to their service as police officers."

"How appropriate for his next attempt," Dunham said.

Riggs frowned. "Police officers! Did you say police officers?"

Johnson nodded. "That's right. Luck is finally on our side. Not only is this woman a Buffalo police officer—she and her husband are on the task force!" Johnson waved two police officers over and they approached.

"Dr. Dunham, do you remember Officers Artie and Diane Barnett?" Johnson asked.

Dunham gave them a friendly nod and shook their hands. "I certainly do. This is excellent. Are you prepared to snare this guy?"

"Absolutely!" Diane said animatedly. "This guy needs to go."

"Now, his method of attack in each case begins with strangulation, so I would recommend you to get some sort of reinforced collar—impeding his ability to choke you." Dunham noticed Captain Johnson beaming elatedly. "What's up, Captain?"

"Diane here is a black belt in judo! She's an expert on chokes!"

Riggs chuckled. "Not only is she an expert, Dr. Dunham, she just received a gold medal at the AM-CAN judo tournament; one of the largest tournaments on the east coast."

Diane blushed. "My husband and I have been doing judo for fifteen years. Hopefully this has prepared me for this type of attack."

"Of course, we'll apprehend him before it comes to that, anyway," Riggs added. "You'll do great, Diane, especially with Artie and me there to back you up."

"We need to set this trap in such a way that he doesn't slip through our fingers," Dunham raised his hand, "and if he does, he doesn't realize we've figured out his method of victim selection."

"Agreed," Johnson added and scanned the group. "Ladies and gentlemen, we have work to do—and we only have two days to do it! Get moving."

The task force members began to leave.

"Let's go grab breakfast, Dr. Dunham," Riggs recommended.

"Great idea," Dunham replied as he watched the officers leave the room. "So, you know Diane and Artie?"

"Yes, we're close friends. I was in their wedding. I'm one of the aikido instructors at the same martial arts club they go to, Kin Tora Martial Arts Center. They teach me judo, and I teach them aikido." Riggs exhaled. "Diane's one tough lady." He pointed his finger and smiled. "Hey, I have an idea. We have our aikido and judo classes tonight. Would you like to come and watch, or even participate? We've had a large influx of new students ever since the homicides began, and you might like to see it."

Dunham nodded immediately. "Yes, I'd like that. I've been interested in aikido for years, but I've never taken the opportunity to join a class." He paused. "Tonight I'll just watch though."

"We'll grab a quick snack, and we'll go right after work," Riggs recommended. "Aikido starts at five thirty, and judo follows at seven fifteen. We'll grab a bite to eat afterward."

When they arrived at Kin Tora Martial Arts Club just prior to aikido class, Riggs introduced Dunham to his students. "As you can see by all the colors of the belts, Dr. Dunham, the students range from novice white belts to experienced black belts."

"I see."

Riggs glanced over at someone wearing a foot cast. "John!" he yelled, and the man named John approached them. "Dr. Dunham, this is John, one of my brown belts."

They shook hands.

"As you can see he can't participate today, so he's sitting on the sidelines." Riggs eyed John. "John, do you mind sitting with Dr. Dunham and explaining everything to him tonight while we have class?"

John gave Dunham an easy grin. "Sure."

"We have about twenty students tonight, so my instructors will be busy," Riggs explained. "It should be a good show." Riggs turned toward the locker room.

When Riggs came out, dressed in his aikido uniform, Dunham noticed he stayed at the edge of the mat, bowed, then positioned himself in front of a photograph of the founder of aikido and got into a Japanese-style sitting position facing the photo. The students fell into lines behind him. They bowed in respect and began stretching out.

"John, what's the name of the uniform they're wearing?" Dunham asked.

John nodded. "The white uniform is called a gi—and the type we use is thick, which is designed for judo. Judo is very rough-and-tumble, so they need a thick gi. Karate uses a thinner gi, since there's less grabbing and grappling."

"What's the black skirt the black belts are wearing?"

"The black skirt is Japanese formal wear, called a hakama. Many of the jiu-jitsus and Japanese sword arts also wear it."

After twenty minutes of stretches, exercises, and falling and rolling drills, Dunham watched Riggs demonstrate his first technique.

Riggs called up a senior student to attack him. The student got behind Riggs and grabbed his neck from behind forcefully, in a rear choke hold. Riggs pivoted on his right foot, inwardly positioning himself under the student's right arm and elbow. Riggs' left hand reached to his neck where the student's right hand gripped him. He grabbed the student's hand and secured a wrist lock.

John leaned over to Dunham. "That wrist lock is called a *sankyo.*"

Dunham nodded and noticed that the student was quickly immobilized and thrown to the ground and locked into place.

"Pinning him to the floor like that is called a submission technique," John explained.

A white belt raised her hand. "Shihan, I thought you said we were going to do techniques that'll help against the Niagara Falls Ripper. Doesn't he use a knife?"

Riggs nodded. "Yes he does, but that's not how he first attacks. In each case, he first chokes his victim until they're unconscious. Because of this, I wanted to start out by practicing a number of choking defenses." He glanced over at Dunham.

Dunham grinned and nodded.

Riggs clapped his hands, signaling to his students to select a partner and practice the technique. As the class continued, Riggs demonstrated four more choking defenses.

Soon, more people came into the club.

Dunham asked, "John, are these the judo students coming in for the next class?"

John glanced over at the people on the mats. "Yep, they start their class around seven fifteen."

A few minutes later, Dunham recognized a couple entering the dojo. He waved at Diane and Artie Barnett.

They waved back and joined him.

Diane touched Dunham's shoulder. "Hi, Dr. Dunham! It's great to see you here."

Dunham stood up. "You too. Riggs asked if I wanted to watch the aikido and judo classes, so here I am."

"Riggs is an awesome aikidoka," Artie commented. "He's not too bad at judo either. Are you going to come on the mats for judo or just watch?"

"Thanks, but I'll just watch," Dunham replied. "Riggs told me I'll enjoy watching the two of you."

"Diane's the tough one," Artie insisted. "The Ripper has no idea what's in store for him, but of course, I'll have his head before that happens."

Riggs finished his aikido class and joined Dunham and the Barnetts. "Hi, guys." He gave Diane a hug.

Artie grabbed Riggs' shoulder. "Hey, brother, are you jumping on the mats or hanging with Dr. Dunham?"

Riggs shook his head. "No, I plan on sitting with Dr. Dunham so I can explain what is going on."

The Barnetts left to dress, and ten minutes later the judo class began.

"Just as in the aikido class," Riggs explained, "the judo class begins by bowing in respect to their founder. They stretch and warm up too, but it's different."

After a few minutes the judo class began their rolls.

"Wow, I can't believe how well everyone rolls!" Dunham noted. "Even the white belts."

"Not only do you have to know how to throw, you have to know how to be thrown without getting hurt, and rolls help this out."

Everyone in class paired up and began throwing each other with a myriad of judo throws.

Riggs pointed to Artie. "Watch Artie. He's great at this."

Artie dropped underneath his partner, picked him up, and an instant later, the partner was on his back.

"That was great!" Dunham exclaimed.

"*Ne-waza!*" the head instructor called.

Riggs leaned toward Dunham. "This is where the students sit on the ground and go back-to-back with a partner. It's grappling practice—my favorite. It's kind of like wrestling."

The head instructor called "*Haji-me,*" and everyone began wrestling.

"Arm bars and chokes are allowed, too," Riggs added, then pointed to Diane. "Watch Diane. This is her specialty."

Dunham noticed that Diane was working with another female black belt. The other seemed to maul her from the top position, but Diane patiently went onto her back and gracefully applied an arm bar on her partner, causing the other woman to give up by tapping.

"Did you see that?" Riggs asked. "In only about three minutes of ne-waza, Diane applied two arm bars and two chokes." He grinned and shook his head. "She's awesome."

At nine p.m. the class ended.

Dunham and Riggs stood up.

"Thanks for inviting me, Riggs. I really enjoyed the classes."

"Maybe you can join us on the mats next time," Riggs offered.

"I think I will."

Riggs pointed toward the Barnetts. "Diane and Artie invited us to dinner tonight."

Dunham nodded and smiled. "Excellent. I'd actually like to talk with them about the snare, but I insist on paying the bill."

chapter twenty

Inspector Andrews never tired of experiencing the sights and sounds of Hyde Park on London's West End, especially near sunset. From the entrance, he watched crowds of people maneuvering their way around a multitude of carriages and horse-drawn omnibuses.

"Watch out, Inspector," the detective accompanying Andrews warned as an omnibus sped by.

"Is it always this busy at Hyde Park, Sergeant Elliott?"

Elliott nodded. "Eventful, isn't it, Inspector?"

Sergeant James Elliott was a detective locally assigned to Rochester Row Police Station, and since headquarters was just around the block, Andrews had built an excellent working relationship with him. He was tall and thin, had a full head of reddish-blond hair, and kept a well-groomed mustache, which grew into reddish sideburns.

Andrews closed his eyes and took a deep breath. "I've been spending so much time recently in the East End, I forgot about the fresh smells and the feeling of cleanliness here."

Elliott glanced around. "It doesn't help that the East End is downwind from the nasty London coal-burning factories' billowing smoke." He pointed west. "The West End here receives a constant supply of westerly country air."

Andrews nodded. "It's certainly no coincidence that the wealthy chose the west of London to live and play."

Another omnibus rushed by.

To Andrews' surprise the horse dropped a pile of dung almost on his feet. He shook his head. "So much for enjoying the pleasant smells."

Elliott snickered. "This in an equestrian playground, Inspector, droppings and all."

Andrews glanced around Hyde Park at the people strolling in and out of the high-end shops, cafés, and restaurants. "I can see why our more conservative colleagues claim the West End is no longer 'English,' with all this business catering to affluent foreign tourists. Why, in the last thirty minutes, I've heard dozens of foreign accents and languages."

Elliott shook his head. "The future is difficult for the status quo, Inspector." He peered up at a large building. "With these large hotels, the up-to-date transportation, theaters, and restaurants, it's tailor-made for the tourist industry."

Andrews smiled at Elliott. "Being a musician in your own right, Jim, the relaxed social attitudes, artistry, and free-thinking found in this district fit you perfectly."

Elliott grinned in the dusky evening. "I have to admit, Inspector, it's very appealing, but at night the unsavory side of the West End comes out, and I don't particularly enjoy this part."

"Well, that's why my detective team is in need of your services." Andrews scanned the street. "You know this area better than anyone."

Elliott nodded. "What a transformation the West End has; the pleasant and popular location of Hyde Park in the daytime changes into a location of illicit activities and prostitution at night." He shook his head and frowned. "Troublemakers everywhere, and I certainly do know them by name." He eyed Andrews. "So, did Chief Inspector Swanson wire you about the problems we've been having in this area lately, Inspector?"

"Yes, though he just said that it's a very sensitive issue."

Elliott nodded. "Well, a well-kept secret about London is the rampant man-on-man sexual subculture prevalent in this area. It has actually produced a thriving industry where wealthy men visit to pay for the attention of young males—those 'rent boys.'"

"Is it that bad?"

"You'd be surprised at who's involved," Elliott asserted. "Men of high social status participate in this subculture to such an extent that it's the practice of headquarters to take a—" he paused—"hands-off approach and conveniently ignore the problem. Soon it will come to a head." He glanced up at Andrews. "I'm actually surprised that the assistant commissioner has allowed you to pursue this assignment."

Andrews scanned the entrance of Hyde Park and grinned. "I believe the Whitechapel murders have just become an even bigger embarrassment than this." Andrews looked around. "Sergeant, where is this male prostitution practiced, besides the soldiers stationed at Hyde Park?"

Elliott's eyes opened wide. "Actually, quite a few places, Inspector. We've cataloged deviant male activity in the large hotels, theaters, restaurants, and those new public toilets in Soho, Piccadilly, Green Park, Covent Garden, the Strand, and even the Royal Exchange." He raised his hands in frustration. "It even occurs on the trains and in the train stations."

Andrews stared at Elliott and paused. "So what you're saying is finding young Albert Fisher and other rent boys who've been with Tumblety might take a little while, is that correct?"

Elliott grinned and shook his head. "Not necessarily, Inspector. I have a reluctant informant named James Burton—alias 'Uncle Burton'—who knows most of the more popular young rent boys in the West End, including Albert Fisher. I believe he'll be able to point us in the right direction."

Andrews grinned and gripped Elliott's shoulder. "This is exactly why I needed your help. Will Uncle Burton be difficult to find?"

Elliott pointed toward the entrance to Hyde Park near a crowded location where horse-drawn carriages picked up and dropped off customers paying for carriage rides through the park. They noticed a thin, wiry-looking man wearing a well-worn tweed jacket and a cockney hat, pacing back and forth near the public toilet. Elliot glanced back at Andrews. "That's him, and he's here every Saturday night beginning just at sunset."

Andrews stared at Burton. "What's he doing?"

"He, along with a partner rent boy, engages in a lucrative blackmailing business." Elliott paused. "These young rent boys are fully aware that their client gentlemen have much to lose if their private sexual escapades were made public, so they blackmail their clients. Without any other alternative, these gentlemen pay handsomely. James Burton teams up with a young rent boy in order to 'close the deal,' so to speak, and his favorite rent boy lately has been Fred Atkins, alias Denny, probably the best in the business."

Andrews nodded. "Interesting."

"Good-looking young Atkins solicits an eager gentleman, then takes him back to his lodgings. Once in bed, Burton will barge into the room, pretend to be outraged at the moral degradation of his young nephew, then threaten to contact the police. The gentlemen clients will pay handsomely just to get out of the situation."

"How do you know his methods so well?" Andrews asked.

"Well, the scam has been very successful, but one time it didn't go as planned. Atkins had picked up a gentleman from Birmingham, and he took him back to his lodgings. Uncle Burton barged into the room and began his usual rant. He took the gentleman's gold watch and necklace. Instead of the Birmingham gentleman being intimidated, he argued back, demanding his possessions be returned.

Andrews raised his eyebrows. "This sounds like Dr. Tumblety himself. His file is full of this kind of thing."

"Well," Elliott continued. "The landlady heard the commotion and entered the room to see a half-dressed young man with a middle-aged man, so she called for the police," he eyed Andrews, "which is where I came in. When I arrived, Burton and the Birmingham gentleman told me that 'It had all been a storm in a teacup, and the argument was over a game of cards.' They told me that the argument was resolved." He raised his hands. "Regardless, I marched the three to the station, where statements were taken. I gave Burton some leniency, and he's been helpful ever since."

"Did you get the name of the Birmingham man?" Andrews asked. "Maybe our Tumblety might even be in your records."

"Like I said, I gave Burton some leniency, so I might not have any, but I'll check." Elliott peeked around. "Isn't the rest of your team supposed to be here?"

Andrews nodded. "Yes. You know Sergeants Walter Dinnie and Frank Froest, don't you?

Elliott gave an animated grin. "I sure do. Life is never boring when Froest is around. I remember one time when four loafers made the mistake of attacking him. He knocked their heads together by twos, and when I got there, all I saw was a pile of four men lying at his feet while he was finishing his bitter." Elliott paused. "He would've made the rank of inspector by now, but his antics seem to get in the way."

Andrews grinned and nodded. "I recall bailing him out on a few occasions, but it was well worth it. Not only is he the toughest man I know, he's an impressive detective." Andrews chuckled. "It's great to have him around in a pinch." Andrews glanced across the street opposite the entrance to Hyde Park. "Here they come."

Froest and Dinnie headed toward them. Froest, clearly having noticed them, elbowed Dinnie and cheerfully bellowed something to his partner.

Even from a distance they saw Dinnie grimace in pain. He mumbled something back.

They both headed straight for Elliott.

Froest vigorously shook Elliott's hand with a powerful grip. "Sergeant Elliott, it's great to see you! No one told me you'd be here."

Dinnie just shook his head. "I tell him these things—he never listens."

Elliott genuflected in pain. "Great to see you, too, Frank," he groaned. "It looks like you still have a grip of steel!"

Froest let go, furrowed his brow apologetically, and pulled him up.

Dinnie shook his hand. "It's a pleasure to see you again, Jim."

"It's a pleasure as well, Walt."

Froest put his huge hand on Elliott's shoulder. "Jim, what's the difference between a tube and a foolish Dutchman?"

Elliott tightened his lips hiding a grin. "I haven't a clue, Frank."

"One is a hollow cylinder and the other is a silly Hollander." Froest immediately busted out in a powerful, guttural laugh and patted Elliott forcefully on the shoulder.

Andrews interrupted. "Frank is there a joke you don't know?"

Froest lost his grin. "French jokes, Inspector. Although, I don't think there are any."

Dinnie turned to Andrews. "Tumblety was released on bail by the magistrate at the remand hearing this morning, Inspector. He then quickly vanished into the streets."

Andrews nodded and looked down the street. "I figured. Maybe we'll see him tonight." He glanced back at Dinnie. "When's the committal hearing scheduled?"

"Next week, on the fourteenth, so hopefully we can strengthen our case." Dinnie looked around. "So what's the plan tonight, Inspector?"

Andrews pointed inside the entrance of Hyde Park. "See that man pacing back and forth? He most likely knows the whereabouts of young Albert Fisher, Tumblety's old rent boy. He may also know of other rent boys Tumblety's been with."

"He's been pacing in the same spot now for the last twenty minutes," Elliot added, then stared at Andrews with a curious look. "So, let me get this straight, Inspector. We have this Francis Tumblety, who engages in vile activities with rent boys on the West End. He is now one of the prime suspects in the Whitechapel murder case, but since we don't have enough evidence to convict, we're building a case against him for gross indecency. In doing so, we can at least put him in prison for a few years so that Assistant Commissioner Anderson's prison contacts can influence him into giving a confession. Is that correct?"

Andrews nodded. "Correct."

"Well, if the murders continue while he's in prison, then we'll know he's not the killer," Elliott reasoned.

"That's exactly what Chief Inspector Swanson thought," Dinnie replied.

"And we get to put behind bars a disgusting sexual deviant, just where he should be," Froest interrupted.

"Well spoken, partner," Dinnie replied. He glanced at Elliott. "Frank loathes rich, dirty old cocks having their way with our youth."

"There's nothing lower on earth," Froest replied, then he grinned. "Except maybe rats and solicitors, and rats at least have a few redeeming qualities."

Dinnie peeked a glance at Burton. "Sergeant Elliott, how do you know this guy can help?"

"Burton's a salty ol' master craftsman at this illegal business, and he knows everyone. He also has a healthy fear of prison time, and lately he's become an excellent, albeit reluctant, informant."

Inspector Andrews eyed the man. "Well, it's time we have a conversation with Uncle Burton." He pointed to the right. "Detective Froest, ease off to the right of Burton without being seen, and since he knows Sergeant Elliott, we'll approach him from the left. If he runs, he should fall right into your viselike grip. Dinnie, hang back in case something goes awry."

Froest grinned with a slightly evil expression, then nonchalantly strolled toward the right side of Burton. Once in position, he waved to the detectives.

Andrews and Elliott circled around to the left of Burton, purposely gaining his attention. Just as expected, Burton began moving away from Elliott at a significant rate of speed.

Twenty feet later, Andrews saw that Burton was in the hands of Froest, who quickly and forcefully dragged him into the tree line.

"Hey, what is the meaning of this?" Burton yelled.

"Hello, Uncle Burton." Froest grinned. "My name is Detective Sergeant Froest," Andrews could hear Froest say as he and Elliott came onto the scene.

"Hello, Mr. Burton," Elliott greeted. "Are you having a fine evening?"

Burton, acting anxious and fidgety, muttered, "Oh, hello, Detective. Did—did I do something wrong?"

"I'm sure I could think of something, Mr. Burton," Elliott replied. "This gentleman with me is Inspector Andrews, and I would consider it a favor if you give the courtesy of answering his questions."

Burton nodded quickly. "Uh, OK, Inspector. How can I help?"

"Hello, Mr. Burton," Andrews began. "Are you familiar with a tall, eccentric American customer with a very large waxed black mustache? He usually dons an American slouch hat and goes by the name of Francis Twomblety, Twombey, or Tumblety."

Burton glanced at Sergeant Elliott. "Yeah, I know the bastard. He sometimes he calls himself Smith."

"Why do you say he's a bastard?" Andrews asked.

Froest let go of Burton.

Burton straightened himself up and scowled at Froest. "He hurts my friends, and if he ends up in the gallows, I wouldn't lose any sleep about it."

Andrews eyed him intensely. "Would Albert Fisher be one of your young friends he's hurt?"

Burton nodded and glanced over at Elliott. "Indeed he would, but he's not the only one. I know a half dozen other young men who've experienced his rough treatment."

"Well, Mr. Burton, I can help take this American off the streets for you and stop him from hurting your young friends. Would you like that?" Andrews offered.

Burton thought for a moment. "Would it get these constables off my back?"

"Oh, it certainly would help, Mr. Burton," Elliott replied. "If you take care of the inspector's needs, I can certainly have a talk with my constables."

"Albert and his friends would love to help," Burton replied.

"If you don't mind," Andrews asked, "could you arrange a meeting for me with each and every rent boy you know who's had an experience with Tumblety?"

Burton nodded. "Consider it done, Inspector."

chapter twenty-one

PRESENT DAY: Saturday, October 14. 7:00 a.m.
Buffalo, New York—the Barnett Home: "The Snare."

Artie Barnett drank his last shot of coffee while in the kitchen waiting for Diane to finish dressing. He turned toward the bedroom. "The limo will be here soon, hon!"

"I know, I know," Diane yelled. "You're always rushing me. I do have to put on the extra protective gear, you know."

Artie's cell phone rang, and he answered it. "Officer Barnett."

"Hi, Artie, it's Riggs. Is everything a go?"

"Oh yeah, it's go-time all right!" Artie replied enthusiastically. "Diane's a little stressed, but I'll have a good talk with her before the limo comes."

"We don't know if this quack has bugged the limo," Riggs said. "So remember: Be careful what you talk about during your ride."

Artie nodded. "No worries, mate. See you soon."

Back in the bedroom, Diane's cell phone rang, and she answered it. "Officer Barnett."

"Hi, Diane, it's Dr. Dunham. How are you feeling? Are you still up to this?"

"No sweat, Dr. Dunham," Diane replied excitedly. "Artie's nervous as ever though, but I'll calm him down before we get in the limo."

"You've got your protective gear on, right?" Dunham asked.

Diane nodded. "I just put it on."

"Great, we'll be watching you every step of the way," Dunham added reassuringly. "We have task force personnel set up all along the drive to Arcade. We also have a state police helicopter following you from a distance."

Diane smiled. "You've gone all out."

"That's right," Dunham replied. "We're gonna get this guy. Captain Johnson's already at the Attica Railroad Station inside the ticket office and administration building."

"Thanks, Dr. Dunham. We'll see you soon." She hung up then walked into the kitchen.

Artie eyed Diane. "Who was that?"

"Dr. Dunham just checking on us."

Artie nodded. "Riggs called, too." He approached her and took her in his arms then smiled. "Ready to catch the Niagara Falls Serial Killer?"

She nodded and gave a devilish grin. "He won't know what hit him."

Artie's cell phone rang again, and he answered, "Officer Barnett." He paused. "Sounds great." He hung up and looked at Diane. "The limo's out front. Let's go catch a bad guy."

Diane nodded as they headed toward the limo. "As bad as they get."

A radio call came into Captain Johnson's makeshift headquarters: "Sir, our couple has just been picked up."

"Copy that," Johnson replied and popped his head up facing a crowd of officers. "Here we go, folks! Everyone be on their toes throughout the entire operation. We may not get a second chance." He glanced at a group of plainclothes officers. "All right, all of you who're riding the train, I'd like a quick meeting."

"Be right there, Captain!" one of the undercover task force members yelled.

Johnson waited until everyone had circled around him. "Everyone keep ever-vigilant since the attack could happen at any time. Our guess is the killer will attack Diane at a time when she is alone, most likely when she gets up to use the lav, so ensure that you're positioned for immediate response. His MO is to strangle first, so we should have a few seconds to apprehend him. Not only does Diane have a bullet-proof vest on in order to protect her abdominal area, she's wearing a reinforced collar for protection against the strangle."

"What about these actors?" another task force member asked.

Johnson nodded. "They shouldn't be in the way. Diane won't go to the lav until after the mystery show. That way the actors can leave the area and get out of harm's way." He paused. "Good luck, everyone." Johnson quickly raised his finger. "Oh," he yelled, then lowered his voice. "Try not to look like cops. Just smile and act like you're having fun!"

The drive to Arcade and Attica Railroad was without incident. The limo pulled into the railroad station and dropped Diane and Artie off.

As they moved toward the ticket office, Artie scanned the area then whispered to Diane, "Hey, this is kind of fun. Check out everyone looking at us. They think we're important."

Diane stared, expressionless. "I guess not too many people come in a limo." She stopped for a moment and faced Artie. "My hands are sweating."

Artie glanced at her and whispered, "Smile, Diane. We're supposed to be really happy about this." He looked forward. "I'm right next to you."

"I'm trying," she replied. "But it's an eerie feeling knowing that the Niagara Falls Ripper is probably watching us right now."

"Remember why we're here, hon—to catch this loser." Artie grinned. "That puts a smile on my face. Remember, there are a couple dozen cops surrounding us as we speak, and Riggs will be on the train too."

Diane popped her shoulders back and straightened her frame. "Let's do it, babe." She paused. "Maybe I should use the lav first."

Artie tilted his head toward Diane as they approached the ticket office. "The captain figured you'd need to," he whispered. "Especially since he and Dunham don't want you to use the train's lav until after dinner." He nodded toward the lav. "Notice the two ladies next to the lav? They're task force members, and they plan on entering the lav with you. Strike up a conversation with them as you walk in. I'll register us."

Diane stopped and faced Artie. She smiled. "I recognize them from the meetings."

They kissed each other and separated.

* * *

At two o'clock p.m., everyone boarded the train.

Johnson stared at the video surveillance camera monitors. "Just great," he said facetiously. "I count two dozen-plus male customers who might be the killer. It could be any of them."

Dunham shrugged his shoulders. "And he might not even be one of them," he said as the train began its three-hour ride.

Riggs sat with an undercover female Buffalo police officer. They positioned themselves close to the women's lavatory.

"Are you ready, Bets?" Riggs asked.

Bets grinned confidently. "Ready to shove my Glock up his ass?"

Riggs chuckled. "Oh, I like that." He peeked over at an undercover officer situated on the other end of the dining area train, farthest from the lavatory. "If the attack isn't what we think, at least we're prepared at both ends."

The train's whistle blew a number of times, and everyone jerked slightly back as it started to move on the tracks.

Riggs scanned the area. "Here we go."

The conductor gave a welcoming speech, spoke a little about the history of the World War II-era train, and invited everyone to enjoy the scenery outside. He announced that dinner would be served in a half an hour.

"Since half the people are up, I'm gonna take a quick look around," Riggs said as he stood up. "I'll be right back."

The salad was served, followed by the main course, and finally dessert. Since everyone was seated, the only motion was the train riding on the tracks.

Bang!

Riggs' head shot straight up, and he eyed the kitchen entrance. His drink rolled across the table. A man dressed in Victorian period clothing broke through the door, holding his hands over his chest; he fell onto the floor. As his hands dropped, red stains were exposed on his chest.

Bets laughed. "Riggs, it's a murder mystery train ride, remember?" She pointed at the man. "That's an actor."

Riggs took a deep breath, grinned, and shook his head. "My heart's beating like crazy." He glanced at Artie and Diane and noticed they were laughing at him. He covertly flashed his middle finger at Artie.

The mystery murder was a reenactment of a Sherlock Holmes mystery, which lasted approximately thirty minutes. Upon completion of the show, the actors departed past the lavatory and into the next rail car.

Diane squared her shoulders as Artie checked his watch. "Well, we're about thirty minutes from the station. It's time to go into action, hon." He paused. "Are you ready to catch this guy?"

"As ready as I'll ever be," Diane replied with surprising confidence.

Diane made quick eye contact with Riggs then got up and began making her way to the lavatory. It was evident to her that everyone on the task force was ready to respond.

The lavatory was located in a small hallway perpendicular to the main hallway.

As she got near the lavatory door, a lady exited.

"Excuse me," she said to Diane, smiled, and walked back to her seat.

Diane glanced around and saw no sign of anyone in a position to attack her. She opened the door to the lavatory and noticed that it was very small with no connecting closets or rooms. She took one quick peek behind her and entered the lav, purposely leaving the door unlocked.

After waiting for a few minutes, Diane shook her head thinking nothing was going to happen. Perhaps if there was an attack, maybe it would be after the train ride, she thought. She quickly washed her hands, but as she was rinsing, she heard a loud explosion in the distance—in the direction of the dining area where Artie was sitting.

When she opened the lav door, she saw people running past her away from the source of the explosion. As she rushed out of the lav with a single-minded focus on Artie's well-being, she was grabbed from behind by the neck with such force that her feet came off the ground and she landed on her back.

The attacker was so powerful he shifted her fall so that she landed inside a small closet directly opposite the lav door. He quickly closed the door and immediately wrapped his hands around her neck.

Diane's head had hit the frame of the doorway as she went down, which dazed her momentarily. When she fully returned to her senses, the attacker was attempting to crush her throat, but the reinforced collar was working. She went into action.

Feeling an opportunity, she gripped both of his wrists, shifted her butt to the side, and brought her knees to her chest. This gave her enough room to kick one of his knees out from under him with her bottom foot.

The man's body stretched back and he fell onto his stomach, but he held his choke hold.

She slipped her top leg around the man's arm and placed her foot underneath his chin, which created a *juji gatame* arm lock. As she added pressure against his elbow in an attempt to break his arm, she began to scream for help. She knew a normal man's elbow would have broken by now, but this attacker held on with unbelievable strength.

She could hear hurried footsteps nearing the closet in response to her scream. An undercover police officer jerked open the closet door, shouted, "Oh crap!" and then pounced on the man.

With amazing agility, the man tore himself away from Diane's arm lock, got to his knees, and threw the police officer off his back and into the lav door. The attacker sprang to his feet, snatched up a black cane that was lying on the floor, and ran down the aisle.

Riggs and another officer spotted a large, athletic man dressed in a long black jacket rapidly approaching through the aftermath of the explosion.

The man clubbed the first undercover officer with his cane, knocking him away.

Riggs met the man head-on.

The man swung his cane again, this time in Riggs' direction.

As it made contact, Riggs pivoted on his right foot and shifted his body like a matador evading a charging bull. He gripped the man's elbows in a classic aikido *kokyu-nage* throw, causing the man's momentum to twist him in the air and land on his back.

His cane flew a few feet away. Before Riggs could pull out his sidearm, the man leaped to his feet with amazing agility and threw Riggs down the aisle about ten feet.

Artie and another officer appeared and rushed the man, who picked up his cane and knocked the first police officer out of the way.

Artie buried his shoulder into the man's lower stomach, lifted him, and threw him behind himself in a judo *ura-nage* technique.

Out of nowhere the man took out a knife and stabbed Artie in his thigh, causing him to scream and immediately release the assailant. While Artie grimaced in pain, the man bounded to his feet, used a chair to break a window, then leapt from the moving train.

As police officers came to Artie's assistance, realization set in that their snare had failed.

Riggs crossed to the broken window and stared out at a forest of trees passing by. He quickly turned to another police officer. "Contact the state police helicopter and let them know where this guy jumped off the train." He stared back out the window. "I hope he jumped straight into a tree, the bastard." He turned to Artie and asked an officer attending to his colleague's wound, "How is he?"

"He needs medical attention," the officer said. "I've contacted the train station, and they're calling some ambulances to meet us there once the train pulls in. Luckily, the stab wound is in his thigh and doesn't seem to have hit anything dangerous."

Diane rushed to her husband, visibly shaken. "Are you OK, babe?"

"I'm OK, hon," he replied and touched her face. "How're you?"

She nodded and grabbed her collar. "Fine, Artie, the collar worked. I had an arm bar on him, and he ripped out of it like nothing."

"It was like the guy had superhuman strength and speed," Riggs added. "No one even had a chance to pull out their sidearm."

"When I heard the explosion, I feared the worst," Diane said and glanced at Riggs, then back to Artie. "Are you guys OK?"

"The explosion was in the kitchen," Riggs answered. "There's about six who need medical attention, but no one's seriously hurt. It was clearly a diversion in order to give him time to attack you."

"Riggs knew right off the bat that it was a diversion," Artie interrupted, "so he sent people to check on you immediately." He pointed toward Riggs. "The beer's on me, pal."

Riggs stared out the broken window again. "At least now we know what he looks like."

Diane nodded. "And that Dr. Dunham was spot on about this guy. It's too bad he had a disguise on."

Artie nodded. "That mustache was bumped around in his scuffle with you. It was between his teeth by the time he made it out here."

"All right, everyone!" Riggs directed. "This guy may have left some sweat somewhere, which could give us a DNA sample. Whoever was in contact with the perpetrator, you'll have to surrender your clothes." He glanced at Artie. "He was wearing gloves, wasn't he?"

Artie nodded.

* * *

An hour later, at the train station, Dunham, Johnson, and Riggs watched as Artie was being placed into the ambulance on a stretcher, Diane by his side. Dunham turned to see that the kitchen employees were also being cared for.

"Hopefully they can pick up his trail out there, but this guy's amazingly elusive," Dunham said.

"It was like he planned his escape in such a way that it would be difficult to follow him," Riggs commented.

"My guess is he had it planned to jump from the train once he killed his victim," Johnson added, "so it won't surprise me if we come up empty-handed."

Dunham nodded in agreement. "This guy caught us by surprise by creating the diversion. If it wasn't an all-out trap, he would've easily gotten away with it."

Johnson shook his head. "There was no reason for us to suspect he was going to set off an exploding diversion since he'd never done that before. I wonder why he did it."

"I think I know why," Artie answered from the back of the ambulance. "If you think about it, there was really no time Diane would be completely alone. She was with me all the time, with the exception of going to the bathroom."

Dunham nodded. "Since Diane was in the lav when the explosion occurred, he ensured that she would be the last one to leave the area where he was hiding." He shrugged. "This man thought of everything."

Riggs grinned as the Barnetts' ambulance drove off. "He certainly didn't expect to attack a judo expert. I'm just surprised that the attacker could get out of her arm bar."

Johnson nodded slowly, staring at the ambulance. "Oh, I bet he knew. Once he selects his victims, I'm sure he digs deeper into their lives." He shook his head. "The cocky bastard. Bit off more than he could chew."

Riggs nodded and snickered.

"It's too bad she couldn't get to her sidearm," Johnson added.

Riggs glanced at Johnson. "None of us could. The man was amazingly agile. My guess is he's young. Between twenty-five and thirty-five."

A sheriff's car pulled into the parking lot and stopped in front of Riggs, Johnson, and Dunham. A deputy sheriff got out of the driver's seat, then opened the back door to let a middle-aged man and a young man out. He told the two males to stay next to the car and approached Captain Johnson.

"Captain."

"What's up, Deputy?"

The deputy turned and pointed south. "After getting the call that the perpetrator jumped the train, I began searching east on Carpenter Road about a mile south of here, and when I drove by this farmhouse," he pointed to the older man, "Mr. Gates, here, waved me down." He looked at Johnson. "I believe his son was witness to our attacker coming out of the woods."

"Excellent. Great job, Deputy," Johnson replied, approaching the witness.

Johnson extended his hand. "Hello, Mr. Gates, my name is Captain Johnson. I hear your son may have seen someone coming out of the woods?"

Gates nodded. "Andrew Gates, sir." He faced the young man. "This is my son, Bobby."

Johnson turned his attention toward the son. "Hi, Bobby. What did you see?"

Bobby's head was down, and he was silent.

"Go ahead, Bobby," his father said. "Tell the captain everything."

"Well, sir," Bobby began, slowly. "Me and my girlfriend were hanging out in my car at the parking area just down the road from the farm."

The deputy sheriff interrupted, "That would be west of the farm on Carpenter Road, which is only about a quarter of a mile from the train tracks."

Bobby nodded and continued. "We were looking at last year's school yearbook when I heard a noise in the woods."

"Were your windows down?" Johnson asked, considering the unusually warm fall day.

"Yes, sir. I thought it might be a bear or something, so I was about to start the car, but my keys fell out of the ignition. As I was fumbling around the seat, I noticed a tall man in a dark, long coat come out of the woods with a black cane in his hand. It had a large clear crystal on the end."

Riggs glanced at Dunham. "I saw him with the same cane," he whispered, then glanced back at the boy. "Bobby, did he have a black mustache and goatee?"

"Yes, sir, and he seemed really mad." Bobby paused. "He came straight up to our car next to the driver's door. My girl-friend freaked out and grabbed onto my arm. He stopped for a second, then continued past my car and walked down the road about a hundred yards to this blue car. He got in and drove away." He looked over at his father. "That was the freaki-est thing I've ever seen."

"Do you know what make the car was?" Johnson asked.

Bobby shook his head. "No . . . I'm not too good with cars."

"Thank you, son," Johnson said reassuringly. "Do you mind if the deputy sheriff gets a statement from you before you leave?" Johnson glanced at the deputy sheriff.

The boy turned toward his father, who nodded to him. "OK."

The deputy sheriff took the father and son into the building.

"We should have the boy and girl work with a sketch artist as soon as possible," Dunham suggested, then he paused mo-mentarily. "My bet is he's on his way back to the Buffalo area. Let's call it in. Maybe we'll get lucky."

"We can only hope," Johnson added.

"The good news about no one being able to take out their firearms on the train is that he may not have known it was a trap," Riggs reasoned.

"True," Dunham added. "Hopefully, if one of the women on the list receives a gift, they'll contact us. The only concern I have is that the original Ripper stopped after about six homicides. If he follows this pattern, we might not get another chance."

"This guy seemed to be on a mission, but he didn't get what he wanted," Riggs said. "He'll be looking for another opportu-nity, and the next time we'll get him."

Johnson patted Dunham's shoulder. "Thanks to Dr. Dun-ham for figuring this guy out, Diane wasn't the next victim."

chapter twenty-two

The owner of the Queen's Head Pub, an elderly gentleman called Mr. Dipple, sat at a table butted to the wall under a window, accompanied by another old man. He noticed three prostitutes surrounding a table of drunken male customers. Dipple waved at a large man standing next to the door, who was caught up in a conversation with a patron. "Bart! Kick those three out! No unfortunates are going to ply their trade in my tavern!"

Bart hurriedly broke off the conversation and glanced around the room. "Yes sir, Mr. Dipple." He crossed the crowded tavern, hurried the women out of their seats, and pushed them out onto Commercial Street. He then stood, barring the door with a wide grin on his face.

One woman turned, spotted him in the window, and cursed at him.

Dipple glanced back at his drinking companion. "If the police knew I was lettin' unfortunates work here, they'd close me up for good. So what if it's rainin' a bit. There's a reason they're called street walkers."

The other man stared at Bart. "Why's Bart's arm all wrapped up?"

Dipple shook his head. "Awe, he and Jimmy kicked a couple a drunks out last night, and one of 'em pulled a knife on him. Bart fixed him right good but was cut durin' the ruckus. He likes the action though. Every scar or bruise he gits, I pay him double."

The man nodded. "Brilliant. Lucky Bart and Jimmy 'ers big as horses." The man thought for a moment. "A knife, you say. Maybe Bart just gave Jack the Ripper a tannin'."

Dipple grinned. "I'd triple his pay if that were the case." Dipple shook his head. "Nah, it's been over f'r a month since the last killin'. The Ripper's done, at least f'r this season." He peered out the window and pointed. "Take, f'r example, that man across the street leanin' on the wall at the storefront, just loiterin' in the rain."

His drinking partner glanced out the window and nodded.

"If it were last month, and if he'd a b'n the killer, wearin' a dark cape and a large hat coverin' his face so suspicious like he's doin', I'd have Jimmy and Bart drag him kickin' and screamin' to the nearest police station."

His drinking partner nodded and drank from his stein. "Y'got that right."

Outside, the same caped figure noticed two old men in Queen's Head Pub staring at him, so he decided to move to a new, more private location. It was a cool and rainy evening in Whitechapel, which put Commercial Street under a thin mist. The man thought to himself: *Ah, the thick October fog is no more; just the usual fall mist. Even with the entire world's attention on Whitechapel, the detectives are clueless.*

A couple walked by him but did not acknowledge him.

"I am completely invisible to them," he mumbled under his breath. "What better proof of my divinity? I wait in the shadows for an unfortunate in the company of her male escort, then I follow them as she finds a private spot for their disgusting business. Everyone believes I am the escort, but why would I want to be the last one seen with her? Why would I want to be caught in a trap set up to spring on me? Why would I want to even associate with the disgusting lesser sex? Fools."

He moved in the shadows to another location as a crowd of people ambled by, and he blended in with them.

Even in the cold rain, the main thoroughfare near Dorset Street was quite busy.

"I have looked these detectives directly in the eye, yet they are powerless to stop me. Soon, I will be finished with my harvest and achieve true divinity. Even though circumstances have forced a delay, the gates of Hell are still open."

At that moment, the dark figure saw a man in a long dark coat and a soft felt hat approach an unfortunate and whisper something to her.

They laughed, and she said, "All right." They talked a little more, then walked across Commercial Street and headed down Dorset Street. Pedestrian traffic was high on Dorset Street, and as usual, the dark figure merely disappeared in the crowd as he followed the couple.

When they came to McCarthy's Rents, he saw the couple approach an apartment. The unfortunate reached her hand into the broken section of a window next to the door and unlocked it from the inside, then led the way.

"Excellent!" he whispered to himself excitedly. "Instead of a quick outdoor sacrifice in the cold rain, I will wait until the punter leaves, unlock the door as she did, and enjoy a long and private ceremony."

About an hour later, the punter left.

The dark figure followed his plan and opened her locked door. As he did, the unfortunate was sitting at the side of her bed.

She glanced up and saw the man holding a knife and screamed, "Oh, murder!"

The dark figure grabbed her by the throat and choked her unconscious within seconds. He closed the door, positioned himself behind her, then began the demonic ritual. Once he had given her body and blood to his divine master, he dragged her up onto the bed. He saw the smoldering fire in the hearth.

"If this is Hell on earth, then let's make a fire worthy of his presence!"

A dog barked outside in the distance.

He took off his hat, added more wood to the fire, then stoked it until the fire began to blaze. He approached his sacrifice and continued the ritual. "*Fructus arbor vitae sumo*—I take the fruit of the Tree of Life." He removed her heart and placed it into his bag. The dark figure was so engrossed in his sacrifice that his hat burning next to the fire barely registered in his consciousness.

"Yes, now that my offering and harvest is complete, it is time to immortalize this hallowed ground. Every museum around the world will demand a wax recreation of it, and it will be the centerpiece attraction. A real-life Anatomical Venus overshadowing all other Venus displays."

With methodical precision, the man repositioned the woman in the bed to his satisfaction and purposely placed each organ that he'd removed in a certain location around her body. He grabbed his knife and further mutilated the body. He picked up his bag and stood back near the hot fire, staring at the woman.

"It is perfect," he said, satisfied.

The man then took off his bloody shirt and threw it into the fire; he took out another shirt from his bag and put it on. He glanced out the window and noticed it was near sunrise. He collected his things and left the room just as quietly as he'd entered.

Friday, November 9. 10:50 a.m. London, England—East End, Commercial Street Police Station.

Inspector Beck was on duty at the Commercial Street substation, having taken Inspector Chandler's watch. He glanced at the constable sitting at the duty desk, scowling. "Chandler owes me one, he does," Beck grumbled.

The constable snickered, glanced at the other police officers in the room, but said nothing.

Beck's thin frame, short blond hair, well-groomed mustache and sideburns, and glasses gave him a very academic look, especially when he was at his desk, where he was now working on his daily paperwork.

Two men burst into the station. The smaller man ran straight to the duty desk. "There's been another Ripper murder! There's been another Ripper murder!"

The constable shot out of his seat and turned toward Beck.

The other officers rushed over.

Beck leaped from his chair and rushed the two men. "Inspector Beck here. Who are you, and what do you have for me?"

"Sir, my name's John McCarthy." McCarthy gasped for air. "I'm the landlord at 13 Miller's Court, and this is Indian Harry," he took a deep breath, "I mean Thomas Bowyer. There's been a ghastly murder at my lodging house."

"Go on," Beck insisted.

McCarthy nodded. "I sent Harry to collect payment from Mary Kelly. Through the window, he could see that terrible things had been done to her and got me to see it for myself."

Beck moved toward the front door. "Come, show me." He turned around at a large man in front of the crowd. "Sergeant Thick, notify Inspector Abberline." He faced another officer. "Sergeant Badham, contact Dr. Phillips." He looked at the others. "The rest of you, follow me."

McCarthy and Bowyer took the police officers to Miller's Court and straight to the window of the room. "Here, Inspector."

Beck gazed into the window of the room and was taken aback by a horrific scene. He turned, lowered his head, and closed his eyes. "Ghastly!" He turned again and tried to open the door, but it was locked.

A group of constables were watching.

Beck faced them. "Gentlemen, we need to block off the court and begin searching the entire area." He waived a constable over to him. "Wire Scotland Yard immediately. Headquarters will want to know about this."

Fifteen minutes later, the coroner, Dr. Phillips, arrived at the scene and peeked in the window. "Atrocious! Simply awful."

"As per our standing orders, Dr. Phillips, I've allowed no one in until the bloodhounds arrive. Hopefully, they'll arrive sooner than later," Beck declared.

"Agreed, Inspector Beck. Has Inspector Abberline been informed?" Phillips asked.

Beck glanced up the street. "Yes, he should be here any minute."

At eleven thirty a.m., Inspector Abberline arrived and gazed into the window.

"Good morning, Inspector Abberline," Beck greeted. "As per our orders, no one has entered the room until the bloodhounds arrive."

Abberline continued to stare into the room. "Good morning, Inspector Beck. Thank you for taking charge of the murder scene so quickly and efficiently. I was hoping the dogs would have been here by now." He noticed the coroner heading toward them. "Good morning, Dr. Phillips."

"Good morning, Inspector," Phillips replied then peeked into the room. "Just by looking through the window, it's clear to me that the victim has expired, and the murder was most likely caused by the Whitechapel fiend. The pattern is the same, just to a more extreme level. He's eviscerated the victim completely this time."

"Truer words have never been spoken, Doctor," Abberline agreed as he wiped the sweat from his brow.

"The killer certainly spent more time accomplishing his atrocious agenda," Phillips continued. "Obviously, he was hidden within the confines of this room."

"I have no doubt that you are correct, Dr. Phillips," Abberline said, still staring through the window at the fireplace. "It looks like he enjoyed a warm and cozy fire."

Just then a police constable escorted a middle-aged lady over to Inspector Abberline. "Inspector, this is Elizabeth Prater. She lives up there in the room just above the murder scene. Mrs. Prater heard something around three a.m."

Abberline turned toward the witness. "Hello, Mrs. Prater. Do you know who lives here?"

Prater nodded as tears flowed down her face. "Yes, sir, the sweet child's name is Mary Kelly, an unfortunate down on her luck, but very young—twenty-three she told me. Mary's tall and pretty, and fair as a lily." She shook her head. "So sad, really."

"Did you see her last night?" Abberline asked.

"The last time I saw her was about nine o'clock," Prater answered. "I spoke with her here at the bottom of the entry. She went her way and I mine. I said, 'Good night, dear,' and she said 'Good night, my pretty.'" She smiled. "She always called me that."

Abberline glanced up at Prater's room. "When were you back in your room?"

Prater thought for a moment. "Around one o'clock in the mornin'. I stood over there waitin' for a gentleman. He didn't show, so I walked to McCarthy's shop for a minute then went to me room and finally off to bed."

"Did you see anything suspicious?" Abberline asked.

Prater shook her head. "No, nothin'."

Abberline glanced back at the window. "Was Kelly's light on?"

"No, no, it wasn't."

Abberline nodded. "So, what happened at three a.m.?"

"Between three and four o'clock in the mornin', me cat, Diddles, woke me up." She put her hand to her mouth, fear in her eyes. "I heard a lady say, 'Oh, murder!'" She shook her head. "It wasn't loud or nothin'. It was most likely her."

"Did you look into it?"

Prater shook her head. "No, but this kind of stuff happens all the time around here, so I ignored it and went back to bed til about five o'clock. When I got up, I went to the Ten Bells for a shot of rum, then came back and went to bed til eleven this mornin'."

Abberline nodded. "What time did you leave the Ten Bells?"

"I was only there for about thirty minutes, so most likely 5:50 or 5:45." Prater paused. "Still, nothin' was out of the ordinary."

Abberline gave Prater a kind smile. "Thank you, Mrs. Prater. You've been more than helpful. The detective constable will be getting a full statement from you. Is that OK?"

"Oh yes, Inspector." She lowered her head. "So sad, so sad."

The police constable led her away.

At 1:20 p.m., Superintendent Arnold arrived.

Inspector Abberline and Dr. Phillips met him.

"Good afternoon, sir," Abberline greeted.

Arnold gave a short nod. "Good afternoon, Inspector and Dr. Phillips. I just received word that the hound dogs will not be arriving. I'm not sure if you know this yet, but Commissioner Warren just resigned, and the home secretary has accepted his resignation."

Abberline's eyes opened wide. "Quite an interesting state of affairs, sir, and to have this happen just at the time the killer struck again."

"We need to get into the room as soon as possible," Phillips interrupted. "Each minute we're delayed will make it more difficult for me to estimate a time of death."

"Well then," Arnold replied. "I'll make the command decision. Let's go in."

"The door is locked," Phillips added.

Arnold scanned the area. "Who owns the residence?"

"Mr. McCarthy, sir," Abberline replied. "I'll bring him over."

McCarthy approached Arnold.

"Mr. McCarthy, do you have a key to this room?" Arnold asked.

"No, sir," McCarthy replied. "No one knows where it is."

Arnold glanced at the door and nodded. "Then I need you to break the door down, Mr. McCarthy. We are wasting precious time."

McCarthy nodded and turned away. Minutes later, he returned with an ax handle and broke in the door. Dr. Phillips and the police entered immediately and began to examine the body.

After a few minutes Phillips glanced up at Abberline. "The victim's heart is missing."

Abberline eyed Phillips. "Oh?" He thought for a moment. "We see the fiend taking organs again."

Phillips nodded. "It's clear the killer spent more time eviscerating the victim this time." He shook his head. "Very methodical. Notice the destruction of her face."

"It's as if the killer didn't want the poor lady to watch him disembowel her," Arnold reasoned.

"Superintendent," Phillips said, clearly exhausted. "This mutilation is extensive. My task here is so overwhelming, and I don't want to miss any important details. I need assistance from additional coroners."

Arnold rushed straight to the door. "I can arrange that," he said as he left.

Abberline grinned slightly. "I can certainly understand why the superintendent didn't want to be in this horrific place." He pulled out a parchment. "I'm going to start inventorying the room." He glanced at the fireplace and noticed an unusually large amount of ash and embers still hot from the previous night. "The fire must have been rather large last night. I'm sure the room was excessively hot."

"Hell's fire," Phillips added.

Abberline noticed a piece of burnt hard cloth and picked it up. "This is a burnt piece of brim from a man's hat." He thought for a moment while staring into the hearth. "I think the killer has burned some of his clothing."

Outside, a crowd began to gather, which became a difficult task for Inspector Beck to control. "Back up, everyone, back up!"

As a half dozen constables formed a line, reinforcements from Commercial Street and Leman Street police stations trickled in to give assistance.

A voice whispered, "Hello, Inspector Beck."

Beck turned around and gave a slight grin of recognition to the powerful-looking man who'd stepped up behind him. "Hello,

The Ripper's Hellbroth | 185

Detective Froest. It's been quite a day, especially when we have many of our police officers at the Lord Mayor's parade."

"It looks like there's a bigger crowd here," Froest observed.

Beck glanced back at the large crowd. "Why are we blessed with your presence here, Frank?"

Froest glanced at the crowd, then back at Beck. "See that tall, dark-haired man with the large mustache looming in the back of the crowd?"

Beck took a quick, unassuming peek. "I see him."

Froest glanced away. "He's a suspect in the case. Inspector Andrews' team was assigned to him. He was arrested a couple of nights ago for suspicious activities on Commercial Street. When we found out who we had, we quickly released him and began to follow him. I expected him to be wearing his usual Yankee hat, but he's not."

"Do you need help arresting him?" Beck offered.

"No, he's scheduled to be in front of the magistrate next week. We lost his trail last night, and I figured he might be here."

"How curious he's at the scene of our latest murder," Beck remarked.

Froest nodded and grinned. "Isn't it?"

The tall man turned and hurried from the crowd.

Froest and a number of other men headed off in the same direction. Froest flashed a grin over his shoulder and said, "Have a good day, Inspector."

"Happy hunting, Frank," Beck said with a nod.

chapter twenty-three

PRESENT DAY: Saturday, October 14. 10:00 p.m. Buffalo, New York—Lafayette Hotel.

Riggs stopped the car in front of Dunham's hotel.

"As always, thanks for dropping me off, Riggs," Dunham said.

"Never a problem, Dr. Dunham." Riggs glanced at the lobby. "You know, this hotel's bar and restaurant has an excellent reputation."

"I'm definitely going to take advantage of them," Dunham replied. "It's time for a fine lager. I need to wash down some frustration anyway. Care to join me?"

Riggs smiled. "I was just going to recommend that very same thing." He knew that Dunham was taking it personally that the snare was unsuccessful. "My lady's out with the girls tonight, so I'm free. I need a good beer."

"Perfect."

Riggs parked the car, and they found their way to the bar. "I'm buying the first round," Riggs insisted as they bellied up to the bar.

"Be my guest."

They ordered their drinks.

Riggs' iPhone buzzed, and he glanced at the display. "I just received a text from Diane. It looks like Artie's fine, and he's back home. The knife wound wasn't as deep as they thought." He snickered as he returned a text.

"What're you laughing at?" Dunham asked.

"I texted Diane to tell Artie that a real man wouldn't have wimped out and gone on an ambulance ride, let alone to the hospital. Me? I would have rubbed some salt on it and walked it off."

Dunham grinned and shook his head.

The bartender brought their drinks.

Riggs took a swig. "Hopefully, one of the swab samples taken in the train will nail this guy."

"I'm doubtful," Dunham began. "With the hundreds of people in those compartments in the last month, even if they did get someone's DNA, chances are it's not his."

"True," Riggs replied. "But if we do find the needle in the haystack, so to speak, we may finally have a suspect to connect to the murders. We have no one at the moment, aside from the sketch artist's creation, and since he was wearing a hat the sketch doesn't have enough detail."

Dunham frowned and shook his head. "We were that close."

Riggs paused. "Dr. Dunham, are you always this hard on yourself when the plan goes awry? I think of you as the epitome of level-headedness."

"You're not the first to notice," Dunham said, rubbing his hand. "My wife has raised her eyes at me a time or two. Most of these emotions occur during missed opportunities with these damn serial killers. She's a brilliant lady, my wife, and I believe she's figured out why."

"Why?"

Dunham took a long drink then stared at his glass. "A forensic scientist, such as me, is generally not part of serial killer task forces out in the field, but is stuck in the lab in support." He grinned. "We introverts actually like it there. This is kind of like going to a party. While extroverts thrive at parties, introverts stress."

Riggs took a drink. "Well, if you're an example of lab coats joining the task force, I'm all in favor of it, even if you have to hang out with a psychiatrist afterward." He thought for a moment. "How did you start becoming part of task forces, anyway?"

Dunham's eyed opened wider. "Well, it all started about twelve years ago. At that time, a task force investigating a serial killing spree along the Grand River in Grand Rapids, Michigan, had asked for my professional assistance. I was extremely excited to assist, for two reasons. First, it was to be my first, and possibly the only opportunity I would get to demonstrate that my training and experience would be useful in the field. And second, my close high school friend, Jack Bernard, was a member of the task force, and I wanted the opportunity to work with him." He raised his finger. "It was Jack who had personally requested my assistance, and I felt, and still feel, forever indebted to him for this."

Riggs pointed his finger at Dunham. "Little did you know that this was the beginning of your remarkable streak of success—a success that has traveled to Buffalo."

Dunham smiled.

"So, we can thank Jack for this." Riggs raised his glass to Dunham. "Here's to Jack, Dr. Dunham."

Dunham nodded, and they tapped glasses.

"Well," Dunham continued, "Jack was a Kent County sheriff and was raising his family in a small town just north of Grand Rapids. He had a beautiful wife and two daughters, Amy and Marie. Amy was the oldest and in her second year of college at Grand Valley State University, located next to the Grand River in the city."

Riggs glanced up at the ceiling in thought. "You know, I seem to recall this case."

"There had been four killings, and the case was going nowhere," Dunham said. "The four victims were found along the Grand River, and each was murdered at a separate location, then dropped off along the river. All four victims were abducted while away from their homes—near a grocery store in one case and at a bowling alley in another. Jack had advised the task force that they needed assistance from the FBI—specifically an FBI forensic scientist—and I was asked. Actually, I have a few skills unique to even forensic scientists, which was most likely one of the selling points. Namely, profiling."

"Very helpful," Riggs agreed.

Dunham nodded. "Once the team debriefed me on the investigation, I attempted to identify any patterns in the killings that they may have missed. The team had settled upon the belief that the offender was a disorganized serial killer, satisfying his evening impulses through opportunistic encounters. I initially agreed with this assessment, since the murders fit the textbook definition of a disorganized serial offender." Dunham raised his finger and shook his head. "But something was nagging at me."

Riggs grinned. "I've witnessed this before."

Dunham smiled. "There was a similar MO with all four victims, but each had a unique characteristic as well. For example, the last victim was discovered with a crushed rose-type flower under her body, yet none of the others had had this. I decided to focus upon these unique characteristics. I noticed in the report that there was an unusual statement made by the victim's husband, something to the effect that the scene of his wife's murder had similarities to the movie she had just watched. I contacted the husband by phone to ask what he meant by that statement."

"What did he say?"

Dunham took a drink. "He said that his wife had just watched the *Wizard of Oz*, and in the movie Dorothy fell asleep in a field of poppy flowers. He told me that a detective had shown him this crushed poppy flower discovered underneath her body. They had put it in a clear Ziploc bag and asked him if she had purchased poppy flowers the night she went missing, and he told them she had not."

"So, did that mean anything?"

Dunham eyed Riggs. "It did, and it was the key piece of evidence that broke the case. My revelation was that maybe this killer was more organized than we believed. It seemed the offender knew she just watched the *Wizard of Oz*, thus he could very well have been in their back yard, watching her."

"Stands to reason," Riggs replied.

Dunham nodded. "If so, he may have left evidence. I had the task force initiate a massive search around the homes of all four victims. They discovered a number of cigarettes butts located behind the back yard of each home, although the butts were well-deteriorated at the residences of the first three victims. They also discovered lip marks on the outside of the sliding glass door of the last victim's home."

Riggs frowned. "The bastard was watching."

"DNA analysis was successful," Dunham continued, "on the sample saliva found on the butts from the last victim's residence and on the lip marks. They compared the DNA sample with the prison database, which was the database they used at the time. It matched up with a known violent sex offender living in Grand Rapids. The task force obtained a search warrant for the sex offender's home and vehicle and collected enough evidence for a solid conviction."

Riggs nodded. "Good news."

Dunham paused, then choked up. "Well, on the day they arrested the sex offender, a fifth victim was discovered. When I reached the location of the victim's body, it became quickly apparent who the female victim was. It was Jack's oldest daughter, Amy."

Riggs' jaw dropped. "Oh, I'm so sorry."

Dunham nodded. "Jack was present at the scene and in hysterics. I was so distraught that I vomited and nearly passed out."

"Totally understandable," Riggs consoled.

Dunham took a drink. "The next two weeks were horrible for me, feeling immensely guilty, because I knew Jack and his family were feeling even worse. I couldn't imagine losing a daughter." He paused. "I actually held myself responsible for not saving her. If I had only found the pattern two or three days prior, she would still be alive. Jack told me that the only one responsible for his daughter's death was the killer, and that I shouldn't take anything personally."

"Jack had that right!" Riggs exclaimed.

Dunham shook his head. "That's easier said than done. He actually thanked me for discovering who he called, 'the despicable waste of human flesh.'"

Riggs held his beer up to Dunham. "Well, how about we kick the Niagara Falls serial killer's ass for Jack and his family."

Dunham presented his glass to Riggs in mutual agreement.

Dunham glanced up at the list of beers. "It's time to try another selection. Have you ever tried the Oktoberfest Ale?"

Riggs nodded enthusiastically. "Oh yeah, you'll love it."

The two spent another hour talking and, although Riggs switched to water, Dunham continued trying out the selections of craft beers.

"Thanks for drinking a few beers with me, Riggs," Dunham said. "I'm feeling the effects a little too much though, so I'm going to call it a night. Thank goodness tomorrow is Sunday."

Riggs got to his feet and shook Dunham's hand. "Anytime. I'll catch up with you next week, Dr. Dunham."

Dunham smiled with renewed confidence. "We'll buckle down and catch this guy once and for all."

chapter twenty-four

Sergeants Dinnie and Froest entered the courtroom along with the solicitor for the prosecution, Tumblety's solicitor, and Tumblety himself. The case just prior to Tumblety's was being heard by the presiding magistrate, James Lennox Hannay. Sitting to the magistrate's right was the chief clerk.

Froest recognized the man next to the solicitor for the prosecution and whispered to Dinnie, "Hey, I know that guy. He's Hank Leek. Walter Dew arrested him last month because he was bragging in a bar how much he hated women, especially unfortunates. He released him the next day since he had a solid alibi, but he's one peculiar fella."

The chief clerk stood up. "Quiet in the court!" He paused until there was silence. "William Avenall, twenty-six, chimney sweeper, Adam and Eve Court, Oxford Street; and Frederick W. Moore, twenty-eight, carver and gilder, Carlisle Street, Soho, are charged on remand for behaving in a disorderly manner and assaulting Henry Edward Leek, an oil-and-color man, of Gilbert Street."

Froest leaned over to Dinnie again. "The way these clerks and solicitors talk in court bores me to tears. Kick me if I snore."

Dinnie merely shook his head.

The clerk continued. "Upon entering a public house in the neighborhood of Berner Street and Oxford Street, someone in the bar suggested the assaulted was Jack the Ripper. Upon Mr.

Leek leaving the house, the two defendants seized hold of him, and Mr. Avenall said he was a detective, and both behaved very violently toward him. The defendants proceeded to drag Mr. Leek along the street, pretending to take him to a police station."

The solicitor for the defendants stood up. "Your Worship, my clients truly believed Mr. Leek was the real Jack the Ripper, thus, they were justified in taking the accused to the police station. Mr. Avenall and Mr. Moore are hardworking, respectable men and are willing to make compensation as far as their means will allow."

"As far as the assault is concerned," Magistrate Hannay concluded, "this might better be settled by a civil action—if the accused desired such a course to be taken."

Frederick Moore stood up. "Sir, I would prefer that you deal with the case."

The magistrate thought for a moment. "If people take upon themselves the responsibility of making practical jokes, they must put up with the consequences. In the present excited state of public feeling, it is a highly dangerous thing to drag a man about the streets saying that he is the Whitechapel murderer, and such conduct might actually lead to loss of life."

The solicitor for the defendants stood up again. "Your Worship, my clients are willing to give Mr. Leek a sovereign each."

Magistrate Hannay glanced at the arresting constable. "Constable, did either of the defendants introduce themselves as police detectives?"

"No, Your Worship, but Mr. Avenall did tell me he was a private detective."

The magistrate paused, then said, "As regard to the charge of impersonating a detective, the evidence is somewhat conflicting, therefore I shall dismiss it. As to the charge of assault, however, I hereby inflict the full penalty. Although the defendants did not beat the accused, they frightened him so badly that they caused him to become ill and enter a state of nervous depression. The defendants shall pay the maximum fine allowable and serve one month imprisonment." Magistrate Hannay performed the gavel strike. "Next case."

The clerk allowed time for the parties to leave and for Francis Tumblety and the solicitors for the prosecution and defense to take their places. Tumblety was sent to the dock of the court and ordered to stand.

The clerk began, "Francis J. Tumblety, fifty-six, physician, summoned to Police Court Magistrate James L. Hannay on this fourteenth of November 1888, following a bail set by said magistrate at the remand hearing, dated 7 November 1888. The prosecution is requesting the case be transferred to the Central Criminal Court per the Criminal Law Amendment Act of 1885. As to the original indictment, the defendant is charged with committing an act of Gross Indecency under the Criminal Law Amendment Act of 1885, Section 11, and indecent assault with force of arms under the Offenses Against the Person Act of 1861, Section 62, in the cases of John Doughty, occurring on the second of November; of James Crowley on the fourteenth of October; of Arthur Brice on the thirty-first of August; and of Albert Fisher on the twenty-seventh of July."

Magistrate Hannay glanced at Tumblety. "Identify yourself to the court."

Tumblety raised his chin and closed his eyes arrogantly. "Doctor Francis James Tumblety."

"Are you the defendant being charged in this case?" the magistrate asked.

Tumblety nodded. "Yes, Your Worship."

Magistrate Hannay stared at Tumblety. "How do you plead?"

"Absolutely not guilty," Tumblety replied angrily.

The magistrate reviewed the file for a few minutes. "Transfer to the Central Criminal Court is justified and hereby granted pending a grand jury." He glanced at a calendar. "The next time it is seated is 19 November 1888." He glanced at both solicitors. "Is there anything I should take into consideration before I make a decision upon the issuance of a warrant of committal and corresponding bail?"

Tumblety's solicitor stood up. "Your Worship, my client is a medical professional held in the highest esteem. The defense requests bail to be set in order for my client to properly serve our citizens."

The solicitor for the prosecution stood up. "Your Worship, the prisoner is an American, and we must take into consideration the possibility of him absconding. He is clearly a flight risk. The prosecution requests no bail."

Tumblety's solicitor raised his hand. "My client could have easily absconded after bail was set at the remand hearing, Your Worship, yet he did not."

The magistrate thought for a moment, then faced both parties. "In view of the seriousness of the indictment, I hereby place you on remand, although, concern for you being a flight risk is not justified. Bail is set at three hundred pounds. You will remain in custody until your pretrial hearing at Central Criminal Court. If you acquire the funds for payment of bail prior to this, we will readjourn in order to execute bail." The magistrate performed the gavel strike. "Next case."

November 19. New York City, New York—Byrnes' Office.

Detective Crowley burst into Byrnes' office. "Sir! This private cable just came in from Scotland Yard addressed 'For your Eyes Only'! It's from Assistant Commissioner Anderson again!"

Byrnes grinned. "Of course you didn't read it."

Crowley shook his head. "Of course not . . . I mean . . . well, I am in charge of cable dispatches."

Byrnes laughed. "No worries, Detective. What's it say?"

"They're asking for more information on the suspect they contacted you about a few days back."

Byrnes read the dispatch:

Police Detective Bureau Chief Inspector Thomas F. Byrnes: Request all available records on Francis Tumblety, who is under arrest in England on charges of indecent assault. He was arrested some weeks ago for the Whitechapel murders. Have already been in contact with the Pinkerton Agency, and chiefs of police in San Francisco and Brooklyn. All assistance would be appreciated. Confidentiality is of the essence.

—Anderson, Scotland Yard.

Byrnes glanced up at Crowley. "I had suspicions they'd be in contact with me again."

"The press certainly did swamp our office yesterday, only a day after someone in Scotland Yard leaked the story to the *World* reporter."

Byrnes handed the *New York World* newspaper to Crowley. "It's in the paper today. Read it."

Crowley read the article.

HE IS "ECCENTRIC" DR. TWOMBLETY, The American Suspected of the Whitechapel Crimes Well Known Here.

A special London despatch to THE WORLD yesterday morning announced the arrest of a man in connection with the Whitechapel crimes, who gave his name as Dr. Kumblety, of New York. He could not be held on suspicion, but the police succeeded in getting him held under the special law passed soon after the "Modern Babylon" exposures.

Dr. Kumblety is well known in this city. His name however is Twomblety, not Kumblety. Twenty-four years ago he made his advent in this city and was since then known only as "Dr. Twomblety" a most eccentric character. He formerly resided in Nova Scotia, where he practiced medicine under the name of Dr. Sullivan. About the time of his appearance in this city he was a fugitive from justice, having fled his Nova Scotian home to escape punishment for malpractice.

Ever since his identity became known here he has been under surveillance of Inspector Byrnes's officers, who rarely lose sight of him or knowledge of his whereabouts. For twenty years he has been widely known as the manufacturer of Twomblety's pimple banisher, from which he professes to gain a livelihood. His own face is covered with pimples, and although his features are otherwise regular, his appearance on this account is somewhat repulsive. He is a large and heavily built man, standing fully six feet in his stockings. The doctor's dress and appearance upon the street were remarkably eccentric. He had an office on Broadway, near Eighth Street, and another in Jersey City, but he spent most of his time in this city.

Every afternoon, for years, he was seen with a huge buttonhole bouquet in the lapel of his coat, walking up Broadway, then later in the day promenading up and down in front of the Fifth Avenue Hotel. On all these occasions he would be followed at a distance of about ten feet by a valet, a short and stocky built fellow, who led by their collars two monster greyhounds. The doctor also drove a gorgeously equipped turnout.

One day a brief history of the man appeared in Frank Leslie's paper, showing him up in his true colors. A few evenings later Editor Ralston, of the journal, was enjoying a tete-a-tete with a friend in the Fifth Avenue Hotel cafe, when in popped Dr. Twomblety. The latter immediately accused the editor of writing his history and followed up the abuse by assaulting Mr. Ralston. The doctor was arrested, but discharged the next morning, as Editor Ralston refused to prosecute.

During the past few years Twomblety has opened a branch office in London and has been making regular trips across the ocean at intervals of five or six months. He was last seen here about five months ago, when he appeared on Broadway, just as he did twenty years ago, with his leather-peaked cap, white over-gaiters and button-hole bouquet.

Crowley glanced up at Byrnes, smiling. "I think the press was a bit surprised we had so much information on this guy just one day after the story hit the papers."

Byrnes sat back in his chair. "Scotland Yard certainly has an interest in this man. Only time will tell if he's Jack the Ripper." He paused. "Let's give them what they ask for, Detective."

Crowley nodded. "I'll take care of it, sir."

chapter twenty-five

**PRESENT DAY: Friday, October 20. Buffalo, New York—
Lafayette Hotel.**

Riggs pulled his car up to the front entrance of the hotel and
found Dunham waiting.

"Good morning, Detective Riggs. On time as usual, I see."

Riggs handed him a cup of coffee as Dunham entered the
car. "Good morning, Dr. Dunham. Where're we headed?"

Dunham handed Riggs an address on a sheet of paper.
"Thank you for the coffee. Let's go to 416 Delaware Avenue."

Riggs glanced at the note. "I know where this is. We'll take
Elmwood Avenue first." He eased out into the road. "This guy
must be rich. This section of Delaware Ave. is the old money
section of the city." He turned the corner. "Stand by to see some
gorgeous century-old mansions."

"Interesting."

Riggs glanced at Dunham, who was staring out the side
window. "Don't beat your head against the wall too hard, Dr.
Dunham. Yeah, he slipped through our fingers, but the mere
fact that you predicted his movements means you have his
number."

Dunham looked back at Riggs. "True." He thought for a moment. "But I should've known he had an exit plan. Although it's
a misconception that most serial offenders have above-average
intelligence, this one certainly seems so." He paused. "I can understand why he's been elusive for so long. Hard to believe, after
all the planning for the snare, we've just spent the last week
starting over."

"I was thinking about it last night," Riggs remarked. "I'm pretty sure that the killer didn't realize we had set a trap, so we may be able to catch him off guard again in the future." He raised his finger. "That was an excellent idea of yours, to hide that fact as best we could."

Dunham stared out the side window again. "The problem is, we may not get another opportunity like that. None of the other women have received a gift or anything violet-colored yet. We've already told them to change their daily habits. The fact that there are no other women on the list who've received a gift might mean he's done. Maybe there is no next victim." Dunham paused for a moment, then smiled. "But that's a pessimist talking. We'll nail him."

Riggs grinned and pointed to Dunham's coffee. "Drink some Timmy Ho's. That'll perk you up."

"You're right," Dunham replied, inspecting the cup of coffee. "I'm getting addicted to it."

Riggs glanced over at Dunham. "Like we talked about last week, if he does have an agenda requiring a specific number of victims, he didn't get it. I think he's not done." He paused before changing the subject. "So, who is this guy we're seeing, anyway?"

"His name is Jonathan Bradbury," Dunham answered. "A very important and influential man, but you wouldn't know it except from the fact that he's very wealthy. He prefers to stay behind the scenes, and it's only because of one particular covert investigation that the FBI knows of him and his activities. He's the Grand Master of the Fraternity of the Ancient and Mystical Order of the Rose Cross in this area, which is an international Masonic-style organization of modern-day Rosicrucians."

"Ah, Rosicrucians!" Riggs replied in recognition.

Dunham nodded. "If you recall what Ryan Stanton said about Rosicrucianism, it seems our killer is following Rosicrucian beliefs—or the mirror opposite of them—so I wanted to speak with Mr. Bradbury to see if he has received any suspicious visitors in the last year. I called him, and he's offered to speak with us first thing this morning." He looked over at Riggs. "Apparently, he's an early riser."

"Do you think the killer is affiliated with these people?"

Dunham shook his head. "No, I don't. The offender seems to be exploiting Rosicrucian rituals and practices in a very ruthless, personal way. The Rosicrucian Order would find this most troubling and would've intervened. Not only do they abhor the act of murder, they hate anything that gets them in the news, such as a gruesome series of killings." He took a nip of coffee. "They're very private people. "

"Even so, I wouldn't reveal too much of what we know," Riggs suggested.

Dunham nodded. "Agreed."

They turned onto to a side street from Elmwood Avenue, an area marked by quite luxurious homes. "Here's the address."

The home was a beautiful, three-story rectangular mansion, and the front had a tall metal gate.

Riggs pointed at the front of the home. "The gate's open." He pulled the car into a wide, U-shaped driveway and parked near the front door.

As they got out of the car, a well-dressed man exited the building.

Riggs whispered, "Is that old money, or what?"

"Good morning. Are you Dr. Dunham?" the man asked.

Dunham shook his hand. "Yes, and you must be Mr. Bradbury?"

Bradbury nodded. "Welcome."

Riggs shook his hand. "Hello, I'm Detective Riggs."

"It's nice to meet you, Detective Riggs." Bradbury waved them to follow. "I prefer to escort my guests into my home. Please come in."

They entered through the front door.

Dunham gazed around the entranceway. "Your home is beautiful, Mr. Bradbury."

Bradbury smiled and looked around. "Thank you. It's been in the family for quite some time." He led the way into what appeared to be his study.

The room had an old Victorian atmosphere, the walls lined with cherry bookshelves containing a vast library of very old bound books.

"May I have your home, Mr. Bradbury?" Riggs joked.

Bradbury chuckled. "Have a seat. Won't you?"

They sat down in very comfortable seats with armrests and tall backs.

An aged butler entered the room with refreshments. He first handed Bradbury a drink and a napkin.

Bradbury nodded to him. "Thank you, Winslow."

Winslow then handed a drink and napkin to Riggs, who nodded to him. "Thank you."

Lastly, the butler approached Dunham and handed him a drink. As he began to turn from Dunham, the butler caught his foot on the rug and stumbled. Dunham caught the elderly gentleman, saving him from an embarrassing fall.

Winslow, horror-struck, faced Dunham and said, "Excuse me, sir. I am so sorry."

Dunham smiled kindly. "No problem."

Winslow left the room.

"Nice catch, Dr. Dunham," Bradbury remarked and paused for a moment. "I was very intrigued by what you said on the phone. May I inquire as to why you believe the Niagara Falls Ripper might be somehow guided by Rosicrucian philosophy?"

"At the moment," Dunham replied apologetically, "I'm not at liberty to say much because the investigation is ongoing, but I can tell you the offender isn't following the beliefs your organization holds so dear—rather an aberration of those beliefs. Instead of gaining universal knowledge and understanding for the betterment of humankind, he's exploiting Rosicrucian knowledge for selfish reasons, and doing so in a very ruthless manner."

Bradbury grinned at Dunham. "I am actually quite impressed. Few understand our philosophy."

"What exactly is a Rosicrucian?" Riggs asked, then noticed Dunham searching his pockets. Riggs quickly whipped out a new notepad and pen.

Bradbury mused at the exchange. "First," Bradbury answered, "if one claims to be a Rosicrucian, chances are they are not. It's more appropriate to say we are students of the philosophy. We believe humans have within themselves the capability to understand everything, including the divine."

"Is it a type of Christianity?" Riggs asked pointedly.

"From the way you are asking it, yes, but we interpret the Gospels differently than Catholics or Evangelical Christians do." Bradbury raised his finger. "Note, the difference is not the written word but the interpretation of it."

"I apologize for asking so many questions, but it's very intriguing," Riggs interrupted.

Bradbury smiled. "No problem at all; you are a detective." He took a deep breath. "In the Pauline Christianity that most are familiar with, Jesus was God that became man. Many in our Order believe the Gospels say that Jesus was a man who became God." He leaned back. "We also believe Jesus was the highest initiate—one who attained complete enlightenment, or illumination. He is the perfect role model and the goal of many students of the philosophy. They want to be Christlike; they want to be full initiates."

Riggs nodded. "So, Rosicrucianism, or the philosophy, is grounded in goodness."

"Yes!" Bradbury exclaimed, beaming. "Not all of us in the community adhere so strongly to this belief and instead support the Pauline tradition of Jesus as both God and man." He slowly wobbled his head and stared at the ceiling. "We enjoy the many other qualities of the Rosicrucian Order."

"Why the secrecy?" Riggs asked.

Bradbury grinned. "Such as the secrecy. Today, secrecy is merely tradition—and it's kind of a thrill to be part of a secret society, wouldn't you agree? But in medieval times, the Church would burn people at the stake for believing as we do, which forced us to go underground and practice secrecy."

Riggs nodded. "That makes sense."

Bradbury continued. "I assure you, our rituals and initiations today are designed to cultivate intrigue, a feeling of tradition, belonging, and fraternal brotherhood, rather than being expressions of a true belief in the ancient esoteric mysticisms." Bradbury shifted his gaze toward Dunham. "Now, from what I've read about this killer, it sounds like he has embraced the dark areas of the mystical knowledge. Rituals involving the mutilation of women have no place in our philosophy."

"I certainly agree," Dunham replied. "He has unquestionably ignored the ancient warnings of the Illuminated Brotherhood, and we have discovered a crack in his armor—though we don't think he's realized we have discovered his pattern." He paused. "Because of this, I'd be indebted to you if you could keep this knowledge in your confidence."

Bradbury nodded slowly. "Of course. Again, you surprise me, Dr. Dunham. The Illuminated Brotherhood's warning is not even known by most of our members."

Dunham continued. "This brings me to why we have imposed upon your day. Although I certainly understand your reasons for confidentiality, I am pressed to ask you if you have encountered anyone in the last eight months that has given you need for suspicion within the Rosicrucian community."

Bradbury sat back in his chair and stared up at the ceiling. "At the moment, Dr. Dunham, no one comes to mind, but let me think about it for a while." He leaned forward. "If it becomes public that this killer's motive is based upon our philosophy, it doesn't fare well for our Order. I hope you understand."

"I certainly do," Dunham agreed. "I have one more card up my sleeve, which is using the press to our advantage—and this will stay in reserve until we've exhausted all of the other strategies." Dunham pulled out a business card. "Here's my card, and please contact me at any time. May I do the same?"

"Yes, and I certainly will as well," Bradbury replied. "I will walk you out."

Dunham and Riggs stood, shook hands with Mr. Bradbury, and they exited through the front door.

As Riggs and Dunham got into the car, Riggs said, "Well, the conversation was very interesting, but it didn't seem productive."

"That's not entirely true," Dunham replied. "Masonic-style organizations like this are composed of an overt outer circle of openness and altruistic community awareness, yet they are run by a clandestine inner circle of men with a much different agenda. He and I were speaking the language of outer circle Rosicrucianism, but he clearly knew I was communicating with the inner circle of leaders. I wanted them to know that I, as a representative of the FBI, will find this killer even to the ruination of their secret inner circle. If they do know anything about the killings, my guess is they will find a way to assist us—especially since the inner circle truly does abhor the actions of this murderer."

Riggs grinned. "Brilliant, Dr. Dunham."

Bradbury watched Riggs' car disappear down the driveway. He closed the door and headed for the basement. Through a series of locked doors, he entered a high-tech room.

In the center of the room was a table with four older gentlemen who had been waiting for Bradbury's arrival. Monitor screens in front of each of them showed a video image of the den that Riggs, Dunham, and Bradbury had just vacated.

One of the older men was reading Dunham's notepad. The man said, "Winslow certainly has many talents, Jonathan, including pick-pocketing." He paused. "Well, I guess you were right. Dunham has connected the killer with our philosophy. Specifically with the attempt to create an elixir of life." He glanced up at Bradbury. "He's even had a personal meeting with Ryan Stanton, but I see nothing about the French immortal. Do you think he'll realize we have possession of his notepad?"

Bradbury shook his head. "Dunham is a brilliant man, but because of his absentmindedness, I believe we're safe. Thanks to your sources, Frederick, we know the task force has almost caught the killer—and did so by predicting his next move with information gained from a blood donor list."

"I believe we're in agreement that we should help at all costs," a third man interrupted. "This murderer could seriously undermine our agenda. Better yet, if he does actually possess a working elixir, or even the *Magnum Opus* itself, and gets captured, we just might be able to take over ownership."

"Do we have our people prepared to confiscate such a cache from the evidence room, Fredrick?" Bradbury asked.

"Yes indeed, Jonathan," Frederick replied. "We need to invest all of our resources into discovering the identity of this man."

"One way we can do this is to have some of our resources follow the progress of Dunham and the task force," Bradbury responded. "He is an amazing investigator. They don't call Dunham 'the Watchmaker' for nothing."

chapter twenty-six

Sergeants Froest and Dinnie boarded the train in London's West End at Charing Cross train station. The estimated duration of travel to the east coast city of Folkstone on the English Channel was two hours.

An hour into the trip, Dinnie, sitting across from Froest, popped his head up from the daily paper. "Maybe you should give me your expensive cane—you know, the black one with gold trim."

"Enough already!" Froest blurted out. "How many times do I have to apologize? I had no idea that the chief inspector would force you to come with me on this trip and ruin both our weekends."

Dinnie returned to his newspaper. "You're the one getting disciplined. You spoke to the American reporter and let slip that we were after Tumblety for the Whitechapel murders. The chief inspector himself is even in hot water."

Froest leaned forward. "Hey, it was a weak moment, Walter. He's taken care of me on a few occasions, so I thought I would help him out a little. How was I to know it would become major news in America?"

Dinnie glanced over his paper. "Well, Tumblety is the only strong candidate we have at the moment. He's an extreme woman hater." His voice trailed away, and he thought it best to change the subject. "Can you believe Inspector Andrews saw us off at the train station?" He shook his head. "You know he did it just to get a good laugh."

Froest popped out a slight grin. "The bloody idiot."

Their trip came to an end at the Folkstone train station.

Froest peeked out the window and noticed their escort waiting. "There's Captain Ruxton."

Kent County Police Chief Constable Captain John Ruxton had been telegraphed by Chief Inspector Swanson regarding their mission and to watch out for Tumblety attempting to board a ferry at Folkstone bound for France. Ruxton had cabled back stating that he would personally meet Froest and Dinnie at the station and assist them.

Dinnie glanced out the train window. "Huh, he looks like the assistant commissioner."

He was elderly and had a thin frame, white hair under his hat, and wore a relatively short white beard and mustache. There were two young police constables with him.

Froest and Dinnie departed the train and hurried toward the well-dressed man.

"Captain Ruxton?" Dinnie asked.

The captain nodded, then clasped his hand in a hard shake. "Good afternoon, Detective Sergeants Dinnie," he shook Froest's hand, "and Froest. I trust your trip was satisfactory?"

"It was. Thank you, sir," Dinnie said, using his country gentleman charm. "Chief Inspector Swanson sends his greetings. He told us the two of you worked together on the force years ago."

"Yes," the captain agreed. "How is that ol' coot, anyway? I was at his wedding years back."

"Excellent, sir," Dinnie replied. "He still has that smile on his face."

The captain pointed to the two constables. "These are Police Constables Albert Adams and Miles Henry."

Froest and Dinnie shook their hands.

Both were tall, dark-haired, and athletically built.

"I've assigned them to you for the weekend," the captain explained.

"Excellent. We certainly appreciate it, sir," Froest replied.

The captain began walking away. "Follow me. We have a cab."

He looked around as everyone followed. "Chief Inspector Swanson has informed me that we'll be escorting you to

Folkstone Harbour to review the ferry and ship manifests and to watch out for a Whitechapel murder suspect trying to make his way out of the country."

"Yes, sir," Dinnie confirmed. "Allow me to give you the details. Chief Inspector Swanson fears the suspect—an American named Dr. Francis Tumblety—may be trying to leave the country. We don't have enough evidence against him for the murders, so we charged him with two misdemeanor offenses—indecent assault, and gross indecency—offenses he's clearly guilty of. He knows he's going to lose the case and most likely be sentenced to Holloway Prison for a few years."

"So, he's not in custody without bail?" the captain asked.

Dinnie shook his head. "Last week, the local magistrate placed him in custody awaiting trial at Old Bailey Courthouse and set bail at three hundred pounds. Two days later, two bondsmen bailed him out. He's free, and he hasn't been seen since. He was a no-show at the Old Bailey Courthouse two days ago, and his solicitor has no idea where he is. He convinced the judge to postpone the trial until December."

"Interesting."

Dinnie nodded. "Chief Inspector Swanson fears the worst and believes he'll make his way west to Liverpool and board a steamer to America. It makes sense, since this is his usual point of entry and departure, and his sister lives in Liverpool." He paused. "So far, he's not been seen."

"Which leads you here," the captain reasoned.

Dinnie eyed the captain. "Assistant Commissioner Anderson suggested the possibility that this Irish-American might try to sneak out of the country with the assistance of Irish Nationalists opposite of Liverpool and get onto a ferry here en route to Boulogne, France."

The captain grinned. "We're excited to do our part in this investigation."

The four got into the police cab, and the cab started its way to the harbor.

Captain Ruxton took his hat off, wiped his forehead, then placed his cover back on. "Folkstone Harbour is owned by South Eastern Railways, and there's a memorandum of agreement that the police department is responsible for the port's safety and security. Our relationship with the company is actually quite good, but there's one small problem—the supervisor in the administration building."

"Oh, how so?" Froest asked.

"He's pompous," the captain said bluntly. "It irritates me every time I have to deal with him."

"I see," Dinnie replied. "This may help. The assistant commissioner has actually given us the authority through Home Office to confiscate any material. Apparently, he's quite close with the heads of South Eastern Railways and has received prior approval."

The captain nodded. "Good to know, Detective Sergeant."

Dinnie pulled from his breast pocket three pictures and handed them to the captain and the constables. "This is the most recent picture we have of our suspect. If you see anyone attempting to board a ferry who looks remotely like him, hold him until Sergeant Froest or I can identify him. We've been in his presence on several occasions."

The police cab arrived at the harbor and stopped in front of the administration office. They entered the building, then crossed to a teller.

"We need to see your supervisor, please," the captain requested.

"One moment," the teller replied as he turned and hurried away. A few minutes later, he returned. "Follow me please, gentlemen."

They followed him to an office located to the side of the main room. They entered the room and saw a well-dressed, balding, overweight man staring down at a manifest. They stood there for several moments.

The man slowly flipped the page and continued reading, clearly ignoring them.

Froest glanced over at Dinnie and rolled his eyes at the man's attempt to send the message that he was in control of the situation.

The man peeked up. "Yes, Captain, may I help you?" he asked in a condescending and impatient tone.

"Good afternoon, Mr. Wainwright," the captain began. "May I present Detective Sergeants Froest and Dinnie from Scotland Yard. They have been directed by their superiors to search through your ships' manifests, beginning on November sixteenth, up to today."

206 | Michael L. Hawley

Wainwright took a fleeting glance at Froest and Dinnie. "I see." He paused for a moment. "Being that we are a private company, in accordance with the Private Act of 1836, you'll need to follow the proper procedures and have your superiors make a formal request through our home office in London. Once I receive permission, I'll have my secretary contact your office via telegraph, and you may return." He dropped his gaze and resumed his reading. "Good day, gentlemen."

Froest glanced over at Dinnie, grinned, then nodded his head.

Dinnie crossed to the door and closed it as the two constables positioned themselves in front of the door.

Froest slowly approached Wainwright, reached over the desk, and grabbed him by the lapels.

Wainwright popped his head up in surprise.

In one powerful motion, Froest lifted the heavy man out of his seat, dragged his body over the desk, knocking everything off of it, and dropped him in front of the captain.

The man's eyes went wide in utter shock.

The captain spoke softly. "Now that we have your undivided attention, Mr. Wainwright, I am going to repeat my demand: all of your ships' manifests, beginning on November sixteenth, up until now. If we do not have them in our hands and a room for us to review them, I am going to arrest you for obstruction of justice and impeding an ongoing investigation of national security. You will then be spending the evening in the jailhouse, sharing a cell with a lowlife dandy named Hank, whom I just arrested last night. I further recommend that while we're examining your manifests, you telegraph your headquarters telling them exactly what we're doing, and also inform them that they have Assistant Commissioner Anderson's gratitude for allowing us to review your manifests."

Wainwright stared at the captain with fear in his eyes. "I'll get the manifests right away, gentlemen. You may use my office."

Froest grinned.

Moments later, a pile of ship and ferry manifests were placed on the supervisor's desk.

Dinnie looked at everyone. "On the back of the pictures I gave you are lists of aliases that this American suspect uses when he travels, so search for these names on the manifests as well."

The captain looked out the window, then at Froest and Dinnie. "It looks like there's a ferry leaving for Le Havre, France, within the hour. How about the four of you check out the passengers before they board? I'll stay behind and review the logs."

"Excellent idea, Captain," Froest agreed, then glanced at Dinnie. "How about we split up? Constable Adams, you're with me, and Constable Henry, you're with Sergeant Dinnie."

The four left the administration building and headed toward the ferry.

"Good, no one's been let on board yet, so that should help us with the search," Dinnie said as they approached.

"Let's start with the people waiting in line at the ferry, then make our way outward," Froest suggested, studying the large crowds around the dozen or so buildings.

The harbor was a bustle of activity with stores, hotels, carriage services, and taverns.

Dinnie nodded. "How about we section it off in two parts. You two take the northern section, and Constable Henry and I will take the southern section."

Froest nodded. "Let's be off."

The four made their way through all the passengers waiting in line and to the wooden sidewalks connecting many buildings. They split up as the ferry blew its horn and passengers began to board.

"Sergeant, are there any other characteristics I should be looking for?" Henry asked.

"He's a tall man with dark hair. He waxes his long mustache in order to make himself look younger," Dinnie replied. "Since he's on the run, he may have changed his look a bit. He will be on guard for trouble, so look for anyone acting suspicious."

They approached a large stable.

"Henry, I'll go through the inside of the building, so why don't you walk around it?"

Henry nodded and left. He slowly ambled around the building into a secluded section, which had a path adjacent to the building with bushes and woods on the other side. As he turned the corner, he immediately came face-to-face with a tall man in a hat, dark-haired with a large mustache, who was pulling a chest.

The man froze.

"Excuse me, sir, may I see your identification?" Henry asked.

"What? Certainly," the man replied nervously and pulled out his ferry ticket.

Henry read the ticket. "Hello, Mr. Townsend. Frank Townsend." He compared it to the aliases on the back of the picture, but Frank Townsend wasn't one of them. His face, though, looked almost identical to the picture, in Constable Henry's opinion. "Mr. Townsend, you'll need to come with me, please."

The man moved closer to the ferry, causing Henry to face away from the path. "Officer, I need to make my ferry."

Henry gripped the man's arm. "It's not going anywhere. I'll see to that."

Henry was suddenly grabbed from behind by a second person and pulled backward off his feet. His helmet was dislodged as he hit the ground.

A third person clubbed Henry over the head, leaving him unconscious.

A few minutes later, Dinnie exited the building, searching for Henry. He frowned. "I told him to stay close to the bloody building." Dinnie cursed, then entered a crowded store and continued his search.

Ten minutes later, the ferry released its mooring and set off across the channel.

Eventually, Dinnie met up with Froest and Adams and noticed Henry wasn't with them.

Dinnie glanced around. "I thought Constable Henry would be with you."

"Where was the last place you saw him?" Froest asked.

Dinnie pointed behind him. "Over there at the stables. I told him to walk the perimeter of the building while I went inside."

The three hurried toward the stables, and when they came to the secluded path, Adams looked inside the bushes. "Over here, Detectives! I found Henry! He's alive but all tied up!"

Adams removed the bindings. "You have a nice welt on your head, Miles. You all right?"

Henry touched his head. "Ow, someone clubbed me over the head, and I blacked out, then I woke up gagged and all tied up."

"Start from the beginning. What happened?" Froest asked.

Henry pointed to the path at the corner of the building. "I questioned a tall man with dark hair and a mustache right there." He looked at Froest. "His eyes were darting back and forth just as you said your suspect did." He touched his bruised forehead again. "When I was reading his ferry ticket about three or four men grabbed me from behind, and one of them clubbed me on my head."

Adams shook his head. "You didn't have your helmet tightened, did you?"

Henry glared at him. "I did so!"

"Well, the ferry left," Dinnie said. "So I'm sure he's on it. Did you see the name on his ticket?"

"Yes I did," Henry replied. "Frank Townsend. I remembered it because it was close to the name of Francis Tumblety."

"It had to have been him," Froest snarled, snapping his fingers as his face tightened in anger. "Blasted! We were so close."

Dinnie grabbed Henry's arm. "Come on. Let's get you into the building and check out your head."

The four made their way back to the administration building and updated Captain Ruxton.

"He's left for the Port of Le Havre in Le Havre, France." The captain grabbed a book on the bookshelf entitled *Compagnie Générale Transatlantique (CGT) 1888 Departure and Arrival Schedules.* "They have these new ocean steamers that sail out of Le Havre for New York City. My wife's uncle just came back from there." His eyes opened wide. "Here's something. The *SS La Bretagne* departs for New York City on November twenty-fourth—that's in two days!"

"I'm sure he's headed for the Le Havre. Tumblety hails from New York. I'll need to send a cable to headquarters immediately. They'll have to contact Inspector Bill Melville, our Scotland Yard operative stationed in France."

"Do you think he'll get to him in time?" the captain asked.

"I'm sure he will, but that's not the problem," Dinnie explained. "Assistant Commissioner Anderson was right—Tumblety used the same escape route as the Irish extremists. The French government is quite sympathetic to the Irish cause in England, and if extremists are helping him, Melville might be powerless to apprehend him."

"It looks like the trip across the Atlantic is about eight or nine days," the captain interrupted as he read the arrival schedule. "The estimated arrival time into New York City is December second."

Froest stood up. "Thanks for your excellent assistance, gentlemen." He glanced at Dinnie. "It looks like we're headed back to headquarters tonight."

November 25. New York City, New York—Byrnes' Office.

Detective Crowley opened Chief Detective Inspector Byrnes' office door. "You asked for me, sir?"

"Come in, come in."

Crowley stopped in front of Byrnes' desk.

Byrnes looked up. "In a few minutes, Robert Pinkerton of the Pinkerton Detective Agency will be here to see me."

"Robert Pinkerton? The same Robert Pinkerton who had lunch with the president? That Robert Pinkerton?"

Byrnes grinned. "None other. He's had considerable correspondence with Scotland Yard and Commissioner Sherwood from the Canadian Dominion Police about Francis Tumblety. Apparently something has come up, but he will only speak to me privately about it. I told him I wanted you present, since you've been handling the Tumblety case for me. He agreed."

A man knocked on the door and popped his head in. "Sir, a Mr. Pinkerton is here to see you."

Byrnes stood up. "Send him in, Detective."

Robert Pinkerton entered the room

Byrnes smiled. "Robert! It's a pleasure to see you again."

"Thomas, it's a pleasure to see you, too," Pinkerton replied. "I believe the last time we saw each other was during the arrest of a number of Dynamiters bound for London."

"We botched their plans, didn't we, Robert?" Byrnes added enthusiastically.

Crowley watched the way Byrnes and Pinkerton greeted each other and noticed that they actually looked very similar, with their portly bodies, receding hairlines, and thick dark mustaches. "How do you do, sir." Crowley said with an outstretched hand.

Pinkerton shook his hand. "Fine. Nice to meet you, Detective."

"Come take a seat, Robert, and tell me what's so urgent." Byrnes sat.

Pinkerton took his seat. "You're aware of our New York Whitechapel murder suspect, Dr. Francis Tumblety."

Byrnes nodded.

"Well, he slipped through the grips of Scotland Yard, and he's going to land on our shores in one week," Pinkerton explained.

"What?" Crowley bellowed. "We heard he was arrested."

Pinkerton shrugged his shoulders. "He apparently sneaked out of the country. Keep in mind, they charged him with indecent assault against four young men, which is only a misdemeanor offense."

"Do they need us to arrest him when he pulls into port?" Crowley asked.

Pinkerton shook his head and glanced at Byrnes. "We have our hands tied. Tumblety hasn't violated any US laws nor is the offense he was charged with in London extraditable." He raised his finger. "However, if Tumblety finds his way into Canada, Commissioner Sherwood certainly does have the authority to send him back to England."

"That is a predicament, isn't it," Byrnes acknowledged.

"So, Assistant Commissioner Anderson requested I personally speak with you and ask if you'd be able to maintain Tumblety's whereabouts while we undergo a background investigation on him. Maybe we can dig something up. Now, they are not entirely certain this Dr. Tumblety is the Whitechapel killer, but he is a suspect nonetheless."

"We certainly can tail him, Robert," Byrnes said, glancing at Crowley and nodding to him.

"My partner and I will take care of it, Mr. Pinkerton," Crowley insisted.

"Excellent," Pinkerton replied. "He's on board the *Le Bretagne* out of La Havre, France, and will pull into the New York Harbor on December second." He glanced back at Byrnes. "There is one more request."

"Oh?"

"Dr. Francis Tumblety is a person of interest in Scotland Yard's Special Branch division. Therefore, they've classified the investigation and have asked if we could respect their decision to keep it confidential. San Francisco and Brooklyn didn't do so well in that regard."

"Certainly, Robert." Byrnes turned his gaze toward Crowley, who nodded back.

Pinkerton stood up to leave. "We will be in touch." He shook both their hands and left.

chapter twenty-seven

PRESENT DAY: Friday, October 20. Buffalo, New York—
the Anchor Bar.

"So, where are you taking us to dinner?" Dunham asked as
he and Riggs drove north on Main Street in downtown Buffalo.

"You told me you wanted a taste of Buffalo while you were
here, so we're going to eat at the home of the original Buffalo
chicken wings—the Anchor Bar!"

Dunham beamed. "Is that right? Great idea." He glanced
at Riggs. "I have a story about Buffalo wings. An old, know-it-
all boss of mine once told me Buffalo chicken wings actually
started in Cincinnati, Ohio. I said, 'Is that why they call them
Buffalo wings?' He never liked me for some reason."

Riggs snickered. "Well," he began, "the story goes that in
1964 the owners' son, nicknamed 'the Rooster,' was tending
bar, and had a few of his friends come to the restaurant late one
night. He asked his mother to prepare something for them to eat,
so she deep-fried chicken wing scraps in a homemade sauce. It
became such a hit that instead of saving all the chicken wing
scraps for soup, they put chicken wings on the menu. Today,
Buffalo wings are found on menus across the United States."

Dunham paused for a moment. "That sounds a bit more
convincing than my old boss' story."

Riggs nodded. "They have a number of different sauces they
use on the chicken wings, from the original, to barbeque, to
even a sauce called suicide. But watch out—the suicide wings
are hot!"

"Do they have anything else on the menu besides chicken wings?"

Riggs nodded. "Oh yes, it's an Italian restaurant, so they have a big selection."

"How about beer?" Dunham grinned. "As you know, I love a good craft brew."

"Oh, I remember," Riggs recalled. "I believe they have a selection of about thirty different types, from the common national types to a few specialty beers. My girlfriend was supposed to meet us there, but she can't make it. Her cousins are in town from San Antonio, so they went to Clifton Hill at Niagara Falls on the Canadian side. There's a bunch of tourist attractions there, like a wax museum and a Ripley's Believe it or Not museum."

Dunham pulled out his iPhone and checked his email. "No problem. I'll meet her someday." He glanced over to Riggs. "Maybe there's a wax display of Jack the Ripper. That'd be ironic."

Riggs nodded as he stopped at a red light. "How true. Wax museum displays seem so real."

"Actually," Dunham added, "I came across a ripperology article that suggested Jack the Ripper found inspiration for his murders by visiting Victorian Era wax museums. There was even one of these Chamber of Horrors wax museums in the East End district a few hundred feet from one of the murders, and that museum had, on display, wax representations of his murdered victims."

"Wow that sounds like a little more than just a coincidence," Riggs reasoned. "Did they have a wax model of Jack the Ripper?"

Dunham nodded. "Yes, and just after each murder happened, a wax model of the victim—mutilation and all—was displayed. Apparently, in the corner they had a model of Jack the Ripper looming over them." He shook his head, glancing out the window. "If the actual Ripper didn't visit that museum, immortalizing his handiwork, I'll eat my hat."

Riggs glanced over at Dunham. "You don't wear a hat."

"Yeah, well, I'm not a betting man," Dunham mumbled. "Still."

They reached the Anchor Bar, parked, and went in.

Dunham stopped inside the entrance and gazed at its unique décor. He grinned.

Hanging from the ceiling were six motorcycles and similar objects, and the walls were completely filled with framed pictures and photos of famous patrons as well as nautical objects such as harpoons and a large steering wheel from a sailboat. There was a large wooden bar that dominated the room.

"What a great-looking place," Dunham commented.

They sat at a table and perused the beer selections. The waitress arrived, and Riggs glanced up at her. "We'll take two Ellicottville Blueberry Wheats."

The waitress smiled as she wrote. "My favorite."

Riggs glanced at Dunham. "Are you going to try the wings?"

"But, of course." Dunham glanced up at the waitress. "I'll take the assorted wings. Does this include a number of different sauces?"

"Yes it does," the waitress replied.

Dunham glanced back at the menu. "Great."

Conversation continued as they received their drinks and meals.

"I certainly don't like the idea of waiting around until another woman on the donor list receives a gift of some sort, or worse yet, he kills one with a predictable pattern of behavior," Riggs said while wiping wing sauce from his face. "I wish we could be more proactive."

Dunham nodded. "I couldn't agree more, especially because he may hold off or could have even stopped his killing spree." He shook his head in frustration. "There is a solution to this, but it's just out of reach. I'm racking my brain trying to reach it." Dunham wiped his hands, then patted himself down. "And wherever that revelation is, I bet my notepad is with it. It seems I've lost another one."

Riggs grinned, wiped his own hands, and pulled out a new notepad for Dunham. "Don't worry. I've got your back."

"Thanks. I probably owe you a fortune for these notepads and pens," Dunham jested.

"You owe me nothing. Courtesy of the City of Buffalo Police Department." Riggs snickered. "I raided the supply storeroom. Captain Johnson knows."

Dunham picked up another chicken wing. "I truly appreciate all of the help you and Captain Johnson have given me." He took a bite of the chicken and immediately opened his eyes wide as tears leaked from his starry gaze, then he drank half his glass of water.

Riggs' chuckle echoed around them. "That would be the suicide wings. I told you they're hot. Drinking milk is the best way to stop the pain."

Dunham coughed. "I like it," he mumbled. "But I was just caught off guard." He took another, more cautious bite, eyes squinting.

"I say Mr. Bradbury knows exactly what we're looking for," Riggs continued, "but doesn't want us to know that he's aware of a Rosicrucian connection."

Dunham swallowed. "Maybe so, but I have a feeling he wants this guy caught just as much as we do. My guess is he'll pull through with something."

"Well, maybe he was just showing us his good side," Riggs reasoned. "But behind the kindly-gentleman smile just might be a ruthless sociopath."

Dunham's eyes widened. "That's it!" he yelled in recognition.

Riggs stared at Dunham. "What's it?"

"You just figured it out! We've been so focused on Mr. Hyde, we forgot about Dr. Jekyll."

"Sorry?" Riggs asked, confused. "You got me."

Dunham leaned toward Riggs. "Well, the original 1888 newspaper article that discussed Scotland Yard investigating an elixir-of-life motive for Jack the Ripper stated that the theory suggests the killer was a 'medical maniac'—keeping in mind our killer may be imitating this predecessor. If true, then we're dealing with a Dr. Jekyll and Mr. Hyde scenario. During the original killings, the play *Dr. Jekyll and Mr. Hyde* was showing at the well-to-do Lyceum Theatre, the same place Tumblety's old boyfriend—a man named Henry Hall Caine—Bram Stoker, and Oscar Wilde socialized."

"So, where does that leave us?"

"We may just find our killer enjoying some of his evenings at the local high-end theater." Dunham paused. "The anchor point for this serial offender is Buffalo, so what's the name of a prominent theater in Buffalo?"

"Shea's Theater, and it is just south of here on the same street, but closer to downtown Buffalo." Riggs checked his watch. "There's probably a show going on as we speak."

"After dinner, do you mind if we visit Shea's Theater?" Dunham asked.

"No problem. We're only five or ten minutes away." Riggs took a long drink, then beamed. "I love figuring things out, even when I have no idea I did."

chapter twenty-eight

1889: Wednesday, July 17. London, England—East End.

The police cab stopped, and Inspector Andrews peered out the window at a dark, drizzly early morning, only a few hours past midnight.

A rather large crowd of pedestrians had already formed with police constables holding them at bay.

Andrews climbed down from the carriage and made his way through the crowd. He noticed Inspector Reid and the surgeon, Dr. Phillips, standing over a motionless woman lying facedown on the pavement with her head toward the curb and her feet almost against the wall.

Blood could be seen around her neck and abdomen.

Reid glanced up at Andrews. "Good morning, Inspector Andrews. It looks like Jack the Ripper has decided to resume his terror after almost a year's hiatus."

Andrews stared at the body. "Good morning, Inspector Reid. And to think Scotland Yard took Inspector Abberline off the case last spring. A tad bit too soon, apparently." He turned toward the surgeon. "Dr. Phillips, does it look like the work of our Whitechapel fiend?"

"I believe so, Inspector," Phillips replied. "But I won't know for sure until I inspect the body. She does have a knife wound on her neck, and there are signs of abdominal mutilation indicating this is the same killer. Some things do not add up, though, as in the wounds seem to be much more superficial."

Reid interrupted. "Even though the doctor is taking a cautious approach, I'm convinced." He handed Andrews a clay smoking pipe and pointed an open hand to the body. "Let me introduce you to 'Clay Pipe Alice,' a known unfortunate." Reid nodded toward a lady in the crowd who was speaking with a constable. "According to an acquaintance of hers, this is Alice MacKenzie. The mutilation of another prostitute, in a similar way, and in the same district." He paused and turned toward Andrews. "This can't be a coincidence."

Andrews nodded, then tightened his lips. "If this is indeed another Jack the Ripper murder, why the big gap in time?"

"Hmmm."

"Maybe he decided to take the winter off?" Andrews shook his head. "And to think I believed a suspect long since gone from our shores was Jack the Ripper."

Reid's eyes opened wider. "Oh, that's right, I can certainly see why this murder has taken you by surprise, since you spent so much time investigating the American doctor. Francis Tumblety, wasn't it?"

Andrews nodded. "Yes, and there were many reasons why we were convinced of his guilt. You'd be surprised at how much the doctor hated women, especially prostitutes, and what he did to express his anger." He shook his head again. "I know more about his life than I care to."

"Come to think of it," Reid said tapping himself on the chin, "I recall headquarters sent you over to Canada last December to discover anything incriminating from his past. How did it go?"

Andrews tilted his head. "I brought back loads of documents. Inspector Jarvis and the Pinkertons assisted in collecting material all through the States for me, but we found nothing definitive to warrant an extradition." He paused. "Sad, really. Even if he wasn't the Ripper, he certainly decoyed impressionable young Englishmen."

"Maybe he'll slip up and find himself in jail," Reid added. "Those types always do."

"We can only hope," Andrews wished. "He has certainly been keeping a low profile lately, but his vices will catch up to him someday." Andrews pointed to the female body on the sidewalk. "As far as your newest victim, I'll not be assigned to assist you. I'm here because the assistant commissioner asked me to tell you face-to-face that he agrees that the Ripper is back

in business, and he has approved three additional detective sergeants and more police constables on the investigation."

Reid nodded. "Please tell him it's much appreciated and that
we have a couple of leads already. I'll wire headquarters with
the details."

Andrews shook Reid's hand. "It's been great working with
you this past year, Edmond."

"I enjoyed it as well, Walter. When you get to headquarters, please give Inspector Abberline my greetings. I hear his
investigation into the brothel on Cleveland Street is becoming
complicated."

"I certainly will send your greetings, and yes, Cleveland
Street is quite the scandal," Andrews said as he got back into
his police cab and left the East End.

New York City, New York—NYPD.

Chief Detective Inspector Byrnes sauntered up to Inspector
Crowley's desk and dropped a paper in front of him. Crowley
peeked up and grabbed the paper. "Oh, hi, sir. What's this?"

"Another Ripper murder just happened in East End London,
and our New York suspect is in Brooklyn," Byrnes replied.

Crowley began reading the letter:

*Dr. Tumblety, the alleged Whitechapel murderer. I had
seen several pictures of that notorious gentleman, which
were published in the Herald about the time he fled from
London, and the man sitting beside me closely resembled
them. . . . Well, to make a long story short, one thing led
to another, his every remark convincing me more and
more that my guess at his identity was correct, until at
last I asked him his name. "Dr. Francis Tumblety, you
may have heard it before," was his quiet reply. I replied
somewhat significantly that I had. He said he had been
greatly wronged by the press, and gave me a pamphlet
containing his picture and a number of notices of a book
he had just published. We parted at the Brooklyn end of
the bridge. Shortly thereafter the last Whitechapel murder
occurred in London [Alice McKenzie], and as Tumblety
was without doubt in Brooklyn at the time, he is evidently
unjustly suspected of being 'Jack the Ripper.'*

"Well, that answers that," Crowley replied.

Byrnes shook his head. "That fact that the murders stopped when Tumblety sneaked out of the country and they took their lead inspector off the case . . . I was starting to be convinced Tumblety was Jack the Ripper." He shot a glance at Crowley and grinned. "Of course, don't quote me on that."

"It looks like they're back to square one, sir," Crowley said.

chapter twenty-nine

Dunham and Riggs strolled into Shea's Theater about an hour after the completion of the evening's show and approached the first employee they saw.

Dunham took a step back as Riggs showed his badge. "Excuse me, my name is Detective John Riggs. Where might I find your manager?"

The employee pointed to a side office. "He's in his office, I think."

Riggs glanced over then nodded. "Thank you." They hastily made their way to the office, and Riggs knocked on the door.

"Come in," a voice replied from inside the office.

Riggs led the way in and flashed his badge again. "Hello, I was told you are the manager. My name is Detective John Riggs of the Buffalo Police Department, and this is Special Agent Dr. Edward Dunham of the FBI."

The manager stood up and shook their hands. "Nice to meet you. Henry Scarpena. Is something wrong?"

"Not at all," Dunham answered. "Actually, you might be able to help us out."

Scarpena gave a quick nod. "Do you mind following me around the theater as we speak? I need to do a final walk-through before I let my employees go. They would kill me if I was delayed."

"Oh, not at all," Dunham replied as they followed him out of the office and into the main area. "Mr. Scarpena, you have a beautiful place here."

"Thank you. It's the flagship of the theater chain," he proclaimed. "Designed to resemble the old opera houses and palaces in sixteenth- and seventeenth-century Europe. The original designers, Rapp and Rapp, out of Chicago, modeled it in a unique way. They combined both Spanish and French Baroque and Rococo styles."

"They did an excellent job," Dunham complimented.

Scarpena pointed to the walls and ceiling. "The interior was designed by the famous designer Louis Comfort Tiffany, and the place was open for business in 1926."

"I hope I don't have to take a test after this," Riggs joked.

Scarpena laughed. "I've been told I like to ramble. What can I do for you two?"

The trio stopped near a concession stand, its attendant cleaning and closing up for the night. Dunham noticed that she paused—either to rest while her boss was distracted, or to eavesdrop—as he cleared his throat and began.

"This will only take a few minutes, Mr. Scarpena. We're part of a task force in the case of the Niagara Falls serial killer, and we're following every possible lead. There is a possibility the offender enjoys the theater." He glanced up at a huge marble pillar. "Since Shea's Theater is the most prominent theater in the Buffalo area, we've decided to bring our investigation here first."

Scarpena nodded, lifting his shoulders proudly. "Well, if there's anything I can offer, I certainly will."

"Our suspect is around six feet two, dark eyes and dark hair, with an athletic build. He may or may not be wearing a mustache and goatee," Dunham explained. "He has most likely gone to more than one show in the last few months, and probably comes alone."

"Wow, that's not much to go on," Scarpena replied. "We have so many patrons."

"I've seen him," the concession attendant interrupted.

All three simultaneously eyed the young woman.

Dunham glanced over at Riggs then back at her. "Excuse me?"

Scarpena approached his employee. "Uh, this is Celine Faulks." Scarpena stared at Celine. "Did you say you've seen him, Celine?"

Celine nodded boldly. "Yes, just two weeks ago."

Dunham and Riggs approached her.

"Hello, my name is Special Agent Dunham from the FBI, and this is Detective John Riggs of the Buffalo Police Department."

"Hi, Celine," Riggs greeted.

Celine nodded.

"You seem to be very confident that you've seen our suspect. Why are you so certain?" Dunham asked.

"My brother followed him. Robbie's a senior in high school," Celine stated matter-of-factly.

"He followed him?" Riggs asked, surprised.

Celine nodded. "A month ago, this guy in the concession line next to mine gave me serious creeps. He was staring at me with these gray-color eyes like he had x-ray vision or something. He looked exactly like the description you gave Mr. Scarpena. Mr. Deckman told me he has been at Shea's a few times."

"Would you happen to know his name?" Riggs asked.

Celine shook her head. "No."

"Was there anything else unusual about him?" Dunham asked.

"Actually, yes," Celine replied. "He was wearing a huge diamond ring, and his cane had a huge diamond-looking crystal on its handle."

Dunham and Riggs glanced at each other, each clearly recalling that the attacker on the train had carried a cane.

Celine continued. "I was so concerned by him, I told my brother about it. Robbie is sort of this amateur detective, and he's good at it. Anyway, he was convinced this guy was the Niagara Falls Ripper, so we set up a tail on him the next time he showed up to Shea's—two weeks ago. Robbie and his two friends, Ralph and Kyle, followed the guy to his yacht."

"So you know his whereabouts!" Riggs blurted out in excitement.

Celine nodded.

"Where did he have this yacht docked?" Riggs asked.

"It's at the Erie Basin Marina, just a few minutes down the road on the river. It's the biggest yacht there at the end of the big dock, Robbie says. You can't miss it. I think he said the name was Magnum something."

"*Magnum Opus*?" Dunham asked.

"That's it!" she blurted out.

Dunham turned to Riggs, stunned, realizing Celine had just identified their suspect—and likely the killer.

"I'm leaving right now to meet my girlfriends at the Haunted Catacombs," Celine said. "I'll direct you there before I go."

"Thanks, Celine, but I know where it is," Riggs replied. "We'd like to speak to your brother, Robbie, though."

"He's home right now. I'll give you my parents' address and phone number." Celine grabbed a sheet of paper off the counter and began writing. "Robbie actually met the guy. When they tailed him, the guy was dropped off by a limo and went into his yacht. Robbie, Ralph, and Kyle sneaked onto the next yacht in order to peek in his windows. The security guard caught them and forced them to speak with the guy. The guy thought it was funny and told the security guard to let them go." She handed Riggs the piece of paper.

Dunham shook Celine's hand. "We cannot thank you enough, Celine."

Dunham and Riggs quickly left and drove straight to the marina.

"This is the break we've been waiting for!" Riggs said enthusiastically. "I texted Captain Johnson before we got in the car."

"Our next steps have to be well thought out," Dunham reasoned. "We don't want to lose this opportunity."

"For sure."

As they reached the marina, they noticed the yacht was still docked in its mooring and had all of its lights off. Riggs parked the car.

Dunham glanced around. "He's either sleeping or gone. Before we speak to this guy, we need to speak to Robbie." He looked at his watch. "It's quite late, but I'll give him a call."

"How about we set up round-the-clock surveillance on this yacht?" Riggs suggested as he grabbed his iPhone and dialed.

"Perfect." Dunham dialed Robbie's number and the line picked up on the other end. "Hello, this is Special Agent Dunham from the FBI. Is this Robbie Faulks?"

"Yes, it is," Robbie replied.

"Yes, we just spoke with your sister, Celine. I'd like to come and talk with you and your parents about your experience with a man you followed to his yacht two weeks ago. Are you available to speak tomorrow?"

"I'm available any time!" Robbie blurted out. "Celine just called to let me know you guys will be coming here. Actually, how's right now? My mom and dad are home."

Dunham nodded. "Excellent, the sooner the better."

Dunham and Riggs reached the Faulks' home and were greeted at the door by Robbie's father and mother.

"Thank you for letting us speak with Robbie. It's critical we do so," Dunham explained.

"Not at all," Mr. Faulks replied. "Anything to help. Celine told us what's going on, and this guy needs to be taken off the streets."

Dunham turned to Robbie. "Robbie, take us through the entire evening, and start right from the beginning. Tell us everything, even if you think you might get into trouble, because I promise you won't."

Robbie grinned, then gave Dunham and Riggs all the details of that evening.

"Was there anything unusual about this man?" Riggs asked.

"He seemed like a nice enough guy, especially since he let us go. He did have a weird room, though."

"What do you mean?" Dunham asked.

"We saw him in this room, which was painted light purple with flowers and diamonds all over it."

"Might they have been violet flowers?" Dunham asked.

"Could be . . . I have no idea what violets look like though." Robbie thought for a moment. "I take that back. They actually look like the bouquet of flowers Celine got two days ago."

Stunned, Riggs grabbed Dunham's arm, noticing Dunham had stiffened up by Robbie's news.

"They were the same light purple—or violet—flowers," Robbie continued. "She told me they were violets, and she has them at her apartment."

Dunham eyed Riggs. "Thank you very much, Robbie. This may be the break we've been looking for. Did Celine receive a gift with these flowers?"

"Yeah, that's where she's at right now. She got three free tickets to the Haunted Catacombs for tonight. She went with her two college roommates."

Riggs shot out of the house, cell phone to his ear.

Dunham started backing up to the door and pointed at Robbie's father. "Mr. Faulks, I need you to call Celine right now on her cell and tell her to get into a public area and find a security guard until the police arrive! Stay here, and we'll contact you within the next two hours!"

Dunham jumped into Riggs' moving car. Riggs hit the accelerator, leaving half the rubber from the tires behind, as he said, "Police're on their way. No one is answering at the Haunted Catacombs. It's just a recording of the times it's open. Dispatch is attempting to find another phone number to call. My guess is it's too loud for them to hear anyway. Good news is, we're only a few minutes away."

"The Haunted Catacombs—is it a haunted house attraction?" Dunham asked.

"Yes. It's one of the largest haunted house attractions in the area. It's set up in a huge building and has five separate haunted houses inside. It's usually packed with people, so it's going to be difficult to find her if she doesn't answer her cell. Hopefully we can have them close all of the attractions and evacuate everyone."

* * *

Celine and her two roommates, Ellen and Amy, gave their tickets to the lady behind the booth at the entrance and entered the main area of the Haunted Catacombs.

"You should get anonymous gifts more often, Celine!" Ellen said enthusiastically.

"You're not kidding!" Celine agreed and scanned the large room. "It's certainly busy tonight—and loud, too."

The area was filled with adults and kids finding their way to, and being in line for, each of the five haunted house attractions. It was dark and noisy with Halloween sounds of screams, menacing laughter, and the occasional noise of chainsaws.

"I bet Jared gave you the flowers and tickets," Amy guessed.

"What!" Celine yelled as she leaned over to Amy.

"I said I bet Jared gave you the flowers and tickets!" Amy repeated. "He's got such a crush on you!"

"He's a cutie!" Ellen added loudly.

They continued into the main area. Signature music themes from some of the best-known Halloween movies were emanating from speakers. In this particular spot, the theme from the movie *Halloween* was most audible. A huge, fifteen-foot, moving mechanical T. rex was attached to the wall between two haunted houses, making lots of noise.

"I love the foggy atmosphere at haunted houses!" Celine exclaimed as she noticed the fog hugging every section of the ground. She breathed deeply and took in the distinctive smell from the many smoke machines.

Mingled in the crowd were about a dozen paid actors dressed in frightening costumes trying their best to scare the customers, especially the women.

"Hey, check out the screaming lady!" Amy yelled.

A seemingly panicked woman was running at full pace across the main area with a monster right on her tail.

"Don't look now, but we've been noticed!" Celine yelled.

A surprisingly real-looking red devil with huge horns approached the three girls as if they were his prey. They grasped each other, screaming, but grinning from ear to ear.

Amy glanced at Celine. "Celine, take a picture of me with him!" Celine pointed her iPhone at Amy and the devil, and right on cue, he assumed a scary pose behind Amy, pretending to choke her.

After the camera flashed, Amy smiled at the red monster. "Thank you, Devil!"

"Would ya look at the size of that clown!" Ellen yelled, staring across the room. "He must be at least seven feet tall and easily five hundred pounds. That's not just the costume."

A massive man in a clown costume moved in a slow, methodical pace, seeming to bother no one.

"You can see why they use him," Celine replied. "Hey, he's going into the clown house. Let's go in!"

The three girls joined the line for the clown house. Once they were at the front of the line, the employee gave them 3-D glasses. Inside the house, the walls were painted psychedelic colors, and the glasses produced a three-dimensional look. Carnival music was playing in the background. Ellen was in front and nearly crushed Celine and Amy when she abruptly backed into them as a scary-looking clown rushed out of a hidden door, brandishing a bloody knife.

"Watch it!" Amy screamed.

They eventually made their way through the clown house and back into the main area. Celine thought she heard her cell phone tune mixed in with the corny carnival music as they were leaving the clown house. She reached down toward her purse, but Amy caught her hand and yanked her out the door, shouting, "Oh my God, let's go to the haunted forest next!" Celine laughed and grabbed onto Ellen's hand, and the three ran off toward the forest's entrance.

"Hi, Celine!" yelled a security guard.

Celine glanced toward him. "Oh, hi, Jeff. I didn't know you worked here!"

"The best job I ever had!" Jeff replied loudly. "I'm actually supposed to be at the front door! Where're you headed off to?"

"We're going to check out the haunted forest!" Celine replied enthusiastically.

"Have fun! I'll see you later!" Jeff waved, turned, and made his way toward the building's entrance.

Ellen grinned at Celine. "Oh, a little hottie! You are certainly the popular one lately, Celine!"

All three giggled at each other.

The entrance to the haunted forest was lined with trees and bushes mixed with scary objects, and actors dressed in various costumes suited for a haunted and dangerous forest. One was even dressed as a scary-looking tree with two hooked branches designed to grab passersby.

Ellen backed away from the moving tree.

"Don't worry, Ellen, his bark is worse than his bite," Celine joked.

Amy shook her head. "I hate your puns, Celine."

Celine and Ellen chuckled.

Black speakers located throughout the forest played sounds of hooting owls, crickets, and bodiless screams.

Upon entering, they noticed a path, which they assumed they were supposed to follow.

The first scary scene was in a tree-filled area with a werewolf in chains that seemed to barely hold him.

"He looks pissed," Amy commented.

As they carefully trod past the werewolf, he abruptly tried to attack them but was held off by the chains. Just at that moment, when all eyes were on the werewolf, another werewolf growled at them from behind, though he was chained like the first.

All three of the girls screamed in surprise and then rushed on forward.

"I'm not too fond of werewolves," Celine replied.

"Me neither," Amy agreed.

A third of the way through the haunted forest, just after the werewolf encounter, the trees opened up into an old-looking cemetery filled with coffins engulfed by ground-hugging fog. Some of the coffins opened up and robotic skeletons with decaying skin sat up, making eerie noises.

"Check him out!" Celine noticed at the opposite end of the cemetery a man dressed in black clothes and a black cape.

He had on a black wide-brim hat, which caused a shadow to cover the upper part of his face, but she could somewhat make out that he had a good deal of facial hair. He was leaning against a tree and looking directly at them.

As the girls crossed the cemetery, Celine noticed that the dark man didn't move from his location but kept on staring at them. Perhaps they weren't walking close enough to him for the actor to do his bit—they all seemed to act only as patrons walked into their respective vicinities. As the girls exited the cemetery, Celine peeked back and saw that the dark man was gone, and she supposed they would never know what scary trick the man in the cloak was to have performed.

The next area had a very long, creaky boardwalk with decrepit-looking artifacts lying all around. The girls passed a couple of old wooden cabins on both sides of the boardwalk. Surrounding trees created a forest atmosphere. A mechanized old forest witch with glowing red eyes was in one of the cabins, and she started moving and cackling from behind a huge black pot as they neared her area.

"Cool!" Ellen said excitedly as she broke away from her friends to get closer to the cabin.

Amy jogged forward to catch Ellen, while Celine lagged behind, farthest from the old-lady attraction; all three still had their backs to the adjacent cabin.

At that moment, Celine was forcefully grabbed from behind with a hand firmly covering her mouth. She was snatched off her feet and pulled behind the cabin, out of view from her friends. The man pounced on top of Celine, straddling her, still covering her mouth.

Celine opened her eyes, a little dazed, and recognized the man from the cemetery. She couldn't scream, nor could she move a muscle within his powerful grip. Her heart was beating fast; real fear gripped her now.

With his free hand, the man stroked the side of Celine's neck and slowly grabbed her by the throat, adding unbelievable pressure. He released the hand over her face and began choking her with the other hand as well.

Celine's fear now turned into panic. The powerful grip on her throat had an immediate effect. Just as she was blacking out, the large ceiling lights turned on and she saw the man's angry, intense, and unusually gray eyes glaring at her. She recalled these same eyes as being owned by the creepy guy from Shea's Theater—and then she passed out.

Moments later, Celine began to regain consciousness. Someone was leaning over her, tapping her cheek, and calling her name.

"Celine, can you hear me?"

She recognized voice as being vaguely familiar. Dr. Dunham. She opened her eyes, and his face came into focus.

"Hi, Celine. Don't move," Dunham ordered. "The medical people are coming over."

"What?" Celine asked, then she coughed. "What happened?"

Dunham gave a comforting smile. "We got here as fast as we could. Once the manager turned on the lights, we saw him on top of you through the trees. Detective Riggs and two other police officers leaped onto the man who attacked you, knocking him forward and off of you." He paused. "The place is now crawling with police officers. You're safe, Celine."

Jeff the security guard was just behind Dunham. "Celine, are you OK?"

Still coughing, she nodded. "Yes, I think so. Where are Ellen and Amy?"

"The police escorted them out of the building," Jeff answered. "They're OK. The police came in just after you guys entered the haunted forest. They ordered everything to be shut down and to begin an evacuation. We were looking for the manager when one of the police officers asked if anyone saw a Celine Faulks. I said I just saw you, so I brought them here as fast as I could."

Dunham glanced up at Jeff, smiled, and nodded. "And if it wasn't for you, young man, things might have turned out for the worse. You should be proud of yourself."

Jeff beamed.

Riggs approached Dunham and whispered in his ear.

Dunham turned and met Riggs' eyes, then gritted his teeth. His look betrayed his disbelief.

"Hi, Celine," Riggs said. "How do you feel?"

"I'm OK now, thanks to you guys."

"You need to stay here until the medics check you out," Riggs directed. "We'll be staying with you until they come. I hear they're in the building now. Also, we called your family and let them know you're safe. Thanks to your brother, Robbie, we made it here in time."

Dunham looked down at Celine. "Your brother is an impressive young man, Celine. He's naturally observant."

Celine nodded. "Did you catch him—" Celine paused and swallowed hard—"this guy?"

Dunham dropped his gaze and his face resumed a look of disbelief.

"As I just informed Dr. Dunham, the perpetrator escaped," Riggs answered. "The man fought everyone off and slipped into another one of the haunted houses. He's exceptionally powerful, and at the time there were too many people around to get off a safe shot. We have the police searching every nook and cranny." He put his hand on her shoulder. "Excuse me, Celine. I need to borrow Dr. Dunham for one second." He pointed to a spot ten feet away. "We'll be just over there."

Celine nodded as Jeff knelt down next to her.

Riggs eyed Dunham as they approached the spot. "He's definitely the same guy from the train who attacked Diane Barnett," he whispered. "He had the same clothes, facial hair, cane, and was just as athletic and powerful."

Dunham thought for a moment. "His method of attack was identical in both cases as well, and it's identical to the MO of our serial offender." He paused. "Besides, it's beyond coincidence that we predicted he'd be here if he wasn't the guy."

Riggs glanced over at the exit. "My guess is, if he slips out of the building and gets away, he'll make his way back to the yacht."

"Hopefully that doesn't happen," Dunham replied. "Do we have people at the marina?"

Riggs nodded. "Yes, I told them to keep their eyes open but to keep hidden even if he shows up. They're to arrest him only if he tries to leave."

"We need to get a search warrant ASAP. I don't want to give him any possible opportunity to dispose of precious evidence."

Riggs grinned. "Captain Johnson's already on it."

"Good. We'll stay here and keep on searching in the meantime."

They approached Celine, who was now sitting up.

Dunham bent down next to her. "Celine, did you get a good look at the man?"

She nodded. "Oh, yes. Those were the same crazy-looking gray eyes as the man I saw at Shea's. Just before I blacked out, the lights went on, and I got a good look at him. He was wearing a black mustache and goatee, but they looked fake to me."

"Soon we'll be asking you to identify him in a lineup. Will you do that for us?" Dunham asked.

"Of course."

"Also, the medics are required to take you to the hospital," Dunham explained, "and we've asked your mother to bring a change of clothes. We'll need you to give us these clothes. The attacker may have left sweat on them, and if he did, we may be able to obtain a sample of his DNA." Dunham glanced over her head. "Here come the medical personnel with a stretcher."

Celine touched Dunham's face and smiled. "Thanks for everything, Dr. Dunham. If it wasn't for you coming to Buffalo and helping out, I might not be here."

The medical personnel moved in front of Dunham and began to take care of Celine.

As Dunham backed up, he gave her a smile. Celine's thank you was the perfect medicine for what he believed to be his failure in saving his close friend's daughter, he thought. The feeling of peace then switched back to concern. There was still the problem of catching this killer.

Three hours later, Riggs received a phone call.

"Riggs," he answered then paused, listening. "Thanks, we're on our way." He popped his head up. "Dr. Dunham! The suspect just returned to his yacht. He didn't return to the marina in a vehicle. He walked."

"Let's go," Dunham replied.

Twenty minutes later, they entered the marina and found Captain Johnson standing next to his vehicle.

"Hello, Captain," Riggs said.

The captain turned around and nodded. "I just received verbal approval from the judge to execute the search warrant. The SWAT team's in place and ready for boarding."

Dunham looked over at the team. "Excellent."

Captain Johnson gave the go ahead to the team leader. From a distance, the three watched a coordinated approach by the SWAT team members.

Three team members boarded the yacht simultaneously from different positions, and within ten minutes the team had secured the yacht and arrested the suspect without incident.

"All clear," the team leader called over the radio.

Johnson started toward the yacht, followed by Dunham and Riggs. "It's time to meet this man face-to-face."

The team members escorted the suspect off the yacht and began a search. As Johnson, Dunham, and Riggs approached, the team leader finished reading the suspect his Miranda rights.

"That certainly looks like the guy on the train," Riggs whispered to Dunham, "with the exception of not having a mustache and goatee."

As the three approached, the suspect noticed Dunham. "Well, Dr. Dunham, how are you?"

"I don't believe we've met," Dunham replied.

The man smiled. "Your reputation has reached many circles. I've known about you for many years. My name is Michael Sullivan." He looked at Captain Johnson. "Now, what is the meaning of my evening's interruption? I am not accustomed to this kind of treatment."

"You're under arrest for the attempted murder of Celine Faulks, Mr. Sullivan," Johnson explained. "You'll have the opportunity to contact legal counsel at the station." Johnson nodded to the SWAT team members holding the suspect. "Take him away."

As the suspect was escorted to the SWAT vehicle and out of hearing range, Riggs turned toward Dunham and Johnson. "Detective Simpson watched him board his yacht and is convinced he arrived at the marina in the clothes he's wearing." He eyed Dunham. "If he is the attacker, he must have changed before he came back, meaning incriminating evidence is most likely hidden at a separate location."

Dunham nodded. "I think you're right. Also, Mr. Sullivan had a very calm demeanor throughout this entire episode. He clearly has no fear of us discovering anything on board his yacht."

Johnson shrugged his shoulders. "Well, maybe we'll find something he didn't plan on us discovering."

"At least we'll be able to acquire a sample of his DNA," Dunham replied. "The chain of events from Celine approaching us at Shea's Theater, to her brother leading us to Mr. Sullivan, then back to Celine being the killer's selected victim, is too much to be mere coincidence."

"We should call this entire case, 'Beyond Coincidence,'" Riggs reasoned. "What do you think?"

"The judge thought the same thing when he issued me the search warrant," Johnson added.

"Celine's pretty confident her attacker is the same man from Shea's Theater," Riggs said. "The problem is she passed out just seconds after the light turned on—along with his face being blocked by the mustache and goatee. The team of lawyers this guy can afford will pick up on that and exploit it in a heartbeat. I'm convinced he was the attempted murderer on the train, but I can't argue against a possible mistaken identity due to the facial hair."

"Well, we have enough to hold him," Johnson said. "Especially if the girl picks him out of a lineup. If worse comes to worst, and we don't find anything on the yacht, maybe the background investigation on him and a time line will reveal something." Johnson nodded confidently. "He's the offender, all right. Dollars to donuts the killings stop now, and that will also help our case."

Dunham shook his head. "We need to find his second location. It most likely has the weapon, his dark clothes, the gloves, and DNA evidence. I don't believe he knows we'll be looking for this place, so let's keep this information from him as long as we can."

Riggs looked out to the road. "At least Mr. Sullivan has unknowingly narrowed down our search of his secret location. It has to be in walking distance to the marina. We know he usually commutes in a limo, and I'm sure he doesn't want his driver to know where the place is." He paused. "I'll have our team look for security cameras in the area. Maybe he was picked up walking."

"We should check with the cab services, also," Johnson remarked. "Just in case he was dropped off a few blocks away."

Dunham eyed the back of the yacht. "His yacht is registered in Toronto. It looks like I'll be contacting the FBI's Canadian counterpart, the Canadian Security Intelligence Service, regarding a Mr. Sullivan."

chapter thirty

PRESENT DAY: Thursday, October 26. Buffalo, New York—Erie County District Attorney's Office.

Dunham, Riggs, and Johnson sat in the waiting room of Erie County District Attorney Alfred Stein's office. Johnson leaned over toward Dunham. "The district attorney is awesome. He's a well-respected attorney and very popular within the community."

"That's great to hear," Dunham replied.

Johnson eyed Stein's office door. "He's in his, I believe, tenth year as the Erie County chief prosecutor."

A thin, middle-aged man with a full head of dark hair entered the waiting room from the hallway. Carrying a large file, he walked right up to Captain Johnson, and as he stood, the man gave him a friendly handshake and a huge grin. "It's great to see you, Fred."

"You too, Dennis," Johnson replied.

The man faced Riggs. "Riggs, looking squared-away as ever."

"Thank you, Mr. Hanson," Riggs replied and shook his hand. "You're looking dapper yourself."

Johnson interrupted. "Dennis, I'd like you to meet Dr. Dunham." He faced Dunham. "Dr. Dunham, this is Assistant District Attorney Dennis Hanson—the best ADA in Buffalo!"

"Hardly, Fred, but thanks." Dennis Hanson turned toward Dunham, shook his hand, and stared at him. "We've been waiting to meet you, Dr. Dunham. Your reputation precedes you. I'm excited about this meeting."

Dunham smiled. "It's nice to meet you, Mr. Hanson."

A secretary entered the waiting room from the district attorney's office. "Hi, Dennis." The secretary eyed the others. "Gentlemen, Mr. Stein will see you now."

They filed into Stein's office.

Stein stood up from his desk and approached them.

Dunham registered that Stein was a very tall and imposing man, well over six feet.

Stein greeted Johnson with a big handshake, his other hand on Johnson's arm. "Fred, it's nice to see you again."

Johnson nodded. "It's nice to see you too, Mr. Stein."

The DA maintained eye contact with Johnson. "How's Alice?"

"She's keeping me fat with her awesome cooking, sir."

Stein laughed heartily. "That's the sign of a great wife."

Johnson pointed toward Dunham with an open hand. "Sir, I'd like to introduce you to Dr. Edward Dunham, senior chief forensic scientist at the FBI lab, and task force team member."

Stein approached Dunham and gave him a strong handshake and a huge grin. "It's nice to finally meet you, Dr. Dunham, and we certainly appreciate you joining the task force."

"It's a pleasure, sir," Dunham replied. "I'm honored to be a part of this task force."

Stein glanced at Riggs and shook his hand as he addressed Johnson again. "Fred, I appreciate you having Detective Riggs here keeping my office updated on the case, especially since the arrival of Dr. Dunham." He glanced back at Dunham. "Because this case has created national attention, the governor has asked me to be involved, but Dennis will be handling all the details. As you know, he's the best prosecutor in the office. Everyone, please take a seat."

Hanson glanced at a file on his lap as everyone seated themselves. "It looks like Mr. Sullivan is a dual US/Canadian citizen, so there shouldn't be any issues specific to citizenship, but I see he's seventy-two years old. This is clearly a weakness in our case, and we must address it." He looked at Johnson. "Did Miss Faulks make a positive ID in the suspect lineup this morning?"

Johnson nodded. "Yes she did, and she feels confident Sullivan is our man."

"In her statement, she said that the attacker had on a mustache and goatee. Assuming this was a disguise, Sullivan's defense team will surely highlight this at the arraignment," Hanson continued.

"Also, five of our police officers," Johnson pointed at Riggs, "including Detective Riggs here, have made a positive ID as to Sullivan being the perpetrator of the Arcade train attack on Officer Barnett."

"Was the ID from a lineup?" Hanson asked.

Johnson nodded. "Yes. Every one."

"Good," Hanson replied. "The volume of positive witness IDs should trump his old age, at least in the arraignment this afternoon." He raised his eyebrows. "But the grand jury indictment later on—that will be an entirely different matter."

"Understood," Johnson replied.

"As expected," Hanson continued, "he's got a powerful legal team, the Looney Law Firm from here in Buffalo. They're expensive and good, especially Jack Looney." Hanson paused. "Has any new evidence been uncovered from the suspect's yacht yet?"

Riggs shook his head. "Nothing linking him directly to the attempted murders or the previous murders, but the search is only in the preliminary stages."

Hanson nodded. "You state here that you believe he most likely has a secret hideout where he keeps his gear for accomplishing the murders."

"That's right," Johnson replied. "When he returned to the marina, just after the Haunted Catacombs attempted murder three hours earlier, he was wearing a different set of clothes." He shook his head. "So far, we've been unsuccessful in discovering its location, but there's a lot of ground to cover."

"If he is the offender," Stein interrupted, "then Sullivan having a secret hideout makes sense. But I can see Mr. Looney arguing that a more plausible explanation is a case of mistaken identity." He looked down at his own file. "It says here this Michael Sullivan is out of Toronto, Canada. Do we know any more about him?"

Dunham shook his head. "Not yet, sir. Information exchange across the border is relatively slow, but the Canadian authorities tend to be very supportive."

Hanson glanced at Stein. "Sir, I recommend we charge him with the two incidents of attempted murder, and hold off on charging him with the serial killings until that part of the case is a little more solid. The strongest card we hold is the fact that Dr.

Dunham here predicted his move on two separate occasions, which then came to fruition. This is beyond coincidence."

Johnson, Dunham, and Riggs glanced at each other and grinned, all recalling Riggs' nickname for the investigation.

Hanson continued. "This is a direct connection to the attempted murders, but only indirectly to the actual murders. We can add these charges once we've collected enough direct evidence to support Dr. Dunham's persuasive circumstantial evidence. The Niagara Falls serial murder case is now a national news item—actually an international news item if we take into account Canada—so we don't want to make any embarrassing mistakes." He grinned. "Also, we'd like to keep our relations with Canada positive, and if this wealthy guy turns out to be someone important to them, things may go south quickly."

Captain Johnson raised his hand. "Do you think we have a good chance that bail will be denied at the arraignment?"

"With this being such a serious offense and Sullivan living on a yacht with the ability to make it to Canada on a moment's notice, absolutely. We have a very no-nonsense judge. We'll definitely play the 'fear of absconding' card. Awarding a high bail is meaningless since he's a multimillionaire. Again, our advantage now is we don't have to try the case at the arraignment, but when the grand jury finds out a seventy-two-year-old beat up five or more strapping police officers on two separate occasions, our problems begin."

Stein stood up. "Well, let's not keep you gentlemen from fixing this problem."

Everyone else stood.

"Just keep us in the loop," Stein requested. "Dennis will do the same."

Johnson nodded. "Thank you, Mr. Stein, we certainly will."

chapter thirty-one

Riggs rushed into the task force situation room toward Captain Johnson and Dr. Dunham, who were engrossed in a conversation.

Johnson's head popped up. "What's up, Riggs?"

"Good news—bail was denied."

"Great, but why the glum face?" Johnson asked.

Riggs sat down next to them. "Captain, I think there has to be something wrong with Sullivan's credentials."

"How so?"

Riggs paused. "Even though it says he's seventy-two, my bet is he's no older than forty. The guy who threw me across the room and ripped through all those cops was not geriatric in the least bit, and yet I assure you, the man we arrested is the attacker."

"It's not a mistake," Dunham insisted. "Sullivan's birth certificate says it, and the Canadian authorities confirmed it."

Riggs dropped his head. "No jury will ever believe a seventy-two-year-old man threw around five or six healthy, young police officers, on two separate occasions, especially when the famous attorney Jack Looney does his lawyer thing on the jury."

"It's not impossible," Johnson remarked. "There've been other tough seventy-two-year-olds. Jack Lalanne, the godfather of fitness, lived to ninety-six, and he could've kicked all our asses, even in his eighties. Come to think of it, maybe we should give the DA a few Jack Lalanne videos as evidence."

Dunham interrupted, eyeing Riggs. "To further add to the confusion," he paused, "although, it just might help, the results of the DNA test on Sullivan are back." He pulled out a document. "In the remarks section, Dr. Chesterfield, the chief forensic scientist at the Erie County forensic lab, wrote:

"Telomeres are specialized DNA strands at the ends of linear chromosomes functioning to protect the chromosome from recombination and fusion during cell division. The 'Telomere Hypothesis' states that there is a continuous shortening of the telomere throughout the life of the organism. Telomeres are like the plastic ends of shoestrings—and through time, they wear down. Because of this, telomere degradation can be used as a forensic tool in order to estimate the age of a particular subject.

"Genetic testing and fingerprinting analyses have confirmed our subject to be Michael Sullivan, but at the same time a major discrepancy has been observed. The age of the subject is 72 years, which conflicts with the real-time PCR analysis of telomere degradation. Based upon analysis regression, a man of 72 years should have a telomere length consistent with his age, but our subject has a telomere length consistent with males around the age of 20. A value of 0.4, as what our subject has, has never been observed in a subject over the age of 28. The results are highly suggestive of a statistical anomaly, which would account for the discrepancy.

"It's signed,

F. E. Chesterfield, PhD
Chief Forensic Scientist
Erie County Central Police Services (CPS)
Forensic Laboratory"

Dunham glanced up at Johnson and Riggs. "This guy's an enigma; although, having the telomere lengths of a twenty-year-old does conform to the physical prowess he displayed."

"I still believe this physical prowess issue is going to be our Achilles heel, even if he's Mr. Athletic," Riggs predicted. "The district attorney's office will not like it if we can't find additional evidence. The only other thing we have connecting him to the attempted murders are Dr. Dunham's theories and predictions—awesome as they are."

"Interestingly," Johnson added, "he has requested a dialogue with Dr. Dunham—and Dr. Dunham only. He doesn't even want his legal team around."

Riggs thought for a moment. "At the marina, he told us he's known about Dr. Dunham for years." He glanced at Dunham. "I think he's intrigued with you, Dr. Dunham."

Dunham raised his eyebrows. "It does sound like he likes the idea of a cat-and-mouse game with me. Hopefully we can take advantage of this. Maybe I can get him to slip up a bit. I don't want him to know we're on an all-out search for his secret location though. I'd hate to have the place suddenly get torched."

"Agreed," Johnson interrupted. "No time like the present. Let's set up the meeting and see where it leads us. Now, he and his legal team don't know of our linking him to the Niagara Falls Serial Killer Case yet, so let's keep him thinking he's arrested only for the attempted murders."

Sullivan was escorted in arm and leg shackles into an empty interview room by two deputy sheriffs, and placed in a chair situated next to a small table. He stared into the large mirror and gave a small grin, indicating that he knew full well that law enforcement officers were observing him from the other side.

Johnson elbowed Dunham. "Talk about enjoying the moment."

"You're right, Dr. Dunham," Riggs agreed. "He is in the mood for a cat-and-mouse game."

"Let's hope he inadvertently reveals something we can use against him," Dunham added. "I want him feeling confident and in control. I'm going to stroke his ego so much that he'll want to give us something to work with."

Dunham strolled into the interview room, then took the chair opposite Sullivan.

Sullivan glanced up and gave a big, confident grin. "Hello, Dr. Dunham. We meet again."

Dunham nodded. "Hello, Mr. Sullivan. Are you sure you don't want your lawyer present? Anything you say in our discussion may be held against you."

Sullivan shook his head. "I'm an innocent old man, Dr. Dunham. By now you must have discovered my age. My lawyer actually commented to me that I should be outraged at this treatment, but to be honest, I'm enjoying the experience. As I said at the marina, I've known about you for quite some time. I enjoy real-life mysteries—and your name always pops up as a success story. The Niagara Falls serial murder spree has received an unusual amount of attention, even in Canada." He paused. "I suppose it's one of the reasons why I've extended my Buffalo vacation."

"Why are you in Buffalo?" Dunham asked.

"It's more that I enjoy traveling in my yacht on the Great Lakes, really," Sullivan explained. "I usually hit the bigger cities, from Detroit at the west end of Lake Erie, to Kingston on the east end of Lake Ontario."

"I've always wondered how ships get from Lake Ontario to Lake Erie when Niagara Falls sits in between. How is that?" Dunham asked.

"Through the Welland Canal," Sullivan explained. "It bypasses Niagara Falls and Niagara Gorge. It's an all-day trip through the canal. Buffalo's one of my favorite stops. When I'm here I enjoy the theater and the fine cuisines this city has to offer. I stayed a little longer this year because I've become somewhat interested in the Buffalo Bills."

Dunham peeked down at a file. "I see you're a dual citizen, Mr. Sullivan. One of the companies you own out of Toronto is an antique business."

"Yes, I have a passion for old things, especially objects from the Victorian Era. Early on I realized the only way to make money in this business is to handle high-end antiques." He tilted his head. "It takes money to make money, Dr. Dunham, so once I became wealthy it just made me even wealthier. I now have managers who operate my businesses, so I can enjoy the pleasures in life."

Dunham glanced up at Sullivan. "Mr. Sullivan, for being seventy-two-years-old, you seem very healthy and spry. What's your secret for such vigor?"

Sullivan laughed. "Oh, I feel every year, but besides a strict regimen of healthy food, I take long walks," he leaned forward. "Which was what I was doing just before being arrested at the marina."

"Of course," Dunham replied. "Can anyone corroborate your story? Did you stop at a convenience store, or speak to anyone?"

"No," Sullivan answered, then sat back. "I'm somewhat of a recluse and don't really enjoy conversing with strangers. It shouldn't be a problem." Sullivan grinned. "My attorney, Mr. Looney, has just received word that the charges against me do not reflect your true agenda, and that I'm actually a suspect, or person of interest, in the Niagara Falls Serial Killer Case. Am I correct?"

Dunham, although slightly taken aback by his discovery, maintained a relaxed exterior. "That should not be a surprise, since all attacks on women in the western New York area within the last few months immediately raise flags." He paused. "We've considered this possibility, but nothing more. Our focus is on the attempted murders."

Sullivan smiled as if he knew more than he was saying. "Sure, Dr. Dunham. If you say so." He paused for a moment. "I'm curious, though. Since we're on the subject of serial killers, do you believe your past success at discovering their identities is because of your intelligence, or your education, or even your unique training?"

Dunham thought for a moment and shrugged. "It's probably a mixture of all of those things, plus a little luck."

"Oh, I highly doubt luck is involved," Sullivan replied confidently. "And actually I doubt it has anything to do with intelligence, education, or unique training. After all, some of your fellow law enforcement officers must equal or even surpass you in a number of those traits." He smiled. "Although I do see unusually high intelligence in your eyes. No, it has nothing to do with learning or environmental influences."

"What else could there be?" Dunham asked.

Sullivan grinned. "I suggest that you have successfully tapped into a reservoir of hidden knowledge in the human brain—undiscovered by most everyone else. I would love to speak to you in depth about it, in order to find out how you did this without the assistance of ancient knowledge." He paused. "Maybe you read some kind of ancient text in the past? Have you?"

"Not that I can recall," Dunham replied. "All this sounds very Gnostic, Mr. Sullivan. It sounds like you're a student of Plato or Pythagoras."

Sullivan nodded. "Excellent, Dr. Dunham. I am, but the Truth predates these men. It predates even the seven sages of the ancient Greeks, including Thales of Miletus—the first Greek student of the ancient Egyptians."

Dunham stared at his notepad. "I'm an empiricist, Mr. Sullivan. A student of Aristotle, if you will."

"Ah, the flaw of induction," Sullivan argued. "Just because an answer best follows the path of logic does not make it the truth. Ignore what I say if you must, Dr. Dunham, but sooner or later you'll realize I'm correct. Somewhere in your past, you've read a special manuscript."

Dunham tilted his head, recalling a time when he was around twelve, when he did indeed read old texts for an elderly neighbor scholar going blind. He shrugged it off as nonsense. "It sounds like you have an in-depth knowledge of this particular flavor of Gnosticism." Dunham paused. "Rosicrucianism—are you a student of the philosophy, Mr. Sullivan?"

Sullivan's eyes widened as if Dunham had struck a nerve, but then he glanced away. "Oh no, I'm merely well-read." He glanced around. "I'm a bit tired. If you don't mind, I'd like to retire to my temporary quarters."

"Of course. Thank you, Mr. Sullivan."

Dunham left the room and approached Johnson and Riggs. "He will definitely be using the age card for his defense." He watched the guards take Sullivan away. "He's planned it like this all along."

Riggs shook his head. "Did you notice how he's now acting the part of a true seventy-two-year-old? He certainly took his time getting into and out of that chair. My guess is he's going to dye his hair salt-and-pepper for the grand jury."

Dunham thought for a moment. "We foiled two separate murder attempts by the serial offender based upon the assumption that his motive was the Rosicrucian belief in an elixir of life." He stared at Johnson. "A very convincing set of circumstances. We have now connected a murder suspect with this belief. Mr. Sullivan may have incriminated himself with his reference to hidden knowledge—at least in my mind."

"So, what's this tapping into hidden knowledge mumbo-jumbo?" Johnson asked.

"Students of Rosicrucianism believe that both trees of the Garden of Eden—the Tree of the Knowledge of Good and Evil, and the Tree of Life—symbolize total attainable knowledge, and God kicking Adam and Eve out of the Garden after tasting a fruit from one of the trees symbolizes man's exclusion from attaining this knowledge by himself. Hence, hidden knowledge."

"Wow, I think I understand what you're saying," Johnson mused.

Dunham continued, "In other words, all human beings have inherited in their brains total knowledge of the universe, yet no one can tap into this knowledge thanks to original sin—except if one reads a certain ancient book. I believe our serial offender's quest is for the elixir of life, i.e., the Tree of Life, which represents immortality. This quest is the same quest Jack the Ripper suspect Francis Tumblety may have been on. Because I've been successful in understanding evil, or serial killers, Sullivan believes I've tasted fruit from the Tree of Knowledge of Good and Evil, and he wants to know how I unlocked this secret." He shook his head. "He believes I've read from this book."

Johnson laughed. "The jury will most likely get lost in those details. There's nothing like direct evidence presented in court, so we need to find this secret location, and soon."

"Where are they holding Sullivan?" Dunham asked.

"The Erie County Holding Center," Johnson answered. "It's a maximum-security detention center with an inmate capacity of up to six hundred eighty. More than twenty thousand inmates are processed through the holding center annually. Inmates incarcerated for serious crimes, such as Sullivan's, are transferred from the courthouse to the holding center via an underground tunnel, which travels underneath Delaware Avenue."

Dunham's eyebrows rose. "That's interesting. An actual tunnel?"

"There's a little bit of intriguing history there, as well," Johnson added. "It was constructed in 1880 to limit the opportunity for dangerous criminals to escape while being transferred. When President William McKinley was assassinated in Buffalo in 1901, the tunnel was used to transfer the anarchist assassin, Leon Czolgosz, away from an angry mob of citizens calling for a lynching."

"That's good to know," Dunham said.

Riggs grinned and placed his hand on Dunham's shoulder. "You surprised him in that interview, Dr. Dunham. I bet Sullivan just realized he had better not get too cocky with his plan."

chapter thirty-two

PRESENT DAY: Tuesday, October 31. Buffalo, New York—Buffalo Police Headquarters, Task Force Situation Room.

Riggs rushed into Johnson's office. "Sullivan's defense attorney will be giving a press conference in two minutes! It was on a breaking news broadcast."

Johnson lifted his hands up in disgust. "Amazing." He tilted his head. "Actually, I'm not surprised. Looney will do anything to get publicity. Not only is he a great lawyer, he's a great businessman." Johnson pointed behind Dunham. "Dr. Dunham, would you hand me that remote behind you?"

Dunham did so, and Johnson turned on his TV as Riggs continued. "That's not all. It looks like the press knows we're interested in him in the Niagara Falls Serial Killer Case. The reporter prefaced the announcement of the press conference with Sullivan's apprehension as being the first big break in the serial killer investigation."

Johnson shook his head. "Just great. Exactly what the district attorney's office did not want. Of course they'll blame our department for leaking this."

"Looks like its starting," Riggs interrupted as he stared at the TV. "Jack Looney certainly looks like he's enjoying being in front of all those cameras on the steps of the courthouse."

Onscreen, Looney tightened his expensive tie and glanced around. "Good afternoon. My name is Jack Looney of the Looney Law Firm, and we are representing esteemed millionaire

Michael Sullivan. My client has been implicated in, and is being charged with, the separate attacks of two women in the locally well-known Arcade Mystery Train and Haunted Catacombs cases. But these assault and battery cases are not the reason why you've joined me at this press conference today."

"This guy's smooth," Riggs observed.

"As the press has been reporting all day," Looney continued, "my client has also been implicated in the notorious Niagara Falls Ripper Case. Apparently, Mr. Sullivan is the very first suspect in the brutal murders of six innocent women in and around the Buffalo area."

"Notice how he's hooking his audience," Johnson remarked. "He knows we haven't officially labeled him a suspect, so he carefully phrases it to sound like we have, but correctly states it came from the press. Brilliant guy. He wants this national news, and he's going to get his wish."

Looney continued. "With regard to my client's implication in the Niagara Falls Serial Murder Case . . . there is no case. And to even suggest Mr. Sullivan—a wealthy seventy-two-year-old millionaire—to be involved in such an atrocious series of mutilations borders upon incredulity." He paused and scanned the crowd, clearly enjoying the fact that he had everyone's undivided attention. "Now, with regard to the two formerly mentioned assault and battery cases, my client will be pleading not guilty. In addition to this, I will be requesting District Attorney Stein's assistance regarding Mr. Sullivan's bail. Being an elderly gentleman of seventy-two years of age, his requirement for medical care, such as a unique regimen of medicines and physical therapy, will clearly not be satisfied in county jail."

Dunham nodded. "Looney is a smart attorney. He's chosen his words carefully. Notice how he's speaking directly to the DA's office and pressuring them to drop the case prior to it reaching grand jury."

"How so?" Riggs asked.

"Look how he elaborated on the point about getting his bail dropped because of old age. He's telling the prosecutors he knows that the weakness of this case is a lack of physical evidence, and he's putting them on notice that his plan is to publicly embarrass the duly-elected DA. My guess is we'll be hearing from the ADA to get additional physical evidence or they will drop the case."

Johnson's secretary knocked on the door. "Dr. Dunham? You have a phone call from a Ryan Stanton. It's on line three."

Dunham jumped up. "Maybe this'll help." He crossed over to his desk and answered the phone. "Dr. Dunham."

"Hello, Dr. Dunham, this is Ryan Stanton. I promised I would call you up once I received the results of the DNA analysis involving the London Jack the Ripper case."

"Thank you, Mr. Stanton. Is there anything interesting?"

"Yes, and the ripperology world is buzzing with activity," Stanton replied. "The results are quite unusual. None of the suspects we tested match the DNA sample found in the Ripper victim, including the body found in Francis Tumblety's grave. But here's where it gets strange—Francis Tumblety's father and brother are near-perfect matches with the DNA found in the victim! The analyst stated that the male DNA sample found in the Ripper victim's abdominal region must have been no greater than one generation from Tumblety's father and brother. Since the DNA sample was from the Y-chromosome, the killer could only have been male, and a male Tumblety. The only conclusion that can be deduced is Francis Tumblety is the Whitechapel fiend, especially since he was a suspect."

"Yet you just said the body in Tumblety's grave did not match," Dunham interrupted.

"Exactly, and this leads to the question of whose body is in Tumblety's grave? The body, which we all agree is the remains of Francis Tumblety, shows no genetic relationship with his own family."

"That is strange," Dunham agreed.

"The only plausible option we can think of is that Francis Tumblety was Jack the Ripper, yet the remains in Rochester, New York, are not that of Tumblety. Apparently, Tumblety's body never made it from St. Louis to Rochester in 1903. His death certificate certainly states he died in St. John's Hospital in St. Louis, though, and he did use the same alias he'd used while escaping from England during the Ripper murders. "

Dunham thought for a moment. "Maybe he faked his death in 1903."

"That's a thought," Stanton replied. "He was very eccentric and wanted so much to be left alone in his old age."

At that moment, a far-fetched idea came into Dunham's head, so bizarre that he decided to keep the details to himself for the moment. "Mr. Stanton, I wonder if you could have a DNA test comparison of the sample in the original Jack the Ripper victim with one more sample."

"That could easily be done."

"Great. I'll have someone from the lab here send it over."

"Who's the subject?"

"His last name is . . . was Sullivan," Dunham answered.

"You're kidding, right?"

"Why?"

"Dr. Dunham, the name Sullivan was one of Francis Tumblety's aliases in his early years. A Michael Sullivan."

Dunham's jaw dropped, almost causing him to fumble the phone. Could this far-fetched idea be true? The wild thought made complete sense.

"What have you discovered, Dr. Dunham? Who was this Mike Sullivan, and where is his grave site? Have you gotten yourself into ripperology or something?"

Dunham realized that Stanton hadn't connected the Sullivan name with the Niagara Falls Serial Killer Case.

"If you can be patient for just a little longer, I'm going to purposely withhold the identity of this person for objectivity's sake. I'll tell you everything once the comparison is done."

"Fair enough," Stanton accepted. "But my interest is piqued!"

"Thank you, Mr. Stanton."

"So, have you made progress on the Niagara Falls Serial Killer Case?"

"Yes, we have a possible person of interest, but we're not out of the woods, yet. If you haven't seen it on the news yet, you will."

"Outstanding!" Stanton replied.

"You've been very helpful, Mr. Stanton, and thank you."

"Once I receive word on the DNA test, Dr. Dunham, I'll call you."

Dunham nodded. "Thanks, Mr. Stanton. It is a time-critical issue."

chapter thirty-three

Dr. Dunham saw Ryan Stanton enter the task force headquarters. He overheard Stanton apprehensively mumbling to the secretary something about being expected to call rather than just showing up, and Dunham rescued the man from his own ramblings by calling across the room, "Mr. Stanton, what an unexpected surprise." He ambled over and extended his hand in greeting to the ripperologist.

Stanton relaxed and smiled. "Hello, Dr. Dunham, the DNA results are in, and I thought I should speak with you personally about them."

"Excellent, let's go to my office." Dunham escorted Stanton to his office, and they sat.

Stanton glanced around the room nervously. "I apologize for not calling first, but I decided to drive straight here. The results are—" he paused—"unbelievable."

Dunham perked up. "That's fine. What did you find?"

Stanton glanced down at his briefcase. "OK, the DNA results." He pulled out a folder and handed it to Dunham. "This Sullivan DNA sample you sent me is a perfect match with the Jack the Ripper of 1888." He shook his head. "It's a near match with Francis Tumblety's father and brother."

Dunham popped his head up and stared at Stanton for a moment, then he examined the results.

Stanton leaned forward. "It can't be a Tumblety descendent either." He shook his head again. "It can only be him!"

Dunham said nothing and continued to review the results.

"It looks like you found Francis Tumblety and Jack the Ripper!" Stanton blurted out.

Dunham sat back in his chair and stared at the ceiling. "Unbelievable." He maintained a blank expression.

Stanton eyed Dunham. "Dr. Dunham, I've been catching the news on your Niagara Falls serial killer suspect. His name is Michael Sullivan." He paused and stared at Dunham. "It's his DNA sample, isn't it."

Dunham paused for a moment. "Yes."

Stanton sat back in his chair, dumbfounded. "So Tumblety found the elixir of life." His expression also remained blank.

Dunham shook his head. "It certainly looks that way."

Stanton glanced back. "No one's going to believe this."

Dunham nodded. "Aside from the absolute shock of the realization that we have an immortal man on our hands, note the quagmire I'm in. Sullivan . . . or Tumblety, is the Niagara Falls Ripper, but there's no physical evidence that links him to any of the western New York murders, yet we have a direct link to the 1888 London murders."

"I see."

Dunham rocked back in his chair again. "The Niagara Falls serial killer is not a copycat Jack the Ripper serial killer—he is Jack the Ripper." He shook his head again. "No jury in the world will believe this, regardless of the DNA evidence."

"Especially when DNA analysis is based upon statistical probabilities," Stanton interrupted. "Even though the DNA results give a billion, or even trillion, in one chance of it being someone other than Sullivan's." He sat back.

"Exactly."

Stanton continued. "The choice is either accept improbable odds or accept a science-fiction-type conclusion." He paused. "Someone truly being immortal."

"Sullivan's lawyers will definitely exploit this," Dunham reasoned aloud.

Stanton shook his head and smiled. "Francis Tumblety actually created an elixir of life." He paused for a moment. "He made a true Ripper's Hellbroth."

Johnson and Riggs hurried into Dunham's office.

"There you are," Johnson blurted out. "We can't have the meeting without you."

Dunham glanced at his watch. "Oh, sorry. Captain Johnson, this is Ryan Stanton, the ripperologist Riggs and I met in Rochester. Ryan, this is Captain Johnson, head of the task force."

The two greeted each other.

"Do you remember Detective Riggs?" Dunham asked.

Stanton shook Riggs' hand. "Yes. Hello again, Detective Riggs."

Riggs gave a quick nod. "Hello, Mr. Stanton."

"Ryan has been updating me on new discoveries in the original Jack the Ripper case," Dunham explained. "I was hoping something might help us out, but nothing yet."

Stanton glanced over at Dunham. His quick change of expression conveyed that he understood that Dunham wasn't ready to discuss the elixir of life revelation with anyone else. "I'll help in any way I can," he said.

Johnson nodded to Stanton then quickly ignored him. "I just called for a break, so everyone's going to meet back in the task force room in twenty minutes. Let me update you on what you've missed."

As Johnson spoke with Dunham, Dr. Dunham noticed Stanton glancing over at his desk, eyeing a small gift-wrapped package he'd received but hadn't yet gotten a chance to open. Stanton glanced back up at Dunham and interrupted Johnson, who was still speaking. "Excuse me, excuse me."

Johnson halted and stared, irritated, at Stanton. "Yes?"

"Excuse me," Stanton repeated. "Where did this gift come from?"

Dunham picked up the gift. "Well, because of our first meeting with you in Rochester, we recently made a visit to Jonathan Bradbury, the president of the local Rosicrucian organization, in hopes that he could shed some light on our investigation." He shrugged his shoulders. "Apparently, he enjoyed our meeting, and he sent me this gift yesterday. In the note he thanked me for the visit and wished us the best in the investigation. He's a kind man."

"Even though it was very interesting to be in Bradbury's mansion and to be served by a butler, it hasn't helped us out yet with the case," Riggs explained.

"Maybe it has," Stanton remarked.

260 | Michael L. Hawley

Johnson quickly shifted his body toward Stanton in surprise. "Oh?"

"Yes," Stanton replied. "The address on the gift is interesting—actually beyond coincidental, really."

"Why is that, Mr. Stanton?" Dunham asked.

"The address says the gift contents came from Townsend Street. Francis Tumblety used Townsend as an alias when he jumped bail in 1888 during the Ripper murders, and when he checked into a hospital in 1903 to die."

Dunham's eyes widened, and he shot a look at Johnson and Riggs. "Is Townsend Street within walking distance to the marina?"

Riggs' attention became acute as he recognized the implications to the question. "It certainly is!" He pulled out his iPhone. "Let me pull up the map."

Dunham grabbed the gift and opened it up to find a small box of Weis' Chocolates.

Johnson's mouth dropped. "I live two miles from Townsend Street, and I've been to Weis' Chocolates. It's a small, family-run chocolate store on the first floor of a two-story building."

"What's on the second floor?" Dunham asked.

"I think it's an apartment," Johnson replied.

"Let's go check it out," Riggs suggested.

Both Dunham and Johnson nodded.

Johnson bounded into the meeting room and began barking orders to everyone in the task force, initiating command and control. "OK, ladies and gentlemen, we have a huge lead. Stop what you're doing and listen up!"

Everyone stopped and stared at Johnson.

"We may have found Sullivan's hideout, and we need to treat it as a secondary crime scene, so let's get into CSI mode." He pointed to one task force member. "You! We need to contact all pertinent law enforcement agencies. Team up!"

Dunham interrupted. "I wouldn't put it past Sullivan to rig some kind of booby trap."

Johnson nodded, then eyed a red-haired female police officer. "Janette, contact the SWAT team and bomb squads and have them meet us there!"

"Yes, sir."

"Let's go, ladies and gentlemen!" Johnson ordered. "We've got work to do!"

As Johnson, Dunham, and Riggs left the room, Dunham stopped and glanced back at Stanton. "Oh, thank you again for everything, Mr. Stanton. I'll call you later."

Stanton nodded. "No problem. I'll see myself out—and good luck!"

Johnson, Dunham, and Riggs beat the SWAT team to the Townsend Street apartment. They parked on the side of the road a safe distance away.

Johnson pointed at the apartment. "There it is, above the chocolate store. It looks like you get into the apartment by those outside stairs situated on the side of the building."

Riggs peered at the apartment through a pair of binoculars. "I see a security camera pointed right at the door. Sullivan's yacht has a security closed-circuit TV, remember?"

"Good memory, Riggs," Johnson said. "If I were Sullivan, I'd also keep an eye on my secret location from a safe distance away in my cozy yacht." He paused. "And even remotely push a button to engage some kind of bomb or something. I bet you're right, Dr. Dunham."

"Not that he can do that from prison, but he still could have set traps in the event his apartment is breached by someone other than him," Dunham observed.

"The chocolate store looks open," Riggs noticed. "Let me get these people out of the building."

Johnson nodded. "Excellent."

Riggs got out of the car and headed toward the chocolate store. Minutes later, four people rushed out of the store with Riggs behind them. He stopped, turned around, and flipped the 'Closed' sign on the door.

Johnson grinned. "Riggs thinks of everything, doesn't he?"

Dunham smiled.

Once the people drove away, Riggs returned to the car.

"Nice call on the sign, Riggs," Johnson complimented.

Riggs nodded. "Nice people. The owner of the chocolate company owns the building and remembers the guy renting the upstairs. He fits Sullivan's physical description. He gave me verbal permission to enter the apartment."

Johnson eyed Riggs. "Judge signed the arrest warrant."

"Yeah," Riggs replied. "Just making the guy feel like he's helping."

At that moment, the SWAT vehicle pulled up and contacted Johnson on the radio. "Captain Johnson, this is Sergeant Mancini."

Johnson grabbed his walkie-talkie. "Perfect timing, Sergeant. Everyone has evacuated the chocolate store. We see a security camera on top of the steps leading to the apartment. Our fear is that there's some kind of booby trap set to go off when the door opens."

"Copy that. Our bomb squad's with us. We'll take it from here."

Johnson, Dunham, and Riggs watched the SWAT team leave their vehicle and take up strategic positions around the apartment.

"It looks like they're taking no chances," Riggs observed.

Once the SWAT members made it up the stairs, they peeked into a small adjacent window. Minutes later they used a glass-cutter on the window glass, inspected the inside of the window, and then opened it. A SWAT member entered the apartment through the window, followed by two more members.

After about ten minutes, Johnson received a radio call from Mancini, "Captain Johnson, you were correct. There is an incendiary device attached to the door, which has an on-and-off switch. It looks like it's set up to turn it off with a pass code within thirty seconds of opening the front door. He resets it when he leaves. If someone opened this door without turning the device off, the entire building would have gone up in flames."

"Copy that," Johnson replied.

"It's disengaged and disassembled. The rest of the apartment's been cleared, so it's safe for your team to come up."

"Thank you, Sergeant. We'll be right up," Johnson replied.

They left the car and went into the apartment.

Dunham stopped inside the entrance. The apartment seemed to have been converted into a laboratory, with medical gear, a full refrigerator/freezer stocked with jars and containers of obscure substances, a pill-making kit with empty and full pill containers, canisters of powdered substances, and a couple of electric ovens.

"Make sure everyone has their latex gloves on, but don't touch anything anyway," Johnson reminded everyone. "The CSI team is on their way."

"Captain, check this out," Mancini said, examining the inside of a closet.

They peered into the closet and found a dark trench coat, a mustache-goatee disguise, dark boots, gloves, and a black cane with a clear crystal on the top.

"I recognize this stuff," Riggs said and pointed at the coat. "I see bloodstains."

Dunham, wearing latex gloves, grabbed the cane at the midsection and turned it, exposing a ten-inch blade. "I think we may have found the murder weapon." He placed the cane back where he found it.

They crossed to the table with a pill-making machine on top.

"You were right, Dr. Dunham," Riggs said. "This guy has been creating an elixir of life concoction, and it seems he's been ingesting it in pill form."

"Actually, that's quite ingenious," Dunham remarked. "In pill form, there's no need to store his elixir in a refrigerator. Pills last much longer than fluids. Also, the pills can be hidden inside a pocket and taken anytime."

"Check this out," Riggs announced as he pointed to the far wall. "Photos of each murder." He glanced down at a table and noticed small wax displays of each murder scene.

Dunham approached the table. "He's immortalizing each murder location." He shook his head. "He thinks he's a god."

"I know that we still need to collect DNA samples for comparison, but I believe we just caught our man. It's been a long year," Captain Johnson said with an air of satisfaction and finality, as if a huge weight had just been lifted off his shoulders. He shook Riggs' and Dunham's hands, congratulating them, "Excellent job, gentlemen."

chapter thirty-four

**PRESENT DAY: Thursday, November 9. 8:00 a.m.
Buffalo, New York—Erie County Forensic Laboratory.**

Dunham neared the Buffalo forensic lab with Johnson and Riggs, and they were also accompanied by ADA Dennis Hanson. Everyone seemed unusually anxious, he thought, but for obvious reasons. They had the goods on the offender, but now began the legal phase, and anything could go wrong.

"Dr. Chesterfield, your forensic scientist colleague, seemed quite excited on the phone about the DNA samples retrieved from Sullivan's secret location on Townsend Street," Johnson began, glancing at Dunham.

"Let's hope for the best," Hanson interrupted. "I'm sure you'll feel at home here, Dr. Dunham."

Dunham smiled. "True. I love the lab. It's all about the physical evidence. Facts speaking for themselves," he paused. "Although, there's still the human element of interpretation."

They entered the forensic lab, and Dunham glanced around as if he were a kid in a candy store.

A short elderly gentleman, white-bearded and wearing a lab coat, hurried toward them. "Dr. Dunham?"

Dunham nodded and smiled.

"I'm Dr. Chesterfield. It's nice to finally meet you." He shook Dunham's hand.

"I'm thoroughly impressed with your lab, Dr. Chesterfield."

"Thank you, Dr. Dunham. Does it compare with the FBI lab?"

Dunham nodded. "In every way, other than our lab being retrofitted for international terrorism."

"Ever since the Bike Path Rapist Case years ago," Chesterfield explained, "our lab has been well-funded. I'm certainly not complaining."

"Dr. Chesterfield, you said you have some significant results from the Niagara Falls serial killer samples?" Johnson asked.

"Yes, come over here." Chesterfield led everyone over to the forensic biology section of the lab and picked up a computer-generated document.

Hanson peeked over at a glass-covered shelf with labeled samples. "Are these the samples we gave you?"

Chesterfield nodded. "Yes, we used a type of polymerase chain reaction DNA technique on the samples, utilizing short tandem repeats called STRs—a part of human DNA strand that is different in each individual."

"Not too complicated, please," Johnson requested glancing over to Riggs.

"Of course," Chesterfield agreed. "Because we're comparing STR loci with known individuals as opposed to an entire database, analysis time was significantly reduced." Chesterfield pointed to a DNA analyzer. "We opted for the gel electrophoresis separation and detection method for numerous reasons that I will not bore you with."

"So, what're the results?" Johnson asked.

"So far," Chesterfield explained, "we've matched four of the six Niagara Falls serial killer victims with samples taken out of the powdered substance and pills found at Townsend Street with a false-positive probability of one in a billion."

"Yes!" Riggs blurted out.

"That's outstanding!" Hanson added.

Chesterfield grinned. "That's not all. We've also matched Sullivan's DNA with samples taken from the cane and from the goatee disguise." Chesterfield scanned the excited faces around him. "Congratulations, gentlemen, you've caught your man."

"I love the sound of that!" Johnson said, beaming. He shook Dunham's hand, then slapped his shoulder. "You did it."

"That's right, we did it," Dunham corrected.

"I should have further results soon," Chesterfield added.

Dunham shook Chesterfield's hand. "Thank you very much for all your help, Dr. Chesterfield. You do class A work here."

Chesterfield smiled humbly.

Hanson glanced at Johnson. "Not only do we have enough for the grand jury indictment—this may have just sealed the fate of Mr. Sullivan at trial, as long as we cross our Ts and dot our Is."

Riggs took a deep breath and exhaled. "Wow, what a weight off our shoulders."

Hanson approached Dunham. "Dr. Dunham, I'd like you to question Mr. Sullivan one more time, seeing as he has a certain level of respect for you. I would hate to spend extra time and taxpayer dollars on this piece of trash by going to trial, so maybe you can get a confession out of him."

Dunham nodded. "Certainly. I'll do my best, although I believe there's a low chance for success."

"Hey, at least we get to watch his reaction to us discovering his secret hideout and making a DNA match between him and the victims," Johnson interrupted. "I can't wait to watch that condescending smile drop off his face."

"Dr. Dunham? I'd like to show you some of the technical details over here," Chesterfield requested.

Dunham nodded. "Sure."

Chesterfield led Dunham over to a private corner of the lab. Once he had Dunham alone, Chesterfield whispered, "Dr. Dunham, as you know, I discovered Mr. Sullivan's telomere condition to be that of a 20-year-old."

Dunham nodded.

"I've discovered another anomaly with that of all four victims I've identified so far, along the same lines."

"Oh, what is that?"

"When I compared the DNA samples of each victim from their respective murder sites with the corresponding samples found in the powder at Townsend Street, I noticed telomere repair with all four victims' material."

"The victims were experiencing telomere repair?"

"No, I'm not saying the victims were experiencing telomere repair," Chesterfield clarified, "but their ground-up tissue matter within the powdered substance. It's like the ingredients in the powder had the ability to repair telomeres. Taken further, it just might be a substance that increases the lifespan of an organism." Chesterfield stared at Dunham. "It seems this does not surprise you."

"No, it doesn't," Dunham admitted, but he wasn't ready to talk to a fellow scientist about an elixir of life, so he moderated his comments. "This substance is what allowed me to connect Sullivan to the murders. Do you recall the bloody parchment found a block away from one of the victims?"

"Yes, we analyzed it here."

"I discovered that it was a recipe for a medicine to improve one's health," Dunham explained. "I had read about it in an unpublished article last year from an acquaintance of mine. It is years away from FDA approval, if it even gets that far. It seems our Sullivan had gotten wind of it and financed the manufacture of it in secrecy."

"I would certainly like to know more about it."

"I'll see what I can do," Dunham replied.

chapter thirty-five

PRESENT DAY: Thursday, November 9. 1:00 p.m.
Buffalo, New York—Erie County Courthouse.

Sullivan, in ankle and wrist shackles, was escorted to the Erie County Holding Center by a team of deputy sheriffs. The team of four deputy sheriffs and one sergeant brought him into the interrogation room, where his lawyer was waiting for him.

Behind the mirror were Hanson, Dunham, Johnson, and Riggs.

"Are you all set, Dr. Dunham?" Hanson asked.

Dunham nodded. "Yes. I'm sure his lawyer will tell him not to speak, but I'll see what I can do." He headed for the interrogation room.

Inside, Sullivan glanced up at Dunham with a welcoming grin. "Dr. Dunham, it's a pleasure seeing you again."

His lawyer stood up and met Dunham. "Hello, Dr. Dunham. My name is Jack Looney. I'm Mr. Sullivan's attorney."

Dunham shook his hand. "Hello." He sat in the seat directly opposite Sullivan.

"I have to tell you up front that I've recommended to Mr. Sullivan not to speak with you."

Dunham nodded. "I understand. I wanted you here as well, in view of the additional evidence we've uncovered."

Sullivan maintained his silence but kept his confident demeanor.

"Oh, what do we have?" Looney asked.

Dunham glanced at Sullivan. "Mr. Sullivan, on the night of the murder attempt at the Haunted Catacombs, you told us that you were taking a long evening stroll, which of course is the reason why you've kept such excellent health."

Sullivan merely stared Dunham, grinning slightly.

"Additionally," Dunham continued, "you told us that you have no witnesses to corroborate your story, because you stated you avoid contact and communication with strangers."

Looney interrupted. "Dr. Dunham, you seem to be wasting our time. I fail to see . . ."

As Looney was speaking, Dunham leaned toward Sullivan, maintaining eye contact. "We found your secret hideout on Townsend Street, Mr. Sullivan."

Sullivan's smile immediately dropped, replaced with a stunned expression.

Looney glanced at Dunham then at Sullivan. "His secret hideout? What hideout?"

"That's right, Mr. Sullivan," Dunham remarked as he ignored Looney. "And we also disarmed your makeshift firebomb before it could go off. Thanks to the evidence collected, we now have linked you directly to not only the Arcade train and Haunted Catacombs attacks, but also to at least four of the Niagara Falls serial murders."

The shock slid from Sullivan's face as rage took its place.

Dunham realized he was now looking into the eyes of a pathological killer; a person who wouldn't think twice about mutilating him.

Looney raised his hand. "I expect to have access to each and every piece of evidence that you've cataloged, Dr. Dunham. Also, I'm hiring an independent private forensic team to analyze all incriminating physical evidence, including DNA samples collected."

Dunham shifted his gaze from Sullivan to Looney. "Of course, as long as you follow the proper procedures and go through the appropriate channels. Once you realize how damning the evidence is, I would suggest you discuss with your client the advantages of a confession. I'm sure the DA's office will offer a deal."

Sullivan sat up in his chair and leaned toward Dunham. "I can tell you the answer to that now, Dr. Dunham."

"Mr. Sullivan," Looney interrupted. "I'll handle—"

"Quiet!" Sullivan roared as he continued to stare at Dunham. "The answer is never. I recognize authority from no mortal inferiors."

"Why is that, Mr. Sullivan?" Dunham asked. "Or should I call you Dr. Tumblety?"

Sullivan snapped his head back in amazement.

"Dr. who?" Looney asked in utter confusion.

Dunham leaned forward. "I know your secrets, Francis," he whispered. "Every single one of them—and the carnage stops here in Buffalo."

Sullivan regained his composure and put on an evil grin. "Oh, I highly doubt that, Dr. Dunham. We'll see how the trial goes. I'm not convicted yet." Sullivan changed the subject. "Now that you're aware of certain realities, do you still question me about the origins of your own talents? What more proof can you have of it working?"

Dunham sat back. "You may be right, but that's irrelevant now, isn't it?" He stood up and glanced at Looney. "Consider the confession." He turned to exit the room.

Sullivan screamed at Dunham's back, "Enjoy the moment, Dr. Dunham. It will not last!"

Dunham entered the room behind the two-way glass. He noticed Johnson, Hanson, and Riggs watching Sullivan being escorted from the interview room.

"Well, that went just as expected," Johnson said.

"He sounds pretty adamant about rejecting any possibility of a confession and plea bargain," Riggs remarked.

Hanson eyed Riggs. "I believe you're right." He then looked at Dunham. "But who's Dr. Tumblety?"

Dunham noticed Johnson and Riggs looking just as curious.

"Detective Riggs and I realized Sullivan was imitating not only Jack the Ripper, but a particular Ripper suspect named Dr. Francis Tumblety." He paused. "When we entered Sullivan's hidden room, we noticed his display of photos and wax recreations of the victims in their death positions." He paused again and glanced at Hanson. "He believes he's a god reincarnate. In his last life, he believes he was the actual Jack the Ripper, or Dr. Tumblety. I was merely feeding into his ego—or alter-ego in this case."

Hanson nodded. "That makes sense."

Dunham noticed Johnson and Riggs also nodding in agreement. "His last comment concerns me," Dunham said, purposely changing the subject. "It's almost as if he's going to attempt a jailbreak. How secure is the Erie County Holding Center?"

"Very secure," Hanson answered with confidence. "Knowing their procedures, I just don't see how he could escape, even if he did have outside help. To pass through any doors or gates, inmates, as well as employees for that matter, need to get buzzed in by a deputy sheriff sitting in a room on the first floor. No one's ever escaped in the past."

Dunham felt more at ease. "That does make me feel better." He shook his head. "But what a strange comment he made."

chapter thirty-six

**PRESENT DAY: Thursday, November 9. 7:00 p.m.
Buffalo, New York—Erie County Holding Center.**

Sullivan had his hands tucked behind his head as he re-clined on the narrow mattress. His cell was only a little larger than the torture chamber they called a bed. He quickly sat up as the duty deputy sheriff passed his cell. He bunched up the orange coverall so it added bagginess to his frame and watched for the deputy to glance into his cell. "Deputy, this seventy-two-year-old body is not doing so well today. May I go to medical and get checked out? I have a deep sliver in my hand." He held up one hand.

The deputy sheriff wrapped his fingers around a steel bar and glanced at the outstretched hand. "I'll be back in a couple of minutes, right after I finish my rounds. Then I'll take you to the infirmary."

Ten minutes later, the deputy sheriff came back to Sulli-van's cell with the duty sergeant and another deputy sheriff.

"Your medical escort, inmate," the sergeant said.

The deputy opened the cell door and placed shackles on Sullivan's hands and ankles.

Sullivan slowly toddled out with slumped shoulders, acting every bit of his alleged seventy-two years.

One of the deputies grabbed Sullivan by the arm to help him to the infirmary. "Come on, old man."

The sergeant stared at the two other large deputy sheriffs next to the frail old man, then said, "Deputy Manning, this is overkill. We don't need everyone escorting him to the infirmary. I need you to go back to your floor."

"Are you sure, Sergeant?" Manning questioned. "Captain's orders state that an inmate needs to be escorted by three deputy sheriffs."

The sergeant glared at Manning. "I'll take the hit. Take off."

The medical wing was the entire third floor of the holding center, and the two escorts took Sullivan to the elevator. Once on the third floor, a designated medical security officer met the escorts and Sullivan at the elevator, then ushered them to the infirmary. Inside the infirmary were a female attending physician and a female nurse.

"What do we have here?" the physician asked.

"Our elderly inmate, Mr. Sullivan, has a deep sliver in his palm," the sergeant replied.

The physician turned away from them, continuing her previous task. "I'll be with you in a moment. Take a seat in the chair, please, so the nurse can take your vitals."

Sullivan sat in the medical chair with the nurse attending him, while the deputy sheriff, medical security, and the sergeant stood a few feet away.

Once the nurse was finished and wrote the information down on a clipboard, the physician approached Sullivan. "Let me see your hand, Mr. Sullivan." The doctor glanced over at the sergeant. "Sergeant, could you take off the shackles around his hands please?"

The sergeant approached Sullivan. "Sure."

After the sergeant unlocked his shackles, he placed the key back on his belt.

The physician inspected the wound in his hand. "Yes, you certainly do have a large sliver buried deep in your palm." She met his eyes. "I'm going to have to give you a local and then incise it. Are you OK with that?"

Sullivan acted insecure and shaky. "Just be careful, Doctor. I'm not too fond of seeing my own blood."

"Don't worry, Mr. Sullivan. You're in good hands."

Both the physician and the nurse began to collect medical implements and bandages. The physician gave Sullivan a shot near the small wound, then pulled out a packaged, sterilized scalpel.

Sullivan began to act dizzy as if he were going to faint.

The physician glanced up at the escorts. "Could a couple of you hold onto him so he doesn't fall and hit his head? He's quite a large man."

The deputy sheriff and the medical security deputy sheriff grabbed Sullivan under each armpit and held him up.

Just as the physician was opening the package containing the scalpel, Sullivan reached up and grabbed both escorts by their hair and slammed their heads together.

The force was so great that the two deputy sheriffs lost consciousness immediately and dropped to the floor.

"What!" the sergeant yelled, and rushed Sullivan, but was grabbed by the neck just under the jawline.

Sullivan picked him up off of his feet with one hand and slammed his head into the concrete ceiling. The sergeant's body went limp, and Sullivan threw him to the ground. The physician and the nurse were stunned, motionless in fear.

Sullivan calmly turned around, ripped the scalpel out of the physician's hand, and grabbed both the physician and the nurse by the hair. "Sit on the ground."

They sat immediately.

Sullivan approached the unconscious sergeant, pulled off a key from his belt, then removed his ankle shackles. He then removed the uniform from the sergeant and put it on.

He faced the doctor and nurse. "Come with me, ladies. If you utter one word or scream, you're dead."

Sullivan, now in uniform, escorted the two women out of the infirmary and down the long corridor to the stairwell.

The stairwell door was controlled from the other end by a deputy sheriff.

The door had a small window in it, and when Sullivan approached the door, he merely stared at the deputy sheriff and waved to him.

Glancing up from his book and seeing a man in uniform, the deputy sheriff automatically buzzed the door open, then went back to reading.

Sullivan marched his two hostages down to the first floor. As he did with the first stairwell door, he stared at the next deputy sheriff through the first floor door window and waved. Again, the deputy sheriff merely buzzed the door open.

Sullivan picked up his pace and forced his two hostages toward the entrance door to the underground tunnel that connected the holding center to the courthouse on the other side of the street.

The deputy sheriff operating tunnel door hesitated when he saw Sullivan. Recognizing something was wrong, he stood up and sounded the alarm.

When Sullivan arrived at the door, the deputy sheriff said, "Now, let the doctor and nurse go. You don't want to get yourself into more trouble than you're already in."

Sullivan grabbed both women by the hair with his right hand and revealed the scalpel in his left hand. He thrust the scalpel into the neck of the physician.

The physician squealed with pain while blood spattered all around.

Sullivan turned and devilishly grinned at the deputy sheriff. "Open the gate now or she's dead."

The deputy sheriff's eyes opened wide and his jaw dropped, stunned by the vicious and gruesome attack. "Oh my God!"

Even before the deputy sheriff could open the door, Sullivan slit the physician's throat deeply and dropped her to the ground.

The physician died a few seconds later, right in front of the deputy sheriff's eyes.

As Sullivan put the scalpel to the nurse's throat, the deputy sheriff buzzed the door open.

Sullivan took his hostage into the tunnel and moved as quickly as possible to the courthouse end. When he arrived, he approached the door window and calmly waved to the courthouse security officer and grinned. The security officer buzzed the door open without question, as his duty phone was ringing.

Sullivan slammed the door open and two security guards turned to see Sullivan holding a scalpel at the nurse's throat.

"Come any closer and I'll slice her up just like I did the doctor," Sullivan warned.

One of the officers held his arms up. "Hold on now . . . we can talk this out."

Sullivan thrust the scalpel in the nurse's shoulder. She let out a piercing scream.

The security officers backed away immediately.

Sullivan shoved the scalpel in deeper, and the nurse screamed even more desperately. He glared at the deputy sheriffs. "Follow me outside and she's dead!" He backed out the front door of the courthouse with the nurse. As he rushed down the steps toward Delaware Avenue, he saw a small dark car approaching. When he got close to the street, he threw the nurse into the road, forcing the car to skid.

Just before it stopped it struck the nurse, and she was knocked onto the sidewalk, unconscious.

Sullivan had the front door of the car open before it came to a complete halt. He forcefully pulled a male driver out, then struck him with such force that he immediately went limp, falling to the ground, facedown. Sullivan quickly took the man's wallet, grabbed him by the hair, and viciously slashed his throat, ensuring the blood spattered away from him, then jumped into the car and drove off.

The courthouse security immediately poured out of the building in an attempt to assist the nurse and the man.

Sirens in the distance got louder as they approached the courthouse and holding center.

Back at the task force office, Johnson, Dunham, and Riggs sat in Johnson's office eating Chinese takeout, staying late with the rest of the task force.

Johnson's phone rang. "Captain Johnson," he answered. Seconds later he shot out of his seat. "What? You've got to be kidding me!" He stayed silent, listening to the person on the other end of the phone. "Thanks—and did you contact the state police and federal authorities? We'll be joining in the hunt." Johnson hung up the phone and glanced at Dunham and Riggs. "Come on."

As they got up to follow Johnson, Riggs and Dunham eyed each other.

"I wonder what's up?" Riggs asked Dunham.

They strode into the middle of the task force office. "I need everyone's undivided attention!" Johnson yelled. Dunham, Riggs, and everyone else gave Johnson exactly what he asked for. "That was the sheriff's department. Sullivan just escaped from the holding center, killing several people along the way, and has just stolen a small, dark vehicle outside of the courthouse."

"What?" Riggs bellowed.

Johnson continued. "They've already contacted the Buffalo police dispatch and the state police."

"Unbelievable," Riggs mumbled. He glanced at Dunham. "Dr. Dunham, your fears have again been realized."

Dunham shook his head. "If he's got a car, he could be quite a distance away by now."

Johnson turned to Dunham and Riggs. "Sullivan killed the driver, so we can't solicit information about the make or model of the car, or the license plate number. He also took the victim's wallet, so it's going to take awhile for us to ID the driver."

Riggs pulled out his iPhone and tapped rapidly with his thumbs.

Johnson continued. "By the time we know what vehicle we're chasing, he'll probably have dumped it off and taken another car. Sullivan certainly knew what he was doing. Damn!"

Johnson noticed Riggs grinning at his iPhone. "Riggs, what are you smiling for? Our suspect has just escaped!"

"Sullivan's still in the Buffalo city limits, and it looks like he's driving southeast," Riggs proclaimed while still staring at his phone.

Johnson glanced at Dunham. "Wha—How do you know this? And how is it on your phone?"

Riggs glanced up at Johnson and Dunham. "Sullivan's wearing black loafers with a GPS installed inside them. GTX Corp makes them for Alzheimer's patients."

"Holy crap!" Johnson shrieked. "When did this happen, and why didn't you tell us?"

"I forgot, actually," Riggs explained. "A sergeant at the holding center is a buddy of mine. I told him how this seventy-two-year-old is a high priority suspect. He told me the department was experimenting with Alzheimer GPS shoes for their aged minimum-security inmates who go home on weekend passes. He thought, just on the outside chance that Sullivan's lawyer succeeded in getting him a weekend pass, why not have him issued a pair?"

Dunham grinned from ear to ear.

"You never cease to amaze me, Riggs," Johnson replied.

"What's more," Riggs continued, "I just downloaded the corresponding GPS tracking app on my cell phone. That's what I'm reading right now. It looks like he just stopped his car. The lat-long is no longer changing." Riggs manipulated his phone. "And that location is," he paused, "Exchange Street."

Johnson shot a glance at Dunham. "The Amtrak station is on Exchange Street. It looks like he may be trying to escape on a train." Johnson scanned the room. "OK, ladies and gentlemen.

Let's notify everyone and begin coordinating his capture." He glanced at Riggs and Dunham. "Let's go."

They rushed out of the office.

Sullivan parked the stolen car in the Amtrak station parking lot and made his way into the building. He looked down and noticed a few blood spatter marks on his pant leg. The train station was relatively empty, so he didn't think anyone would notice the spots on his trousers. He calmly entered the room as if nothing out of the ordinary had occurred and went directly to a lavatory located next to a wall of lockers. He hurried into the very last stall.

Two men entered the lavatory and headed for the urinals. "Do you have any aspirin on you, Ralph?" one man asked the other.

"What? Do I look like a drug store, Hank?" The other man paused. "I think the wife has a couple."

Sullivan waited patiently for them to leave, then stood up on the toilet and reached up into the false ceiling. Moments later, he pulled out a hidden key. He left the lavatory and opened a locker. In the locker was a set of clothes in a bag, a large sum of money, and an ID with the name Frank Townsend. He returned to the lavatory, went into a stall, and changed into the new set of clothes. Included with the new set of clothes was a knife, which he pocketed, and a pair of shoes, which Sullivan put on his feet. He stuffed the uniform and loafers into the bag, shoved them in the trash, and hurried from the lavatory. As Sullivan headed toward the ticket booths, he noticed multitudes of law enforcement officers briskly searching the station. He wasn't the only one who noticed the influx of police.

The two men who had visited the lavatory stopped and stared. "What's up with the cops?" the man named Hank asked.

"What do I look like, a detective? I dunno," his friend replied.

Sullivan quickly stepped behind a group of men sitting together near the lavatory, apparently waiting for their train. He hoped they would be ready to board soon so he could move with them toward an exit without being noticed.

"Check the bathrooms," a police officer ordered two other officers.

The sudden presence of so many police officers in the train station had completely caught Sullivan by surprise. Somehow they had been tipped off. Anger and frustration began to cloud his judgment.

The men in the group next to him noticed the police officers, and one said, "I wonder what's happening."

As the men stared at the police, Sullivan did as well, effectively camouflaging himself. He knew they were searching for a lone man in a police uniform, and being a member of this crowd seemed to be working. But now, he decided, it was time to move. Hugging the wall, he edged away from the group. His hand gripped the handle of a maintenance closet that a number of police had already checked out and cleared. He casually opened the door and ducked inside. He left the door open just a crack so that he could observe the police. He unscrewed the light bulb in the closet just in case someone opened it up and flicked the light switch. Sullivan watched the police who'd earlier entered the lavatory come out with the bag and uniform.

A number of them were talking on their radios and cell phones.

He knew he had to get out soon; his chances for escape were diminishing. He watched the progress of a couple of police officers escorting a half dozen people away. He gripped the door handle as they made their way by the closet door.

"What's going on, Officer?" someone being escorted asked.

"Just keep going. I'll explain once we're outside the building," the officer said.

As the group passed by, Sullivan quickly opened the door and joined in with them. It worked! He continued with the group, being escorted by the police. As they were marched outside, he thought it ironic that these police were his ticket out of the building.

Just as the group neared the entrance, Johnson, Riggs, and Dunham entered. Riggs immediately recognized Sullivan within the group. He pulled out his handgun and bellowed "Freeze!" so loudly that the whole group froze.

Sullivan quickly grabbed one of the females in front of him and put his knife to her throat. He dragged her to a second entrance to his left.

Her screams caught everyone's attention.

Just before he got to the entrance, he was body-slammed from his blind side by a police officer.

Sullivan lost his grip on the woman, then regained his footing and attacked the police officer.

The police officer dropped his weight, placed his arm on Sullivan's back, pivoted both feet, and threw him with a judo technique known as *o-goshi*.

Even though he had twice the strength of the officer, Sullivan found himself thrown onto his back.

After throwing the fiend, the officer backed up, took out his handgun, and said rather calmly, "Get on your stomach, and put your hands on your back! Now!"

As the other officers converged, Sullivan slowly crouched down as if to get onto his stomach, then leaped with amazing speed and caught the police officer's handgun and ripped it out of his hands. His body collided with the police officer, who soared backward, crashing onto the floor, leaving Sullivan with the gun in his hand. He pointed the handgun at the officer.

At that moment, a shot from another handgun sounded, and the bullet impacted Sullivan right between the eyes.

His head flew back, and his body followed. He landed on his back. The gun fell out of his hands, and his body was motionless. Sullivan was dead.

Riggs approached the scene, then he saw that the police officer who'd shot Sullivan was none other than Diane Barnett, the woman Sullivan had attempted to kill on the Arcade train ride. He beamed.

A number of police officers surrounded Sullivan's body.

The police officer on the ground slowly got to his feet and turned toward Diane. "Nice shot, dear," he said, breathing hard. "You just saved my life. I owe you dinner."

"Are you OK, Artie?" Diane asked him.

"Never better," he replied with a big grin. He grasped his wife's trembling hands and gathered her up in a tight hug. "We're safe, dear; we're safe."

"No one messes with the Barnetts!" Riggs roared jokingly. "You guys are the bomb."

Dunham and Johnson rushed through the crowd then stopped in front of the Barnetts.

"It looks like we missed the excitement," Johnson joked. "Are you two OK?"

"Yes, thanks to Diane's dead eye," Artie replied.

Riggs glanced at Sullivan's body. "Nice shot placement, Diane. How appropriate that it was you who took this loser out."

Diane took a deep breath, still trembling. "What an awful feeling it is to shoot someone."

"The Niagara Falls Ripper is no longer, Diane," Dunham spoke up. "Because of you, he will no longer kill innocent women. Remember that."

Diane, nodded, glanced at Artie, and hugged him.

chapter thirty-seven

PRESENT DAY: Monday, November 13. 10:00 a.m. Buffalo, New York—Buffalo Police Headquarters, Task Force Situation Room.

The task force room was filled with all of the members of the Niagara Falls serial killer task force. Balloons, celebration signs, and other party items completely filled the room.

Captain Johnson made his way up to the podium. "Hello, everyone. This is our last briefing in the Niagara Falls Serial Killer Case." He paused and raised his fist. "Mission accomplished!"

The roar from the entire task force was deafening. Everyone high-fived each other, yelled, clapped, and cheered.

Johnson raised his hand to quiet everyone. "Quiet, please, quiet. There are still many loose ends to tie up, but because we're not preparing for a court case due to the death of the prime suspect, our primary mission is complete." He paused. "A number of the family members of the victims wanted me to pass onto everyone their sincere appreciation for your hard work."

The entire task force cheered again.

Johnson raised his hand again. "It was a team effort. I would like to single one person out, however, and that's Dr. Dunham."

Everyone in the room shot from their chairs and gave a standing ovation.

Dunham blushed and gave a smart wave to recognize everyone's appreciation.

Johnson continued. "Before he joined our task force we were spinning our wheels, but less than two months after he joined, the killer has been identified and taken off the streets." He faced Dunham. "Dr. Dunham, your reputation is most certainly deserved."

"The Watchmaker!" someone yelled from the crowd.

Everyone joined in. "The Watchmaker!"

Dunham stood up and raised his hand to make a comment. He waited for a full minute before the cheering died down. "I would like to say that of all of the task forces I've been privileged to be on, this one has impressed me the most."

His audience cheered.

"Yes," Dunham continued. "I may have opened up a good lead, but this truly was a team effort. Sullivan was the most elusive character that I've ever seen." He pointed to the crowed. "Great job, everyone."

The cheer sounded again.

Two people carrying dozens of pizza boxes walked into the room.

"Rarely does a serial killer task force end on a good note," Johnson said. "So the pizza's on me!"

Cheering erupted again.

Johnson leaned over to Dunham. "I believe the cheers are louder for the free lunch than for you, Dr. Dunham," he teased.

Dunham laughed. Johnson raised his hand again. "Besides pizza, I've ordered an assortment of subs and refreshments. The rest should be here in a moment, so please stick around. Thanks, everyone."

Riggs and Johnson approached Dunham.

Riggs shook Dunham's hand. "It was a pleasure working with you, Dr. Dunham. I've learned so much."

Johnson shook Dunham's hand again. "It certainly was a pleasure. I hope we keep in touch."

"Thanks, both of you. The professionalism and friendship here were outstanding," Dunham replied. Then he smiled. "Aside from the fact that I'm now addicted to Timmy Ho's!"

Riggs laughed. "By the way, this has been bugging me ever since you joined our task force. Why do they call you the Watchmaker anyway?"

Dunham grinned. "Well, I've always been notorious for explaining things ad nauseum, or in great detail."

"Do ya think?" Riggs joked.

Dunham laughed. "Once, years ago, one of my forensic-psychologist colleagues and long-time friend used to tease me about my habit of belaboring a point, so he said to me jokingly, 'Edward, I'm going to ask you a question. Now, if I ask you what time it is, are you going to build me a watch?'"

"Ha!" Riggs belted out.

"He said it in front of a bunch of special agents, and it stuck."

Johnson laughed. "Actually, I couldn't agree more, but in my twenty-plus years on the force, I've never seen someone so good at routing out the bad guy. How long is the FBI going to let you stay, now that the task force has accomplished its mission?"

"Only a few more hours, I'm afraid. My flight back home leaves at four o'clock this evening."

Johnson and Riggs exchanged disappointed looks.

"Your presence will be missed," Riggs said, placing a hand on Dunham's shoulder. "Oh!" He reached into his pocket. "Here's your iPhone. You left it on my desk."

Dunham smiled and shook his head. "If you guys will excuse me, I need to call Ryan Stanton." He entered the hall and selected the ripperologist's contact.

"Ryan Stanton."

"Hello, Mr. Stanton. It's Dr. Dunham."

"Hello, Dr. Dunham. Congratulations! It's all over the news that the Niagara Falls Ripper was shot during an escape attempt."

"We had a close call," Dunham explained. "Just as they've been saying on the news, Sullivan broke out of the Erie County Holding Center but was eventually shot and killed at the train station. I wanted to call you and thank you. Your information broke the case for us."

"You're welcome," Stanton said. "I'm glad to have helped. In view of the fact that Tumblety actually did discover a true elixir of life, the world may change."

"Well, maybe not . . . at least for a while," Dunham replied.

"What do you mean?"

"The elixir hellbroth concoction found in Sullivan's hideout has just gone missing from the evidence room."

"Wow! Is that normal? How can someone walk into an evidence room undetected?"

"It's near impossible, but I have a feeling I know which secret organization may have done it, and it suggests they have long arms."

"I don't think I want to know who they are!" Stanton commented. "Sounds like they could make people disappear, too."

"I don't think they want the world to know their business," Dunham answered.

"Well, I have no interest in letting the world know about a true elixir of life. Not my cup-o-tea. Anyway, I hope to see you more often in the papers catching serial killers, Dr. Dunham. Take care."

"You too, Mr. Stanton."

chapter thirty-eight

**PRESENT DAY: Monday, November 13. 3:00 p.m.
Buffalo, New York—Buffalo Airport.**

Dr. Dunham was sitting at the gate terminal waiting for his boarding call, reading.

An older gentleman approached him, then sat down in the next seat.

Dunham glanced up and smiled. "Hello, Mr. Bradbury. It's a pleasure to see you again."

Bradbury nodded. "Hello, Dr. Dunham, and you as well. I wanted to speak with you personally one more time before you left for Virginia." He paused. "Did you like my gift?"

"Not only was it an excellent gift, the timing was perfect." Dunham nodded. "Thank you, Mr. Bradbury. The information was immensely important for the success of the case. You're the reason he's off the streets for good."

Bradbury shook his head. "Oh no, you did that, Dr. Dunham. We had no idea who it was, but once you discovered him, our investigators got lucky."

Dunham gave Bradbury a subtle smile. "Sullivan's, or Tumblety's, elixir of life ingredients seemed to have gone missing from the evidence room. You wouldn't happen to know about that, would you, Mr. Bradbury?"

Bradbury grinned. "No, of course not, Dr. Dunham, but my guess is it's now in the rightful hands, out of reach of anyone with an evil personal agenda—and for that matter, the entire world."

"My thoughts exactly," Dunham agreed. "No reason for me to investigate any further."

Bradbury nodded, then paused. "He's right, you know."

Dunham glanced at Bradbury. "Who's right?"

"My police sources told me that Sullivan spoke to you about tapping into hidden knowledge." Bradbury paused. "He was convinced that your gift came from this hidden knowledge, somehow revealed to you in your past by reading a very old book."

"Oh, that," Dunham recollected, then shrugged his shoulders. "Maybe you're right. After all, the fact that he discovered the actual elixir of life through 'the philosophy' certainly attests to its veracity. The problem is I'm not ready to embrace the philosophy. Science has been good to me so far, and I think I'll stick with it."

Bradbury laughed. "No problem, Dr. Dunham." He leaned closer. "But, just to further put your empirical mind into a tizzy; the last Jack the Ripper murder in 1888 was on November ninth. Sullivan murdered for the last time four days ago," he paused, "on November ninth."

Dunham popped his shoulders up, slightly stunned by the amazing coincidence. "You're not trying to say Sullivan selected this date, are you Mr. Bradbury?"

Bradbury grinned and shrugged his shoulders. "Sullivan was an amazing man, Dr. Dunham, but at the moment, it's all speculation."

Dunham rubbed his chin and stared at the floor.

"If you want to learn more, just contact me." Bradbury stood up to leave.

Dunham's iPhone alerted him to a text, and he glanced at its display.

"Oh, one last thing," Bradbury began. "If you recall which old book you read as a young man, I believe I know the perfect custodians for it."

Dunham nodded. "I have a feeling you will be entertaining me as a guest one more time, Mr. Bradbury. By the way, I just received a text from Captain Johnson. It seems Sullivan's body went missing. I guess the body does have the elixir in it, and disposing of the body would eliminate all traces of it." Dunham glanced up at Bradbury. "You wouldn't happen to know about *this*, would you?"

Bradbury's smile dropped. "I must go now, Dr. Dunham." He turned and began walking away. "We certainly will be meeting again."

Dunham stared at Bradbury leaving. "Maybe sooner than later," he whispered.

www.ingramcontent.com/pod-product-compliance
Lightning Source LLC
Chambersburg PA
CBHW030527030726
47495CB00004B/891